I0760258

GUARDIAN OF TALONS AND SNARES

THE ZHENINGHAI CHRONICLES

GUARDIAN OF TALONS AND SNARES

THE ZHENINGHAI CHRONICLES

ANASTASIS BLYTHE

GUARDIANS OF TALONS AND SNARES

www.AnastasisBlythe.com

Hardcover ISBN: 978-1-960606-01-3

Cover design by Moorbooks Design.
Interior Design by Dragonpen Designs.

FOR HANNAH, LEIGH, JACQUELINE,
ANNA, LEISA, AND CASSIE.

THANKS FOR BEING PART OF THIS STORY
FROM DAY ONE.

CHAPTER 1

"HAVE YOU SEEN my boots anywhere, Ye Ye?" Aranya growled, tripping over an unpacked box and catching herself on the splintering doorframe. "I *know* I left them by the door!"

The white cat blinked sleepily up at her from where he was curled by the empty fireplace, fluffy tail over his nose. Aranya would have to get more firewood for tonight, after work. Right now, there were much more pressing things to worry about.

"Can you shift back to human form?" she said, trying not to huff too much. "I can't be late for my first day at my appointment, so I have to find my boots, which I need your help for, and you can't talk to me when you're a cat!"

"Mmreow!" Ye Ye chirped in response, stretching and arching his back.

"I know, I know. It's just easier to communicate when you're human—ow! I wish I'd had more time to unpack these phoenix-scorched boxes!" She let out a long gust of pained breath as she waited for her stubbed toe to stop hurting. "How do they expect us to graduate from the Academy, move halfway across the empire, *and* get settled in only a week, all before the first day of my appointment?"

A raspy chuckle sounded from the mat by the fireplace, and Aranya turned to see her grandfather sitting cross-legged, in human form. His long white hair looked more mussed than usual, with strands fallen out of his queue ties and into his face. His eyes crinkled in a smile. "Such a blessing from the fathers, this appointment of yours, Sunflower."

"Well, it won't be a blessing if I can't get there on time! I can't risk them dismissing me just for tardiness. That would ruin everything! All the appointments are given out now that Graduation is over, so I can't get a different one, which means we'd starve, and even if I could, it would involve moving *again*—" At this, she paused, glancing up and over her shoulder at Ye Ye. He wasn't looking at her, or the mess of their tenement, with robes strewn over unpacked crates and a cheap lattice screen tilted against the far wall. He was looking at the first gleams of sun shining through the window. It shone on the folds of his leathery skin, on his knobby hands, his hunched shoulders.

One move had been hard enough on him. She doubted he would survive another. She swallowed the lump in her throat and turned back to her rummaging. "Now, have you seen my boots?"

"Where was the last place you left them?"

Aranya let out a long, slow breath, closing her eyes, and then bent to shove this box aside. "I was wearing them yesterday. I could have sworn I left them by the door!"

"Is that them over there?"

She jerked upright, nearly hitting her head on the corner of another box. "Where?" But she followed the trajectory of Ye Ye's pointed finger, and . . . *there*! The scuffed toes of her well-worn boots peeked out from beneath the screen.

"You found them, Ye Ye!" Relief gusted out of her, and she leapt across the small room, snatched up the boots—nearly knocking over the screen in the process—and hopped around on one foot as she yanked the first boot on, then the other.

He was chuckling. And Aranya couldn't help her own smile, feeling suddenly ridiculous about her panic. Even if she'd been late, it was probably silly to think they'd dismiss her just for that. No matter. She had her boots, a bowl of steaming congee for Ye Ye to eat, and just in time for the sun's cresting over the horizon.

"Fathers bless your first day," said Ye Ye cheerily when she set the warm bowl before him. "You're a good girl, taking care of your old grandfather."

"Just returning the favor," Aranya replied, bending down to kiss his brow. "I'll make you proud."

"I already am. Now let me see that big smile of yours."

She flashed her biggest grin, warmth filling her chest at his praise. He reached out and flicked her nose. "Hey!" she cried.

"Off with you, now!"

"Are you sure you'll be fine by yourself all day?" She couldn't help the sudden tightening of her chest when the words left her mouth.

He waved his hand dismissively, staring down at the sun shining across his breakfast. He would be fine—he would. And it wasn't like she had a choice. They needed money, and she was the only one to earn it.

She tripped twice on her way to the door, resolutely yanked it open, and refused to glance back at her grandfather as a loud *slurp* echoed from his mat. She shut the door firmly behind her and headed out to her first day at her very first appointment as a warden at Zushui Wardpost.

Kai closed his eyes, drew in a deep breath. Let it out with a long, low sigh. He sat on the edge of his bed, staring at the light shining through his window as day dawned. In but a few moments, the bustle of the city outside would begin, and the early morning peace and quiet would be gone.

He dragged his eyes away from the window, letting them skim over his sparsely furnished tenement, the low table, his clothes still packed in a crate by the window. There was no dressing screen, and as long as he lived alone, he had no need for one. The pots and a kettle were stacked beside the stove with a single bowl and set of chopsticks.

Finally, his eyes slid down to the sealed letter in his hand. There was his name, written with a flourish of thick, black ink.

Shi Kai.

He closed his eyes again and crumpled the letter in his fist. Shooting to his feet, he strode over to the table where three more missives awaited. The handwriting on one of them was distinct from the others, which all bore unnecessary decorations. He didn't have to open them to know who sent them or what they said.

In one decisive motion, he swept the rest of the letters up, marched toward the fire, and threw them into the dying blaze. It sparked and leapt in response to the unexpected fuel, crawling over the once flawless parchments and turning them black around the edges before devouring them whole.

He tossed the crumpled one in last.

Then, with a last deep breath, he turned and strode to the door, pulling it open and shutting it firmly behind him, the crackling of the fire fading into nothing.

Today was the day he would finally, *finally* start anew.

CHAPTER 2

SHE WASN'T EXPECTING a fancy welcome. She didn't expect her fellow wardens to grant her a cordial bow and ask what mark she graduated with—though she would have told them with pride. Whatever she was expecting, it sure was *not* the welcome she got.

"What's this?" growled her new supervisor, eyes squinting in clear irritation, as he chewed a blade of sugar grass between fat lips. "*Another* fresh-faced, starry-eyed idiot for me to train?"

Aranya blinked, surprise catching her tongue.

The supervisor nestled his knees into the mat before his low desk, but somehow, he had leaned all the way back so his shoulders rested against the wall. It looked painful, yet he did not adjust his position as his eyes roved the length of her. Measuring her.

She tried not to let her eyes wander around the small office she stood in, at the bamboo beams supporting the ceiling, the creaking wood beneath her boots, or the morning sunlight shining through the open shutter and catching on the purely decorative, gold-studded *jiaun* mounted on the wall above the supervisor's desk. The weapon was doubtless an award for military service.

Instead, acutely aware of his scrutiny, she straightened her spine and flashed a grin before bowing forward. "Sun Aranya, shapeshifter and new resident idiot, apparently—"

"You have broad shoulders," the supervisor said, lifting his hand to twirl the sugar grass in his mouth. The only movement in his thoroughly unimpressed face was the smacking of those lips.

Aranya's smile froze. She almost snapped, *"They're very functional."* She forced the smile back bigger than before. "Indeed, my shifting abilities are . . ." Not *limited*—that would hardly make a good impression. ". . . of a more unique variety that requires significant upper body strength," she finished, breathing through her teeth, her gaze fixing above his head on the *jiaun,* not wanting to stare into that critical gaze longer than necessary. Two arrows were slotted in the firing mechanism of the weapon. What if it *wasn't* purely decorative? Perhaps it was there, loaded and within arm's reach, for the supervisor to grab and shoot at any moment. At any threat that walked through his sliding office doors.

"I have no need of you."

Her breath caught in her throat, died upon her tongue. Her attention snapped to focus sharply on the supervisor, who rolled the grass to one side of his mouth so he could sip from a teacup with a prowling dragon painted across its front. She blinked, trying to collect her suddenly scattered thoughts. This time, when her smile faltered, she let it disappear entirely.

"I beg your pardon? There must be some mistake," she said.

He raised an eyebrow, spat out his sugar grass, set his teacup down with a clang, and stood. He was not a tall man, and his age was catching up to him, slightly stooping his shoulders and winding gray hairs through his beard, yet the way he moved gave her the impression that she wouldn't want to engage with his magic in battle. Whatever his magic was. She hadn't been told in advance, and it was usually impossible to tell someone's magic from their bearings alone.

"Indeed, there has been a mistake," he agreed.

"But how could there be a mistake? Is this not Zushui Wardpost?" she sputtered. Her hands were already reaching, almost of their own accord, to the scroll tucked in her robes. "My appointment—"

"I already accepted the appointee for this position a few minutes ago."

Her hand froze just as it closed around the scroll. How was this possible? She forced herself back into movement, withdrawing it. Her mouth was dry when she handed it to him.

He unrolled it, grunting as he read. His brow furrowed lower and lower.

"The appointment I was given after graduating from the Academy," she began tentatively, "is to become a warden at Zushui Wardpost."

"I submitted *one* opening," he growled to himself, rolling the scroll back up. "*One* opening." He flung wide his hands, still holding her notice of appointment. "So why are there *two* fresh graduates scratching at my door this morning?"

What? "I do not know, sir."

"Maybe the first is mistaken," he muttered. "Follow me, girl."

She followed silently after the man, nearly tripping over her own feet several times because she paid little heed to the wardpost's ill-placed steps. They passed several wardens, armed for the day's work and conversing with one another, striding down barebone hallways of wood plank floors and dirty, white-plastered walls. One or two eyed Aranya, but she couldn't muster the courage to meet their gaze and offer a smile. Not when everything she'd worked for might be crumbling to pieces.

This could *not* be happening. She had spent her entire life at the Academy preparing for this. She'd devoted herself to grueling training sessions to hone her magic and combat skills until she was worn to the bone, to countless arena battles against opponents with stronger magic than her, to endless hours studying in the stuffy library with wax candles dripping everywhere. All this to get a respected appointment as a magic-wielder of the Zheninghai empire so she could keep food on the table and care for Ye Ye.

She had earned this appointment. It was *hers*. And she couldn't afford any "mistakes" with it. Now that Graduation was over, all the appointments were given out. If there had been a mistake with this one . . .

They'd be ruined.

Aranya shoved down the tension building in her chest and forced what she hoped passed as a mild expression onto her face. She doubted it was convincing, but she just couldn't let anyone know how truly terrified she was.

This was only a misunderstanding. It would be resolved soon enough.

Everything would be fine.

The supervisor marched through one of the side doors and barked loudly, "Shi Kai!"

A masculine voice from outside responded, "Yes, Master Qigang?"

"What is your appointment?"

"Shi Kai?" Aranya blurted, unable to help herself. Thankfully, the supervisor paid her no heed. Her mind spun faster than before, and for a moment, it was like she viewed the world upside-down, walking on the bamboo ceiling beams as if they were flooring. Shi Kai was the one who was here to steal her appointment?

Memories flashed before her, memories of a lopsided smirk, observed from a distance across the Academy's mess hall. She'd never been close to him—and that was intentional. He was an infamous troublemaker. Half the pranks at the Academy were his, but the masters were never able to catch him. Worse than that, however, was his reputation as a notorious flirt. Wherever he went, he always left a string of broken hearts behind him.

Just the sort of boy a girl should avoid when trying to succeed in a rigorous environment like the Academy, and just the sort of young man to avoid in a professional sphere like this one.

"My appointment?" said the masculine voice again. "A warden at Zushui Wardpost."

"Let me see it. Either those fools at the Appointment Office messed things up again or one of you can't read."

She peered around Qigang to see Shi Kai sitting on a bench outside in the courtyard, tugging on a pair of wardpost-issued boots. Sheathed knives lay next to him, along with a long broadsword and a two slotted *jiaun*. He withdrew a similar scroll from his robes and handed it to the supervisor.

The young man looked past the supervisor and saw her. Aranya blinked as those unusually light brown eyes met hers, set in a handsome face with a strong jaw and straight nose. He maintained the gaze for a breath, and then his mouth curved up in the slightest smirk.

Everything inside her revolted.

"Harumph!" was Qigang's response to whatever was written in the scroll. He tossed it down to the bench beside Kai. "What a mess."

Was it really true? She was speaking before she realized it, her voice threaded with mounting anxiety: "There was only one opening, but they appointed both of us?"

At that, Kai's smirk vanished, and his eyes widened, darting immediately to the supervisor. He twisted on the bench to face the supervisor, gesturing at Aranya. "What in all the seven valleys is she talking about?"

Qigang leaned back against the doorframe, heaving a great sigh, and glaring at them both. As if dealing with this problem first thing in the morning was bothering him as much as it bothered Aranya to lose her livelihood.

"Our incompetent bureaucracy has *apparently* issued the same appointment to both of you. I must send one of you back."

No, no, no. She couldn't be sent back.

There wasn't a trace of a mirth on Kai's face now. He clamped his jaw shut, a vein standing out in his neck as his hand fisted around the sheath of the knife he was holding. It seemed like his breath was coming almost as fast as hers.

"Why not keep both of us?" Aranya said, forcing a sunny smile that was probably more effort than it was worth. "I'm sure having an extra warden is not the worst—"

"We only have the funds for one new warden," the supervisor replied crisply. "And I certainly have no interest in training two idiots at once."

Kai's eyes flashed at the insult, but he said only, "I arrived first."

"Indeed, you did."

Her stomach dropped. Wretched boots! But she gritted her teeth and barely contained her growl. She would not let some *"I arrived first"* nonsense beat her out of the appointment that was rightfully hers.

"What about a competition?" she blurted.

Kai's eyes shot to hers, his nostrils flaring. As if in challenge, he began picking up the knives beside him and tucking them into his belt. Daring her.

"A battle," Aranya continued, keeping her focus on Kai. It had been a long time since she'd faced someone with his type of magic, but she didn't doubt her training. "No weapons, only magic. We could—"

"I have a better idea," Qigang drawled, his huge lips tilting up in a menacing smile.

Oh no. She widened her stance, bracing herself for his words with something between elation, hope, and dread.

"I will make you both temporary wardens," he continued, smile growing. "No training for either of you—yet. I will expect you to go about the regular duties of a warden until I decide which of you to accept and train."

"As delightful as a competition sounds," said Kai, "I'm confused about how this differs from accepting us both."

Qigang lifted a brow and turned on his heel to leave them. "You will split the single salary between each other. If you're unhappy with my decision, you can leave and find work elsewhere."

Aranya stared after him as he strode away. He practically glowed with what he doubtlessly supposed to be a brilliant plan. Split the salary? She wanted to cover her face with her hands and groan. That would not be nearly enough.

There was only one option: she had to win her appointment back, and she had to do it fast.

Taking a deep inhale through her nostrils and setting her shoulders, she faced her rival.

Kai stared after Qigang, his jaw hanging open, and his hand still where it had been busy buckling on his weapons a moment ago. He clamped his mouth shut and swiveled his attention to her.

"I suppose *this* will be just loads of fun," he growled.

Aranya gave him a patronizing, wrinkly-nosed smile in response. But then she blinked, a thought suddenly occurring to her. "What in all the seven valleys are *you* doing at this appointment? Surely you had better options!"

"I see my reputation proceeds me," he said, a sarcastic tilt to his mouth.

As if he didn't know her! Or . . . *did* he not know her? Sure, they'd never spoken before, but she was in his graduating class. How could he not know her?

"How did someone with your magic end up with a warden appointment? Were your grades that bad?" She wouldn't be surprised if they *were*, considering how much time he'd spent causing trouble and dodging the repercussions.

The idea that someone with his type of magic could get this appointment with bad grades, an appointment she'd slaved for, fought for, sent her stomach curling like she'd just drank spoiled milk. People like him, with his privileged magic and pristine bloodline, could get any appointment they wanted, and with it, all the status and wealth they could dream of.

He fixed those hazel eyes on her, and for a split second, she could see why she'd seen so many girls crying over him. Instead of getting lost in those eyes, she watched them narrow. As if her comment about his grades had slid right beneath his skin.

That meant she was right, and he'd done poorly at the Academy—which wouldn't surprise her—or he was here for a different reason. Him trying to take this wardenship was the equivalent of a magic-wielder like herself stooping to being a tailor's errand girl.

He shot to his feet, sweeping up the rest of his weapons into his arms, and strode toward where she stood in the doorway. Fathers, but he was so tall. He seemed to savor his height as he towered over her and spat, "Get your big man shoulders out of my way."

Get her *what* out of his way?

So this was how it was going to be.

Somehow, Aranya managed a grin and bowed, unfolding her arm in a grand gesture as she stepped aside. "A delight to formally make your acquaintance, Shi Kai."

He gave her a sticky smile and strode past her without another word, leaving her alone in the wardpost's doorway.

Then he was gone.

She paused only one moment, her mind finally clearing enough to run a cursory glance over the courtyard, the way the large complex was built around it, with doors letting out into the flagstone paving. She took note of each exit—just like she'd been taught. Except she was taught to do this immediately upon entry. *Whatever.* She'd been occupied. Better late than never, right?

First things first. She needed weapons. Kai had found them somewhere. It would certainly do her no good in this competition to enter her first day of work unarmed. But where . . .? She pursed her lips, glancing back out toward the courtyard. Maybe the weapons were in one of the other buildings.

She had been wandering for a few minutes when she ran into another warden. A middle-aged woman, broad-boned but lean, stepped out of one building as she strapped a knife to the belt she wore over her dust-colored robes. She did not even blink when she saw Aranya.

"What are you?" she asked, her voice rough and gravely.

Aranya quickly smiled and bowed. "I'm a shapeshifter—"

"Not that." The woman waved a hand and straightened, grimacing like she prepared herself for a long day. "Warden? Recent graduate?"

Aranya nodded. "My name is Aranya."

"You from this area?"

"No, I'm from the Wang Valley, though I've lived in Suguan most of my life for training."

"Naturally," the woman said dryly.

Aranya continued nodding, her smile slipping into a pair of pursed lips. She shuffled before catching herself and forcing her limbs to be still. "Is this where the weapons are?"

"Yes, though I'd be careful if I were you. We have not had a new graduate at this posting in over five years, and the wardens around here tend to be possessive about their favorite weapons and routines. Keep your hands off the nicer ones for now. And keep your head down. You'll be fine."

The woman did not know about Kai and their competition, then. She stalked off, slightly favoring her left leg.

"Thank you! What is your name?" Aranya burst out before it was too late.

The woman did not stop walking as she tossed over her shoulder, "Na."

With that, there was nothing to do but step through the darkened doorway of the armory. It was a narrow room, with some weapons piled atop each other on the long tables framing the walls, other weapons hanging from hooks, and waxwood staffs chunked in a tall clay holder. She had only just finished fumbling through the different stacks, frowning at the disarray that would never be tolerated at the Academy, when the door burst open and another young man—this one a little older than Kai—stumbled in. Maybe their most recent addition before Kai and Aranya?

"Hello?" she offered when he noted her, disregarded her, and ran to the hanging broadswords.

He clipped, fastened, buckled, and tucked half a dozen weapons onto his person, panting all the while. In his haste, he kept knocking or dropping weapons that clattered loudly to the floor before he cursed and scooped them up again, only for them to fall inevitably once more.

Aranya caught a knife by its hilt before it landed, holding it out to him. He blinked at it, then at her, and with a sucked in gasp, grabbed it and stuffed it into his belt.

"I'm Aranya," she said, craning her head to catch his eye.

"I'm late!" he spewed in response.

She reined back her snarky, *"Nice to meet you, Late,"* response and instead asked, "Late for what?"

"If I don't hurry, I'll get put on south patrol *again.*"

"South patrol?"

But he was already racing out the door, his heavy footsteps loud and near frantic. If he was worried about being late . . .

"Dragons blast it!" Aranya fastened her last buckle and raced after him.

She would *not* be late and let Kai get ahead.

CHAPTER 3

THE MOMENT ARANYA skittered out to the front of the wardpost, fifteen pairs of eyes turned to look at her in various shades of curiosity, amusement, and irritation. The latter being the most common. And most prominent on Qigang's face.

"Sun Aranya," he drawled, eyeing her. "South patrol."

The scattered chuckles confirmed her fear that she'd gotten the worst duty on her first day. She shoved it away with a polite nod toward the supervisor. At least she was going to be on patrol, not just polishing boots at the wardpost.

She glanced around and noticed Na's indifferent expression, then found the young man who was so desperate to avoid south patrol. He stared at the supervisor, eyes wide with pleading.

Qigang's gaze flicked up and met the young man's stare. "Xian Chen, south patrol."

Chen let out a dejected sigh, his shoulders stooping. He looked toward Aranya and sighed again. She shot a sidelong glance at Kai, who was standing straight and tall, his expression unreadably serious. Until his face twisted to one side, enough for his eye to meet hers. The faintest trace of a smirk played on his lips.

That—that smugness! The nerve!

"Shi Kai, eastern market patrol."

Na raised an eyebrow and folded her arms across her chest. Chen glowered.

Apparently, the supervisor already had a favorite.

After the rest of the assignments were handed out, Aranya sidled up to Chen as he jabbed his hands up his sleeves to check his weapons.

"Hello!" she chirped, bowing. "I'm glad we can officially meet now. I suppose we'll be comrades for the day."

Chen sighed again, forcing his hands down rigidly at his side. He bowed. "Xian Chen. Aranya? What type of wielder are you?"

"Shapeshifter."

"What sort of animals do you shift into?"

Don't be embarrassed. She plastered a grin on her face. "I'm more of a partial-shifter."

Chen jerked his head down the street. "Come on then, partial-shifter." He set off, heavy boots shuffling on the dirt road down between the rows of homes and storefronts, kicking up dust that caught the morning sun rays.

She scurried to match the quick pace he set. "What's so bad about the south patrol?"

He waved his hands vaguely, wincing. "It's just . . . It's a rougher part of town, so there are a lot of brawls. We're always breaking up fights."

"Doesn't that make it exciting?"

The look he gave her clearly indicated the answer to her question was a definite *no.* "Everyone hates it. You always get scuffed up, and it's easier to make mistakes, which means you get in trouble with

Qigang. Which impacts whether you get a raise or if you get put on a better part of town."

"How does Qigang decide who goes where? It certainly seemed rather arbitrary this morning."

Chen ran a hand through his hair, grimacing again. His other hand kept patting down his chest, his hips, feeling the quivers and buckles and blades. "Well, *I* think it's arbitrary, but some others, like Na or Yazhu, are always defending him. I think he just doesn't like me, so he keeps sending me here, hoping I'll make a mistake big enough to merit being dismissed."

"Dismissed?" she said, her stomach dropping even further than before. "He would try to dismiss you?"

Qigang must have put her on this patrol because he already didn't like her. The thought that she wouldn't be safe in her position even if she could beat out Shi Kai for it . . . She shook her head, drawing in a deep breath. No, she wouldn't think like that. Because she *couldn't* think about failing Ye Ye ever again.

Chen shrugged. "Everyone says he's the best supervisor this wardpost has had in ages, because he came from the battlefront in the north. I think he was a lieutenant or captain—something important. Fought against the barbarians and all that. Or so I've been told. I think they're just intimidated by him, so they think he's everything and a cup of tea. I mean, the barbarians are already back to crawling along our borders, so apparently he didn't do the best job."

Aranya found herself mumbling, "Oh." She winced against the rising sun, glancing at the silhouettes of townspeople beginning their day. A wagon rolled down the street, making them hop off to one side. In the distance, the smiling eaves of the pagoda rose high above the rest of the buildings. She glanced sidelong at Chen, who was muttering something unintelligible under his breath.

So far, of the people she'd met today, Na was the only remotely encouraging one. This boded well for her future.

"What did you say your magic was?" she asked.

"I can breathe underwater."

She craned her neck further so she could get a better look at him. "Breathe underwater? Are you a shifter, too?"

"Shifter? Oh, no. My magic is feral. But the only ability I have is the water breathing. No bone-crushing strength over here, unfortunately."

She laughed.

He frowned, glancing at her. "What?"

She swallowed her laugh and faced forward, arching her eyebrows and firming her steps. "So . . . how do you use your ability to your advantage on the job?"

"You mean, why is someone like me so far from a significant body of water? Same reason you're here; because the bureaucracy is stupid."

Hearing so many people criticize the empire was starting to grate on her. No one spoke like this in Suguan or at the Academy. Of course the empire wasn't perfect, but Emperor Nianzu and his father had devoted their lives to peace and safety for their people. She, for one, was glad they didn't have to worry about northern raids or battles with marauding barbarians over harbors and springs. She didn't mean to make her response harsh, but it had an edge to it, anyway.

"Stupid?" she said. "Maybe you're great at combat."

He withdrew a knife and began twirling it in his hands, making her brace herself and glance warily over at him every few seconds. "I'm not good at anything."

Aranya stopped, faced him, and planted her hands on her hips. "You got a respectable appointment, didn't you?"

He snorted, sheathing his knife only to withdraw another. A woman nearby shuffled her son to the other side of her, frowning fiercely.

When he said nothing, Aranya continued, "I'm sure there are plenty of other things you're good at. Besides, that's why the Academy doesn't *just* train us how to use our magic, but how to be warriors and scholars so we can fill any variety of roles in the government. That's actually what I love about the Academy system. There are people with all sorts of magic. I mean, there are the overarching categories, like elemental manipulation, feral abilities, shapeshifting abilities, mind powers, curse casting, and so forth, but the fact that no two sets of magic are exactly identical—"

Chen waved his hand impatiently. "It's impractical, really. Because it makes it harder at the Academy to train everyone in their magic if everyone is different. It requires more specialized, individual training."

She might explode if this conversation continued much longer. Instead of snapping at him for all his negativity, she resorted to saying briskly, with a rueful glance down at her hands, "I suppose it's impractical, but it's reality. I might wish I was taller, but I cannot help that my parents were short, so there's no point in bemoaning my height."

And no point bemoaning about how the magic we have isn't the magic we want.

Melancholy washed over her, even as the day brightened around them, and gravel crunched pleasantly beneath her boots. What she wouldn't give to be a full shapeshifter like Ye Ye . . .

"Where are we going?" she said, forcing herself to abandon her line of thought.

Just then, out of an alleyway, a man came hurtling straight into an empty barrel. The barrel broke on impact, cracking and splintering. The man moaned but rolled to the ground and landed on all fours as another man came flying and shouting out of the alley.

"Right there." Chen sighed.

But she was already in motion, the sudden action washing away all unpleasant thoughts in an instant. Adrenaline surged through her blood, flooding to her toes and fingertips. Her heart leapt to her throat, her knees almost weak with the sudden thrill. *This* was what she'd trained for all these years.

"Stop where you are!" she shouted at the second man. "Not another step!"

He ignored her, not even glancing up as he tore toward the man on the ground. Violence glittered in his eyes.

Aranya ran.

She flung her hands to either side of her, and they burned as she shapeshifted. The sight and feel of talons protruding from her hands awakened something primal inside of her. Something wild and untamed. With a battle cry, she leapt upon the second man coming for the first. His eyes went wide as moons in his sockets, seeing those claws coming for his face.

She darted to the side at the last minute, flinging out her left arm to catch the man round the neck and shoulder. She used her momentum to swing herself onto his back, and that, combined with the force of her swing, landed him flat on the ground. He let out a loud, "Oomph!"

Just in time to keep him from leaping upon the injured man.

"Stop!" Aranya said, yanking his arms behind him as she straddled his back.

The man gasped, trying to raise his head to twist and look at her.

"Do not fight me," she said, pushing his head back down. "Or it will be much worse for you."

He spat out dirt. "He's getting away!"

"Who?" She tightened her grip.

"Him! He stole my wages!"

She paused, suddenly hesitant. The man must have sensed her doubt because he kept wailing about his lost wages. She looked up, saw the broken barrel, but no sign of the other man.

No sign of Chen either.

"My comrade will get him," she said. "But I must arrest you for disrupting the peace."

"What insanity is this?" the man bellowed, wrenching at her hold on him. "He *stole my money*!"

"We will sort this out, sir," she said and stepped off him. "Come with me to the wardpost. If you're innocent, they will release you shortly."

The man got to his feet, angrily dusting himself off. Outrage boiled in his reddened face.

She paused again. Was this the right thing? Qigang had apparently meant it when he said he wasn't going to train her yet, not until she proved her worth—which seemed backward to her, but he was the one who could retract her salary and appointment at any second. Chen would get the other man, and they would take them both in. He'd help her learn the procedures, and they could figure out who was innocent before a judge. Her job was to maintain the peace and protect civilians.

Throwing other citizens into barrels was *not* keeping the peace.

Thus resolved, Aranya beckoned the man to follow her. "Do not run," she said darkly, brandishing her talons in his face in an unspoken threat.

"You're new, aren't you?" he said, wrenching away from her. "Warden Na is—"

"Warden Na is not here," she snapped. "Quit dragging your feet."

By the time they'd made it back to the wardpost, there was no sign of Chen. She stopped and glanced around warily, eyeing the different doors that led to the law enforcement sector, the others that led to the incarceration units, and the last ones that led to the courts. She bit her lip. Where was Chen?

"Don't know where to take me?"

She gave him a withering glare and marched straight into the front office, where she knew Qigang would be. Her heart hammered in her throat, but she doubted her supervisor would be too upset about her bringing her captive to the wrong place, considering she'd been on the job for about twenty minutes and had already brought someone in.

Aranya flashed her best grin and swept a bow the moment they crossed the threshold. "Master Qigang, I have brought—"

Qigang, sitting on the same mat as before, swiveled his head from where he had been caught up in conversation with . . . with Kai?

Qigang's eyes flicked from Aranya to the man about to spout off next to her. Kai's brows rose, his mouth twisting slightly.

Her grin faltered, but she did not let it slip for more than a mere second.

"What have you brought me?" Qigang asked, folding his arms across his chest. "Where is Chen?"

Aranya's elbow to the gut was not enough to keep the man from spewing his tale to Qigang, claiming he'd been robbed, and he was only trying to retrieve his money.

"You threw a man into a barrel!" she cried.

"After he punched me!" the man shot back.

Qigang sighed, shaking his head, and covered his face with one hand. His other hand flicked a dismissive wave toward Kai, who bowed. When he rose, his eyes met Aranya's, and just before he turned on his heel to leave, a full, devilish grin split his face. He winked.

Her jaw dropped.

Despite herself, a familiar burning overtook her hands. Her tongue twisted as her mind fumbled with an infuriated response.

"Put your claws away!" Qigang spat, wiping his hand away from his face. "Where is Chen?"

"Chasing down the other culprit," she muttered.

"Wonderful," he said sarcastically. "Well, why don't you take your hook out of this one's throat and toss him back?"

"But what if—"

"You are free to go," Qigang said to the man.

She balked as the man turned a triumphant expression upon her before storming out of the wardpost. The door slammed shut with a resounding bang.

"You're just going to let him go? But I—"

"I know how this went," Qigang replied coolly, tenting his fingers. "You came upon them fighting and without thinking, without asking Chen what to do, without assessing the situation, you threw yourself upon it. You dragged this poor innocent man in here—"

"He might be lying!"

"Do not interrupt me!" he snapped, letting out a loud, frustrated exhale. "I have half a mind to dismiss you here and now."

Dismiss her now? Her lungs compressed so tightly she nearly couldn't breathe. Panic flared across her senses, and for a heartbeat, she wasn't standing before Qigang, staring at that stupid *jiaun* mounted on the wall behind his low desk, but instead standing in the doorway of a tenement. Before her wasn't a glowering, fat-lipped supervisor, but a collapsed, white-haired form on the ground. Weakened from hunger.

But in that moment, she hadn't known he was half-starved. Hadn't known he still breathed, and blood stuttered through his veins. She had thought her grandfather was dead. And it had been her fault because she wasn't there when he needed her.

She blinked, drew in a shaky breath. And then, that stabbing bolt of fear twisted in her gut. Twisted into something hotter, sharper. She flung a finger toward the door her rival had just disappeared through.

"Kai has been sitting on his backside instead of going to his patrol!" she said.

"Shi Kai has made zero mistakes to your five. I suggest you shut your yapping mouth before you dig yourself into a hole too deep to climb out of. Get back to work, listen to Chen, and maybe I won't dismiss you by the end of today."

Aranya stared at him. He couldn't . . .

She shoved away the crowding vision of her unconscious grandfather. She couldn't let her supervisor see how pale she'd probably gone. So she pursed her lips tightly and executed her best bow. "Very well. I will not disappoint you."

"Harumph."

She turned on her heel and marched out of the building, taking care to not slam the door behind her. She stood for several minutes on the step, letting her eyes adjust to the sunlight, and staring at the people and animals milling around.

Well, things were going just swimmingly.

"Spitfire," she cursed, grinding her heel into her boot. "*Spitfire.*"

She tore off into a run toward the south end of the city. The rest of today would simply have to go better if she were to have any hope of winning this rivalry.

CHAPTER 4

KAI STRODE OUT of the wardpost, rolling his eyes and shaking his head as he went. So far, catching a glimpse of Sun Aranya's stupidly shocked face a few minutes ago was the only fun he'd had all day. Everything else was a bloated dragon's gut of all that was cursed by the fathers in Zheninghai.

One thing! Couldn't he ask for *one thing* to go right? All that work—washed away in an instant. By something as stupid as bureaucratic error. He'd so carefully maneuvered his plans into place, and then some bright-eyed idiot with a fake smile waltzed in and said this appointment was supposed to be *hers*.

He needed this appointment. Sure, she probably thought she needed it too, but not like he did. It wasn't even like he needed it for very long. Just until he could make a better plan. Maybe find a way to get out of the empire, sprawling as it was. He wrinkled his nose at that thought. Leaving the empire meant learning a new language, and just thinking of the effort made him exhausted. Besides, he'd have to travel so far. Butagin in the north wasn't viable if he wanted to avoid the looming potential of war with the barbarians. Which, as delightful as war was, he could bring himself to go without.

The longer he could stay here before his cover was blown, the better. And that started with keeping this phoenix-scorched wardenship.

Not that he was worried about losing it to *her*. No. Not at all. If his memory from the Academy served him, she wasn't even that skilled. The more he thought about it, the more ridiculous it seemed to worry.

Gravel shifted beneath his boots as he set his face east, where Na had told him to meet her after he finished explaining his *situation* to the supervisor.

He vanished like a shadow at high noon.

Aranya had often imagined what it would feel like to come home from her first day of work. Tired—famished!—but nevertheless satisfied in the accomplishment of a hard day's work.

Instead, her feet dragged, aching and blistering in her new ill-fitting boots. The dying sun taunted the reddened skin of her face and neck. She was indeed tired and famished, but satisfied she was not.

"How was the first day?" a roughened woman's voice said from behind her.

Aranya whirled to find Na trudging up the street after her, favoring her left leg more than she had been this morning. The woman's mouth was set in a firm, straight line, the furrow between her eyes a permanent fixture.

"It was . . ." Aranya shrugged, not exactly sure what to say. The only thing that would have made today worse was if she'd been dismissed on the spot. So she resorted to shrugging again and attempting a small smile.

Now was not the time to indulge in tears and self-pity. No, she needed to keep her head screwed on straight so she could figure out how to win this competition.

Na gave a short, grim huff as she caught up to her. "I heard about the mistake. There's no way to handle issues like this without someone getting the short end of the stick. But don't let it get to you and don't listen to a single thing that fool Chen says. Save your questions for the wardens like me who have been here for a long time. And be glad you still have a chance."

Aranya swallowed the lump in her throat and nodded. "I *am* glad I still have a chance."

When Na made to turn down another street, in a different direction, Aranya said quickly, "Does your family live down there?"

Na didn't even turn around when she called over her shoulder, "Just me."

Aranya stopped walking. The older woman made her way through market stalls as owners packed up their wares for the day, loading them into donkey-hitched carts. Would that be Aranya in ten years if she kept this position? A warden, respected by others, but with no one to go home to?

Ye Ye wouldn't live forever.

She trudged up the street, her hollow stomach aching, until she reached an old but well-maintained building.

Home.

Not the entire thing, of course. Just one room. The tenement that she shared with Ye Ye. She wiped her sweaty, dirty face on the back of her sleeve and cringed. But Ye Ye probably would not notice her filth. She pursed her lips as she entered the building, navigated the halls until she found the right room, turned the key in the lock, and pushed open the door.

It was dim. No fire had been lit in the fireplace, but the curtains were open, and the last rays of sunlight turned the creaky floorboards orange. And, sadly, the morning's chaos hadn't fixed itself over the course of the day.

"Ye Ye?" Aranya called.

A soft purr met her ears.

She smiled, a true smile this time. She hobbled through the doorway and shut it behind her, leaning heavily against it for just a moment. "I'm home."

More purring met her ears.

She pushed off the door and dodged around boxes toward the windows, pushing aside the rest of the curtains. The white cat stretched out on the windowsill, purring uproariously. He gave a series of happy chirps and reached soft bean-padded paws in another long stretch.

"Hello, Ye Ye." Aranya grinned, petting him as he butted his head against her shoulder, her chin. "I see you've had a lovely day."

Ye Ye trilled, his tail curling into a happy crook.

"Are you hungry? I've brought food. Why don't you shapeshift so we can eat together?"

Gently, she picked up the soft, fluffy bundle and set him on his favorite mat near the empty hearth. He set to grooming while she arranged the last bits of wood for a fire. She bit back a curse. She'd planned to chop more wood this evening, but she had already forgotten. And the last thing she felt like doing right now was wielding an ax.

Except against Kai, perhaps.

"Well, if it isn't my lovely granddaughter come to make me something delicious to eat," that familiar crackled voice said from behind her.

Aranya smiled, twisting away from the half empty hearth. She was met with a crinkling pair of eyes and a wide, yellow-toothed grin, framed by white hair that he'd attempted and failed to re-tie.

"I don't know about delicious," she said. "But I'll have something for you to eat. Regardless, you're not allowed to complain."

He chuckled. The rasping, wheezing sound clenched around her lungs, but she absolutely refused to let her smile slip in front of Ye Ye.

"Everything you make is delicious, little sunflower."

That was certainly not true, but she had suspected years ago that his taste buds had perhaps grown a bit . . . *desensitized*.

"How was my brave warden's first day at her appointment, hmm?" Ye Ye asked, eyes almost enveloped in merry crinkles.

Aranya sat back on her heels. What could she tell him? She couldn't give him any cause for worry. He had taken care of her when she was a wee thing, and she had never wondered where her next meal was coming from or where they would sleep. And ever since that horrible day she'd found him collapsed on the floor, she refused to give him any reason to fear.

But Ye Ye knew her better than anyone. Even if he sometimes forgot they were in Zushui now, and not Suguan, he always seemed to know how she was feeling. So she settled on a compromise. With a frown, she lifted her gaze to meet his before letting it drop. "I did everything wrong today, Ye Ye."

No mention of Kai or their competition.

He tilted his head, knobby fingers tapping the weathered but clean floor. "Well, it *is* only your first day. And mistakes help you learn."

Aranya gave a consenting nod. "Yes, I suppose. But Ye Ye, all I learned was what *not* to do. Don't jump into a fight before you know what's happening. Don't take anyone to the supervisor. Don't take anyone even to the wardpost because it's apparently a *'waste of resources'* to bring in every brawler. Don't make decisions without Chen's approval. Don't listen to Chen's decisions because he's wrong half the time. Don't listen to what anyone says when you have your claws to their throat." She threw up her hands, shifting fully to face her grandfather. "This morning, I dragged this worthless fellow in because he'd knocked someone into a barrel, and then my supervisor took his side and made me let him go. Then guess what happened?

I run into him *again* and he's pinned some poor wench to the wall. I intervene, of course, and then Na tells me later that he gets arrested every single week. After that, Chen tells me I've gone and broken protocol that nobody thought to inform me of. Through it all, Kai is just over there smirking like a gloating idiot—"

"I bet your supervisor is delighted to have such a dedicated new warden." Ye Ye smacked his lips, giving a gummy grin.

Aranya stopped, finding herself unable to meet his gaze. Failure burned her tongue, her gut.

"I'm going to get some more firewood." She stood and gave him her softest smile. "I'll be back in a little while. I promise I'll have food ready soon."

"Not to worry, girl. Not to worry."

She swallowed with effort. Then she stood, hefted the axe from the doorway over her shoulder, and dragged her aching feet back outside. If things hadn't gone the way they had today, she would have simply bought firewood. But with only half a salary now? She tromped into the street. At least they lived on the edge of the city. She wouldn't have to go far, but how many trips would it take to get a sizeable stock for the next few days? If only she had a cart. Or a donkey.

"Hey! You! Sun girl!"

Aranya turned as a spindly man with a long face, long neck, and even longer hair came charging out of the door, an apron tied around his waist. His jutting chin crooked to one side, cheeks sallow and sunken under razor sharp cheekbones.

"Xu Lim." She bowed. "It is a pleasure—"

"Don't gush pleasantries at me, girl. Look at all this dirt you've tracked in! I don't care what position your fancy magic has gotten you, but while you're one of my tenants, you keep things clean. Shoes off at the door like any other tenant. No special treatment for magic-wielders."

"Oh! Sorry!" she said hastily. "Forgive my carelessness. I'll clean it up when I get back."

Lim shook his head sharply. "I cannot accept that. The fee is a tangu."

Her smile swept away immediately. "You're fining me for a bit of dirt? Here, step aside and I'll sweep it right now—"

"A tangu or I'll have you evicted!"

"Evicted?" she echoed, shock rendering her tongue almost useless. "Are you mad?"

"I am your landlord!"

Aranya stared at him, blood humming in her veins. It took all her self-control to not imagine five different ways she could land him flat on his back in the street. She met his gaze, meeting fury with fury, until she finally spewed a frustrated breath of air.

It wasn't that important. Not as important as preventing Ye Ye from having to move yet again. Besides, it would be difficult to find a place like this, in a safer part of town for this price. Now they couldn't afford anything nicer.

Begrudgingly, she undid the knot around her throat and pulled her string of coins out from beneath her tunic. She slid one of the copper coins off the string and smacked it into the landlord's palm.

"Now get in and clean it up," Lim said.

It was stupid. She was exhausted, hungry, and still had plenty of work to do. The dragon-eaten fine was paid. She shouldn't be this angry—it had been a long day. The sweeping would hardly take five minutes.

Regardless of all her reasoning that this *did not matter,* Aranya's hands started burning. Shifting. Lengthening.

"It's illegal to use magic outside of the emperor's service," a voice drawled from behind her.

She spun.

Kai leaned against the fence, ankles crossed, and arms spread out on the posts. He looked as pristine as she'd last seen him. Not a scratch or smudge of dirt on his handsome face or immaculate clothes. He'd probably sat at the wardpost all day while she wrestled with scoundrels.

"What do you want?" she snapped.

He shrugged and pushed off the fence. "A reason to arrest you would be nice."

"Then why'd you stop me? Why are you even here?" she said, standing up straighter when he reached her.

The fire in his gaze from this morning was gone. In its place? A lazy step, a gleaming pair of eyes, and a half-twisted mouth. Remnants of that devilish gloat he'd given her when he'd left Qigang's office.

Kai shrugged easily. "I live here."

He lived here? He lived *here*? So they were to be rivals—and neighbors?

She just couldn't catch a break. But she couldn't let him see that or he'd know his advantage. So, with her eyes half lidded because she was too tired, she flashed a smile his way and bowed grandly—though it was more like a forward flop—and swept her hand toward the glowering landlord and open door. "Then welcome home, Shi Kai."

His eyes met hers, golden flecks dancing. Then, before she had even fully straightened, he strode right past her, knocking into her shoulder as he did so.

"Hey!" she cried, stumbling back.

"Hey!" the landlord interjected.

Kai stopped on the threshold, turning a patronizing smile on the landlord. Without letting that gaze falter, he lifted his leg and yanked off one boot, then the other. Wordlessly, he strode inside and shut the door behind him.

The landlord sniffed and growled at her, "The *floor*," before disappearing inside after Kai.

Sweep the floor. Chop the wood. Haul the wood. Feed the grandfather. And do it quickly before Ye Ye had a chance to be worried.

Aranya groaned and pressed a hand to her face. The day couldn't get any worse.

CHAPTER 5

HER BOOTS WERE sopping wet the next morning.

Aranya stared down at them and the puddle seeping into the wood floor. The shafts flopped down, positively *ladened* with water. Cringing, she lifted one sodden boot up, only to find the soles were full of sitting liquid.

She glanced toward Ye Ye, curled up innocently in his cat form on the mat by the near-dead embers. A frown creased her forehead.

She certainly hadn't gotten her boots wet.

Had Ye Ye done it accidentally? Had he gotten up in the middle of the night to get a drink . . . and then spilled it?

Nothing else was wet. Just the boots.

She would simply have to ask him about it later when she came back from work. For now, she raced the sun to arrive early at her post. South patrol had been a disaster, but she decided to blame it on Chen. With proper instruction, she doubted it would be so terrible. Maybe today she would be paired with Na. Or better yet—be sent somewhere else.

Dressed and ready for the day, Aranya left a few boiled eggs for Ye Ye, scooped up her boots, and crept out of the tenement.

The sun had not risen, but the outside world was brightening even so. She inhaled a deep breath of crisp, clear morning. An irrepressible smile spread across her face. Irrepressible, that is, until she stuck her foot into the first boot. Soggy cold met her blistered skin. She winced, sighed, and then pulled on the other one.

They'd dry eventually.

Fathers, her feet would stink to the high heavens and down into the seven layers of *diyu* when she removed the boots. She took a squelching step. Winced.

"Today," she muttered to herself, "we're going to fight crime, keep this city lawful and orderly, and we are *not* going to let Kai get ahead." She pursed her lips, then added, "And we're not going to make Qigang mad."

When she reached the wardpost, she bypassed Qigang's office and headed straight for the armory. As soon as she opened the door, the mustiness of leather and dust hit her nostrils. She quickly set to work picking out the worst of the disarrayed weapons, hoping not to step on anyone's toes by selecting their favorites. Just as Na had instructed.

The door opened. By habit, Aranya turned, flashed a grin, and started to chirp, "Good—"

Kai stood in the doorway.

"—morning." The last word fell out of her mouth significantly less brightly than the first.

He blinked quickly, as though startled to see her too. His hair was a little mussed, despite the apparent attempt to tie it back cleanly. His sleep-fogged, half-closed eyes met hers and darkened before stepping to the opposite side of the armory.

Well, this was certainly a different side of Kai from the one she'd seen last night. She couldn't let this advantage pass her by.

"Fancy seeing you here," she said. "Sleep well?"

He grunted.

She paused her arming, stepping back so she could fold her arms across her chest, and leaned back against the wall. "So talkative in the morning."

Her boot squelched loudly when she took a step. He looked up, turning enough to glance down at her feet.

"I know." Aranya waved a hand. "My grandfather got my boots all wet sometime during the night. He's harmless as a rosefinch, but sometimes I think he doesn't always know what he's doing."

"Your grandfather?" Kai repeated, that one eyebrow lifting even higher. He returned to buckling a knife to his thigh. He suddenly seemed more awake, though his voice remained deepened with grogginess.

She grinned wider and continued. "Yes, my grandfather. Ye Ye. He's a shifter, too. We're all shifters in my family."

"Is he a partial-shifter like you?" Kai asked.

So he did remember her from the Academy.

She couldn't see his face, and the question was innocent enough, but the slight change in his tone and emphasis on the word *partial* made her blink. Was he . . . deriding her? She barely maintained her smile, suddenly self-aware of her broad shoulders. The outward testament to the limits of her magic.

At her silence, he twisted to look at her. Something sparked in his hazel eyes. Fire. Challenge. Daring.

Her hackles raised, realizing that this wasn't a sleepy version of Kai who was more open to politely conversing with her. He was goading her, testing her—and reminding her. Reminding her he was her rival, not her friend or comrade.

As if she would forget.

Aranya pushed off the wall and snatched a leather sling from the pile. “He is a full shifter.” She shoved the sling into her belt. “He was in the military, and eventually a lieutenant in his day.”

She spoke the words with pride, but Kai gave no sign of being impressed. He merely returned to his weapons. She chewed her lip, trying to find another topic of conversation. It had been a while since she’d seen it in action, but she still remembered that he was an evanescer—a magic-wielder who could teleport at will.

“Is everyone in your family an evanescer?” she asked.

He grunted.

She rolled her eyes at his back and squelched in her wet boots toward the door. But she paused a few steps away from the exit. She glanced his way again as he strapped on his broadsword and couldn’t help her curiosity. “*Were* your grades really bad?”

He said nothing, only finished the last buckle and straightened.

Whatever. She didn’t have time for nonsense. Shaking her head, she turned back toward the door. And found herself nose to nose with a smirking Kai.

She jumped, stumbling backward into one shelf of weapons. “Qilins!” she snapped, her scare turning to anger fast enough for her to shoot a glare up at him.

“Good warriors don’t startle easily,” he said smoothly. With that, he turned and stalked out of the armory.

She stared after him, gaping like a plucked chicken at the Harvest Festival. “What in all the seven valleys did those Academy girls see in him?”

Aranya took another step. Squish, squish.

Oh.

It took everything not to let the burning overtake her hands and shift them into weapons. Her face flushed hot even as her jaw dropped for the third time this morning.

Kai was an evanescer. Which meant . . .

Which meant he would have no problem getting through a locked door to soak her boots. And she'd told him that her grandfather had done it! She covered her face with her hand and winced.

"So *that's* how it's going to be," she said through clenched teeth. "Very well, Shi Kai. Challenge accepted."

When she left the armory, it was still early. The night wardens had not returned from their patrol, and the sun only barely poked over the horizon. She breathed in the crisp air deeply, enjoyed the cool morning air before the summer heat sweltered her to death in the afternoon. At least it was almost autumn.

She strode out into the courtyard and stopped, looking around the empty space. Qigang was likely in his office, and she definitely did not want to disturb him. And wherever Kai was, she didn't want to be there.

She was still standing there, trying to decide what to do when a shout rang out from the front steps. She didn't hesitate—she broke into a run and raced through the wardpost.

A youth was bent double against one of the supporting beams outside, gasping for air. He wore a sun-bleached set of robes and trousers. They clung to his skin with sweat, and his round face poured rivulets that dripped off his chin. His topknot drooped to one side, little flyaway hairs sticking out.

He was a scout, one of the youths that patrolled the city along with the wardens. The scouts' job was to fetch wardens and alert them to problems. Unlike the wardens, the scouts had not attended the Academy and possessed no magic. They were simple peasants who needed the money.

"What's the matter?" Aranya asked, instantly in front of him.

His eyes were wide when he said, "Lord Meng's daughter was kidnapped!"

She jerked back, her mind reeling. "Kidnapped?" She gripped the boy's shoulder to prevent him from bending over again. "What do you mean? Tell me everything!"

He winced and grabbed his side. Fathers, had the lad never run in his life?

"Lord Meng . . . his daughter—she vanished! Sometime in the night, they don't know . . . when," he gasped.

"What kind of magic does she wield?" she asked. If her father was a lord, then he had magic, which meant his daughter would have inherited it too. Knowing what type could help track her down.

"She doesn't have magic."

Aranya's eyes snapped to his. "What? A lord's daughter with no magic? Where is their estate?"

An entirely different voice said from behind her, "Lord Meng's residence would be in the Dangui district on north patrol."

That voice made fire rush down Aranya's spine. She closed her eyes for the briefest moment, then let go of the boy's shoulder and turned to glare at Kai. "You are *not* coming. I was here for this one first!"

Kai leveled chilly eyes to hers and snorted. "I'll let you join me. *If* you can keep up."

He vanished.

Simply *vanished* right off the wardpost steps, leaving her and the scout gaping behind him. But only for an instant. Aranya scrambled around the boy and tore off at a run into the streets of Zushui, fuming as she went. Kai was likely already there by now. Insufferable evanescer.

Finding the Dangui district was simple enough; she ran north until the houses looked less like huts and more like palaces. Identifying the particular house was no more difficult, as she only had to ask a breadman on his early morning circuit where the lord lived, and the closer she got, the louder the commotion grew.

The lord's yard was full of fussing servants, weeping children, and frantic women. Shouting orders in the middle of it all was a pink-faced, blunt-nosed man still in his silk dressing robes, leaning on a cane despite having a full head of jet-black hair. Had this case been too serious to run off too? Qigang should have been informed.

But if they had told Qigang, he would have sent someone else. How was she to prove her worth if he only ever sent her to the south patrol?

There was no sign of Kai, so Aranya plodded straight up toward the man she assumed to be Lord Meng. He kept shouting orders, telling some servants to take his other children inside, to board up the windows, double the guards, and to please get those dragon-eaten wardens over here.

"Lord Meng," she said and bowed with a winsome smile. "I am Sun Aranya, a warden of Zushui, at your service."

The lord's attention shot to her, and she almost took a step back at the strange light flaring in his eyes. "They only sent two wardens?" he growled, quickly giving her a disapproving once-over. "This is outrageous! Someone send another scout—we need a crew of wardens here!"

She was just about to brush past him and get to work when a voice spoke in her head. Low, threatening.

You bring my daughter back alive, warden, or I will personally see that you never set foot in a wardpost again.

Aranya almost leapt out of her skin, glancing back at the lord. He was not looking at her, occupied with shouting at someone else. But that light flared in his eyes, too bright. She turned on her heel to climb marble steps into the mansion. Her heart pounded in her chest.

A mind-speaker. It made sense, after all. Noblemen possessed magic, since it was magic and not birth that dictated the upper classes in society. The stronger or rarer the magic, the more noble. Thus, it was to be expected that Lord Meng would wield powerful magic, but she hadn't expected him to be a mind-speaker. Or such a menacing one at that.

Yet his daughter had no magic?

Involuntarily, her spine crawled. She rarely thought of herself as superstitious, but her skin tingled as she crossed the threshold into the house and onto the sprawling scarlet rug. Some said the loss of magic in a generation indicated a family curse. The more powerful the parents of the magicless offspring, the darker the curse.

Their very own great emperor had a daughter born with no magic, and he was a mighty fire-wielder. His other children were fire-wielders like him. But not his middle child, Princess Meiling. Her lack of magic was even more distressing than Lord Meng's daughter. The shadow of that curse had plagued the empire since her birth.

But curse or no, the reality remained that without magic, a son or daughter could not lift their family higher in society. And if they weren't climbing the social ladder, they were slipping down it.

No one wanted to be the weak link. Aranya knew that fear all too well.

She only had to ask a few bustling servants before they directed her up several more flights of marble stairs and through ornate, dark-wood corridors until she reached the missing girl's rooms. She forced herself not to falter as she stepped over the threshold. Curses and superstition had no place at this job.

Aranya expected to see a smashed window, a disheveled bed, and furniture bashed against walls. But the room was pristine. She swallowed her surprise with a few blinks, taking in the neat array, the slightly ajar door that revealed a well-maintained inner chamber, the gentle downturn of the jewel-blue quilt on the bed. Even the tea setting at one of the low tables hadn't broken. No signs of struggle.

There was, however, a pair of feet and a back. Kai crouched on all fours, his head stuck under the bed.

"What are you doing?"

He made a hissing sound that might have been a curse and carefully eased his head out from under the bed. Enough that he could arch an eyebrow at her. "I see you finally made it." His gaze took in her sweaty face, how her hair and clothes stuck to her skin, while his were perfectly pressed and dry. As if he couldn't help it, he smirked.

Her returning smile was as sticky as sap. "So why are we hiding under the bed?"

Kai gestured vaguely at the room. "You've got eyes and a brain—or so one might presume. Figure it out yourself."

"Doesn't seem very efficient to have us both doing the same work," she said.

He rolled his eyes. "Very well—I will give you a hint."

"A *hint*? Is this a game to you? We're hunting down a kidnapped girl!"

"You want to know what I've found or not?"

Aranya's silence was answer enough. Arms akimbo, she waited with a glare. He met it evenly and said nothing. Making her wait. It took everything inside her not to huff an exasperated sigh. But that would only give him the reaction he wanted.

"What sees without eyes, breaks under pressure, and—"

"You're giving me a riddle," she deadpanned. "Right now?"

"Can't figure it out?" He smirked again.

"You made it up, didn't you?"

"Of course I did. This level of brilliance can only come from—"

"You clearly mean the window, but a window *sees* nothing itself, only the people looking through it, and literally everything breaks under pressure."

"Not diamonds."

She nodded very slowly as he tilted his head innocently to one side. "Right. I'm glad to know you're still twelve years old." She strode to the intact but open window. Frowning down at the three-story drop, she asked, "Was she taken out of the window? There's no roof or lattice to climb down. It's just wall. A very difficult descent."

Especially for someone who wasn't trained at the Academy.

She leaned further out, trying to puzzle out how one could accomplish such a feat. A skilled kidnapper could have scaled the walls, but to carry a flailing prisoner with him? Perhaps if the kidnapper were a magic-wielder, it could have been accomplished. If a magic-wielder, that meant they were dealing with brigands—those who illegally used their magic outside the service of the emperor.

Could it have been a *mó guǐ* attack?

That seemed unlikely. Most *mó guǐ* usually stayed out of the city. Why bother with a victim asleep on the third floor of a mansion? Surely there was much easier prey for a midnight snack. She hopped up onto the windowsill, about to swing her legs over the side, when Kai interrupted her.

"Don't be an idiot. Look at the floor."

Aranya shot him a glare but dropped from the sill into a crouch on the ground. She squinted, got to her hands and knees, and peered closely at the wood floor and the edge of the red and gold trimmed rug.

"Dirt," he said, and she could have sworn she heard him roll his eyes.

"I don't see any—"

"There!" Kai jabbed his finger right in front of her nose. "Dirt!"

She squinted again. *Maybe* that was a speck of dirt she saw? She sat back on her heels and nodded toward the bed. "I assume you found more dirt there?"

He only rolled his eyes again and went back to his own investigation.

Aranya reined in her impulse to growl under her breath, and returned to the window, frowning down at the drop. She hopped back onto the windowsill again and swung her legs out. At Kai's furrowed brow, she smiled sweetly and said, "Since you're determined to be unhelpful, I'll scale the walls for my own clues."

"Scale the walls?"

What had he thought she was going to do when she almost climbed out of the window a minute ago? Jump?

In a burning flash, she used her magic to shift her hands. She grinned at his wide-eyed stare taking in the lizard pads now lining her palms. "What? Did you think I only had talons?"

She began lowering herself down the wall from the sill, unsure if she was pleased or irritated that she had been so beneath his notice at the Academy. "You keep your clues to yourself, and I'll keep mine to myself."

His eyes darted between her on the sill to the bed where he crouched, his mouth opening and closing once. Was Shi Kai almost *sputtering*? Did he finally see the stupidity of his bid to keep his discoveries to himself? Did he realize that no matter how fancy his evanescing magic was, he couldn't scale a wall like her?

"Unless," she said, "you want to show me what you found, and then I'll share what I learn when I climb the wall."

Kai's eyes darkened as he pursed his lips, but he begrudgingly pointed at the floor near him. "There was dirt here and here, but the carpet here," he pointed near the edge of the bed, "was not dirty. The rug is matted in these three places. Two knees and an elbow."

Aranya raised two eyebrows as she pulled herself back onto the windowsill. "I think you're making this up to throw me off the trail so you can steal the glory."

Kai flashed a quick, patronizing smile. "Just be glad I'm letting you in on this lead."

She waved a hand dismissively as he again crouched beside the bed. Whatever—she would hear him out. Perhaps he was right.

"So . . . your point is that a nobleman's daughter probably wouldn't have dirt on her slippers, so the dirt came from elsewhere," she said.

"There is no dirt by the door to these rooms, which would be the case if she tracked it in."

"We know the kidnapper used the window, then?"

That would explain his reaction that she would withhold what information she found scaling the wall. He let out a low, frustrated breath through his nostrils.

"I know you think I'm stupid," Aranya said. "But you don't have to be *quite* so condescending."

He didn't respond, only ducked his head back under the bed and supported his weight with one elbow, like he must believe the kidnapper had done.

"If the kidnapper had been after the girl, why did he take time to kneel under her bed? Why not just snatch her up and run out the window?" she asked.

"That's what I was trying to figure out when you interrupted—seven valleys!"

"What?" She jumped down and hurried to his side, getting on her knees, and tried to see what he was reaching for. "What did you find?"

Kai grunted, winced, and rolled out from the bed. He blinked, finding her face close to his, and she jerked backward. He tossed something to the ground between them.

A polished black stone, perfectly flat and round. It was glassy enough that when Aranya leaned over it, she saw her own widened eyes and gaping mouth in the reflection.

"There is no way," she breathed.

Now it was Kai's turn to grin wryly. He swept up the stone and slipped it into his pocket, gathering his long limbs and standing. "This just got far more interesting."

Maybe also far more dangerous?

"A siren," Aranya said softly, still aghast.

Kai was already by the window, peering down the vertical wall. "A siren committing crimes. We've got a brigand to track. At least the girl is more likely to be alive than if a *mó guǐ* abducted her."

True. Which boded better odds for their warden careers if Lord Meng's threat was to be believed.

"Why . . ." She trailed off, scrunching her face in concentration.

"What?" he asked impatiently.

"If the stone was used to subdue the girl, then why is it still here? Why not on the girl's person?"

Kai paused, his back to her. He was silent long enough to indicate he hadn't given any thought to the oddity. "The siren might have used multiple," he said at last. "One under the bed to make sure the girl didn't wake before she was fully spelled."

"If the siren left it by accident, then that was certainly careless. Either way, please excuse me." Aranya bumped past him and shifted her hands in a flick. With practiced agility, she lowered herself out of the window. Her muscles braced at the effort, her abdomen flexing tight, but she had trained for this. Even though her feet couldn't shift and were near useless except for finding footholds in the stone, she could still hold herself up entirely by her hands.

This was why she needed so much upper body strength.

Kai stared down through the window at her, his mouth open and eyebrows knit, as she began climbing down. She peered closely at the stones, looking for smudges of the dirt he claimed he found inside. Nothing. But she *did* find something else.

"Hey!" she called, her core clenching at the effort. "There are some scuff marks on the stone. It looks like he took her down the wall this way!"

But *how*?

Aranya pulled herself closer to the wall, palms flat against the stone and toes wedged into the jutting edges. She glanced over her shoulder, down the long drop to the ground below. Already, her arms and stomach burned. How could a siren brigand—especially one not gifted with feral strength or shifter abilities—have scaled this wall with a captive?

At least the siren part explained why the girl hadn't screamed. The siren's spell-stone planted under her bed would have made her a mindless, willing victim. Prone to do whatever the brigand instructed.

"No sign of a rope lowered out the window," Kai called from above.

"None?"

"None."

"Are you sure?"

He glared down at her, and she glared back. She focused her attention back on the wall, scaling down further. The scuff marks stopped. Wait, no, they didn't stop, they simply did not directly descend downward. They went . . . diagonal?

Aranya shuffled sidelong, her hands giving the softest popping sound when she lifted them. She followed the scuffs until she could see a direct trail going diagonally down the wall. "Who scales a wall diagonally?" she mused under her breath. "Or rather, *why* would someone scale a wall that way?"

Lifting one hand so she hung precariously from the other, she brushed a lizard finger over the scuffed stone's edge. Dusty. The grout looked loosened, like someone had replaced the stone.

Her shoulders burned. Sweat beaded on her forehead, dripped down her temple. But she gritted her teeth and kept moving.

"Fathers!" she gasped. "Kai! I think I figured it out!"

He vanished from the window, only to reappear below her on the ground. She scurried down the rest of the wall as quickly as she dared before dropping the last few feet.

"I think our siren had help," Aranya announced.

CHAPTER 6

THERE WAS DEFINITELY only one brigand in the girl's room." Kai frowned, crossing his arms over his chest and sticking his leg out in an unnecessarily dominant stance.

"The second brigand didn't enter the room at all. His job was to get the siren up to her room without anyone detecting it," Aranya said. She couldn't help her triumphant grin. "An earth-wielder, I'm almost certain of it. See these stones?" She brought him to the lowest stones with scuff marks. "They've been moved. The grout is all displaced. A certain type of earth-wielder could displace stone, correct?"

"That is absolutely ridiculous."

"No—look! They go diagonal up to the window, and see at how far apart they are? A pace's width. They probably weren't brought out far—six inches, perhaps?—because of the scuffs. The earth-wielder could have made the staircase and left the siren to kidnap the girl and bring her back down."

Kai looked momentarily uncertain, but it was gone in a blink. "Still ridiculous," he tossed over his shoulder, turning in the direction the steps had begun in the stone. "Why would the siren even be necessary then? Just knock the girl out."

"Perhaps they didn't want her hurt. Blunt force trauma to the brain can cause a concussion."

"I know what blunt force trauma can do to a brain. I don't need a walking, giggling textbook to tell me that," he growled icily. "There are ways to knock someone out besides hitting them."

What had he just called her?

Aranya stared at his back as he knelt to inspect the ground. How easy it would be to inflict blunt force trauma on the back of *his* head at this moment. Instead, she gritted her teeth and took off at a run, leaving Kai behind her.

"What are you doing?" he called.

She only ran faster, the pounding of blood in her head clearing her fury. The more they talked, the more they fought, and fighting wasted precious time. There was no need to explain herself to him. She would simply go ahead and rescue the girl by herself while he was stuck back—

Suddenly, Kai appeared right in front of her.

She couldn't stop herself in time and barreled straight into him. She grabbed hold of his tunic to catch herself, but his arms wheeled precariously, and her momentum sent them sprawling into the dirt, Aranya landing with a hard, *"Oof!"* on top of him.

He grunted and opened his eyes to look down his double chin at her. A smirk tilted his mouth as his hand came up to brace her waist. "Well, hello there," he said.

Aranya lay frozen there for a heartbeat, eyes far too wide, clenching her fists, dust from the fall getting into her gaping mouth. Then she leapt to her feet. "What is *wrong* with you?"

He sat up, flicked dust off his shoulder. "Why are you running off like a maniac?"

She wiped her mouth on her sleeve, gaping at him. The heat of embarrassment burned in her blood, mingled with coursing anger. She stood there, covered in sweat, considering shifting into her talons and relieving him of his face.

Don't let him get under your skin. He's being difficult to scare you off. Which just shows he's afraid you'll succeed before him. And that's his problem, not yours, she thought to herself.

Taking a deep breath and mustering every ounce of self-control she possessed, Aranya smiled at her rival and brushed herself off. He would not undo her.

"We're running out of time," she told him evenly as she set a quick walking pace. "They might be mounted on horses. I figure they probably wouldn't want to bring her deeper into the city and risk being spotted by a patrol, which cuts off three directions." She pointed toward the east, west, and south patrols. "This leaves north as their only option to enter the wilderness. They clearly came from this direction, since they didn't enter her room from the opposite side. That outcropping of trees over there is very close to Lord Meng's mansion, so if they wanted to run in quickly without being spotted by anyone, they would most likely come from that direction. They could have left horses tied up, the remnants of which should be easy for us to spot. They wouldn't have kept them too close though, otherwise anyone could have heard them fleeing. If it happened recently, we might overtake them."

She paused, then flashed a smile his way. "That is why I was running in this direction, Shi Kai."

She expected another insult, a fight from him—some reason he thought they should go back to find a firmer trail.

He was silent, however. Briefly, he reached up to scratch his neck, then stopped as if he realized what he was doing.

"You're welcome to go back and keep sniffing the dirt back there," she said. "I'm going to catch a couple of brigands."

After several minutes of walking with no response, she glanced back over her shoulder, then halted in surprise. Kai wasn't there. She looked in every direction, but there was no sign of him. At first, she frowned, but then merely shrugged; if he wanted to vanish into nothing, then she wouldn't argue. It wasn't like she had wanted him to come in the first place.

Her spine prickled nevertheless as she reached the line of trees that melted into wilderness. She could almost hear her Academy masters berating her yet again for being impulsive. Closing her eyes for only a second, she bit her lip.

Perhaps it was foolish to think she could beat two brigands in a fight. But the way she saw it, most brigands were deserters—magic-wielders who abandoned the Academy or their appointments—and deserters rarely left because they were the best at something. These particular ones might never have finished their Academy training, *if* they had even attended. Leaving behind the siren stone was a mistake she wouldn't expect from well-seasoned wielders.

Besides, she fully believed Lord Meng had the power to do exactly what he threatened. And the thought of that . . . The worst moment of her life flashed before her eyes again, and she shoved it away. Now was not a time to think. It was a time to *act*.

Just as she suspected, finding evidence of horses was easy. Bark was broken off a tree branch where tethers must have been looped, below which lay a pile of droppings and a chewed-up patch of grass. Still no sign of Kai anywhere. Unless he thought her reasoning completely idiotic—which it *wasn't*—then he should have followed her or gone ahead. Yet he was nowhere. He couldn't have gone back, could he?

Aranya broke into a jog, following the horse trail. Unlike her original guess, however, it didn't look like the brigands galloped off. Finding the horses' hoofprints in the grass was much more difficult, which indicated a slower pace. But every time she feared she was about to lose the trail, she found more droppings and hurried on faster.

No twists and turns. Due north.

If she were a full shifter, she could shift into a horse and gallop her way there. Or, for something stealthier, a jaguar.

She was reminded of Academy hunts when they were thrown out in the *mó guǐ*-overrun wilderness at dusk and told to survive until dawn. Some students would run and hide, while others hunted throughout the night for the monsters. Only a few of the top students hauled back *mó guǐ* carcasses—Tan Shangdi, Cao Renshu, and Hu Fen. She'd tried but had not stumbled upon a single *mó guǐ* all night long.

Suddenly, she caught a whisper of voices in the morning wind. She instinctively crouched lower as she slowed her pace and quieted her steps. Though her heart pounded in her chest, she forced herself to take soft, even breaths. With a quick flick, her hands burned like fire and grew long, razor-sharp talons.

She moved swiftly toward those voices. Her muscles coiled tightly, dying to spring free. Her blood hummed as she ducked through the trees. She tried to make her hands stop shaking.

Cool, calm, lethal. That was what she would be.

There, ahead!

Two horses, walking at a relaxed pace, with three riders. Aranya darted between tree trunks, staying hidden while trying to ascertain what she could about the brigands. She peered between the foliage of a katsura tree enough to make out that the brigand closest to her was a woman and the other one was a man.

They were . . . laughing?

Yes, they laughed and bantered. She couldn't make out what they said, but it seemed *lighthearted.*

Aranya blinked, cocking her head to one side. Perhaps she simply had not seen enough brigands to know how they usually behaved.

Maybe this unhurried gait was how kidnappers usually were, and she only imagined the low hooded, galloping-across-the-plains type.

Regardless, it was obvious that they were the kidnappers. The male brigand held the victim in front of him on his saddle. Only the girl's head was visible above the man's shoulder, but it was upright. She was no doubt still under the siren's magic.

Rushing headlong into a tense situation hadn't served her well yesterday, so she tried to calm the raging adrenaline in her veins. Tried not to flick her talons repeatedly in nervousness.

Which one should she attack first?

If she attacked the woman taking up the rear, that would leave an easy opening for the man to gallop away with the girl. She ought to attack the man first. It would leave her vulnerable to attack, but that seemed better than her other option.

She slinked through the forest, trying to get ahead of them for a clear shot at the man. Her talons started aching—itching. Instinct flooded her blood.

Should she go for the killing blow immediately?

She swallowed, refusing to balk. She was a magic-wielder of the empire; this was her duty. And what a story she would have to share with Ye Ye tonight! He would be so proud.

She waited, tree bark digging into her back, for the man to reach her. Just another few steps . . .

Aranya leapt.

She hadn't meant to yell, but an animalistic roar came ripping from somewhere deep inside her. She jumped straight for the man's arm to drag him off the horse.

The moment her talons sunk into the man's arms and side, something faltered within her. The feeling of flesh and bone and muscle and skin—of blood spurting onto her hands and into her face . . . She gritted her teeth and yanked hard, as her killing instinct swept away her qualms.

Shouting filled the air. Screams too.

Then Aranya landed flat on her back on the ground. She stared up at blue sky, not comprehending what had just happened save for one conscious thought: she couldn't breathe.

While she gasped for the breath she'd lost, a face covered the blue sky above her. A woman's face. Aranya gasped again, clutching at her screaming lungs, and tried to scoot away. In one half-aware, fully frantic moment, she found her talons had vanished. She reached for a knife.

The woman pulled a smooth, black stone from a pouch at her side.

Aranya choked, trying to scramble to her feet to get away, to run. But the woman smiled and bent down to drop the stone into one of Aranya's still soggy boots.

"Sleep," the woman smiled again, backing up. She twisted her hands into a circle and focused it on Aranya. "Sleep and do not pursue us anymore. You never found us."

Blackness closed in on her vision. The girl and the man she'd injured were gone. The horses, too. All she could see was the smiling woman, rotating her hands and speaking soft, lulling words.

"Sleep."

She forced her eyes open, fighting the sweeping magic, but it was too strong. Only her panicked, tightening chest kept her from immediately losing consciousness. It was the one reason her eyes were still open to see a tall form appear right behind the woman and knock her clean to the ground.

CHAPTER 7

THE SPELL ON Aranya immediately weakened. Enough that she could roll to her side and gasp for tiny sips of air. The world spun around her, the ground tilting precariously.

Kai. Brigands. The girl. She had to get up.

Aranya pushed against the ground, only to feel something cinch tighter around her mind. She almost fell back into the dirt, but she gritted her teeth and lifted her head. When her vision cleared, Kai was straddling the struggling woman's back, knees digging into the ground at her sides. Somewhere, he'd found rope and was trussing her hands behind her. She bucked and kicked, but he only adjusted his position and clenched his teeth until her wrists were bound. Much faster, he bound her kicking ankles.

"Get the stone out of your boot!" he called to Aranya. "She's still working her spells!"

The stone. The stone—yes.

Though the world remained foggy, air finally came easier. Her hands floated like random appendages in her vision, flailing like a newborn babe's. Somehow, she managed to reach inside her boot and draw out the stone. The proximity of holding it in her palm nearly made her black out again. With the last reserves of her strength and willpower, she flung it away.

The world cleared.

Aranya gasped as her vision focused and her mind sharpened. They were in the woods, and Kai had bound one brigand. But Aranya knew there was another one, and *he* had the girl.

Kai was gagging the siren—to prevent her from working more magic—when a strange whirring sound broke into the clearing.

She whirled, finding the other brigand some sixty paces away, crouched behind a tree. His face was drawn, focused, and his hand was outstretched.

The earth-wielder.

As she watched, with a swooping motion of his hands, he lifted a volley of rocks from the surrounding ground. His gaze was not on Aranya, however, but on Kai, who still straddled the siren and was busy stuffing a gag into her chomping mouth.

"Kai!" Aranya screamed and lunged.

He looked up, eyes white-ringed with confusion as she barreled into him for the second time that day. It was just in time—rocks smashed into the tree behind where his head had been only seconds before.

He vanished out from under her before they hit the ground.

She face-planted, earning a mouthful of grass. She barely had time to throw her hands over her head before the earth-wielder launched more stones toward her. They whirred in the air above her and crashed into tree trunks.

Then there was a loud grunt and another cry.

Instantly, Aranya was on her feet in time to see Kai appear behind the other brigand, brace the man's neck between his forearm and biceps, and squeeze. The man fought, using one hand to pry Kai's arms free of his neck, and with the other hand, he lifted another pile of rocks.

Kai's eyes flicked to the rocks about to be flung into his face, and he squeezed harder. His face contorted with strain, but he held onto the struggling brigand.

Aranya couldn't get there in time. They were too far away.

The siren's black stone lay near her foot. Moving on instinct, she scooped it up and yanked her sling free of her belt. Oh, she hoped her aim was good today! She didn't have time for careful precision or even to get good momentum. It was all happening too fast.

She flung the stone as hard as she could and prayed it didn't hit Kai.

Just before the man launched his stones into Kai's face, the siren's black stone hit him square in the belly. His rocks faltered, some fell—and then Kai's hold finally won, and the man went limp.

Kai gasped in relief, rolling the man to the ground and off him. He looked up, his eyes meeting Aranya's across the span of forest between them. She was still braced in her thrower's stance, one foot in front of the other, hand outstretched with her released sling.

They stared at each other for a moment. No pretense, only wide-eyed relief.

Then Kai barked, "Rope. I need to bind him before he wakes up. They have some in their saddlebags."

She furrowed her brow. Not a word of thanks? It was petty, but she snapped anyway: "I just saved your life and that's all you have to say?"

He only snorted. "You wouldn't have saved my life if I hadn't saved yours. Everyone knows you attack the siren first, idiot."

Aranya found herself marching toward the siren's horse, despite how she glowered at Kai. "How was I supposed to know which one was which?"

"You look at them," he snapped in return. "I could tell even before you attacked."

She sidestepped around the squirming and scowling siren to the wandering horse and dug around in the saddlebags. Her fingers burned with the need to shift, despite the danger having passed.

By the time she'd flung the rope at Kai's feet, her blood was boiling.

"And where were you? You left me to face them alone! If you'd been there with me, I wouldn't have had to choose which one to attack first!"

He didn't even look up as he rolled the man onto his stomach and set to binding his wrists behind him. He worked swiftly, expertly. "You are so loud and reckless. I knew you'd get caught. I stayed on the fringe so they would think you were alone and give me the advantage of surprise."

"You used me as bait?"

"If that's how you prefer to think about it, then sure."

He looked up then, his mouth twisting devilishly.

She couldn't keep talking to him. She would lose her temper and do something she regretted. Spinning on her heel, she marched away from him and his grating conversation. "I'm going to find the girl."

"Back that way," Kai said from behind her.

She tossed a seething smile over her shoulder. "I *know*. I'm only going to check on the siren first."

"Good. Then we can find the girl together."

She only sniffed and hurried to the siren's side. The woman had scooted into a half-sitting position against a tree and was scraping her gag and cheek against the bark. She worked her bound hands, trying to reach for the pouch hanging from her belt.

Aranya met the woman's fierce gaze and paused. "You're younger than I realized," she said, recognizing the pouch as the bag she must carry her black stones in. With a swift movement, she whipped out her knife and sliced the pouch free. The woman's eyes bugged as

Aranya stepped back and took the pouch with her. Then she gripped the woman's shoulders and shifted her back to the ground, away from the tree, so she couldn't loosen her gag.

Kai dragged the bound and unconscious man from his hiding spot. At the woman's frantic eyes, Aranya said, "Don't worry, he's not dead."

Kai shot her a raised eyebrow, but she only shrugged.

She hesitated, though, as he heaved the man into the clearing. Kai was an evanescer, yet he dragged this brigand. Which probably meant one limit of his magic was that he couldn't evanesce other people like his more powerful counterparts.

Before she could offer a chipper, *"Let's go find the girl!"* Kai vanished again. She stared at the thin air where he'd stood a second ago and ground her teeth as she marched into the forest.

"This vanishing business is getting very annoying," she muttered, tromping loudly through the woods. Whatever his limits, evanescing seemed quite the luxurious ability when she could only shapeshift her dragon-eaten hands.

When she broke through the forest into another clearing, not caring how her soggy boots cracked underbrush louder than an elephant, she immediately halted.

There was the kidnapped girl all right, sitting on the other horse. She was beautiful, probably a year or two younger than Kai and Aranya, with a long, slender neck and flowing, silken locks. Her sparkling eyes were alight with fear, her full rosy lips puckered, her wrists bound harshly behind her.

Every inch the damsel in distress.

And there was Kai, standing at the horse's side, giving her his smoothest grin as he pulled a black stone out of the pocket of her silk dressing gown and tossed it away.

"I'm Shi Kai, here to rescue you," he said, his smile lifting with a cocky edge as his hand drifted to rest reassuringly on the girl's knee. She nodded down at him, biting her lip. Slowly, seemingly not to frighten her, he drew his knife. "No need to worry; I am only cutting your bonds."

Aranya nearly gagged. Instead, she stomped on a particularly loud twig and folded her arms across her chest. "Daughter of Lord Meng?"

The girl looked up from Kai, her eyes widening again. He twisted to glare at Aranya, who only smiled.

"A pleasure to make your acquaintance. I am Sun Aranya. Kai and I are here to return you to your father."

The girl glanced between Kai and Aranya and nodded stiffly. She touched her tender wrists gingerly, and then . . . Oh fathers, no. Her beautiful eyes welled up, and she burst into a fountain of tears. Poor thing.

Aranya sighed and started toward the girl again.

But Kai was already at her side. "There, there," he soothed. "All will be well. Here, come."

He reached out to her, and she wrapped her arms around his neck as he lifted her out of the saddle and into his arms. She sobbed piteously into his chest. He held her tightly, mumbling into her hair as he turned back the way they'd come.

Was he seriously going to carry her all the way back to the clearing where the brigands were bound? It would have been sweet if she didn't know the type of person Kai was, and that his sweetness always had an ulterior motive.

"Bring the horse," he called over his shoulder to Aranya.

"Bring the horse? Why are you carrying her? Why not leave her on the horse?" she called after his retreating form. Then, when he didn't respond, she gave a frustrated, "Ugh!" and grabbed the horse's lead, trudging after them.

At least she learned several things about her rival. Namely, that he couldn't be bothered to abandon his conniving flirtations even on duty. Perhaps she could use that to her advantage in the future.

As she and the horse tromped after Kai and his rescued maiden, she couldn't help her chuckle. It turned into a snicker, which turned into a full-out laugh. She was almost doubled over, practically stumbling through the underbrush, when she looked ahead and caught Kai's glare.

It only sent her laughing more.

But her lingering snickers died the moment they reached the clearing.

The siren was bent over the earth-wielder, a smooth black stone placed on his chest. She flexed her bound hands as she mumbled words over him.

Her gag was gone.

CHAPTER 8

EVERYTHING HAPPENED TOO fast. Aranya dropped the horse's lead. Kai dropped the girl. He drew his sword, and Aranya flicked her hands into talons. Wild heat flooded her blood, and she charged at the siren with a battle cry.

Kai vanished. She didn't have time to see where he went. All she saw was the instantaneous portrait of betrayed horror on the girl's face as she landed rump first in the dirt. Then Aranya was racing toward the siren.

The siren's panicked eyes lifted from her rousing accomplice. She grabbed the stone she'd been using to wake him and flung it toward Aranya as she barreled toward her. She started mumbling words as she backed up and moved her bound hands in the air.

The siren's aim was off, and the stone didn't land near enough to snag Aranya in its clutches. The power swelled, however, its tendrils snaking out to wrap around her ankles. Bidding her to stop attacking and leave. But her momentum sent her hurtling past it and tackled the siren.

They landed in a tangled heap of *oofs*.

Somehow, the siren had freed her legs and now used them to her advantage. Aranya was on top, but the siren exploited the momentum of their fall to roll them both and grab one of Aranya's wrists with her bound hands. She twisted, smashing her knee into Aranya's chin, driving her boot into her palm, pinning her other taloned hand to the ground.

Stars spun in Aranya's vision from the blow, her teeth jarred. But the siren's position left her entire lower body unguarded. Aranya rolled back suddenly, bringing up her feet to tuck into the siren's side and kick her backward over her head.

The siren lost her grip on Aranya's talons. With a roar, Aranya somersaulted and swiped at the brigand. Blood spurted, mingling with a pained cry.

Then Kai was there.

He crouched behind the brigand, one hand gripping her bloody arm and the other pressing a knife into her throat. "Enough fighting," he said calmly.

She writhed in his grip. He responded, clenching tighter on her injured arm. She let out another cry as her head fell back.

"You kill me, or they kill me," she said. "What is the point of waiting for trial? Just get it over with."

"Justice," Aranya said, climbing to her feet and staring down at the siren.

The siren glared, giving only token resistance to Kai as he bound her ankles again. Her gaze was fierce, and Aranya was struck again by how young she was.

"You talk of justice, yet you know nothing about me. They will kill us if you take us," the siren said, wincing as blood trickled down her elbow. "They will execute us."

"You deserted the emperor's forces. You wield magic outside of the law. You kidnapped a daughter of Zheninghai. You think you don't deserve to die?" Aranya asked. She carefully wiped her bloody talons on her robes and let them vanish.

The siren lowered her brow. Kai retrieved the gag and was about to retie it when she jerked away and snapped, "I'm having a conversation with the shifter, you qilin-spawn. Kindly allow me my mouth."

"And risk you working your magic? I don't think so."

"Wait," interrupted Aranya. "I want to ask her something."

Kai glared between them, then huffed and retreated with the gag. Probably to go find wherever his hapless maiden had hidden herself.

"Why did you kidnap the girl?" Aranya asked.

The siren jerked her head toward the earth-wielder lying on the ground. "I'll tell you if you let him go."

Aranya raised an eyebrow, crossing her arms over her chest. "Was it for your own gain or someone else's?" *Why on earth would you kidnap a lord's magicless daughter?*

The siren glared again, drawing her knees up to her chest and looping her bound hands around them, setting her mouth stubbornly.

"We don't have to deliver the earth-wielder alive, you know," said Aranya.

"Fine!" she snapped. "Fine, I'll tell you! Maybe then you'll believe that we aren't worthy of death and that you should just let us go."

Aranya snorted. The siren glared back.

"Someone hired us. Told us to fetch this girl and bring her to him at dusk tonight. Didn't know anything else."

"Where were you going to meet him?"

"At Kankhai Lake."

Perfect. They could track their quarry there tonight and find the real mastermind. Aranya shifted her stance, rolling back her shoulders. "Why did you desert the empire's force of wielders?"

The siren's gaze hardened. "That hardly matters."

"It matters if you want to live."

"So harsh," she grumbled. "Roll up my left sleeve and see for yourself."

Aranya frowned, her gaze flicking from the siren to the proffered arm, and then around to see that both Kai and the girl were nowhere in sight. Alarm bells tolled in her mind, but she stepped forward to grab the siren's bound hands and shoved up her sleeve.

There, on her inner wrist, was a tattoo.

It was an artistic rendering of a nine-tailed fox, one of the *mó guǐ,* the tips of its tails disappearing into smoke and curling tiny trails onto the heel of her palm. Aranya dropped her hold immediately and jerked back, gasping.

The siren tugged her sleeve lower and shuddered slightly. "See?" she said. "I never went to the Academy. Technically, I never deserted."

"You're a Hidden One," Aranya breathed.

She scoffed again. "I am a *slave* of a Hidden One, though some people don't notice the difference."

Just then, a wail pierced the air. Aranya whirled, flicking her hands into talons. She relaxed, however, upon seeing that it was only Kai leading the sobbing girl after him.

"Yooooou left meeeee," the girl wailed. "All aloooone!"

Kai's mouth was drawn in a straight line. His arm hovered in the air behind her back, never quite touching, while his eyebrows bunched. "You're safe now," he said.

"That's what the brigands said too!" the girl snapped, angry for the first time since they'd found her on the horse. But as soon as the words were out, her lip quivered, and she pressed her face into her hands as she hiccupped around another sob.

Aranya cast a sidelong glance at the siren, who shrugged.

"She was like that with us too," the siren said. "The only way to get her to shut up was to spell her."

Kai paused, his gaze flicking meaningfully to Aranya's. She knew *exactly* what he was thinking. Silently, she gave a stern, *"Don't you dare,"* look. But then she had to turn so he wouldn't see her sudden burst of irrational delight. Because really, they definitely should *not* spell the girl. But the fact that Kai had even considered it in jest . . .

Maybe she *could* work with him after all.

"You should be glad the spell didn't hold, otherwise we'd have to use the Yanzhao technique on her," said Aranya. "Or, rather, *you* would have."

Kai shot her a devilish look. "And you think I would mind kissing a pretty girl to break a spell?"

Of course. Why had she expected anything else?

The girl stopped crying just long enough to peek through her fingers covering her face, blushing brightly.

He shrugged, strode ahead of the hysterical girl, and grabbed one of the horse's tethers. "The prisoners should go on the horses." He cast a quick glance over his shoulder at the weeping girl. "The rest of us will have to walk."

"It's so faaar to waaaalk!" the girl wailed, setting into a fresh bout of tears. "And they didn't bring my shoes when they took meee!"

She was indeed barefoot, her pale little toes sticking out from under her pink dressing gown. Making her walk a few li through the forest without shoes wasn't going to work. They could give her the siren's boots, maybe?

Kai let out a long exhale. Then, ignoring the girl, he stalked toward the siren, who was busy shooting venomous looks at him. "This can be easy or hard. Your choice."

Aranya stepped to the siren's side. "Don't listen to him," she said, rolling her eyes and earning a sharp look from Kai. "We'll see if we can help you once we take you into town."

"There's no help to be done," the siren said, shaking her head. "You take me, and I'm dead. Simple as that. If the courts don't have me killed, then my slaver will."

"Whatever for?"

"Because I know his name. It is hard to be a Hidden One if you're known."

Kai's head whipped to the siren and Aranya could have sworn he paled. "Y-you're a Hidden One?" he asked, stumbling over the words. His eyes shot straight to her wrist, where her tattoo hid beneath her sleeve.

The siren sighed dramatically. "Yes, yes."

Kai looked away, catching his lower lip between his teeth. Yes, he was definitely visibly paler than before. Apparently, he was even more unsettled than Aranya by this turn of events.

As a magic-wielder who never attended the Academy, the siren could never reenter society normally. She could never *not* be a brigand now. The notorious "Hidden Ones" were a subgroup of brigands. Anyone could be a brigand, whether Academy deserter or a supposedly loyal wielder by day and rogue by night. But the Hidden Ones were those undocumented magic-wielders with no record of birth.

The girl, and her companion, would die if they brought them in.

She looked to Kai, who opted to help the girl mount a horse, asking him silently with her face, *"What do we do?"* He responded by turning his back to her.

She looked back down at the bound siren, helpless without her stones and spells. It didn't seem fair, but determining fairness wasn't her job as a warden. Her job was to maintain civil order and protect civilians from brigands and *mó guǐ*. Not to mete out judgment. Something writhed in her chest, but in the end, she bent down and pulled the siren up.

Surprisingly, she didn't resist. She held her head high but made no attempt at escape when Aranya cut the bonds on her ankles and helped her mount the other horse.

That left Kai and Aranya staring down at the unconscious earth-wielder between them.

"He looks pretty heavy," she said.

Kai's gaze swiveled up to hers, and though his face was still pale, he lifted an eyebrow. "Too heavy for you?"

Too heavy.

Those words, an echo of the past, sliced so sharply into her chest that a gasp snagged in her throat and all the blood drained from her face. Her vision flashed backward, and it was another unconscious man she was trying to lift off the ground. Strong as she was, built low and dense like a tiger, he'd been too heavy for her. She remembered tasting her own tears as she heaved, his arm slung limply over her neck.

Kai was looking at her, brow bunched, like he was suddenly concerned about her. Or maybe he found her ridiculous for taking his taunting so seriously. Had her face shown that much?

She gritted her teeth. She *was* strong enough. And she wasn't giving Kai a chance to see anything that would indicate the contrary. She bent down and rolled the unconscious man over. She pulled him up to a sitting position, focusing her attention on her actions and *not* on that memory.

Looping his arm around her neck, she hoisted his weight up, nearly buckling beneath it. She flashed a tight smile at Kai and puffed a stray hair out of her face. "See?" she managed between clenched teeth. "*Not* too heavy for me."

She'd hoped for a pursed lip or something from him, anything that indicated he was impressed. Instead, he stared at her with his head tilted to one side, as if he were wondering if she'd gone crazy.

I am strong enough, she told herself as she reached the side of the girl's horse. The girl whimpered, as though she was terrified by the idea of being so close to her unconscious captor.

"I can't trust him with the siren, and I'm not dragging him all the way back, all right?" Aranya said and then flashed a grin for good measure. She just had to find the strength to get all this muscle on top of the horse, and the girl wasn't going to make it easier.

"Careful there," said Kai, appearing next to her and catching the man before Aranya nearly lost her grip. His face was startlingly close as he leaned in to help. Close enough that she could see the sweat beading on his brow and shining above his cupid's bow. His attention twisted toward her, and their eyes locked.

His expression remained serious except for that one stupid eyebrow that was perpetually higher than the other. A question? Challenge? Whatever it was, Aranya wasn't about to back down. She met the force of his gaze with her own . . . and grinned.

Together, they heaved the man onto the horse's shoulders, face down, so his limbs dangled on either side of the animal. Like he was a sack of rice.

It was well into the late morning when they arrived back behind Lord Meng's house. Weeping and cries of, "I was sooo scaaaaared! I want to be hooooome!" announced their arrival.

Kai guided her horse silently, his shoulders tense and his fingers fidgeting with the collar of his robes. Aranya guided the siren's horse, mulling over the plight of the scowling siren she escorted to her death.

Could Aranya help her? *Them?* No matter how hard she racked her brain, she came up empty. The only viable options would land her in the same boat as the siren—tried for desertion.

When they broke through the trees, the breath fled her lungs.

Crawling all over the area and poking out of the girl's window were wielders from the wardpost. She hadn't seen many of them before, though that was likely because some were night-duty wielders who had been called in because of the situation. Others looked like special service wielders.

One figure turned. Arms crossed and brow low. Sugar grass stuck out of his fat lips.

Qigang.

Aranya lifted her chin. *See? I'm not wholly useless.* Then she glanced back at the siren, and her gut sank to see the pallor overtaking her features. There was nothing she could do to help her, but if there *had* been, it was too late now.

"Hooome! Hoooooooome!"

Kai's eyes darted to Qigang and then to the girl. He paused long enough to help her down from the saddle, and she tore away from him to stumble toward the mansion. Lord Meng broke free of the crowd, hobble-running with his cane to his daughter. When he reached her, he threw the cane down and wrapped both arms around the girl and drew her to his chest. Then, his voice was suddenly in Aranya's head again, low but edged in profound relief.

I won't forget this, warden. I swear on the grave of my fathers that I will repay you for the service you've rendered to me and mine today.

Aranya couldn't hold in her sigh of relief, or the sudden relaxing of her shoulders. The girl was home, and Lord Meng wouldn't destroy her future and her ability to provide for Ye Ye. That was all that mattered.

Except . . .

She turned toward the siren. "What is your name?"

The siren looked down from her horse, hands trembling slightly in their bonds. She chewed on her lip, hesitating. But then the light in her eyes shifted, and something flashed as though from deep inside her. "My name is Lihua."

Then Qigang was there, jutting his face into hers. "Get to the wardpost this *instant*, shifter."

CHAPTER 9

KAI KNEW THERE would be consequences for tracking down the kidnappers without Qigang's permission. He also knew if he were careful, he could avoid most of those consequences. He just wasn't expecting how quickly the supervisor would blame everything on his rival.

"What were you thinking?" Qigang stormed at Aranya, pacing in front of his desk at the wardpost.

Kai folded his arms across his chest and glanced sidelong at her. Her eyes were wide and narrow consecutively, her face flushed. She kept her hands dutifully by her side, but he saw the flexing of her fingers and how hard she worked to keep from clenching them. Or shifting—she seemed to have trouble controlling her instinct to shift when she was angry. Her legs had unconsciously taken up a fighting stance, braced wide, one slightly in front of the other.

Her defensiveness made sense. What he still wasn't understanding, however, was the moment he teased her about lifting the unconscious earth-wielder when her pretty face had gone white as snow. She'd looked upon that man as though upon her own death. *That* made about a dragon's sneeze of sense to him.

Good thing he didn't have to understand everything about his rival to beat her.

He had much more pressing things to worry about, like the fact that there were two Hidden Ones incarcerated next door, which meant there were more in the vicinity, and that both would either be gone or dead by morning. Couldn't it have been any other network of brigands beside the Hidden Ones? If his cover was blown because of this . . .

"We rescued the Lord Meng's daughter," Aranya said, as though that were defense enough.

Qigang exhaled through his nostrils.

Maybe this would be the end of the competition; Kai wouldn't have to anxiously lie awake at night, running through other potential solutions if this one fell through.

"You rescued the girl, yes," Qigang growled. "But you rushed off on an assignment without consulting me, which is grounds enough for me to dismiss you."

Here it was.

Aranya's fists clenched. "But we *succeeded.*"

Was she so dull that she did not realize Qigang was a man who couldn't stand being challenged? Could she not see that he wanted silent, capable minions to follow his orders? She could recover easily enough from this incident if she would merely bow her head and submit to his verbal thrashings.

But this was why Aranya was getting the rebuke and not Kai, because she could never keep her qilin-cursed mouth shut. He had to admit, for a partial shifter, she was much more skilled than he expected. But for all the time she'd clearly spent training her body to handle the kind of strain required for her partial magic, she had apparently never learned the art of silence.

Qigang slammed his fist into the desk, making her jump. Kai stayed still.

"But that's the problem, isn't it?" Qigang said. "You succeeded, so now I am forced to send a commendation to the capital for both of you." He shot a look at Kai this time, and Kai lowered his eyes like he was penitent. It was enough to make Qigang return the brunt of his ire to Aranya. "I am forced to reward your thoughtless, impulsive, utterly reckless behavior with a commendation. And I cannot dismiss you, though you can be sure I would have otherwise."

Kai's stomach dropped, but he kept his shoulders straight. It took every ounce of his self-control not to let his thoughts slip into frustration similar to what clearly boiled beneath Aranya's skin.

Very well, if she was not dismissed now, then she would be dismissed later. After all, the temporary low salary was not a true concern for him.

Aranya readjusted her stance, and her boots squelched. He almost let his mask slip. Had she figured out yet who soaked her boots? Or was she too dim to realize even that?

"Why are you railing at me?" she demanded, flinging her hand at Kai. "He was part of this just as much as I was!"

Another mistake. Kai kept quiet, carefully lifting his eyes to Qigang. The supervisor barely regarded him.

"Shi Kai has not proved himself a flighty, impulsive idiot! Lord Meng demanded an army of wielders, *shifter*," Qigang growled. "He is too powerful to disregard, so I had to pull wardens off patrols to go investigate. If you'd had an ounce of patience, you could have ended up sole manager of a patrol. But because of your stupidity, some patrols have no wardens!"

Aranya hesitated, realization widening her eyes.

"Yes, exactly," the supervisor continued. "What's worse, he's now demanding that you two be the ones I send to Kankhai Lake tonight to track down the kidnapper's leader. Now get yourself to south patrol before I lose my temper even more."

She blinked. Kai did not look at her, but in his periphery he could see that she glanced his way.

Something twinged in his gut. Not guilt, exactly, because it was Aranya, and not Kai, who had provoked Qigang into such a rage. If she had been anyone else, he might have intervened. But he could not lose this appointment. If she wanted to dig her own grave, he would not stop her.

No, it was a twinge of pity, not guilt. But it was only a twinge. She was an Academy graduate with decent magic and more skill than average. Especially with that slingshot. She could hold her own.

Aranya bowed stiffly, her attempt at a smile absolutely garish. She opened her mouth, closed it, turned on her heel, and stormed out of the wardpost.

Kai's muscles relaxed as the door shut. Had he really been that tense? He kept his eyes downcast for a few seconds longer before slowly lifting them to Qigang's face.

Qigang glowered, sticking a blade of sugar grass into his mouth. He chomped it and then spat out bits. His narrowed eyes met Kai's.

"Have you heard from your brother?" Qigang asked.

"My brother, and my mother. The former, thrice."

The sound of the supervisor's smacking lips filled the space between them for several long minutes. Kai waited, steadying himself with even inhales.

"I have no intention of sending you back," Qigang said at long last.

He barely withheld his sigh of relief. "I thank you."

"Keep doing your job, don't make any trouble, and this appointment is yours. As soon as I can dismiss the girl, I will. She's not a good fit for this posting. But this commendation might get her picked up for something else."

Kai kept his expression blank.

Qigang settled himself on his mat, kneeling and leaning back against the wall. He folded his arms across his chest, staring at Kai. Apparently, he was not ready to dismiss him back to patrol yet.

"I was in a situation like yours when I graduated," Qigang said with seemingly genuine sympathy. "Family is complicated."

Now would be a good time to end this conversation. When Kai had explained his partially true tale of an overbearing family to Qigang yesterday, he definitely had not thought it would become fodder for casual conversation. He had to restrain himself from spewing out a gust of air and shooting a glare. Instead, he maintained his mild expression and nodded.

"Very well," Qigang sighed and straightened. "Best if you were off to the eastern market. Na should already be there."

Kai bowed and barely curtailed himself from evanescing in relief. It was this—be what the supervisor wanted—or do what Aranya was doing and let his emotions get the better of him.

Neither was ideal, but one led to the preferred outcome.

Slipping back into the chaotic and bustling streets of Zushai was reprieve beyond articulation. Gravel crunched under his heavy footsteps, and the slight summer breeze was enough to take the edge off the heat, even under his heavy uniform and excessive array of weapons. Ripe human and the musk of animal mingled with the sharpness of spices the closer he got to the market.

In crowds, he was invisible. Just as he preferred.

Aranya moved her jaw around, touching it gingerly where the siren had kneed her in the face. Last night, she thought she had experienced the peak of discouragement and exhaustion. She hadn't expected it to be possible that the aching would be even worse today.

Apparently, it *was* possible.

"If only there were more healers in this world," she muttered. But her mild injury was the least of her concerns. Her appointment was secure for the moment, though Qigang had made it very clear that he didn't want to keep her. How was she going to prove to him she could be a good warden?

Her feet were raw, and she knew when she removed the now-dry boots, the stench would overwhelm their small tenement. Somehow she doubted her landlord would be happy if she left them outside by the door to greet the rest of his tenants.

There had to be something she could do to make Qigang like her. She could whine all she wanted about how unfair his scolding was, and how Kai remained silent through it all. But that didn't change the fact that she still had to win this competition. No matter how long it took, she would prove her worth. She would learn to control her temper and recklessness, and she would become a skilled warden that Qigang would be proud of.

But before then, she had to get to Kankhai Lake by dusk to capture whoever had ordered the daughter of Lord Meng kidnapped. She touched the *jiaun* she'd swiped from the wardpost. It would be the perfect tool to incapacitate, but not kill. This time, she was aiming for a more *subtle* approach. Hopefully it would result in a less chaotic outcome.

Maybe if she proved herself tonight, Qigang would hate her less.

She didn't have much time. She would need to eat quickly with her grandfather and hurry to the lake. No time for getting caught up in conversation with Ye Ye, as much as she would like to. When she turned onto her street, she caught sight of the tenement.

Aranya froze.

There was Lim, the landlord, outside again, yelling. His long nose jutted out, his finger shaking, veins bulging in his neck.

Then she saw who that finger was shaking at. *Ye Ye.* His eyes were wide, bewildered. Clearly, he had no idea what he'd done or what was happening. He might not even know where he was. He looked terrified.

Something snapped in Aranya.

She broke into a run, launched herself straight over the fence, and stormed between her landlord and her grandfather.

"What is going on?" she demanded.

Lim's eyes bulged as he pointed an angry finger at Ye Ye. "He was gardening in my yard!" he cried.

"Gardening?" she said, glancing around to see Ye Ye's mouth open where he hunched behind her. He could hardly walk without help these days, but as her eyes searched, she found a little hole in the dirt by the door. How he'd dug it with no tools, she had no idea. She returned her attention to Lim, gritting her teeth and flexing her hands. They itched to shift. "I'm sorry, sir, but I don't see how that was any justification for your treatment of my grandfather! All you had to do was ask him nicely and he would have stopped!"

"That old pile of bones didn't understand a word I said!" Lim shot back. "I'll fine you for this!"

Old pile of bones? *Old pile of bones?*

Aranya clenched her fists, trying to retain mastery over herself, and not let a furious tear slip free. It wasn't right. No one should even dare to talk about Ye Ye that way. *No one.* But she was powerless; clawing their landlord's face off would only mean more trouble for Ye Ye.

Yet before she had a chance to swallow her anger and pride enough to ask for the fine, Lim started spouting off again.

"You'll pay that fine, and if this happens again, I'll take care of him myself. I don't care how old or stupid he is! If he isn't careful, I'll—"

The remnants of her self-control snapped into nothing. She shifted one hand in a flash, not fearing the sudden animalistic urge overcoming her rational mind. "You'll do what?" she snarled, stepping toward the landlord. Snatching his collar with her other hand, she brought her talons close to his face. "You'll do *what* to him?"

It was so fast, she didn't realize what was happening next until she lay flat on her back, gasping and staring up at Kai.

CHAPTER 10

KAI STRADDLED HER waist, throwing his weight forward to pin her wrists to the ground beside her head. Preventing her from clawing his face off as she reacted to his sudden attack.

"Idiot!" he snapped into her face. "What do you think you're doing?"

The fire in her blood exploded. Kai was here now? To what—keep her from getting in trouble after letting her take all of Qigang's rebuke? Suddenly, her pent-up anger and frustration of the last two days focused in on the man pinning her to the ground.

She snarled as she tried to twist her hands free of his grip. Kai leaned forward more, gritting his teeth, and his movement was enough for Aranya to bring her knees up and knock him off balance. "Get off me!"

He vanished.

Her talons tore into thin air. She leapt to her feet, whirling for any sign of him.

Something hard hit the back of her knees, making them buckle as Kai slammed a hand down on her shoulder. The blow knocked her to the ground painfully. She rolled with the momentum, cursing, and swiped her talons straight at his arm. She barely avoided knocking into the landlord.

Ye Ye's voice cut through the blood roaring in her ears. "Aranya, are you alright?"

She was too busy to respond.

Kai evanesced again. She knew instinctively he had appeared behind her again, so she jabbed her elbow hard up behind her. It connected between two ribs, and he let out a grunt. But then he snatched her wrist and wrenched it behind her with a hard twist. She cried out in pained surprise, but flexed her talons, trying to angle them so she could drive them into his flesh.

"Control yourself!" he growled. "You'll get yourself dismissed with this behavior!"

"And wouldn't you love that?" Aranya retorted, hooking her foot around his ankle and hauling him off balance again.

The grip on her wrist and the presence behind her vanished. She yanked her hand back, nearly cutting herself on her own claws.

"I would, but not like this," he snapped, reappearing in front of her and grabbing her wrists.

He wasn't fast enough—one of her talons scraped down his jaw. Blood welled along the thin line. His eyes flashed, meeting hers. Then he snarled and rammed her backward into the tenement wall. She let out an *oof* and curled her hands to stab her talons into his arms. Sweat beaded on his forehead with the effort to hold her back from skewering him.

"I will have you all fined for this!" the landlord shrieked.

Aranya glared up into Kai's stupidly beautiful eyes, so close to hers. His were full of anger, sharpened and glittering, glaring back. They both panted through open mouths, chests heaving in time with one another. Blood dripped off his chin from where she'd sliced him. Her muscles quaked as she strained against his grip, trying to break free.

She twisted her neck to the side, so she wasn't trapped in his attention. She squeezed her eyes shut. Took stock of her position, ignored the roaring of her blood. If she moved fast enough, brought her knee up sharply enough, she could break free—

Something soft and fluffy bumped up against her calf. She tore her attention away from Kai and glanced down to see a purring cat rubbing his face into the top of her boots. The white tail flicked her knee and then wrapped around her calf as he stepped over the toes of her boots to keep rubbing.

Something shifted within her. Not only her claws, but something in her blood changed. The urge to fight faded away into nothing. She gasped, her gaze darting between Ye Ye curling around her feet and purring, Kai still restraining her against the door, and Lim shouting in the yard.

Her head sagged. Her muscles dissolved into quivering.

For a long moment, Kai didn't move. He stared at her steadily, his weight heavy against her. Then he released his grip on her wrists and stepped back, pressing his sleeve against the cut on his jaw. The usual sly glint in his eye was gone, replaced by thinly veiled anger.

Aranya scooped up Ye Ye and held the purring cat in her arms. He nuzzled into her neck softly. A sudden urge to cry hit her, but she swallowed quickly and held her composure. Ye Ye was fine. The landlord hadn't hurt him. And Kai had kept her from doing something she would have regretted.

Could she have actually hurt Lim? Would she have become the very person she arrested during the day? The thought made her shudder and hug the fluffy bundle in her arms tighter. Why was she so *reckless?* Why couldn't she control herself?

"Fines! All of you are fined!" Lim was shrieking. "Nine tangus from you, Sun Aranya, for the gardening, the threats, and the battle in my yard! Three tangus from you, too, Shi Kai!"

"*Nine*?" she cried, one hand moving unconsciously to the coins under her clothes. If she paid the fine now, she wouldn't have enough for rent later. Desperation clawed at her throat, and she had to fight another swell of tears as she set Ye Ye back down on the ground.

Fathers, she was exhausted.

Kai had already unfastened the cord around his neck and was sliding off two, not three, coins. Her eyes bugged at the sight of *four gold* tangus hanging amid the ample supply of copper tangus. Her own cord was pitifully sparse. He had enough to pay both of their fines and not care.

It must have been nice coming from a family like his.

"You're welcome for saving your life," Kai muttered as he slapped the coins into Lim's outstretched palm. Lim frowned at them, but shockingly didn't protest.

Handing over nine whole tangus was agony, and she was forced to set the cat down while she did it, but Aranya told herself she should be thankful that Lim hadn't evicted her. Should be thankful Ye Ye wasn't hurt.

The sun is about to set. A fresh blossom of anxiety unfurled in her chest, adding to the bouquet she already held close. She turned, lip between her teeth, toward Kai as he peeled his boots off by the door. "We need to hurry if we're going to make it to Kankhai Lake in time."

"Mmmmrow?" Ye Ye's head twisted around to look at her.

Kai paused, holding one boot in his hand. He stared at her, expressionless, for a long minute, his sleeve still pressed to the cut on his jaw. She forced herself not to fidget or falter under his gaze. He lifted one eyebrow, then the edge of his mouth quirked.

"You're still up for it after wasting so much energy fighting me?"

She didn't deign to respond.

He broke eye contact to look down at his bare feet, giving a single snort. Then he lifted his gaze back to hers, raised an eyebrow, and vanished out of the doorway.

"Kai!" Aranya burst out. "I still have to feed my grandfather!"

But Kai reappeared at her side while she was still speaking, bent double, and scooped up Ye Ye into his arms. Aranya's eyes went wide as she flung out her hands toward her grandfather, but Kai was already carrying him inside, his back to her.

"What are you doing? Put him down!"

Kai ignored her as she stumble-hopped out of her boots at the door, wincing at her blisters, and hurried after him. Ye Ye's tail flicked contentedly, and she just *knew* he was purring at the attention. To no one's surprise, Kai didn't ask which unit their tenement was; he just marched straight to the right one. If there had ever been doubt about the wet boots, there wasn't now. When he reached the door, he opened it and strode right in.

Aranya's eyes widened again as panic hit her sharply. Their tenement was a disaster! Had she left her undergarments in sight? Oh, fathers, she probably had! They were probably hanging from the screen—

"You can just put him down!" she called ahead, trying not to let her voice sound too high-pitched. "Thank you for bringing him in! I'll take it from here—"

"Let's get you something to eat," said Kai to Ye Ye, giving him a good long scratch under his chin. Ye Ye purred in response, arching his back into Kai's neck and flicking his tail again.

Aranya's face flushed hotter by the second as she stood in the doorway, watching her rival gingerly dodge all the overflowing boxes and piles of clothes. "I'll feed him, Kai. Don't trouble yourself!"

Her eyes darted to the screen by the window, and mortification sent her tripping over boxes to get to the screen and hide the undergarments that were prominently displayed for all eyes to see. But while Kai and his long limbs had easily navigated the disaster, she wasn't quite so lucky, moving as frantically as she was. She stumbled, slammed her toe into a box, and went sprawling. She barely shifted her hands into lizard pads fast enough to catch herself on the wall.

Gritting her teeth against the pain as hair fell in her face, she slowly twisted her neck to find Kai on one knee, his arm dangling from his propped elbow. Beside him, Ye Ye sat in human form on his mat by the fire. They both blinked at her. Kai lifted a brow. Then he turned back to Ye Ye.

"How do noodles sound? Aranya, do you have noodles around here somewhere?"

Ye Ye chuckled, eyes crinkling. "What a nice young man! Where'd you find him, Sunflower?"

At that, Kai—who had gotten up and begun rifling through the boxes near the stove—turned fully to face Aranya as she straightened next to the screen. She swallowed and forced a helpless smile onto her face. *Please don't look at the screen.*

Kai raised both eyebrows at her and said with a grin, "Sunflower?"

Ye Ye chuckled. Aranya winced.

"Noodles are by the eggs," she said. "But really, Kai, I can—"

"Enough of your fussing!" said Ye Ye, waving his hand and gesturing toward Kai's turned back. "Let him join us!"

Just when Aranya was about to grab the garments and fling them behind the screen, Kai glanced over his shoulder. She shoved her arms to her side, trying to not look suspicious. He only smirked at her and nodded as though in agreement with Ye Ye. She shot him a return glare, mouthing, *"What are you doing?"* He grinned and went back to lighting the stove.

She took that moment to snatch her garments and toss them to safety. Then she exhaled, closing her eyes, trying to calm her heart rate. Opening them again, she found Ye Ye smiling happily at Kai as he heated water over the stove. She swallowed, drew in a deep breath, and much more carefully made her way toward her rival.

As Kai began chopping vegetables, she bit her lip and glanced nervously at Ye Ye. Twice, she opened her mouth again to say he should leave this to her, and twice she forced it shut. But *why*? Why was he doing this?

"How was your day at work?" asked Ye Ye.

Not now! Aranya paused halfway between Ye Ye and Kai, scratched her neck, and forced her voice to lighten as she said, "Um . . . well, we . . ." She trailed off, glancing uncertainly at Kai. He just kept working on their dinner. Maybe he knew this would make her feel extraordinarily awkward, and that was why he was doing it. Trying to put her off balance.

She would just have to show that she wasn't flustered. "It was a pretty normal day for the most part," she said, shrugging.

Kai's head swung to the side, enough for him to fix her with an incredulous look.

"This is Shi Kai, by the way," she said to Ye Ye. "He's . . . one of my comrades. We worked together today."

The knife came down on an onion in a particularly loud chop. Aranya couldn't help ducking her head to hide her smile.

"Is that so?" asked Ye Ye.

"That is so," replied Aranya, unable to resist goading Kai further. "I went on an investigation today, and since he's new too, he decided to come along."

Suddenly Kai was right in front of her, a blandly pleasant expression on his face. She jumped in surprise, one hand lifting to shapeshift instinctively. Something poked her stomach. She glanced down to find him pressing the cutting board with a knife and half-chopped onion to her.

"How about you take it from here?" He flashed what she was certain was an imitation of one of her smiles. "*Sunflower*."

She grabbed the board, glaring up at him. Gripping the knife by the handle, she lifted it so it pointed in his face. "Don't call me that."

Kai, unfazed, bypassed her to sit cross-legged next to Ye Ye. Aranya tried not to huff as she made her way to the kitchen area, turning her back on them. When she checked the pot of boiling noodles, she discovered Kai had added enough for himself too. Shaking her head, she went to work.

"Lieutenant Sun—" began Kai. The title made Aranya blink.

"Oh, no need for that," said Ye Ye. "Call me Ye Ye."

What? Aranya sputtered voicelessly over the stove.

"Very well," came Kai's reply, and it sounded like he was smiling. "Where did your military campaigns take you, Ye Ye?"

Deep breaths. Deep breaths.

"Hmm . . . Butagin mostly. It's so cold up there! Couldn't blame them for trying to expand their borders southward, now could you? If my rump was always that frozen, I'd have done the same thing!"

"Ye Ye!"

"It's nice, you know, to have a young one like my Sunflower who can keep me updated on the happenings about the empire. I tell you, the older I get, the more I miss! Back when my legs behaved, I'd always go to the markets in Suguan to hear the news. But now, I just sit here, and if not for her, I'd not know the empire was burned to the ground until this tenement caught fire!"

"Oh, don't exaggerate, Ye Ye," said Aranya, hesitating over the salt bin, contemplating whether she ought to cook up a little meat since Kai was here. "You'd find out long before then."

"She always gives me more credit than I'm due," said Ye Ye in a loud whisper to Kai. "She's a good girl that way."

"I do not!"

"I'm sure she gives credit where credit is due," said Kai diplomatically. Why was he being so nice? Perhaps this was his secret to staying out of trouble at the Academy. She added a pinch of dried tien tsin peppers to a pouch and dropped it into the pot.

That was when an idea hit her. A way to repay Kai's prank. With a glance over her shoulder to make sure Kai's attention was focused back on Ye Ye, she took an extra pinch of the dried peppers and put them directly in Kai's empty bowl.

"She's a good girl," said Ye Ye. "Keeping up with her old grandfather, working so hard all the time. She was such a diligent student at the Academy."

"Ye Ye—"

"Not many young folk would take such good care of their grandfather these days!" said Ye Ye.

"Indeed," said Kai.

"Seven valleys, Ye Ye! You make it sound like you're an inconvenience!"

"Oh, come now—"

Aranya spun to face them, a wooden spoon clenched in her fist. She waved it threateningly at Ye Ye's innocent smile. "You're not an inconvenience, Ye Ye. Don't you talk like that."

It came out much harsher than she intended. Ye Ye's smile faltered, and Kai had an unreadable expression in the hazel eyes he fixed on her. As though he read every thought running through her head. She blinked, turned away hastily. Burning filled her chest—frustration. Why would Ye Ye ever think such a thing when he was all she had? He was her life, her home. Didn't he know that without him, she had nothing?

She chopped furiously, another wave of tears welling up. She swallowed them back determinedly; focused instead on the stinging and aching of her blisters.

"See?" said Ye Ye with another chuckle. "A good girl, that Aranya."

She wasn't going to look. She was going to finish these noodles so they could eat quickly and head off to Kankhai Lake. The last thing she was going to do was steal a peek at why it had suddenly gotten so quiet . . .

Phoenix curse it! She glanced over her shoulder to find Ye Ye staring into the hearth, but Kai—Kai was staring at her. There wasn't a trace of amusement on his face. Just contemplation, as though he'd worked out the solution to a difficult puzzle. She shot him a glare and went back to work, trying to distract herself with worry about the fast-declining sun.

"Yes," said Kai belatedly, sighing and sounding like he was standing up. "She's a good girl."

Aranya's face flushed hot.

CHAPTER 11

KAI TRIED NOT to let his gaze drift too often to the backs of Aranya's feet, which were furiously red and a little bloodied in spots. Surely that wasn't because of the water he left in her boots?

He wouldn't let her see the regret on his face.

When she served their bowls of food, however, he found his regret was misplaced. One sip of the broth sent him coughing, his eyes watering viciously, and his tongue scalding. "What—?"

Aranya blinked innocently. "Are you alright? Not used to spicy food?"

That little—!

"Spicy food?" Kai croaked. He swiped away a tear leaking from his eye. If he accused her of purposefully over-spicing his food, she'd point out the boots. And then they'd get in a fight in front of her grandcat.

So Kai found himself grumbling, "I love spicy food," and carefully began eating, dodging the floating flakes of pepper that *should* have been strained out. The edge of his sleeve was damp from tears after only a few minutes, and he desperately needed to blow his nose.

Ye Ye kept conversation light through their meal, asking all manner of what he probably supposed were harmless questions. It was obvious to Kai that he wasn't aware of their rivalry, which was probably why he kept talking her up to him, as though he thought there was a possibility of something romantic between them. Had he not seen them fighting in the yard just minutes ago?

At least this meal was proving as enlightening as he expected. Understanding one's enemies was the key to beating them. Not that he was afraid of losing to Aranya. But with every word out of Ye Ye's mouth, the thought of winning their rivalry turned his stomach a little sourer.

From what Kai had seen, he was a sharp man in rapid decline. His chopsticks shook in his hands, and he frequently dropped bites that Aranya quickly picked up for him with a bright smile. A few times, she even dabbed his mouth with a kerchief, which always made Ye Ye chuckle.

Kai had meant what he had said. She was a good girl. An annoying one, perhaps, unbelievably reckless, and also merciless in her revenge, but a good-hearted girl. It seemed so ironic to him, watching her and Ye Ye grin at each other, how someone with so little family could have so full an affection.

Ye Ye proclaimed the meal the best he'd ever had and gave Kai a knowing look that he wasn't quite sure how to interpret. Later tonight or tomorrow, when no one was awake, he'd slip in and replenish the food he'd eaten. It seemed they were under enough strain to keep them both fed without his uninvited third mouth eating up their food.

He'd do that *after* he dealt with the issue of the incarcerated Hidden Ones.

As Ye Ye slurped up the last of his food, Aranya watching him carefully, Kai sighed and set down his bowl.

"Thank you for the meal," he said to her, while smiling and dabbing away a tear. Fathers, but his chest burned like it was on fire!

She smiled sweetly as she took his bowl. "Any time."

"You will have to join me in my tenement for a meal one of these days," Kai said as he stood.

Ye Ye's face split in a wide, toothy grin. "Why, that would be a delight!"

Aranya's gaze sharpened suddenly, glancing suspiciously between them, and Kai couldn't help smiling just a little bit. *That's right, Partial,* he thought, only a touch vindictively. *Next time I'll be the one cooking up something exciting for you.* He came round to Ye Ye's side of the table and squatted next to him, elbows on his knees, wrists dangling. "Then you can decide who makes a better bowl of noodles—me or Aranya."

Ye Ye laughed aloud. It was a crackling, almost gurgling sort of laugh, rough, but still pleasant.

He looked up to find Aranya watching them, her brows pinched, her mouth drawn in a straight line. He offered her a polite smile, then stood. She quickly turned away, long enough for him to scan quickly over the tenement, note the measly amount of firewood, and say to her back, "Thank you again for the food. I'll meet you at the lake." To Ye Ye, he gave a warm smile and said, "Stay healthy."

He strode out of the room, resisting the urge to evanesce and ruffle Aranya's feathers. He'd sleep poorly enough as it was from all the upcoming evanescing tonight.

"Wait! Shouldn't we go togeth—" came her call just as he shut the door.

"What a nice boy," said Ye Ye, his quavering voice carrying through the wood. "A very pleasant young man."

His stomach turned queasy. He regretted eating more with every passing moment. What if he just disappeared again? Left the appointment to her so she could take care of her grandfather? He could take care of himself, and it would be easier for him to find other work than for her to do so. Maybe he could move even farther away, abandon the title of magic-wielder, take on a different name—*fathers.* He shook his head. Escaping his family was one thing; escaping the bureaucracy was an entirely different matter. He'd be a brigand himself. The very thing he was trying to avoid.

"Indeed," was Aranya's dry as paper reply. "I'm going to go back out. I'll be back as soon as I can, but don't wait up for me."

That was Kai's cue to evanesce to his own tenement. He couldn't evanesce there in one leap due to the stupid arrangement of the hallway that put more than one barrier between him and his room. He landed just inside his door, his own much emptier room sprawled before him. The fading sunlight shone through the window on the empty table. Where Aranya's tenement was chaos and clattering pans, his was silent.

Silent, except for the crunch of something beneath his foot. He looked down to find the corner of yellow parchment sticking out from beneath his toes. For a split second, he closed his eyes and let his stomach drop. Then he dragged in a deep breath, bent, and retrieved the sealed missive. The once fine paper was dirty from its long journey, made especially long through being forwarded from the fake address he'd given his family. But nothing could disguise the ridiculous flourishes of the writing. In a few steps, he was by the hearth, about to fling the letter onto the coals to burn.

Something made him stop. He stared at that paper, dangling from his fingers over black soot. Then, giving into an inexplicable impulse, he pulled it back, broke the seal, and read it.

My dearest brother, it began. Kai barely suppressed a huff. He skipped past the first paragraph, which he knew would contain nothing but false pleasantries, though it was shockingly short today. He started reading at the second paragraph. The handwriting had lost some of its embellishment and was much more uneven than normal. Apparently, this letter had been written in haste.

How can you treat your family this way? Mother is beside herself. Have I not told you a thousand times how your wayward deeds make her grow worse by the day? I thought you selfish before our father died, but I didn't think you were capable of this. She's dying, and it's because of you. Come back before she loses hope. Unless you truly hate us as much as you act. Then perhaps this letter gives you all the satisfaction you've craved. Perhaps this was your plan all along.

I'll never know what Father saw in you.

It went on, but that was enough for Kai. He tossed it in the hearth, stacked up a few logs and tinder, and used a tinderbox to set the fire ablaze. He stared emptily at the flames as they licked around the parchment, swallowing up the elegant signature.

Shi Yong.

He let out a deep sigh. Lowered his head into his hand. No, no, he couldn't give up this Zushui appointment. He glanced up at the window, at the shadows lengthening around him. There was no delaying any further, even though he just wanted to sleep, not hunt more brigands. But he had to go.

He stood up, sighing, and straightened his shoulders. First, he had to stop by the armory to pilfer some weapons. Then—Kankhai Lake.

"Hope you're well prepared, Partial," he muttered.

By the time she reached Kankhai Lake, Aranya's joints ached, and her muscles quivered with exhaustion and the aftereffects of her earlier adrenaline rush. It had been agony to pull her boots back on, but she'd managed it and walked all the way out here.

The light slipped into darkness, the dusk nearly swallowed by night.

No sign of their target. No sign of Kai.

The thought of him brought a host of bewilderment that hadn't been there before. It was simple before—he was her rival. He was rude and arrogant. She hated him and would do whatever it took to beat him out of this appointment. But he'd been unexpectedly and—dare she say it?—seemingly genuine with Ye Ye. She wished it meant nothing to her. After all, they'd been fighting right beforehand!

His attentiveness to Ye Ye, whatever its motivation, hadn't meant nothing to her. Maybe there was a chance she misjudged him. Maybe he wasn't as bad as he had always seemed. Or perhaps he was simply trying to win her trust so he could stab her in the back when she least expected it.

As she approached the lakeshore, she moved slowly and clung to the shadows. It was so dark now she could barely see where she was going, and she made a few unfortunate twig-cracking steps.

Still no Kai.

He probably planned to stay hidden while Aranya made the first attack.

The waning moon had risen, casting thin silvery light over the tranquil, reflective surface of the lake, before hoofbeats rumbled in the quiet. Her gut clenched, adrenaline surging furiously, as she crouched lower against the base of a stout tree.

Carefully, she leaned out to catch a glimpse.

Over the stretch of water, five black horses and riders emerged from the darkness. From this distance, they seemed more wraith than human. Shudders crawled down her spine, but she gritted her teeth and silently flicked her hands into talons. She got the distinct impression they were a lot more dangerous than she'd originally hoped. She pursed her lips and slunk toward the shadow of the next tree. Closer to her quarry.

A black form appeared right in front of her.

Aranya would have squeaked if two hands hadn't covered her mouth immediately. Then she would have clawed his brains out if a low voice hadn't growled, "It's me, Kai." He removed his hands and crouched beside her.

She glanced sidelong at him, barely able to distinguish his face from the rest of him. Why did she suddenly feel uncomfortable being this close to him? Was it because she was beginning to wonder if there was more to him than what she'd always seen?

"I volunteer as bait," she whispered.

He gave the faintest snort. "If you want to die an idiot, Partial, then by all means."

"What's wrong with you? You're supposed to do your fancy evanescing and catch them by surprise while they're occupied with me."

"With *five*? I'd say your suggestion is stupid, but I'm actually quite flattered."

Never mind thinking he was different. Clearly, he was still rude and arrogant. She shot him a glare and got the impression he was winking at her. She'd protest his insults, but talking too much might give them away. Instead, she growled, "Then what do we do?"

"We get names."

"We spy?"

"*I* spy. You're louder than a New Lights parade."

"I'm quiet!"

"I heard you from several li away, Partial."

"Will you stop calling me that?"

Kai stood slowly, ignoring her and keeping his eyes fixed on the opposite shore. "You can leave now. I'll get the names and bring them to Qigang."

"And take all the credit? I don't think so."

He turned his head down to her, but she couldn't make out his expression. "Then stay here and keep your rear end out of trouble." He returned his attention to the lake, starting to stand.

She grabbed his sleeve, forcing him to look back at her again. "Are you just going to vanish on me again? You've got to at least tell me the plan."

He plucked her grip off him and dusted his sleeve. "The plan is that I will get closer, and you will stay put."

"What if you get in trouble?"

Another quiet snort that was no less arrogant for its softness. Then he muttered under his breath, "I'm not going to be able to sleep tonight."

"What? Why?"

"Hmm?"

She had his sleeve in her fist again, keeping him from standing—but not keeping him from evanescing. He let out an irritable sigh but didn't vanish. "Why won't you be able to sleep tonight?" she pressed. "Because you will be lying awake trying to come up with clever comebacks?"

"Just because you need all night to come up with something clever doesn't mean the rest of us do."

She gave a silent huff. Why had she *ever* doubted her initial perception of him?

Around them, the darkness deepened, the stillness punctuated by the gentle hum of summer bugs and croaking frogs. The shadows across the lake hardly moved, like they were statues made of night.

Finally, Kai said, almost too softly to hear, "The more I evanesce, the harder it gets to fall asleep."

Something about the way he said it made it sound like a confession. And it was one, of sorts. Magic-wielders didn't often trust others with knowledge of their magics' limits. In some cases, like Aranya's, it was basically impossible to hide limits, and in a setting like the Academy, it was even more difficult. But in Kai's case, his limits were less clear. She'd already surmised that he couldn't evanesce other people, but he didn't have trouble evanescing objects on his person like his weapons and the clothes he wore—thank the fathers for that.

But insomnia as a result of evanescing? That sounded ridiculous.

Aranya raised one eyebrow. "I don't know if I believe you."

"Believe what you want."

"Is that why you're not a morning person? Because it takes you a long time to fall asleep after you've been evanescing?"

He gave a short chuckle. Then he vanished.

Her eyes shuttered, a deep breath whooshing out of her. She'd believed it *again* for a second there! That he wasn't just an arrogant qilin-brained jerk. She was a fool to think him sharing one of his evanescing limits meant she had a tiny smidge of his trust. He was probably just pulling her leg after that wretchedly spicy bowl of noodles she'd given him.

It didn't matter. Catching these criminals mattered.

She rose from her crouch and edged closer to the next tree, then the next. She wouldn't attack, of course, but getting a little closer would help her assess the situation better. Maybe she could hear them talking. And if Kai found himself in trouble, she needed to be available to help.

She patted the two-slotted *jiaun* on her belt—a weapon she could shoot from a distance. Kai might be right that having her close would pose more risk than necessary, but that didn't mean she couldn't be prepared if things went awry.

The exhaustion in her body was heavy, but she had never been more awake in her life as she eased along the edge of the lake. She kept to the trees, moving as quickly as she could while remaining silent.

New Lights parade! Whatever. She was *very* quiet.

The black horses stomped their hooves impatiently, one tossing its head and dancing against the restraint of its bit and bridle. She could not tell from here if the five wraith-like forms on the opposite shore spoke. But she *could* tell the moment all of them turned toward the line of trees where she imagined Kai would be hiding.

Her heart sank.

Three of the riders dismounted, stalking toward the trees. One cupped his hands together and when he pulled them apart, light glowed between his palms. *A fire-wielder.*

Were these brigands too? They had to be.

They must have heard Kai. She could not discern the magic of the other forms, but by the way they moved, she doubted she wanted to find out. Swiftly, she unholstered her *jiaun,* slotted two arrows, and snapped it into firing mode.

When she lifted the weapon, her arm shook with fatigue. But bracing and clenching herself steady never worked. She exhaled slowly, and her firing arm steadied. She lowered it until her sights lined up with her target—the fire-wielder.

The brigand pulled back his arm to launch his fireball.

Was the range too far for her weapon? Even if she missed, they would hear the arrows and be distracted from Kai long enough for him to find out the information they needed. Maybe?

She didn't have time to wait.

She fired.

CHAPTER 12

A LOUD CRY ripped through the air. The arrows hadn't hit the fire-wielder she had been aiming at, but one of his companions. He stumbled to his knees, then fell to the ground. The fire-wielder extinguished his ball of flame as he knelt beside the fallen one.

Night sank deeper around her. Yet even in the gloom, it was unmistakable when the rest of the wielders turned toward her direction. She steeled her breath but couldn't help her grin. What a shot! Her Academy masters would have been proud.

Something whizzed in the air a few feet away. She jumped and slid behind a tree as something else whizzed nearby. A loud *thunk* hit the opposite side of the tree. Tentatively, she reached out, and her fingertips closed around the fletching of an arrow.

She ducked closer behind the tree, tucking her shoulders in close. "Where are you, Kai?" she whispered between clenched teeth. "Where *are* you?"

There were shouts. More arrows slammed into trees nearby. She dared not move from where she crouched, even to see what was happening. If Kai didn't—

"What in all seven valleys did you *do*?"

Kai was suddenly right in front of her, huddled close against her in the tree's shelter. The moonlight caught in the furious eyes that were hardly inches from her own.

"What were you *thinking*?" he snapped.

"I was buying you time!"

"You lost all our time!"

"You are *not* putting all this on me. They heard you before I—"

Something crackled and sparked in the air nearby. Kai dropped to the ground, cursing under his breath. Before Aranya could ask what was happening, he grabbed her wrist and yanked her toward him. Her forehead hit his chest. She tried to scramble backward.

"What are you—"

"Get away from the tree!"

Hardly a second after his frantic warning, something like crashing thunder exploded behind her. She shrieked, but the sound was swallowed whole. Kai continued yanking on her wrist, and when she looked up, light shone on his horrified face.

She craned her neck to look behind them.

The tree was split to its center, blackened and burning. A lightning strike. They had a dragon-blasted *lightning*-wielder with them. Now she was cursing along with him.

"They've seen us," Kai said, scrambling up to his feet. "Run!"

They tore off into the woods, leaving the ruined tree behind them. The sound of pursuit was loud and heavy: thundering horse hooves, shouts, whizzing arrows, and crackling lightning.

Aranya was excellent at climbing, scaling walls—anything that required upper body strength and a short, trim frame. But she was horrid at sprinting for her life. She stumbled along behind her long-legged rival, trying to keep up and dodge between trees at the same time.

"*Faster*!" Kai growled, reaching to snatch the back of her collar and yank her after him.

"Qilins, Kai!" she cried, nearly falling on her face. "Let me—"

He wasn't evanescing.

The realization hit her as another bolt of lightning demolished a nearby unsuspecting tree. He could get himself out of this situation in an instant, but he stayed. With her.

She ran faster.

The forest was so dark she could hardly see where they were going. Blood pounded in her ears, her legs, behind her eyes. She gasped for air, her side burning with a stitch. They had to make it back to Zushui. They *had* to.

Kai looked over his shoulder, past her, and cursed as his fist tightened on her collar. "Keep running," he said—and then he vanished.

She nearly fell flat on her face at the sudden lack of his dragging force, but she managed to stay upright as she leapt over a fallen long and ducked under low-hanging branches. Fire exploded to her left. Sparks landed on her sleeve. She glanced back.

"Oh fathers," she gasped.

Three figures on horseback gained dangerously fast. She could never outrun them! Not now that they'd seen her.

She pumped her legs harder, every breath terrifying and agonizing. Any second, an arrow would pierce her chest, a flame would consume her body, or a bolt of lightning would incinerate her life in an instant.

Nothing stood between them and her. Nothing except time.

She wouldn't think about Ye Ye. About what would happen to him if she didn't make it out of this alive. About his purrs and white fluff, about how he would be alone. About how she would have failed him for the last time.

A shout sounded behind her; she wouldn't look. She needed to focus on running as fast as she could, ignoring the burning in her lungs with each gasp.

More shouting, a stumbling of horse hooves.

Aranya looked.

One wielder fell off his horse and hit the ground with a sickening thud. The new rider in the saddle vanished. When Kai reappeared behind the next wielder, however, he received an elbow to the face and fell backward.

He vanished in midair before he hit the ground.

She twisted back around and narrowly avoided running straight into a tree. Choking on her own fear and adrenaline, she veered around it.

She couldn't keep running like this.

Lightning crackled and then exploded into a tree next to her. Her scream was lost in the uproar.

Keep running. Keep running. Keep running.

She tripped. Fell flat on her face in the dirt. Her heart nearly burst open in her chest. Terror knifed through her blood. She should roll, get to her feet, and fight.

But her claws were nothing against lightning.

When she stumbled to her feet, she looked back—and they were upon her. Two horses, the third gone, barreled up to her. *No place to run.* She whirled as they circled her. One was the lightning-wielder. The other could be anything.

Aranya flicked her hands into talons and snarled like a cornered animal.

Darkness shrouded all except movement. Her heaving lungs clenched when one wielder dropped from his saddle, approaching her. The other one closed in behind her. She braced her legs wide, reaching for the knife at her belt. The hilt was ice in her grip.

The air popped and sizzled between the hands of the cloaked form, only two steps away.

"Where is the girl?" came the deep-as-night voice. "What trap did you lay for us?"

Aranya took a step back and bumped into something hard. When she turned, horror sunk into the pit of her stomach. The other one. She'd bumped into his chest.

Neither made a move to grab her or kill her, but the threat in the air was palpable.

Where was Kai?

"Where is the girl?" the lightning-wielder repeated, his voice gravelly.

Perhaps it wasn't the smartest thing to say, but she growled, "How do you know I'm not the girl?"

He was too fast. He darted forward, his hand smacking her arm hard.

The force of the blow wasn't what made her cry out. Lightning shock ripped into her arm. Through the sudden, startling, unfamiliar pain, she had the vaguely conscious thought that this was far tamer than the tree-splitting lightning strikes.

Now that they'd lost Kai, they wanted her to talk before they killed her. She bent over from the shock, clutching her buzzing, aching arm.

"Where is the girl?"

Think, Aranya, think!

Between her gasps, she slowly lifted her eyes. The figure before her was still close, cloaked in midnight, ready to strike. Behind her, the warmth of the other wielder emanated into her back. In her hand, the knife.

If she made her move, would the one behind her lop her head off? But if she delayed too long, the lightning-wielder would strike her again.

Aranya snapped upright. She used the momentum to swing her good arm up and fling her knife at the lightning-wielder. She didn't normally throw like this, so she half expected the blade to fly straight over his head.

The surprised hiss told her she'd hit him *somewhere.*

A blow struck the side of her legs. She landed hard on the ground before she could blink. The first went down to his knees.

"Kai!" Aranya screamed, throwing herself to the side as a knife implanted next to her face. She stumbled to her feet, her arm still aching and buzzing where she'd been electrocuted.

Lightning ripped through the air overhead, smashing into a tree. She gasped and barely jumped out of the way of a falling severed branch. But a huge iron fist closed around her arm and dragged her back. She tried to resist, tried to wrestle herself free from his grip, but the strength flowing in his body was too strong, and her own strength was quickly flagging.

He must be feral—born with animalistic strength and senses.

"Where is the girl?" the feral-wielder growled as he latched on to both of her arms and rammed her backward against his chest. Stars spun in her vision. "Tell me or I will rip your limbs apart."

Where was that dragon-blasted evanescer when she needed him?

"Hands off her, or you both die," came a low voice.

Aranya sagged, nearly choking on her own sputtering relief at the sound of Kai's familiar tenor.

"Where is the girl?" demanded the feral-wielder holding her. He shook her, making her head snap back and forth, and gripped both of her wrists—as if to tear her apart.

"I *said*, hands off her."

A knife flashed, and there was a grunt of pain behind her. The grip on her faltered enough that Aranya kicked her heel backward into his knee as hard as she could. It startled him and threw him further off balance as he whirled to defend against Kai's lightning-fast blade.

A loud crashing sounded from behind them.

She was ripping free of her captor when she turned in time to see a black, riderless horse charging at full speed into the clearing. Straight toward them.

Another burst of lightning ripped into the sky. Behind her, something heavy hit the ground. The wielder? Had Kai made do on his threat? When the horse charged in the midst of them, Aranya ran toward it. The idea that she would somehow leap onto its back—utterly wild. But she had to try.

At the last possible instant, a tall dark form appeared out of thin air on the saddle.

"Kai!" she cried, catching his outstretched arm.

He swung her up behind him. She landed painfully hard on the saddle and wrapped her arms around his waist.

"Hang on tight and keep your head low!" he shouted.

CHAPTER 13

LIGHTNING BLAZED AND crackled behind them as Aranya clung to Kai. Her heart pounded, her body jostled, and her exposed back tingled with the anticipation of blows that never fell.

Even when the lights of Zushui grew brighter in the night, Kai didn't slow the galloping pace of their horse. He kept driving them forward relentlessly.

Holding on for her life, she twisted to look behind them. No sight or sound of their pursuers. Her blood hummed with adrenaline, her body burning with guarded relief. She easily could have died.

Why did that realization fill her less with fear and more with shame?

It wasn't until they reached the city that Kai pulled the horse to a stop. The glow of the lanterns hanging in the doorways made the sweat glisten on his brow. His chest heaved in time with hers.

"Get off," he barked.

She rolled her eyes, but grabbed his proffered arm and swung herself down to the ground. Her mush-like legs stumbled when she hit pavement. Kai dismounted after her, breathing hard as he grabbed the horse's lead and strode into the much quieter streets of the city. He started to go down a darkened alleyway, but she stopped him.

"What's wrong with the main roads?"

"Night wardens," he said. "Maybe you're in the mood to get stuck in long conversations about how our job went, but I'm not. I'd rather report to Qigang in the morning."

She laughed.

He twisted back to look at her, shooting up an eyebrow. Instead of continuing their line of conversation, he snapped, "Thanks for ruining everything back there."

Aranya stumbled over her own wobbly feet, brow pinching. "Ruining everything? I saved your life! They had discovered you and were going to kill you!"

"I was *speaking* to them, qilin-brain. I told them I had the girl, and was trying to get their names, when *you* fired your stupid arrows. Of course, they assumed I'd been followed. I had to drop everything to get you out of there."

She stopped. "What?"

"Do I need to repeat myself?"

"You *purposefully* got their attention?"

"No, I didn't. I just wanted to speak to them without getting their attention," he said sarcastically. "Of course I was trying to get their attention! They were expecting to meet someone, so I filled that role. Sometimes I really don't understand you. One moment, I'm impressed with your skill, and the next, I'm impressed with your stupidity. I can't decide if you're skilled or an idiot. Or a skilled idiot."

Somehow, despite that he practically called her a stupid idiot, she found herself grinning.

"It's nice to hear my skills impress you," she responded smoothly.

"Is that all you heard?"

She laughed again. His eyes narrowed to slits, and he turned back to guiding them through alleyways. How did he know which way to go? Was he just especially talented at navigating beneath notice?

"If you won't tell me what your plan is," said Aranya, "then you can't get angry when I go against it."

He didn't respond.

Her arm ached strangely where the lightning-wielder had struck her. It was not in the mood to be useful and seemed to prefer hanging limply from her shoulder. It didn't quite buzz, though it was something similar. Something distinctly painful.

"So you didn't get their names?" All that for nothing? Even more reason to postpone meeting with Qigang until tomorrow, if possible.

There was quiet. At first, she wasn't sure if Kai had heard her. She peered around the bulk of the horse he led, trying to get a look at his face. She opened her mouth, about to ask again.

"Yes, I got their names."

"Wait, you did? You know who was trying to kidnap Lord Meng's daughter?"

"It was Lord Wun."

"Lord Wun? Like . . . one of Lord Meng's neighbors?"

"Indeed."

She stopped in the middle of the alleyway, furrowing her brows. "That makes no sense. What would they want her for?"

Kai shrugged. "Who knows? Perhaps it's political. The main thing is that we know and can arrest him later. Keep moving; you're slowing us down."

"He had all those brigands with him!"

"There are extensive networks of brigands. Men as powerful as Meng and Wun will, of course, have connections to those ready to do their dirty work."

His voice made her cock her head to one side. He said the word "brigand" with the barest trace of familiarity, though "dirty work" was nearly spat out. But his back was to her, so she could not be sure what he thought. If he meant anything besides the obvious.

"If you got his name, why were you all mad at me like I'd spoiled everything?" she burst out. "We would have had to run anyway once they realized you didn't have the girl!"

"Because you revealed *your* position!" he said. "I can disappear. They couldn't catch me. But they could catch you, and while it would have been utterly delightful to rid myself of your companionship back there," he said as he tossed a wintry smile over his shoulder, "I can't just abandon my comrade. You endangered us both! *That* was why I was—why I am—mad at you."

He muttered his next words so quietly under his breath she almost didn't catch them.

"Should have gone on my own."

Aranya didn't think she had any blood left to pump into her veins, didn't think she had any stores of anger and adrenaline left after that flight.

Apparently she did.

But letting her temper fly free earlier had served no good. As satisfying as it would be to sweep up one of these rocks and launch it at Kai's back, she was exhausted. She'd have to save brawling with her rival for another day.

Instead, she grinned smugly. "You have to admit, though, it *was* an excellent shot. I'd like to see you hit a target at half the distance."

"Watch your step, Partial," he said from ahead. "I can do much worse than leave you wet boots in the morning. Or did you still think that was your fluffy grandcat?"

"I knew it was you," she huffed, her smile suddenly harder to maintain. "I was merely measuring your reaction."

Suddenly, Kai's face was inches from hers. Smirking.

"Fathers, Shi Kai!" Aranya gasped, shoving a hand against his chest to push him away from her. "Will you *quit* this evanescing-in-my-face business?"

His mouth went lopsided, and his fingers wrapped around her wrist, prying her hand off him. He held her wrist between them, deliberately tightening his grip.

"Careful," she chuckled. Her grin matched his—challenging, daring. "Don't forget I have claws."

He lifted an eyebrow, eyes glittering. "Please do keep reminding me how afraid I should be of you, Sun Aranya."

Her smile slipped. She didn't intend for it to, and her attempts to recover it only made Kai's smirk widen. She opened her mouth to spout something back in his face when both of them suddenly froze. His grip tensed, his head shooting up toward the scuffing of boots in the alleyway.

"Hear that?" he whispered.

"Night wardens?"

". . . just a huge mess! Such a mess!" came the too-familiar voice from dangerously close.

Qigang. With another warden.

They should just straighten their shoulders and prepare for Qigang's inevitable rebuke despite doing exactly what they were supposed to. They should just get this report and confrontation over with.

But Aranya and Kai stared at each other for a split second, then at the horse, and finally, at a darkened doorway in the shadows of a rundown awning. As if deciding for them, Kai's fingers tightened around her wrist, and he jerked her toward that doorway.

"The horse!" Aranya hissed.

"They're just going to have to find it," he said.

And then they were both running silently, diving for that bit of cover. He whirled toward her, grabbed her by the shoulders, and swiveled her into the darkest corner. She scooted as far back as she could, ignoring how the splintering wood dug into the skin between her shoulder blades.

Then Kai was squeezing next to her, his back to the street, his weight leaning heavily into hers. "Can't you scoot further?" he hissed, his breath panting against her forehead, his forearms bracing against the doorframe on either side of her.

"Sure, let me just melt into the wall here. Give me a second—"

His hand clamped down over her mouth, his eyes going wide. He glanced over his shoulder as the noise grew louder, then squeezed closer to her. Trying to stay out of the line of sight. She sucked in a sharp breath and wasn't sure if it was from how the footsteps were getting louder or how her face was nearly pressed into his throat.

"What's this?" came an unfamiliar voice, cutting off Qigang's rambling.

Aranya froze. Kai's body went rigid with tension and his chest stopped moving like he held his breath. His Adam's apple bobbed against the soft huffing of her nose.

Why hadn't he evanesced his way out of trouble? Why had he crammed himself in this tiny corner with her instead of leaving her by herself to be found by Qigang?

"Where's your rider?" asked the warden.

"Hmmph," huffed Qigang.

Kai's head tilted down toward hers, ever so slowly, until he could look at her. In the darkness, his pupils had dilated completely, and his eyes looked almost black. They fixed on her with intensity.

Her mouth was sandpaper dry. She didn't care if he held his breath for forever; she was gasping, and her goal was just to keep those gasps as quiet as possible. Hoping that the warden couldn't hear anything over the sounds of the horse's soft snorts and his own boots crunching on gravel, the flip of leather as he investigated the saddlebags.

The warden clucked his tongue, then said, "How strange. I'll take him back to the wardpost with me. Maybe tomorrow we can find who he belongs to. Have a good night, Master Qigang."

Qigang gave a grunt, might have raised his hand in a wave, but she couldn't tell from where she was.

With that, the clip clop of horse hooves started, and slowly eased away down the alley. Another pair of footsteps—Qigang's, presumably—took off in another direction. Aranya let out a sigh, but Kai immediately covered her mouth again. She glared at him. He gave a short shake of his head, staring out at the world she couldn't see.

All she could see was Kai, tall and cloaked in shadow. He blocked off the rest of the world from her sight, and it made her fidgety to not know what was happening around them.

She didn't *want* to have to trust his judgment.

Especially when his judgment was apparently to keep her unmoving and silent against a sharp corner that just might slice through her robes with how much weight he was leaning into her. How was the coast not clear yet? The alley had been silent for many long minutes now. She was quite done getting overly acquainted with the smell of his robes.

Then his head tilted down toward hers until his mouth hovered just above the shell of her ear. "Don't move," he whispered—and then vanished.

She nearly stumbled away from the corner with the sudden loss of his heat and pressure but managed to keep herself tucked into the darkness while her lungs filled and emptied rapidly. She could finally catch a full breath now that the smell of boot polish, well-loved linen, and something else that was distinctly masculine did not accompany it.

"All's clear."

Aranya sagged, then groaned as she peeled her back away from the doorway. She craned her neck to find Kai standing in the middle of the alley, his profile cut in obscurity. Slowly, she eased out from under the awning, and slid to his side, feeling suddenly awkward and bumbling.

"Why'd you wait so long?" she asked.

His head swiveled down to hers. She had the strangest inclination to wrap her arms around her middle, as if he intimidated her. As if she were affected by how close they'd been a moment ago.

But she wasn't. She hadn't been affected. Not by someone who had probably been involved with half the girls at the Academy at one point or another.

He opened his mouth as his eyebrow arched, and she just *knew* he was going to say something intended to make her flush.

"No," she said, beating him to it and pointing a finger at his face. "Whatever you're about to say, it wasn't that."

His teeth flashed in a grin.

"Was anyone waiting for us to come out of hiding?"

Kai heaved out a sigh, his mouth still twisted in amusement, and strode down the alleyway. She scrambled to keep up with his long legs. "Yes," he said. "Qigang was suspicious. But I made sure he was gone. Now, do you think you can manage getting back to your tenement without getting caught? Or ought I to stay and babysit you?"

Right, he wasn't staying with her because he *wanted* to, but to make sure he didn't get in trouble. She tossed him her sweetest smile. "Thanks for the offer, but I think I can handle it."

She'd hardly finished the words before he was gone.

CHAPTER 14

KAI SLIPPED DEFTLY through the shadows, as if he were born of night and wind. He tried to evanesce as little as possible, but by this point there would be no sleeping for hours. He'd evanesced too much today already.

But he couldn't let this situation alone or else things could get very bad, very fast.

It wasn't long before he was inside the incarceration unit, past the guards, and sneaking from cell to cell, peering in and looking for a familiar face. He neared the end of the line of cells, all but blind in the darkness, his breath the only sound in his ears. It was almost like this place was completely empty.

It wasn't.

There, in the last cell, bound and gagged because of her magic, was the siren they'd captured earlier. *Lehua.* Not a girl he'd recognized, but the sight of her tattoo burned like fire in his mind, driving him forward and refusing to release him from the tight coils of anxiety.

Lehua blinked when he came into view. Not asleep, but watching and alert. In the cell across from her, the other brigand slept with his head tilted back against the wall behind him.

Kai swallowed, evanesced through the bars, then knelt in front of the siren, who stared at him expectantly. She made no sound, not even a grunt through her gag, even as her eyes narrowed, and her brow furrowed.

"Do you know me?" asked Kai under his breath.

She nodded. Once.

He closed his eyes, chewed on the inside of his cheek. "Then I will make a deal with you."

Her gaze was like a bolt of ice, spearing him straight through the face.

"I'll free you," he said, "and your fellow brigand. In exchange, you'll tell your master that you broke yourself out. If you breathe a word that you saw me, I will personally hunt you down." He paused, gauging that fierce, rebellious light in the siren's face. Then he jerked his head toward the man behind him. "I'll kill him."

The siren's jaw slackened. Good. He'd made a threat that actually meant something to her. He somehow knew that threatening her life wouldn't be enough.

"Deal?" whispered Kai.

She glared at him, grinding her teeth around the gag in her mouth, and then nodded.

Perfect. Now all he had to do was break these two out and stage the area so that it looked like a Hidden One leader had been the one to do it.

Which would be very easy. He'd already done it more times than he'd like to count.

When Aranya finally crept back into her half-unpacked tenement, she could think of nothing except how exhausted she was.

Her boots reeked. Her feet were only worse after all that running. Her arm still ached from being shocked. Not to mention the existing aches and pains of the long days prior. Stepping into the darkness of the tenement she shared with Ye Ye made her brain go muddled with fatigue.

Who was she fooling? Whenever they told Qigang what happened so they could arrest Lord Wun for questioning, she knew she'd get blamed for everything that went wrong, while Kai would get credit for everything that went right. Qigang would proclaim him the hero, and her, the idiot.

And she could take it. She really could. Except that it meant her chances at keeping this position grew slimmer and slimmer by the moment. Her eyes drifted to find Ye Ye curled up on the bed, his tail tucked beneath his paws. Usually, he slept by the fireplace, but tonight she was glad he'd situated himself here.

She swallowed back a thick clog of tears. *I won't fail him again.* She would be strong—as strong as she needed to be.

Her little tenement suddenly seemed much less secure than it had before. She had the presence of mind to tuck her boots away before she changed hurriedly, parking herself in a corner to keep her eyes peeled for any sign of an untimely evanescing rival.

She climbed onto the bed, pulling the quilt up to her chin and settling her head on the firm cushion. Ye Ye's tail was wrapped around his body, covering his face. She shouldn't disturb him. She should let him sleep.

Nevertheless, she reached out and drew the soft white bundle against her. He yawned, stretching out one paw into the air, and then began purring. Even half-asleep, he nuzzled his wet nose against her chin, her cheek.

She held him close, the tension slowly leaking out of her aching body as the sound of purring filled her senses. Tears came unbidden. Ye Ye only nuzzled her more, licking the salty trails on her face, giving her a few burbling chirps.

"I just didn't think it would be like . . . like *this,*" she whispered against him, earning a mouthful of fur. "I didn't think . . . I didn't expect everyone to dislike me so much. And I didn't expect I'd be this *bad* at everything."

"Mrrreow."

"I know I just need to keep working. I am learning. That's what you would say, wouldn't you? That failure is the best teacher."

In response, the cat butted his head against her cheek and flicked his tail against her shoulder. She smiled through her tears, scratching under his chin exactly where he liked it.

She gave a shuddering chuckle. "You would also say that problems are better faced with a good night's rest. You would tell me the most productive thing I can do right now is sleep, not worry."

He chirped again and settled into the crook of her arm, tucking his face against her neck. His cold nose tickled her skin.

"You always have the best advice, Ye Ye."

"Mrrow."

He fell back asleep almost instantly, his fuzzy belly rising and falling so softly.

"I won't let you down," she whispered. "Never again."

She had almost followed him into oblivion when something—some sixth sense—tingled. She opened her eyes. There, in the middle of the tenement, shrouded in shadow, stood a tall masculine form. A familiar form.

His arms were full of something. She snapped her eyes shut as he seemed to glance over to her, trying to hold still as her heartrate pounded. If he was about to play another prank on her . . .

Quiet shuffling sounded by the fireplace. She peeled open one eye, ready to shift into talons at any moment, and tried to figure out what nonsense he was doing.

Something slipped. Wood clinked against wood. Kai froze. Aranya closed her eyes again when she saw his head turn back to her. Several long moments passed, moments when she debated revealing her hand—and waking Ye Ye up in the process—or waiting to see what her rival intended to do.

Was this what he did when he couldn't sleep? Break into other people's tenements? Was this why he was always doing pranks at the Academy—because he couldn't sleep after evanescing all day?

Then, at long last, the faintest scuffs of him moving continued. She opened one eye to see him stand from the fireplace, pull something out of his robes, and set it on the table. With one more glance toward her—during which she hurriedly shut her eyes—he stepped away.

And vanished again.

CHAPTER 15

KAI HADN'T LEFT a prank for her after all, but an armful of logs for the fire and bandages . . . for her feet? Aranya had no idea what to make of this, so she decided not to make anything of it at all. She decided not to say anything about it to him either, because the way she saw it, if he had wanted thanks, he wouldn't have snuck in after he thought she was asleep.

So she bound up her feet and thanked the fathers when she didn't have to chop wood for a few days.

When she arrived at the wardpost that morning, everything was in commotion. Several wardens spoke amongst themselves on the deck outside, and Qigang was red-faced as he gestured loudly and spoke with the incarceration unit supervisor.

Aranya glanced around awkwardly, then hesitantly approached Na, who leaned placidly against a wooden pillar and inspected her nails, boots crossed over each other.

"What happened?" Aranya asked.

Na let out a deep exhale, flicking her eyes up from her nails. "Those two brigands you brought in yesterday broke out sometime during the night. Looks like a brigand leader helped them. This is why Hidden Ones have the worst reputation of all the brigand gangs; it's nearly impossible to keep them captive. They either escape or they're dead the next morning. Qigang is going to positively eat those incarceration operatives alive, though, because he told them to triple guard the brigands and apparently they didn't. An unfortunate misunderstanding. Best to suit up for the day, hunt down Chen, and be off to south patrol before Qigang sees you and yells at you for breathing."

"But I need to report about last night . . .?"

She sighed again and shook her head. "I'll get Kai to report for the both of you whenever he comes in. Off with you now."

Aranya was buckling on her weapons in the armory when Kai walked in. She glanced sidelong at him, saying nothing as she noted the dark circles beneath his eyes, the shadow along his jaw from skipping a day of shaving, and the way his clothes were mussed and wrinkled.

He didn't speak a word or so much as spare her an acknowledging look.

She watched him, her brow wrinkling. She supposed he must have been telling the truth last night, that evanescing gave him insomnia. He looked like he hadn't slept a wink.

She should be glad she finally had an edge over him. Instead, she couldn't hide the hint of concern in her voice when she finally asked, "Are you alright?"

He only grunted, grabbed a broadsword, and didn't even bother taking a *jiaun* as he left the armory with heavy footsteps.

Aranya found out later from Na that when Kai went to report about last night, instead of taking the brunt of Qigang's fury about the escaped brigands or the close calls of last night, Qigang told him to go catch up on the sleep he lost from all the evanescing and come back when he was refreshed.

He didn't come back until the next morning.

A week after their daring rescue of Lord Meng's ungrateful daughter, Aranya was summoned to Qigang's office before reporting for the day's work. She was in the middle of buckling on her knives—Chen scrambling to get his life together nearby—when the summons arrived.

Qigang had sent a few wardens and "stuffy-nosed judicial idiots" to arrest Lord Wun and present him before trial after the findings of their Kankhai Lake adventure. They were still meeting to determine if he was guilty, but Na had told her while they walked back from work each day that it was looking more and more likely they would find him guilty. She said it had been an attempted political move to force Lord Meng to stop pushing a rice tariff that would cut trade with Butagin. An exchange: his daughter, returned to him unharmed, if he dropped the tariff.

"Sounds above my paygrade," Aranya had said to Na.

Na had huffed dryly. "You couldn't pay me enough to play those court games. You'd think Zushui would be far enough from the politics of Suguan, but alas, it appears politics follow us even here. This instance was particularly messy. I haven't seen anything quite like it, but that goes to show the state of the empire at the moment with the barbarians and all the brigands running loose. It's a good thing Emperor Nianzu is reigning now and not his father. Seems like he's doing what he can to fight the inevitable bureaucratic corruption. Just keep your head down, girl, and try to avoid getting involved again with the likes of Lord Meng and Lord Wun. They have too many connections with important people in the government, like the territory guardians."

Now, as she navigated the growingly familiar halls of the wardpost, Aranya wasn't sure what she was expecting from Qigang this time. She didn't *think* she was in trouble, but she could never tell these days. Drawing in a deep breath, and forcing a hesitant smile onto her face, she slipped into his office.

The supervisor paced in front of his desk, his movements languid yet confined. Like a tiger prowling a cage.

Kai was there too, standing at attention. She eyed him, but he didn't look at her. They had not spoken since their Kankhai Lake adventures. For the last week, there had been no wet boots or anything of the sort. Just the occasional flash of a memory of squeezing close in a dark corner whenever they passed, and she caught a whiff of his scent.

She offered him a sunny smile despite the coldness. He did not move a muscle. She faced the supervisor's desk, and her eyes trailed up from his dragon teacup to the beautiful *jiaun* on the wall.

"Well, *this* is a mess I'd never thought I'd find myself in. Least of all with you two!" Qigang spewed suddenly, waving his arms in an exaggerated gesture. "You," he spat, pointing directly at Aranya. "You've put me in a very awkward situation. I'm not happy about it."

"Awkward situation?" she said, brow furrowed.

"Yes! Are you deaf, girl?" He swept up a scroll from his desk and stormed to Kai, shoving it in his face. "Read that, Shi Kai."

Kai blinked, accepted the scroll, and unfurled it. His low voice, free of its typical wry bite, filled the room.

"Upon receipt of this missive, Shi Kai and Sun Aranya are hereby summoned to . . ." he trailed off, peering closer at the scroll. His eyebrows knit together. His focus snapped up to Qigang, as if for confirmation.

"What? We're summoned for what? What does it say?" she asked.

Kai's impatient glare was withering, but he continued. "Shi Kai and Sun Aranya are hereby summoned to report to the Palace Secret Services in Suguan, capital city of the empire of Zheninghai. Utmost discretion is required. Full information on this temporary mission will be disclosed upon arrival."

Aranya stumbled back a step, blinking quickly and pressing a hand to her lips.

"Utter disaster!" Qigang cried, flinging up his hands again. "Now what am I supposed to do? I cannot go against orders like this."

"Go against them?" she gasped. "Why would—?"

"Shut your mouth, girl. I'm in no mood for your prattling. This is ridiculous! You have no experience or skills beyond the Academy; you are just plain *stupid*—seven valleys! What has gotten into these qilin-brains, thinking you two would be suitable for a job like this?"

She clenched her jaw and bit her lip. Her mind reeled so fast she fluctuated between exquisite elation and nearly overwhelming confusion and indignation at being called stupid. This must be the result of the commendation Qigang was forced to send on their behalf after their rescue. But *why*? As much as she didn't want to admit it, Qigang was right. There was no reason they should have gotten a position like this.

Secret Services were so far above her magic, skill, and experience. They only rarely accepted new graduates as it was. Only someone with magic like Kai would have been granted an appointment with them.

Kai looked about as happy as the supervisor at this turn of events. She glanced between them, noticing how they shared a knowing look. Kai—frustration. Qigang—understanding sympathy.

What was between them?

She closed her eyes just for a second, not even caring about the unfairness. Thrill and giddiness threatened to bubble out of her lips in a giggle. She was going to go on a special mission? It hardly seemed possible. It could change everything for—

Ye Ye.

The thought hit her like a physical blow so hard she took another involuntary step backward.

"I can't go," she whispered.

"What?" Qigang barked.

"I can't go."

"You must go; there is no other option. Believe me, I'd demand both of you decline if it were up to me." He let out a long, exasperated sigh and ran his hand down his face. "What a mess," he grumbled. "What a mess."

Her breaths came fast and hard as her mind scrambled through the implications. Her former exhilaration fled, replaced only with dread and panic. This was *exactly* what had happened last time when she'd failed Ye Ye. She'd gotten so preoccupied with her responsibilities at the Academy, had overestimated his ability to care for himself. And he'd only declined more in the years since that day.

She couldn't leave him alone, with no one to pay rent, light his fire, go to the market, prepare his food.

He would die without her.

Her stomach clenched. *No.* While Aranya lived, her grandfather would be comfortable. He wouldn't be alone. He'd be cared for. If that meant she had to offend the emperor himself, or strap Ye Ye to her back while she fulfilled his summons, she would do it.

She would not fail him. Just like he'd never failed her when she'd had no one but him. As Qigang turned around and began ranting at the wall, a quiet voice sounded next to her.

"Ask Na."

"What?"

Kai's shoulders lifted slightly with his intake of breath. "Ask Na to watch over your grandfather. She's sensible and probably willing."

She stared at him, her mouth open.

He cocked an eyebrow at her expression and lifted his gaze to face forward, a rueful smile tugging on his lips. "Or don't."

She swallowed and nodded, suddenly at a loss for words. But she drew herself up taller as Qigang faced them, still growling and muttering under his breath. The tension in her shoulders eased, lightening so much it was like she'd grown wings.

Could Na help? Would this mean that Aranya could fill the summons? Could this change things? For her? For Ye Ye? Could this be an open door for a higher salary?

And a chance to go on a *real* adventure?

She was suddenly aware of Kai's scrutiny and tried to school her features into neutrality so he couldn't begin to guess a single thought that crossed her mind. Wouldn't know how much his suggestion meant to her.

"Get off to south patrol, girl. You both will need to leave tomorrow," Qigang growled. "And remember, if you fail this assignment in Suguan, I'm not taking you back. Get dismissed from them, and you're dismissed here."

A chill swept down her spine, pooling in her gut. This suddenly felt like the riskiest gamble she'd ever faced, and she couldn't even opt to fold. She swallowed. Then she waited for him to issue the same command to Kai. Two breaths later, and he still hadn't gotten a similar command.

She gritted her teeth as she turned to leave the room. Once she'd closed the door behind them, she stopped. Softened her breaths.

"I'd get you out of this if I could," came Qigang's muffled voice.

"It will be fine."

"But your family lives in Suguan, right?"

"Gebei. They will not likely find out."

"And if they do?"

"Then I will disappear, as always."

Kai's tone was so respectful, so formal. Nothing like the grating tenor and barbed remarks he flung at her.

"Evanescing cannot fix all your problems, boy."

Footsteps sounded. She scurried away from the door, but Kai's dark response still carried through the door.

"Evanescing is not the only way to disappear."

She'd barely slipped outside before Kai exited Qigang's office. Squinting against the glare of the rising sun, she hurried out onto the rocky path toward south patrol as the wardpost entrance banged shut behind her. She cast one quick glance over her shoulder to see his tall form take three long strides and then disappear into thin air.

CHAPTER 16

FROM THE FIRST day Kai had shown up in Zushui, nothing had gone according to plan. And tomorrow, he was heading back to the city he'd fled in the first place.

It had been a long day. A long, anxious day of reasoning round and round in his mind, wondering if there was a way to get out of this Suguan summoning. Then when he determined there wasn't, at least not until he arrived at the capital, he tried to figure out what the chances were that his family was visiting the city. After that, he went through his mental map of the city, planning the most efficient way to get through the city to the palace without being spotted by one of his family's scouts. But that wasn't his strong suit, and he ended up only frustrating himself further.

Now, Kai stood outside Aranya's tenement door, fist raised to knock. For several long moments, he couldn't bring himself to actually knock. He just stood there, poised, but unmoving.

The sound of Aranya's voice from inside made him pause.

"I have enough food purchased to last a few weeks," she was saying, presumably to Ye Ye, "but it'll run out, and this is where I'm putting the money. Can you tell Na that for me? That was the one thing I forgot to tell her when she came over earlier. Or maybe I should write a note? And leave it on the table? You won't forget, Ye Ye, will you? To tell Na?"

She didn't give him a chance to answer, but just kept on prattling instructions to Ye Ye and then switching to muttering to herself about all manner of things. The little sniffs and reassurances to Ye Ye that punctuated these words sounded much more like reassurances to herself.

"Na is very reliable and level-headed. She's going to do such a good job taking care of you that you won't even want me to come home!"

Ye Ye chuckled at that, and Kai had to strain to hear his response. "There's no chance of that, Sunflower."

"I hate leaving you with the tenement in this state! But it's not like I can ask Na to move us in while I'm gone!" *Bang!* "Ow! Seven valleys, why are the corners of these boxes *so sharp*?!"

"I can't wait to hear all the stories you'll have," said Ye Ye.

"I suppose we'll see. I don't know what the mission is about yet. It might be nothing. We might be back very soon. Oh fathers, it's getting late and I haven't even made you dinner yet!" Aranya's voice was getting shriller, the sniffles more frequent.

Kai sighed, lowering his head. He knocked on the door.

The clamor of Aranya scrambling through the mess stopped for a second. "Did you hear a knock, Ye Ye?"

"I do believe I did."

"Is it Na? Did she come back? Oh good, because I forgot to tell her about—"

The door swung open. Aranya's face was fixed straight ahead expecting to greet someone of her own height. Kai stared down at her as her head tilted back, her swollen eyes lifting all the way up to his. Her cheeks and neck were flushed, and the sight of him seemed to only make the color brighter.

She set into a series of rapid blinks and looked down, sniffing. Both her hands clenched around the door, and she was half behind it, almost as if she used it as a shield between them.

It was an uncharacteristic display of shyness and uncertainty for her.

Kai looked past her to Ye Ye, who was standing, his back hunched forward, by the hearth. He smiled warmly, and the older man grinned happily in response. He raised a gnarled finger, pointed it at Kai, and declared brightly, "Why, it's that handsome young man who ate noodles with us!"

Kai grinned back, pretending he didn't notice the way Aranya swiped at her eyes with her sleeve. "You are looking well, Ye Ye. How does another bowl of noodles sound? I did promise that I'd have you both to my tenement and you'll have to tell me whose noodles are better."

"No one cooks better than my sunflower."

"I'm a wretched cook and you know it," said Aranya, folding her arms across her chest.

Kai shrugged, still smiling. "I don't know, Ye Ye. I make a mean bowl of noodles if I do say so myself. Come, let me help you."

He was halfway to Ye Ye, dodging between boxes, when Aranya leapt to his side and grabbed his sleeve with both hands. "What are you doing?" she demanded, and then belatedly forced a smile onto her face for Ye Ye's sake. "If this is some scheme—"

He pried her hand off him and returned her smile, leaning down to say quietly to her, "I want the wardenship. Don't mistake that. But that doesn't mean I'm glad for the situation we're in. Besides, just because you have an irksome personality doesn't mean your grandfather does. I find him rather delightful, actually. And all my food is going to go bad if we don't eat it up."

With that, he swept past her, shoved boxes aside to make a clear path for Ye Ye, took his elbow, and guided him out of the room.

Aranya hadn't moved.

"Can you bring a set of bowls and chopsticks for you and Ye Ye?" called Kai over his shoulder, keeping a firm grip on the older man's forearm. "I only have enough for myself, unfortunately."

There was a frustrated huff from behind him, which probably meant he'd successfully angered her enough to keep her from dissolving into tears.

Once Ye Ye was settled comfortably at Kai's table in his tenement down the hallway from Aranya's, he went to the stove and set to cooking. For a split second, he considered repaying Aranya for the bowl she'd made him that, once eaten, had made his entire body feel as though it was on fire. But no. Today's revenge would be making her bowl so delicious that she would dream of it for months to come.

When the room remained quiet except for the sounds of his cooking, he glanced over his shoulder to find Ye Ye still sitting contentedly at the table, and Aranya standing awkwardly by the open door, looking very out of place and uncomfortable. Her gaze traveled over the sparsely furnished room, and he couldn't help but wonder what she thought of what she saw.

He turned back to his work, setting the water to boil as he continued chopping the vegetables. Her padding footsteps were slow as she approached him, and he turned to find her standing to his right, clasping her hands nervously in front of her.

"Do you need help?" she asked.

He side-eyed her, then brandished a green onion in her face. "You aren't allowed to touch these noodles, Partial. Now go sit—"

"You touched *my* noodles!"

"Which was the only reason they were tolerable. Sit down before you breathe too closely to mine."

She huffed, and stood there for a second longer, as though she wanted to keep fighting. But then she gave in and went to sit cross-legged by Ye Ye. Kai kept cooking, only pausing to serve them something to drink while they waited.

"So, Shi Kai," said Ye Ye, breaking the silence with that crackling voice of his, "I take it you have no young lady you're matched to?"

Aranya spat out her water. She set into a fit of vicious coughing. Kai couldn't help smirking as he scooped up a rag and tossed it straight at her face. Her watery eyes met his as she caught the rag, and just as quickly she looked away.

"You alright?" asked Kai.

She nodded, guzzling down the rest of her water and then wiping up the mess she'd made. Then she hissed at her grandcat, "Ye Ye! You can't ask questions like that!"

"Noodles incoming!" said Kai, balancing the three bowls on his arm as he came toward the table, and set one before each of them. Aranya ducked her head and mumbled her thanks, still avoiding his gaze. "Well, Ye Ye, try them. I dare you to tell me these aren't the best noodles you've ever had."

Ye Ye chuckled and lifted his bowl to slurp the broth. He let out a contented "Ahh," then set the bowl down and wound a noodle around his chopsticks.

"Well?" asked Kai.

Aranya said nothing, but she watched intently as Ye Ye took his first few bites. She and Kai waited as the older man swallowed, sighed, and set down his chopsticks, a smile on his face.

"It's amazing, isn't it?" said Kai, a pleased grin spreading across his face and satisfaction blooming in his stomach.

"It tastes the same!" proclaimed Ye Ye. "Delicious!"

"It most certainly does not!" replied Kai, aghast.

Aranya burst out laughing. And didn't stop until tears were leaking out of her eyes and Ye Ye was hesitantly patting her shoulder, asking if she was alright. She nodded, wiping her eyes with her sleeve. Kai just stared at her, his gut sinking deeper and deeper.

If Ye Ye hadn't been here, Kai might have been bold enough to stand up, walk around to her side of the table, and offer her a hug. He had a suspicion she would have turned her head into his chest without complaint and cried.

But Ye Ye was here.

So Kai took up his bowl of noodles and set to eating. After a few minutes, during which Aranya had wiped her eyes a dozen more times between guzzling down the broth in her bowl, she finally looked composed enough for Kai to say, "Well? What's Sunflower's verdict of the noodles?"

She shot him a glare and *there* was the spark that had been missing. Begrudgingly, she admitted, "They're very good."

Kai raised his eyebrows at Ye Ye. "See? Even Aranya agrees mine are better. I'm afraid you're outnumbered, Ye Ye."

"That's not what I said!"

Kai's brows went higher. "You're going to claim your noodles are better than mine?"

At that, she tucked her chin with a scowl and kept slurping up more noodles.

Kai smirked again. "I thought so. To answer your question, Ye Ye, no, I'm not matched. I *was* a couple years ago, though."

Aranya's head whipped up from her bowl. "You were? While you were at the Academy?"

"Indeed. My parents were intended for each other almost from birth, so they did something similar with me. I was destined to marry the purest bred evanescer remotely near my age, which unfortunately meant she was nine years younger than me. But I had no interest in that, so I didn't do it."

"You went against your parents' match?" Aranya asked, mouth falling open.

"The only person who could make me do anything was my father," said Kai, swallowing the bitterness crawling up his throat before he continued. "But he died a few months ago, so there's nothing my brother and mother can make me do, including whatever dragon-blasted arranged marriage they had for me."

"I'm sorry about your father."

"Don't be."

Chopsticks clinked against bowls.

"Why didn't you want it? I thought you were fine flirting with anything that walked on two legs," said Aranya. "Or is it the marriage part that was so unappealing?"

Now it was Ye Ye's turn to cough and sputter. "Now why ever would you say something like that? Please, take no offense from her, Kai."

But Kai laughed. Laughed at the absurdity of this situation, this conversation, at Aranya apologizing for Ye Ye only moments before he apologized for her, at the fact that neither of them actually knew almost anything about him.

He propped his elbow on the table, set his chin on top of his fisted hand, and leaned closer to her. And for the first time tonight, her eyes were glued to his.

"You do realize," he said, "that she is eleven, right? She still plays with dolls between Academy classes. I know most of us can't be as sweet and honorable as you,"—this was said with his most dazzling smile—"but even I have limits."

If Ye Ye hadn't been listening, he would have said his wickedness had limits, but he opted to not freak out the grandfather and omit that particular word.

"I like to keep a policy of withholding judgment when I don't have all the information," continued Kai, clinking his glass of water against Ye Ye's.

She was staring at him, eyes narrowed, as if she did indeed see how his statement was both a lie and a rebuke. But then Ye Ye made a contented noise in the back of his throat and began talking as if Aranya and Kai hadn't been in the middle of a conversation. "Aranya had these dolls she absolutely *loved* as a child."

Aranya's eyes widened, darting from Kai to Ye Ye. Panic flashed across her face. "No, please, not this story again."

Kai lifted a brow.

"Once, when we were leaving for the market—she was probably . . . four years old? That was before her shapeshifting manifested and she went off to the Academy."

"We should probably go back now," said Aranya hurriedly, bouncing to her feet.

"Let me finish the story!"

"I want to hear it," said Kai, leaning forward eagerly, steepling his fingers.

She sat back down, pursed her lips.

"We were leaving for the market," said Ye Ye, "and I said, 'Come on, little sunflower, it's time to go.' And she kept insisting she wasn't ready yet, and finally I relented and asked why she wasn't ready. She ran over to her three dolls propped up on her bed. They were cornhusk dolls, you see. With button eyes. The most hideous things you've ever seen. And she went over to each one, kissed them all soundly, and then came running back over to me. 'Now I'm ready, Ye Ye!' she said. Only then could we leave." Ye Ye chuckled fondly, hands splayed across his belly, as if it were the most hilarious thing ever.

Kai smirked, glancing over at Aranya's pink-tinged cheeks, and said, "How adorable."

"Oh, it was! She was the cutest child, with eyes much too large for her face."

Now Aranya was glaring at Ye Ye, silently pleading with said eyes to stop talking. But Ye Ye only grinned wider.

"When those huge eyes welled up with tears, I just couldn't say no to anything she asked!"

At that, Aranya's mouth twisted. "That is very true. You never said no to me."

"That explains a lot of things," said Kai dryly.

"What is *that* supposed to mean?" demanded Aranya, whipping her gaze up to his as he scooped up their empty bowls.

With that puffy-eyed glare fixed on him, as much as he wanted to keep a straight face and cock an eyebrow, he couldn't help smiling down at her. Genuinely smiling. Neither could he help the very slight bit of warmth in his chest when she quickly looked away.

"It's time to go, Ye Ye. We have lots to do before I leave tomorrow. And you need to get plenty of rest. Thank you for the food, Kai."

He nodded once at her, and then turned to Ye Ye to say, "Now listen, Ye Ye, this bowl of noodles was free, but next time you want more, it's going to cost you."

"Oh, how much?" asked Ye Ye as Kai helped him to his feet.

"One statement. All you have to say is, 'Kai's food tastes better than Aranya's.'"

Ye Ye chuckled. Aranya rolled her eyes. And when they left, Kai stood in the middle of his empty tenement. He'd just eaten, and yet somehow, he was hollow.

CHAPTER 17

KAI HADN'T EVANESCED in hours, yet he laid awake, staring up at the ceiling in the blackness of his tenement, wishing oblivion would swallow him up.

His thoughts swirled in an anxious turmoil. Thoughts of his dead father, of breaking the Hidden Ones out of the incarceration unit, of all the times he'd done that in Suguan, of Aranya's tears, and of the absence of her family besides Ye Ye. Why was she the only one taking care of her grandfather? Why was there no one to care for her?

If only there hadn't been a mistake with this appointment. Then he could have had his escape, Aranya could have her career, and they never would have run off together to solve the case of Lord Meng's kidnapped daughter.

He rolled over, flinging his blankets to one side, letting the cool air wash over his body. It was too dragon-blasted hot during the summer. No wonder he couldn't fall asleep.

And then an image flashed before his mind's eye. Her face uptilted toward his, the shadows unable to hide the glimmer of her dark eyes. How warm and close she'd been, how . . .

He was on his feet the next minute, stumbling on tired legs to the window. He shoved it open, standing there and breathing in the cool draft. Fathers, it was hot in here! Winter needed to come. As soon as possible.

"Suguan," he growled between gritted teeth, his hands braced on the sill. "Did it *have* to be Suguan?"

It was only a slight relief that his family did not live there. They frequented the city, as most distinguished families did. There was always the chance he would run into them or someone reporting to them. Always the risk.

They would find out where he'd gone, eventually. It would only cost a few bribes in the right hands for his mother or brother to infiltrate the bureaucracy, and only a few more to get him back exactly where she wanted him. But for now, they didn't know where he was.

If his mother found him, though . . . If his brother found him . . .

It would be much harder to disappear again. Much, *much* harder.

But he'd managed it this far, and his father wasn't alive anymore to see through his behavior at the Academy. His father had been the only one not fooled by Kai's endless pranks and flirting and poor grades. He saw through the ruse, and Kai would spend his life paying for not playing his part convincingly enough.

If only his father had never died. Then Kai's life wouldn't have been upended. Then he never would have to sort through the strange sense of grief that came when one lost a father who loved none but himself. A despised father was still a father. And when he died, the hope of his redemption died with him.

Aranya had been convinced though. Somehow, that brought a smile to his face. She was many of the things he disliked—rash, squirrelly, so *talkative,* with far too much false confidence. But . . .

Maybe he didn't dislike those things as much as he thought he did.

He returned to his bed, flopped heavily onto it, rolled to his side, and tried to get his eyes to shut. They remained stubbornly open.

He ought to make a plan of escape, should he encounter his family. There were many things he ought to do, and somehow the *ought* always made him far less inclined to do anything.

Mischief would clear his mind. A little mirth went a long way. Besides, he needed to get Aranya back for burning his guts out with those noodles.

He stayed where he was.

He needed an idea. Some inspiration. Yet his mind fogged up, and brilliance refused to oblige itself. He could rig something to the door when she opened it. No, too complicated. Fill her boots with dirt? Too many boot pranks. He was growing lax these days, opting for ease instead of genius. He needed something fresh and unexpected.

Instead of ideas, he saw her face again. So near his own in that doorway. It would have been too easy to uphold his reputation as a notorious flirt, to just lean down and press his mouth to hers. To see if she would melt into his arms, to get even the barest indication that she didn't still hate him for ruining her plans.

He groaned.

This was going to be a long night.

Ye Ye would be fine without her. Aranya's stomach clenched like a small creature was trapped inside, trying to claw its way out.

He would be fine without her.

Na had agreed to take care of him. Aranya didn't have to worry about him. But she couldn't help herself. She wrung her hands as she and Kai rode away from Zushui on horseback the next morning. The reins twisted in her fingers; the leather coming away slick from her skin. She let out a tight exhale.

Slowly, she shifted her gaze to Kai, who was riding just a little in front of her. He wouldn't deign to ride alongside her, apparently, although the road was wide enough to allow it.

"I'm surprised you don't just evanesce your way to Suguan," Aranya said, breaking the silence.

He barked a surprised laugh. "You flatter me," he said, still facing ahead instead of turning to glance at her. "Which I highly doubt was your intention."

"So your evanescing has a distance limit too? Not just the insomnia?"

He seemed to hesitate, his head twisting slightly to the side, as if he debated turning and looking at her, but changed his mind at the last second. "You think I would explain all my magic's limits to you?"

She urged her horse faster, so she was next to him and flashing her biggest grin his way. "I'm all ears."

"My question was rhetorical."

"A rhetorical yes."

He huffed, something that she might have thought was amusement and not irritation, if she didn't know better. But she definitely knew better.

He licked his lips, squinted at the rising sun, still never fully glancing her way. "It's not about distance so much as the number of barriers. I can only evanesce through one barrier at a time, and even things such as trees can be a barrier. So no, I cannot evanesce straight to Suguan."

"Oh! How very fascinating!"

He said nothing. Just clicked his tongue to urge his horse faster, ahead of her. Apparently, pretending she didn't exist was his preferred method of operation at the moment. But if the silence between them persisted, then her mind would have one place and one place only to dwell: anxious worries about Ye Ye. She'd drive herself insane, and before she knew it, she'd have turned her horse around and galloped straight back to him.

"What do you think this special mission is?" she asked, pulling alongside him and refusing to be left at the rear.

He exhaled through his nostrils. "Chatterbox."

"Oh, quit with that," she snapped, waving a hand. "You would've had some Academy classes on Special Services, right? Being an evanescer and all. Now that we have all this time together—"

"The answer is no."

"—then you can explain why you're a warden instead of a spy or something. Did you fail all your classes?"

"Like I said, the answer is *no*."

"You didn't fail all your classes?"

"Fathers," he muttered, dragging a hand down his face. "This journey is going to be so long."

"It's not *that* long," she said, trying to keep her tone from betraying her sarcasm. "There's just the riding today and tomorrow, and then we'll be there."

His answer was silence.

Aranya sidled up next to him, which only made him scoot his horse forward more.

"Where's your family from?" she asked, receiving no small amount of satisfaction at his grunt of annoyance. She'd only overheard that one cryptic conversation between him and Qigang, and now she had *all* this time with Kai. Perhaps she could get him to confide in her, too. She pressed further. "Do you have parents? Siblings? Are they evanescers, too?"

"Poor Chen."

"I think you meant *'Poor Aranya,'* because I promise that Chen being paired with me and my questions are not nearly as bad as me being paired with him and his ignorance."

Kai raised an eyebrow, but beside the tiniest jump of a muscle near his mouth, his face revealed nothing. "I don't do backstory, Partial. Now shut up so we can travel in peace."

He didn't mean it as a dare, but she couldn't resist a good challenge.

"I can be very persistent," she chirped. "We've got a long journey ahead. And I have no one else to talk to, so you can bet—"

She stopped talking as Kai held up a hand.

Suddenly, all was quiet. They reined in their horses, stopping in the middle of the road. Even their horses seemed to hold their breath, waiting. Tension crawling up her spine, Aranya's hand going to her *jiaun* as Kai withdrew the knife at his belt.

If only she could shift completely! She could catch the scent and chase down whatever this was. Instead, she had to rely only on her limited human senses of sight and hearing.

There was that sound again.

Like low, heavy breathing. Alarmingly near.

Any other traveler probably would have hurried their mount onward, hoping to avoid danger altogether. But Aranya and Kai weren't ordinary travelers, and she knew by the twitching in his jaw that he felt the responsibility as keenly as she did.

Whatever their appointment and position in the empire of Zheninghai, as magic-wielders, they were protectors of their people first and foremost.

Kai vanished from his saddle. Careful of her talons, Aranya dismounted hers and hurried both horses to the opposite side of the road. Once they were settled and safely out of the way, she unholstered her *jiaun* and slotted two arrows. With the practiced steps of a hunter, she eased her way toward the tree line off the side of the road, where the sound had come from.

She held the weapon up but didn't peer through its sights. Instead, she searched over the top and evened out her breathing as she approached. The adrenaline surging through her blood made it hard to keep her limbs steady. She could practically hear her old masters smacking her arm or leg and telling her to stop fidgeting.

The worst part of working with an evanescer? She never knew where he went. It would be nice to have some semblance of a plan, considering that Kai always seemed to have a plan extraordinarily different from hers.

Despite her careful steps, underbrush cracked beneath her boots when she left the road. She stilled, waiting. Hardly breathing.

"Cursed fathers!" came a sudden curse from deeper in the woods. "Spitfire! Spitfire! *Spitfire!*"

"Kai?" Aranya called. She opened her mouth again but was immediately cut off by a strange sound.

The tinkling of bells. Tiny, silver, almost mewling. Her blood ran cold.

"Oh fathers, indeed!" she breathed.

Kai reappeared beside her, snatching her free upper arm and yanking her backward. "Get back, Aranya. It's a calf."

Her eyes snapped to his, widening. "A calf? What do we do?"

"We get out of here before the mother comes to find it and discovers us."

"But what if someone else travels this way after we leave? We can't leave this hazard here for some unsuspecting citizen!"

"It won't—"

Bells sounded behind them, but these were like thunderous pagoda bells rumbling in her chest. Kai's grip on her wrist stiffened, his eyes fluttering shut with sudden dread. Aranya whirled, lifting her *jiaun.*

Stalking out of the other forest on the opposite roadside was a beast she had only ever seen illustrated in textbooks. It was something like an elk, but larger, with jewel-toned scales that shimmered ruby in the morning sunlight. Its mane was huge, surrounding its face with hair that looked more like liquid blood than anything else. Fire dribbled from the beast's maw down its crimson beard, sizzling as it went. A pair of great, sharp antlers rose from its head. Cloven hooves pawed at the ground.

A qilin. One of the dreaded *mó guǐ.*

Near, behind them—more bells. Those soft, higher-pitched bells. Aranya didn't have to turn to know that the qilin's spawn was behind her and Kai.

The qilin reared back, shrieking an ear-splitting cry, and opened wide its fire-filled mouth.

She didn't have time to think. She only had instinct. And her instinct made her rip her arm free of Kai's grip, raise her *jiaun* at the monster, and fire.

The arrows went wide. She felt it the instant they released. Her aim was off—and their time was gone.

The qilin fire shot toward them.

CHAPTER 18

SOMETHING GAVE A powerful shove on Aranya's shoulders, too surprising for her to stop her fall. She clutched her weapon, and as fire blazed overhead, wood cracked—her *jiaun*—as she hit the ground.

She rolled, heat blasting too close. Where was Kai? She scrambled up, enough to look back.

He had vanished.

Her relief was short-lived. The qilin screamed, rearing back on its hind legs, and charged. Aranya's mind sputtered, trying to think of what weapon she could use. But those sharp hooves and lethal antlers were coming straight toward her.

She had little but her claws. And those were useless against a charging qilin.

She scrabbled for her *jiaun,* but her hand closed around splintered wood and a broken string. "Spitfire!" she growled, panic flooding her veins. She reached for the knife at her hip and yanked it out.

A hand snatched her upper arm and hauled her out of the qilin's attack with such force she was nearly flung face first into a tree trunk.

"What happened to your sharpshooting skills?" Kai cried. "It was *right there!*"

"I'm better at longer distances!" she retorted, stumbling to her feet.

"That's literally impossible!"

"No, it is *not!* Here, give me your *jiaun!*"

The qilin pawed the ground, its bell-like, thunderous shriek mixing with the baby's mewling.

Kai was already unholstering the weapon and tossing it to Aranya. She caught it out of the air and whipped two more arrows free from her quiver.

"Don't you *dare* miss again. And don't kill me!" he shot toward her before vanishing.

She loaded the arrows into the shooting contraption and lifted it toward the gleaming, ruby-red chest of the horrendous beast. Over the sights, her gaze met ebony eyes.

Without her claws, she didn't feel the insatiable rage and instinct to kill. She took a deep breath, leveling her aim. Her arm shook traitorously.

The qilin charged.

High-pitched bells pierced the air—the qilin calf braying nearby. Anxious horse whinnies surrounded it. Oh fathers, their horses!

If she missed this shot, she was dead.

Though every muscle in her body urged her to stumble backward, to turn on her heel and run, she planted her legs wide and focused on the two deadly tips of her arrows.

The qilin lowered its antlers, and those knife-like tips came plunging toward her at breakneck speed. Now she couldn't hit its chest, and the beast's thick, coarse mane would make it harder to land a killing blow. Somehow, she had to shoot the back of its neck.

It was only a matter of seconds before a dozen antler points impaled her.

She readjusted her aim, hardly able to think around the roaring of blood in her mind, in her body. *Turn, run—stay, fight!—turn, run!* Her instincts warred with her duty.

Just as she was about to release the trigger, just before she was about to be gutted, Kai appeared on the qilin's back, arching over its neck to grab hold of its antlers.

Aranya shrieked, but her fingers were already pulling the trigger. Frantically, she flung her arm wide, and the arrows narrowly missed Kai's head. He hardly had time to send her a face full of outraged, widened eyes before the qilin bucked and reared.

His legs slipped from gripping the beast's midsection, and for a horrible second, he was nearly hanging from the antlers—nearly brought the beast down backward on him. But his leg wrapped around the qilin's neck, dangerously close to its fire-dripping mouth, and he regained his precarious balance.

The qilin smashed itself down to all fours, and an *oof* escaped Kai.

Aranya's fingers wouldn't obey her as she frantically tried to reload the *jiaun*. They fumbled, jumbled, and refused to close around the arrows, refused to slot them into place. In the end, she gave up after loading one arrow.

Her Academy masters had always warned her to not shoot a *jiaun* with only one arrow—something about it being calibrated to require both arrows for balance and aim. They said one arrow in a *jiaun* was unsteady and wild.

Too bad.

The qilin swung its neck wildly, trying to break Kai's death grip and skewer him in the side with its antlers. Sweat drenched his face, contorted with strain, the veins popping out on his neck and forearms.

"Shoot!" he cried. "Dragon-blasted *shoot* already!"

She tried to take aim, but they were grappling so much, her target constantly moving, Kai constantly in the way. Every time she took aim, the qilin would buck and Kai would suddenly be in her line of fire. Even worse, her loaded arrow was unpredictable.

The monster gave a roar and, with a mighty twist, sent Kai flying. Aranya expected him to disappear midair, like usual.

He flew too fast, too suddenly.

And smashed hard into the ground on his back. He groaned.

Aranya didn't have time to worry about him. All she could do was level her *jiaun,* exhale, and let her wild arrow fly.

It hit.

Not where she'd aimed—behind its shoulder, where its heart was—and not where it would kill the beast. It hit on the front of the shoulder, near the base of its neck. Liquid gold blood bubbled from the wound.

The qilin shrieked.

She was already loading another pair of arrows, her hands finally cooperating now.

Suddenly, those ebony eyes met her, glassy like a waterstone. She hesitated.

The qilin calf let out something like a whimper, its high-pitched cry squeaking and tinkling. The sound drew the attention of the mother. It lowered its head, elongating its neck, and bellowed at Aranya. No fire, just loud enough to make her stumble back several steps and brace herself.

But the qilin leapt to her baby's side and, with the arrow protruding, herded the calf into the forest. Aranya watched in disbelief as the *mó guǐ* limped away, hurrying and spitting fire as it went.

She gripped two arrows in her hands. She should load them, chase after the *mó guǐ*. End them both. If she didn't, they could potentially kill people. Other unsuspecting and potentially unequipped travelers.

Yet she stared, her feet unwilling to move.

Even injured, the qilin moved with the elegant grace of a predator. Soon, the sunlight couldn't penetrate the depths of the woods where the qilins vanished, and the last flash of ruby evaporated.

Kai.

Aranya holstered her *jiaun,* shoved her arrows into their quiver, and ran to where he lay on the other side of the road. "Kai!" she said, falling to her knees beside him. "Are you all right?"

He groaned, his face pinched, but he was already rolling himself to one side, propping his weight up on one elbow. Through the mess of his hair, his eyes found hers.

"Took you only a million and a half years to shoot the phoenix-scorched thing!" he snapped. Another moan slipped past his lips, and he raked a hand through dark, loosening strands of hair. "Maybe you would've been more *motivated* if I hadn't intervened on your behalf."

Her anger sharpened, simmering beneath her skin. She should bite her tongue, bite her tongue—

"Then why didn't *you* shoot it yourself?" she snapped. "Just evanesce close to it and blow its brains out! I can't always—"

"Because you're a better shot than me, alright, Partial? But keep missing and nearly blowing *my* brains out and maybe I *will* shoot it myself next time!"

Her talons were out in a flash, but Kai snatched her wrist, glaring ice-cold daggers at her. "Quit being such a *shapeshifter.* Control your dragon-eaten impulses to rip people's faces off."

Aranya's jaw fell open, everything inside her burning hotter, hotter. Flaming—

"We've lost so much time," he growled, flinging aside her wrist and evanescing to his feet. "Let's go before those beasts return. And give me my *jiaun* back."

A thunderstorm was coming as sure as the night, and it only served to make the silence between Aranya and Kai sourer. They were forced to stable their horses for the night at a village inn.

They mounted the wooden steps to the inn, their boots thumping heavily. She kept casting sidelong glances at Kai, but he seemed too busy denying her existence. She opened the door and, with a little smirk, let it fall back into his face. He didn't react. Just caught it before it bashed his nose and let it slam behind him.

Almost immediately, smoke from the fogged tavern swept into her lungs and nearly made her give into a hacking fit there on the threshold.

"Fathers," she choked, waving a hand over her face to clear the air.

Apparently, all the rabble in town gathered here to drink, smoke, and gamble. One sweep of the room, and she could already tell which ones would have given her the most trouble on the streets of Zushui.

There were women too. It was early enough that the place hadn't gotten very wild, but one woman looked up when Aranya and Kai walked in. Something about her expression, the glint in her eyes, and the way they flicked past her and onto her handsome companion made Aranya's spine tingle.

The thick of the crowd blocked the path to the back counter, where the innkeeper was busy taking orders from guests.

Aranya straightened her shoulders and marched forward. "Pardon me," she growled as she practically elbowed her way through, skirting around dishes of baijiu and handfuls of cards. "Move aside."

She got about halfway through before a large, surly man's back blocked her path. She tapped on his shoulder. "Excuse me? Please allow me to pass."

He finally turned. She flashed a grin and repeated her request.

He quickly misinterpreted her smile. The man raised both eyebrows, his own mouth curving up lopsidedly. "Hello, pretty."

Aranya's smile was through gritted teeth. "Allow me to pass, good sir."

"Of course." His leer was practically oozing. He stepped aside, but one of his large, long-fingered hands came around and settled on her low back. She jolted at the contact. "Here you are." He gestured his other hand forward, giving her another disgusting smile. He did not withdraw his touch.

She restrained herself from demanding that he take his paws off her and managed to keep her claws in check. Instead, she strode past him and tried not to cringe as his hand lingered until the last instant. The moment it was gone, and she had broken free of the crowd, her hands tremored slightly.

It wasn't that bad. There is no reason to make a fuss.

But there *was* reason to snap at Kai, who sidled up beside her at the innkeeper's counter.

"Thanks for having my back," she snarled.

When she looked up at him, he wasn't paying attention to her at all. Naturally. His eyes were settled on something above them, on the far side of the room. He frowned.

"What?" she asked, twisting her head to follow his gaze.

There was nothing except all the milling, shouting people on the ground floor, and a few more climbing the stairs up to the rooms. Kai's gaze studied the hooded figures on the stairs. He watched until they disappeared.

"What? Why do you have that look on your face?"

For the first time in hours, his eyes deigned to fall upon hers. Only for a moment. But a moment was all she needed to see the troubled shadow that befell them. Then they returned to the now-empty staircase.

"Hello! How may I help you?" the innkeeper's voice chirped from behind the counter. His beard could not hide his warm smile. Aranya grinned back, her irritation melting away.

"Two rooms," Kai said, already unlacing the second cord of their travel allowance from around his neck. It irked her to no end that Qigang refused to split the allowance between them, instead entrusting the entire amount to Kai. But since there was nothing she could do about it, she simply held her tongue.

"My sincerest apologies," said the innkeeper. "But there is only one room left. I fear the other one was taken just before you arrived."

"There's only one room left?" Aranya sputtered too quickly.

The innkeeper nodded his head sadly, even as his eyes darted between her and Kai. His nostrils flared as he seemed to realize they were magic-wielders.

"One will do," Kai replied smoothly, setting the coins down on the table and retrieving the proffered key from the man.

She shot a glare up at him, only to find his scowl gone. Completely replaced by a spark in his eye he didn't bother to hide. His fist closed around the keys, and he glanced sideways at her. He shrugged.

"I tried to get two," he said innocently.

She rolled her eyes and headed toward the staircase. This would be fine; it didn't have to be awkward so long as she didn't let his goading get to her. As long as she kept her wits about her, it wouldn't be that bad. After all, secret missions and whatnot probably didn't always come with ideal sleeping arrangements. She would likely have to get used to being in close quarters with male comrades.

She just wished it wasn't Kai.

The wooden floor sounded hollow beneath their footsteps as they climbed the stairs and walked down the hallway to their single room. That they would be sharing. Together.

Kai slid the key into the lock, rattling it a few times before it finally gave. The door swung open before them. It was, as expected, a very sparse chamber. Hardly even a place to fit their satchels. A more apt description would probably be a closet.

Of course—*naturally*—there was only one dragon-eaten bed. And it was tiny.

"We paid *how* much for this?" Aranya said.

He waved his hand like it was nothing, and based on the coins she'd seen on his cord, it likely *was* nothing to him.

Then she glanced at the side of his face, at the glint in his light-colored eyes.

Oh no. No, no, *no*. Absolutely not.

She made for the bed, about to fling her satchel down on it. About to flash him her biggest grin and croon some overly confident and probably rather dangerous invitation to join her. Anything to rile away that smirk into a scowl. Anything not to be the underdog here. Anything to make him take the scant bit of floor.

But Kai was an evanescer.

No matter how fast she darted forward, he was faster. In a flash, he vanished from her side. He reappeared less than a second later, sprawling across the bed and letting his satchel fall to the floor. "Ahh," he sighed, closing his eyes and lacing his fingers beneath his head. One knee was bent, creating the most irksome pose when paired with his grin. "So comfortable."

But her momentum was already carrying her, and she couldn't skid to a stop quick enough.

Kai's eyes widened just before she barreled straight into him, the bed sliding back into the wall. She yelped, limbs flailing as she tried to scramble backward. To her horror, instead of screeching in surprise, he caught her flapping appendages and wrapped his arms around her.

She squawked.

"I didn't know it was so difficult for you to restrain yourself around me," Kai said. "I thought we were supposed to be focused on our job. Be professional and all that. But I see that you're determined. If you ask extra nicely, I might even be persuaded into a kiss."

She didn't want to process how close they were, crammed together on this tiny bed, and definitely did *not* want to look up and see the smirk she just *knew* was painted on his face at the moment.

Shoving hard on his chest, she broke his hold on her, and ended up tumbling off the bed and onto the hard floor. She landed with an *"oof!,"* hands splayed flat on the wood plank flooring, glaring up at Kai leaning over the edge of the bed and grinning down at her.

"I never would have thought inns like this would have such cozy beds," he said, then shifted onto his back, as if he were snuggling deeper into the hard surface. His head twisted to the side and his eyes flickered open, fixing on hers with overflowing mirth. "And so small, too. You sure you don't want to join me, Partial?"

Aranya didn't move a muscle.

"Just think," he mumbled, closing his eyes again. "The possibilities for pranks are endless. But if you're in my arms, I promise I won't—"

"Seven valleys, Kai!" she cried, scrambling to her feet and storming to the window. Rain pattered against the foggy, darkened pane. "A little decorum, please? We're professionals!"

So much for keeping things *not* awkward. So much for her plans to make him squirm.

There was a chuckle behind her, and when she glanced back, his eyes were still closed and he still grinned, his hands tucked behind his head.

It was very possibly the largest grin she'd ever seen on him. The only other contender would have been the one he gave her on her first day when he was talking to Qigang as she dragged in that worthless fellow from south patrol.

The bed was decrepit anyway. It was likely home to hundreds of bedbugs.

She would have preferred the floor, even if he hadn't been so *irritating* about it all. But since he continued to smirk, maybe she should give him a taste of his own medicine. Make him uncomfortable for a change.

"Very well," she said, stepping away from the window and smiling what she hoped was a coy smile. "Scoot over."

Kai's eyebrow arched even before his eyes opened. "I'm not sure there's enough room for your big man shoulders here . . ."

She would have cried out in protest. Huffed. Said a snarky, "I suppose we'll see," or perhaps barked an infuriated, "Will you *stop* it?" Maybe she would have done it all as she tried not to curl her shoulders inward.

But she never got the chance.

Just at that moment, a loud smash sounded from down the hallway.

Kai immediately sat up. Aranya flicked her hands into talons and hurried to the door, but he pushed her aside.

"Put your claws away," he snapped. "You don't even know what you're dealing with. I guarantee you it's those hooded figures we saw earlier."

"What could they be? Wielders? Brigands? Ruffians?"

He didn't answer, only shot a look to silence her as he swept up his broadsword, buckled it to his back, and opened the door. He peered down the hallway, and she stood on her tiptoes to see around his shoulders. Far down the length of darkness, one door swung listlessly on its hinges.

Kai vanished. Aranya stumbled back, her breath hitching briefly. Recovering herself, she slipped quietly into the hallway. Her hand moved unconsciously to the knife at her belt, then her sling. She only allowed the brief sinking of her insides at the loss of her *jiaun*.

But if this were some sort of brawl, her claws would do better than any long-range weapon.

The floorboards creaked under her weight, eliciting a wince from her. Nevertheless, she moved swiftly and came round to the door, pausing briefly against the wall. Withdrawing her knife and hefting the weight into her hand, readying herself to throw it if necessary, she darted around the corner.

The room was empty. Save for Kai.

It was identical to their chamber. The only furniture in the small space was a tiny, low bed. Except there was an enormous hole gaped in the wall where the window had once been. Big enough for people to climb through. The edges smoked and sizzled in the rain.

"Brigands," Aranya breathed, hurrying to where Kai stood staring out the window.

Her eyes bugged at the sight and sounds below.

A battle waged in the middle of the village square. Her mind spun, trying to catch up with the blows, the magic flying, the roaring. The darkness had descended even more thoroughly than when they'd arrived, and rain pelted through the torn hole in the wall into her face.

It was so dark she could hardly tell what was happening, except when fireballs were flung and lit up the battle. She thought she saw an orange fur with jagged black stripes. And something that flashed like ice. Was the furious wind ripping through the streets from the thundering storm, or a wielder's magic?

"Are those two of our classmates?" said Aranya. "Tan Shangdi and Hu Fen? What is happening?"

Kai's face was grim, and perhaps a little pale, his grip hard on the torn wall. "This looks like something we shouldn't get involved in."

"What?" She whirled on him. "If that's Fen and Shangdi, we've got to help them! They were our classmates!"

"We don't know what's happening," he returned, brow furrowed as he kept his gaze glued to the battle. "They're fighting brigands, but we don't know why, and this isn't our jurisdiction—"

"Come *on!*" Aranya cried, already spinning to race out of the room. Not waiting to see if he followed her or if he vanished again, she ran into the hallway and down the stairs, taking them two at a time.

She tore into the crowd, caring little how people cursed her for elbowing her way through the tight space and tipping over ill-placed tankards. A few more people tried to reach for her, but she only had to do a quick maneuver once to land an unsuspecting drunk on his back before they stopped bothering her.

She ignored the shouts behind her as she barreled through the exit and into the rain.

She skittered to a stop, immediately drenched to her skin. The rain stung her eyes, and dangerously close flashes of lightning illuminated the darkness, the roar of thunder rumbling in her chest.

They were gone.

All of them.

Kai appeared beside her, gritting his teeth as water poured down his face. "They went west," he shouted, pointing. "Fen and Shangdi escaped with someone else on horseback. The brigands followed."

"What are you waiting for?" Aranya cried and immediately burst into a run in the direction he'd pointed.

"Are you insane?" he shouted.

She stopped, turned to look back at him. Even in the rain, his face was pale as a corpse's, his eyes white-ringed. As though he was genuinely terrified, which made no sense. He was an evanescer; he should have even less to fear than her.

"If they're brigands," she called back, "then we have to hunt them down!"

"We have to journey to Suguan for a separate appointment!"

"Who says we can't be productive on the way?"

She spun on her heel, ignoring his gaping jaw.

CHAPTER 19

TRUDGING THROUGH A thunderstorm on a brigand hunt with Sun Aranya was *not* on Kai's list of things he wanted to be doing that night, for many, *many* reasons. He could think of a dozen more enjoyable ways to pass the time—namely, getting some rest after an exhausting day of travel. If that were not possible, he'd settle for tormenting his rival.

The foremost of said reasons was that those brigands were definitely Hidden Ones, which Aranya didn't know, of course, and wouldn't unless he told her. Which he did *not* want to do, but did he have any other choice at this point?

"Aranya," he said, in a last-ditch effort to stop her. "Those are Hidden Ones."

She stopped, spinning around so fast that her braid slapped her neck. "What?"

He drew a deep breath and succeeded in drawing more water than air into his mouth. For this short moment, he had her full attention, and her dark eyes were fixed on his. They seemed to shine brighter in the rain. "Those are Hidden Ones. They're too dangerous for us to pursue without direct orders."

Her brow furrowed. "How do you know they're Hidden Ones?" The question he was dreading. But she continued, "And if they're so dangerous, then we shouldn't leave our classmates to battle them alone!"

Maybe he wouldn't have to answer that question. Maybe they could just move past—

"How do you know?" she asked again.

Staring down at her, at the rain plastering her hair to her head and face, at the stubborn set of her jaw, his hopes of evading her question was dashed to pieces.

He swallowed, looking away. He couldn't bear to lie straight to her face. "I saw the tattoo on one of them."

No, he'd recognized one of them.

"Oh. That explains why you looked so panicked. Why didn't you mention it earlier?"

He had looked panicked? Oh fathers, her emotional transparency was rubbing off on him. And how was he supposed to answer her next question? Rain dripped between his parted lips. "Um . . . because—"

"We can't leave our fellow wielders to fight them alone," she said, turning to run again.

Instinctively, he reached out and caught her hand, then blinked quickly to dispel the bolt of shock that raced up his arm at the contact. *Focus.* He had to keep her from going after them.

Aranya glanced down at their hands, then back up at him, brow pinched. "What—"

"We can't go after them," said Kai.

Her jaw hardened. She ripped her hand from his grasp. "I'm not leaving them, Shi Kai. You can go back to the inn if you like. But I'm not leaving them to face brigands alone."

Then she was off.

Kai dragged a hand down his face. He couldn't get near the Hidden Ones. It had been risky enough with the siren and earth-wielder back in Zushui, and he'd paid the price for letting them see him evanesce. Even now, they could still betray him, no matter how he'd helped them.

Ahead, Aranya skittered off in the direction their pursuit had disappeared, all determination and good intentions. She'd get herself killed going by herself. Or lost. Or she'd fall in the rain and break her ankle or something, and Kai wouldn't know where to find her.

But one wrong move, one slip-up with the brigands, and his cover would be blown. No doubt every single one of them had been informed of his disappearance and were on strict orders to report to his family the moment they saw him. And now, with this mission in Suguan, it wasn't like he could ignore the summons and disappear again unless he wanted to be labeled a criminal for abandoning the empire's sanctioned use of his magic.

Maybe he should just let Aranya get blasted to bits by a fire-wielding Hidden One.

With a groan, he flexed his hand and followed after her.

The rain was relentless, and despite being summer, it was cold. Wrapping his sodden cloak around him was useless, so he didn't bother. Instead, he tugged his hood low, folded his arms across his chest and sullenly followed his rival out of town.

"Can't you evanesce ahead or something?" she said, spinning to look back at him for the dozenth time. "So we can find them faster?"

There would be no evanescing around Hidden Ones for him. "I'm not here to hunt brigands," he replied, and rain dripped into his mouth when he spoke. "I'm here to keep you out of trouble."

"We can go back faster if we find them faster," she said, flashing a smile when he'd expected a glower.

Did she think he was a mule to be led by a carrot on a stick? "I'll go back whenever I please," he said.

Then, suddenly, he spied movement behind the tree line. His hand flew to his *jiaun*, even though he knew only Aranya could hit a target that far. She hadn't seen the movement, so she prattled on. "But if we can—"

"Hush," Kai snapped, holding up a hand.

She silenced immediately, her gaze darting forward to track his. Her fingers curled and uncurled, but she did not shift yet. Good. Her claws made her more impulsive. If they were actually going to battle a phoenix-scorched Hidden One, or several Hidden Ones, he needed her to not lose her head.

"Whoever is hiding there has a clear shot at us," said Aranya, her hand reaching for her *jiaun*, only to find her holster empty. "You should evanesce and get behind them while I distract them."

Kai shook his head and shoved his *jiaun* at her. "No, we split and run to the tree line and converge on where they're hiding. Run fast so you don't get shot."

"Wait, why aren't you evanescing?"

But Kai was already taking off at a run to the right, heading for the trees and cover. He glanced over his shoulder a couple times to make sure Aranya was running in the opposite direction. It was an oddly vulnerable thing to run through an open field instead of evanescing, but if a Hidden One was watching, it should dispel potential suspicion about his identity. An evanescer would never risk his back like this.

He finally reached the tree line and dove for cover. Just as quickly, he looked back in time to watch Aranya fall flat on her face—making him wince sharply—stumble to her feet, and keep running. He stood beneath the tree's protective branches, leaning on the trunk with one hand pressed to his heaving side.

He didn't move until she made it to the trees, and a deep sigh escaped him.

Then he drew his broadsword, blinking away the rain getting in his eyes, and hurried on through the forest. The closer he got to the spot he'd seen movement, the slower and more careful his movements grew.

Slowly, he crouched behind a thick-trunked oak, peering around it to try to catch a glimpse of what had seen in the trees.

It could be their classmate Tan Shangdi and his crew, or it could be the brigands. He doubted the former, since they had escaped on horseback and would probably ride hard for a while. He would have guessed that the brigands would have been too preoccupied with their pursuit to care about him and Aranya, but *someone* was here.

The rain disguised the sounds of his movements as he craned to see better.

A stone's throw away, a man crouched behind a tree. Exactly like Kai was, except he looked out toward where Aranya had disappeared. His hood was pulled low, but his flashing teeth were visible in a grimace. He leaned heavily against the tree, one hand pressed against a bloody thigh. Definitely one of the brigands.

Another cursory glance revealed no other visible lurkers. Had they left this brigand behind to throw them and any pursuing local wardens off the trail? Kai frowned, cocking his head. What was this brigand's magic that his comrades thought him dangerous enough to stop or slow pursuit, even while wounded?

The brigand's attention didn't leave the line of forest where Aranya must be tromping through the underbrush. Could he see her? Was she not hiding herself properly? Kai didn't have a clear line of sight to tell, but it seemed the brigand knew where she was.

Still, Kai waited, his eyes fixed on the brigand. All he needed was some indication of his magic so he would know how to attack . . .

Suddenly, a cry went up from deeper in the forest. Kai's alertness snapped sharp, his face jerking toward where that sound had come from. That was definitely Aranya's voice. But the brigand hadn't moved, which meant he wasn't alone. This one was wounded, so he should be more concerned by the one attacking Aranya, right? With a growl, he charged back into the forest, arching far around the wounded brigand.

Running was agonizingly slow compared to evanescing. But run he did, as quickly and silently as he could, dodging beneath low-hanging branches. Why did Aranya have to insist on this pursuit? And why couldn't she be the type he trusted to stay out of trouble?

Finally, he came upon her. He ducked behind a fir tree with his sword drawn. His shoulders relaxed just slightly at the sight of her, that she wasn't already collapsed on the ground, but just as quickly, his throat went dry.

She was fighting . . . the same wounded brigand Kai had just left behind.

Her talons blazed against him, swiping viciously and ferociously, but the brigand's movements were liquid, far too smooth. But wasn't he wounded? And he had been back there, not . . . not here!

How was it possible for him to be here?

She shouted inarticulate cries as she lunged and swiped with her claws, her sopping braid flapping around her face. Her eyes flashed predatorily, her lips pulled back in a snarl.

Kai's muscles tensed with the urge to intervene, warring with his patience. But something made him hesitate. He glanced back toward the tree where the brigand had been hiding a minute ago, but it was too far and dense with forest to see. Was this brigand an evanescer too?

No, he couldn't be, because Kai had been staring at him when Aranya had been attacked. So was the brigand *duplicating* himself? In all the years at the Academy, he hadn't met a single master or student with such an ability.

Now that he looked back at the one fighting Aranya, though she was quick and well-trained, she couldn't land a single blow on the elusive opponent. He moved too swiftly.

And yet . . . the duplicate brigand wasn't landing a blow on her, either.

He frowned, bewildered. At least, if she would not get hurt, he could bide his time so as not to lose his greatest advantage—surprise.

But just then, alarm pricked the edge of Kai's awareness. He felt, rather than saw, the attack. He swung his sword by instinct as he whirled.

It was the same man. A grimacing large man with a hefty, haphazard bandage bound around his thigh. Kai glanced back quickly, spying the one attacking Aranya, and was so confused he barely dodged his attacker's blow.

He brought his sword up in a swift arc, but the brigand slipped too quickly to the side. Kai stabbed forward, only to miss again. His opponent swung, forcing him to dodge backward. He barely caught himself in time from evanescing, stumbling back two steps instead. His hood nearly fell from his head, and he had to spare precious seconds yanking it back down.

Back and forth, they fought.

But their blades never met.

What sort of magic was this? It felt *wrong,* and off, somehow, like he knew it wasn't a simple matter of duplication. It was something else, something . . .

He struck out at the brigand with his sword and used that motion to hide when he pulled a knife from its sheath and flung it with his left hand straight toward the heart of the man. He threw it too fast for the brigand to dodge.

The knife sliced straight through the brigand—straight through and plunked into the tree behind him. Realization hit Kai with the force of that knife embedding into bark. And just like that, the brigand melted into thin air and did not reappear.

He whirled toward Aranya, completely ignoring the falling blade of the brigand fighting her, and snatched her wrist. She snarled up at him, pupils dilated almost completely, but Kai batted away her talons before she could slice his face off.

"He's going to kill—!" she shrieked.

Kai grabbed her upper arms, turned his back to the brigand. Aranya's eyes flew wide with panic, looking over his head at what must have been a sword descending straight for him.

"Kai!" she screamed, trying to yank him to the side. At the last second, she squeezed her eyes shut and angled her face away.

The blow never fell. Kai held her, unflinching. Slowly, she twisted back toward him, opening one eye tentatively. Then both her eyes opened, her body relaxing as her brow furrowed and her mouth dropped open. He let her sputter, trying to look around him for the brigand, but Kai already knew it was gone. So he stood there, gripping her arms tightly so she couldn't run off, and waited until her gaze finally met his.

Her pupils shrank, her talons disappearing into the smooth skin of her hands as questions raged in her face. The rain pelted them harder and harder until it was almost stinging. She shivered in his grip.

"E-evanescer?" she asked.

"Illusionist," Kai said.

Aranya's jaw slackened, understanding replacing bewilderment. "What?"

"He was probably left behind to slow down any pursuit like us. Which he succeeded in."

"We need to go after him! After the others! We're wasting time—"

He tightened his grip. She turned a glare up to him. "No, Aranya," he said firmly. "We can't keep chasing them."

She opened her mouth to protest. But just then, mercifully, voices sounded nearby. Aranya jumped in surprise, and together they twisted to see several armed wielders approaching. The badges on their belts identified them as wardens.

Aranya quickly shrugged out of Kai's grip, her face flushing bright red. He drew in a deep breath and pointed. "They went that way. There's an injured illusionist with them. Forgive our impudence for chasing them on your jurisdiction."

"It's no matter," said one of the wardens, nodding. "We'll take it from here. Are either of you hurt?"

Kai glanced at Aranya, but she shook her head. The warden thanked them, and then, when Aranya got *that* look in her eye, Kai took her by the elbow and all but dragged her out of the field back to the inn.

"We should go along! Just to make sure—"

"Not our jurisdiction."

"That didn't stop you earlier."

"I was trying to keep you from dying, Partial."

"I hate it when you call me that."

"Irrelevant to the discussion."

"Even if it's not our jurisdiction, now we know that brigand was an illusionist, and those wardens don't know what he looks like."

Kai didn't respond. He just kept marching through the downpour, wondering how in the seven valleys it was so cold in the middle of the summer. With their luck, they'd both be sick as death in the morning.

"Why were our classmates here?" asked Aranya. "Shangdi received appointments in Suguan, didn't he? And didn't Fen get something up north?"

Kai did not answer. He had never made it his business to know all of his classmates' appointments.

"And if that *was* them—which I'm certain it was—then they're not working their appointments," she continued, frowning. "Maybe they're on some sort of secret mission too? What do you think? Maybe ours is connected to theirs?"

Kai rolled his eyes and let her prattle on. They couldn't know anything about their mission until they arrived at Suguan, and there was no point in guessing. But he had to admit the two wielders *did* look a lot like their former classmates. And though he wouldn't admit it to her, he figured she'd recognize Fen better than him. They were both shapeshifters, after all. Fen was a powerful shifter. The best in their graduating class.

Aranya couldn't dream of winning a battle against a full shapeshifter like Fen.

He itched to get out of this horrid weather, out of these sopping clothes. Perhaps a little more loss of sleep would be worth the time he could save by evanescing to the inn. Yet he continued walking back with her.

"I wonder why those brigands were here. It almost seemed like they were the ones attacking Fen and Shangdi, and not the other way around them. Did you see the third person with them? It looked like a girl, but I didn't recognize her. Do you think she could have been one of our classmates?"

He yawned, earning a mouthful of rain. Finally, the inn was in sight. Maybe he could abandon her now that they were close.

"Fathers, that's going to be expensive to repair," she said.

Kai glanced at her, then followed her gaze upward. There, in the inn's side on the second floor, was that huge hole blasted through what was once a window. He sighed.

"I just don't understand what *happened* with the brigands and our classmates."

As she shouldn't. This wasn't their case or their problem, and they didn't have any of the information about the situation.

"Why didn't you evanesce?" she asked suddenly.

He barely kept his feet from halting. He cleared his throat, facing ahead, away from her. "Because I wanted to be able to sleep tonight. It's been a long day and we've got another long day tomorrow."

She finally grew quiet, whether in awe of the destruction, or puzzling over theories in her head, or perhaps fantasizing about turning around and chasing down those Hidden Ones.

"Riddle me this," said Kai when the silence lasted. "Why would the only caretaker of a beloved family member recklessly risk her life when she was under no obligation to do so—and arguably was under obligation *not* to do so—knowing that if she died, there would be no one to take care of said family member?"

Aranya abruptly stopped walking.

Kai glanced back at her, and something knotted strangely in his gut at how stunned she looked. He'd struck deeper than he'd realized. He stopped, turned around, and took several steps back to where she stood, until a mere foot separated them.

Her lips were parted, her eyes rounded as she stared up at him.

He reached out, took her forearm, lifted and twisted it gently so that her palm faced up. Her gaze never strayed from his, as though she was still too shocked to move. "It's a riddle I haven't quite figured out yet," said Kai, and pressed something into her wet, open palm.

It wasn't until he had mounted the steps to the inn that her voice sputtered from behind him, "Wh-what is t-this?"

He reached the door, rested a hand on the wooden frame, and looked over his shoulder at her still standing there in the rain, holding the key he'd given her.

"It's the key to our room," he said. And then—*oh,* he shouldn't—but he just couldn't resist the twisting tilt of his lips. "I don't need it to get in."

Aranya's face turned scarlet just as her jaw dropped.

Kai vanished.

CHAPTER 20

W*HY WOULD THE only caretaker of a beloved family member recklessly risk her life, knowing that if she died, there would be no one to take care of said family member?*

Those words rung through her mind over and over again until she was dizzy with cold and guilt. What had she been *thinking*? Kai was right. They never should have gone after those brigands. She shouldn't have been so impulsive, so reckless, knowing all that she stood to lose.

All that Ye Ye stood to lose.

So why had she done it?

Somehow, when she stumbled into the room she was doomed to share with Kai for the night, he was already dry and lounging on the bed. Only his wet hair betrayed their recent romp through the rain.

"Try not to drip on the floor," he muttered, eyes closing again. "And don't be too loud. I'm trying to sleep."

She sputtered, flicking her sodden hair out of her face. Her teeth chattered in her jaws. The room seemed even colder than outside. She wrapped her arms tightly around herself and shivered.

"Please step out of the room for a minute," she said, teeth chattering. "I'd like to change."

"There's a washroom downstairs," he mumbled, flinging his arm over his eyes as if to block out light. *So dramatic.* It was nearly dark in the room.

"It's full of drunk men!" she cried.

Kai let out a long-suffering sigh, flinging his arm away from his eyes. "Fine! Only because I'm a gentleman."

"And no evanescing back here until I say I'm ready, understand?" She fixed him with her fiercest glare.

He grinned.

"Understand?" she said.

"You don't seem to trust me." He attempted a pout, but failed miserably.

"I don't."

He stood, cocking an eyebrow and crossing his arms. "I'll leave, and I won't return until you say."

"Promise me—"

"Don't flatter yourself," Kai snorted and vanished.

Embarrassment flashed through her, but she tried to shove it away as she set to work peeling off her soaked garments as quickly as possible. She hung her clothes up next to Kai's by the windowsill, praying they would be dry in the morning, and hastily donned one of the few spare sets of robes that she'd brought.

Plopping herself on the edge of the bed, she fought to get her stockings over her damp feet. She had barely finished saying, "Finished!" when Kai reappeared, taking up his usual spot on the bed.

A squeak burst from her lips as she startled and leapt off the bed, hobbling to the wall as she shoved her remaining foot into the stocking.

He grinned, leaned down, and grabbed the folded quilt at the foot of the bed. With a cocky wink her way, he spread it over himself, turned on his side, and closed his eyes. Without opening them, he said, "My offer still stands."

"What offer?"

The instant the words left her lips, she regretted them. Kai only smirked wider, snuggling deeper under the quilt.

He wasn't looking, but Aranya said anyway, "I'd consider it if I were interested in being eaten alive by bedbugs."

He remained unperturbed.

Growling a curse under her breath, she grabbed Kai's satchel to use as a pillow and emptied hers of its last set of robes to use as a blanket. Then, with one last glare at her smug rival, she lay down on the hard wood.

It was unforgiving on her tired muscles.

She dreamed she was back in Zushui, in her tenement with Ye Ye. He was curled up at her chest, tail flicking lazily in his sleep. Getting fur up her nose. She snorted, wriggled her nose, and nearly sneezed. Tried to scoot away from all the fluff and cat hair that seemed to constantly coat her clothes and find its way into her mouth.

Finally, that tail stopped moving. Stopped bothering her. She could truly sleep now.

But shadows played against the wall of their bare-boned tenement, dancing across Ye Ye's still form. Her eyes followed the erratic movement, a chill creeping down her spine.

Suddenly, a bolt of certainty hit her like lightning. She knew before she knew—as one does in dreams. She knew before she flung herself upright in bed, before she reached for that soft, white bundle. Before her hand caressed fur.

He wasn't breathing.

Panic flared across every sense. No, no, no—*Ye Ye.* He'd been alive only a moment ago. He was still here, still with her, right?

"Ye Ye?" she croaked, heart racing as tears streamed down her cheeks, unbidden. "Ye Ye? Ye Ye!"

Her voice rose to a crescendo, and then she was out of bed, feet bare against the cold splintering wood of their floor. Her hands roamed frantically over the cat form of her grandfather, desperately feeling for any sign of breath, of a heartbeat, of *life.*

Nothing.

Nothing except stillness. Limpness. Even his constant warmth was fading.

The world was dark, primed in silence for the piercing scream she let out as knife-sharp pain plunged into her heart.

"Aranya! Aranya! Wake up!"

Hands grabbed her, shaking her, dragging her upward. She thrashed against them, sweat running in rivulets down her back, dampening her hair and neck. Her pulse raced like a wild stallion galloping for its life.

"Aranya!" came another low, urgent growl. "Wake *up*! Stop fighting me!"

"Ye Ye," she moaned, trying to wrench away from the painfully tight grip. It only tightened the more she fought. "Ye Ye!"

Pain flared across her cheek. Aranya's eyes flew wide with a gasp.

There, crouched before her, wreathed in darkness, was Kai. His face was split in half, one lost in shadow, the other discernable by the sparse moonlight coming through the open window. His visible eye was wide, his brow pinched, his teeth gritted. A vein stood out stark on his forehead, and another running from his neck to his clenched jaw.

He held her face cupped in both hands, hardly a breath from his.

She shut her chapped lips, the pressure in her lungs easing as the knot in her throat lessened. Her face was wet—salty tears sliding between the crease of his knuckles down to drip off her chin.

Their gazes locked, and Aranya thought she'd never felt so vulnerable in her entire life. There were no smiles to save her, no armor she could don for protection. There was nothing, save the raw truth of her tears and pleas for Ye Ye.

Oh fathers.

She might have berated herself for acting the fool, for humiliating herself, and possibly angering the guests in this inn if she'd truly screamed aloud. But all she could do was lower her head and weep harder.

"He's not dead, Aranya," Kai whispered, the warmth of his lips hovering above her forehead. "It was just a dream. Just a dream."

A shudder swept through her from head to toe. The sobs came harder, and she leaned forward to rest her forehead on his shoulder, above his collarbone. Breathed a deep, trembling breath of his increasingly familiar smell. Something about it soothed her sobs to ragged gasps for air. He didn't stop her or pull away.

"Ye Ye is safe in Zushui. He'll be there when you get back."

But would he?

What if he wasn't? What if she missed his last days? What if she finished this, returned home . . . and he wasn't there anymore? What if there was no home to return to?

She wouldn't voice her questions though. Kai had seen too much already.

With a deep, shaky breath, she pulled back, blinking her swollen eyelids. Kai's hands slid from her. Except one, which rested gently, light as a murmur, on the side of her knee.

"Go back to sleep," he whispered.

Then he stood. Left her sprawled there, her back propped up against the wall, shoulders slumped and shivering. He crossed the distance to the bed, ripped his cloak off the poster, and marched to the floor by the door.

He didn't claim the bed. He left it open. For her.

She nearly stumbled to her feet with a groan and toppled into it. Instead, she swallowed and shifted down to the floor, stubbornly. She would take his kindness, but not his pity.

Or was she accepting his pity and rejecting his kindness?

She was too tired to care, and her heart still ached with unrealized loss. A shudder, and she closed her eyes, letting sleep claim her again.

Aranya woke to find herself sprawled on the bed, the quilt half-draped over her and half-hanging limply off the edge in disarray.

She sat up, wincing and groaning as her body protested every movement. She pressed the heel of her hand into her eye socket. Blinked a few times. Her vision clarified to find Kai likewise collapsed on the floor beside the bed, one arm beneath his head, his cloak leaving his feet uncovered. Locks of his hair fell in his face, his lips parted, breath coming in soft huffs and making his chest rise and fall.

He was fast asleep.

How had she ended up in the bed? She was fairly certain she had fallen asleep on the floor, and she wasn't aware that she sleepwalked . . .

Memory of last night, of darkness and tears and warmth, leaked through the early morning fog. *Oh fathers,* she thought, heat rushing to her cheeks and her neck. Had she really—?

Dazed, she stumbled to her feet, carefully dodging Kai's form. This room was so small he took up most of the floor space, making it almost impossible to do anything. She stood precariously on her toes, balancing one foot between his ankles while she tested the wood planks across from him, trying to find the least squeaky place to step. She tested a few places, then set her foot down and leaned her weight onto it.

Creeeeak!

Kai groaned, his face pinching, and rolled to his other side. His calf hit her ankle, making her freeze. Still, he didn't wake up. She stepped over him, pressing herself against the wall to reach her satchel and boots. She'd get ready for the day, then wake him up, and they could—

No, she couldn't. What if he woke up while she was dressing? She squeezed her eyes shut and wished she could scrub that horrific thought from her brain with a fat block of lye soap.

She needed to wake him now.

Drawing a deep breath, she let go of her satchel, twisted, and crouched beside Kai. His mouth had opened more, his forehead still drawn in knots.

He didn't look arrogant and cocky like this, asleep and vulnerable. He almost didn't look like Shi Kai, evanescer and her rival. Instead, he seemed more like . . . like a handsome young man. One that Ye Ye would love to meet.

She reached out a hand toward his shoulder. Gritted her teeth in preparation for those eyes to flash open, for hazel eyes to meet hers, for the memory of last night to come into focus in those irises. He'd look at her, the nightmare between them, and somehow they'd have to pretend it never happened. Because she sure wasn't going to acknowledge her fear to him, and he wasn't going to acknowledge that he'd been kind to her.

She couldn't wake him up. Couldn't find the strength to reach out and shake his shoulders.

Well, changing clothes in this room wasn't an option. That meant she would have to grab her things, sneak down the stairs to the washroom, pray it was empty, and get ready there.

She slung her satchel over her shoulders, scooped up her last change of clothes that was strewn across the floor, and went to grab her boots.

Her eyes widened at the unexpected weight.

And then she suddenly didn't care one bit that Kai was sleeping so peacefully.

"Rocks!" she cried, hefting them up. "You filled them with dragon-blasted rocks! What in all the seven—"

Kai groaned, wincing, and flung his arm over his eyes. "Loud," he mumbled, before letting out another groan and rolling to his other side.

A pair of boots filled with rocks wasn't the only thing he'd left for her, as she soon discovered. The clothes that she'd hung up by the window had been tied in knots, preventing them from thoroughly drying, and her knives were hidden all around the small room, wedged into cracks and buried beneath the bed.

She was still storming around the room loudly, locating each one of her knives, when Kai let out another groan. But this time when she shot a glare at him, he wasn't still lying on the floor, but dragging himself to sit upright against the wall, his shirt ties loose and his head tilted back so his Adam's apple stuck out starkly in his neck.

"You'll wake the dead, insufferable woman," he grumbled. "Can't a man have some peace for just—"

"Look at me, Shi Kai."

He blinked, let his head fall to the side so he could fix his sleepy gaze on her. She was just yanking her final knife out from a crevice in the wall. She tossed it to land with a plunk on the bed with the others. "Funny, are we? Now I'll have to sharpen these all over again, and I'm not even sure that'll undo all the damage! How are we going to get off at a reasonable hour with you slowing us down?"

His foggy eyes cleared, and, when he *should* have been penitent, his mouth twisted into a lazy grin. "I see you found my gifts."

She didn't have words. Neither did she have smiles. She gaped at him, trying to select which of the furious responses collecting in her brain she was about to hurl into his face. If smacking him would have gotten rid of that grin, she'd have done it. But showing him how much she wanted to wring his neck would likely only serve to please him more.

"I thought to repay you for setting my intestines on fire," he said mildly. "Did you sleep well?" His face was unreadable, but it felt like a loaded question.

She shot a glare at him. "It was fine. No thanks to you."

His eyebrows shot up.

Alright, perhaps that wasn't a fair thing for her to say. She glanced away quickly and refused to look back when his gaze burned the side of her face, or when he sighed and stood up, leaning against the wall and crossing his arms. She busied herself with inspecting the tips of her knives. When she stole a peek at him, he was cleaning his fingernails.

"I feel as though I should get *some* measure of thanks," he said dryly.

She shot a suspicious glare his way.

"After all," he continued, blinking slowly as his attention lifted from his spotless nails to her, "you are quite heavy. I think I permanently dislodged some vital tendon in my back."

Her fist closed around the hilt of one of her knives as she whirled on him. "Are you saying *you* put me in the bed last night?"

She didn't realize she was pointing the knife in his face like it was her finger until he reached out, took hold of her wrist gently, and lowered it.

"Well," he said, dropping her hand and smirking, "I suppose you *could* have floated there by yourself."

"You're—" She stopped herself. No insult that came to mind seemed strong enough. She resorted to snapping, "I hate you," and set to untying the knots in yesterday's clothes so she could pack them.

He wouldn't believe those words. Even she knew they weren't true. They came out anyway, propelled by embarrassment about the nightmare last night and irritation from the pranks this morning.

But Kai was silent.

Which was probably because of some other reason that had nothing to do with the thoughtless words she'd just spouted. After all, he hated her even more than she disliked him. So did it even matter if he thought her words were true? Of course not.

"Well, I'm hungry," said Kai, his voice suddenly brisk. "I'll leave you to your,"—he waved his hand vaguely in the air—"whatever girls do in the morning. I'll bring you something to eat. Then we'll be off."

He was opening the door before Aranya blurted, "To answer your question, of course I'm not going to thank you for putting me in the bed. I'm positively covered in bug bites. I told you it was infested!"

She wasn't sure what made her call out after him. Some ridiculous desire to make sure she hadn't irreparably damaged . . . whatever was between them. Except that their relationship was irreparable before it had even begun. So what made her say something like that? She reached up to her braid, feeling all the places that little strands were poking out of their confines.

He stopped, looked back over his shoulder at her. Smiled. It was roguish while still simultaneously managing to be warm and gentle. Her stomach flipped.

This was what they saw in him, Aranya thought about the girls back in the Academy.

Then he was gone, and in the silence left in his wake, she had space to remember she was angry at him. Furious, even. He'd had the gall to pay her back for her payback prank, and to do so in between waking her from nightmares and carrying her to bed.

As she dressed and packed her satchel and dumped the rocks from her boots out the window, it hit her what he had done. He'd given her something to think about this morning, something to be angry about, something to fight with him over, so she didn't have to endure the painful awkwardness of facing him after last night. When he'd soothed her tears and calmed her with the brush of his thumbs, given her a shoulder to weep on in the dead of night when her fears had gotten the best of her.

When she stepped out of their room, it wasn't Kai's cocky grin that flashed before her mind's eye, but his face set in half-shadow, eyes locked on hers, dark and steady when everything else was crumbling around her.

CHAPTER 21

MARCHING THROUGH THE streets of Suguan, listening to the cry of gulls overhead and the bustle of city life around them, brought a strange mix of thrill and heaviness to Aranya's bones. This place felt more like home than any other, her having come here so young to train at the Academy. But it also felt different, being a graduate now.

Not that long ago, she walked these streets, to and from the Academy to the tenement where Ye Ye lived. The other students hadn't been granted the luxury of leaving the grounds, but she'd been given special permission for Ye Ye.

Gravel crunching under the soles of her boots, the jolting rhythm of carts in the street, the bright blue sky above her, the mountain looming to the west, the rising height of the magnificent palace towering at its base over the rest of the city—all of it made her remember what it was like to feel a heavy weight on her shoulders. Whether she succeeded or failed. Whether she passed all her classes, received a good enough appointment.

It felt no different this time.

Her heart fluttered in her chest, her bottom lip twisting between her teeth. Report to the Secret Services with Shi Kai. It didn't seem real. But it must be real, whatever the case was they were being summoned for.

She wasn't going to mess this up.

Kai hadn't uttered more than a couple of grunts the entire day. And that was fine by her. Whenever she looked back, however, his eyes were alert, scanning every which way.

Though the palace was right beside the Academy, she'd never been inside. Thus, walking its hallways now shrouded her in awe. Ye Ye and special assignments and Qigang's threats to dismiss her fled her mind in an instant.

It was the grandest building she'd ever seen, the inside even more magnificent and colorful than the outside. They passed a grand staircase guarded by two life-sized replicas of qilins.

"We battled one of those." Aranya nudged Kai, nodding toward the fearsome statue. "One and a half, if you count the baby. But then again, the baby did nothing except whine, so probably only one."

He didn't even grunt in response.

"This place is covered in so much gold," she said, compensating for his silence. "Do you think it's real? Or simply paint?"

His eyelids lowered slightly, as though exasperated by her question.

"Do you know where we're going?"

He grunted.

"Good. Because I'm lost."

She wasn't actually lost—she could hardly call herself an Academy graduate if she lost herself in a building five minutes after entering it. But sometimes the difference blurred between knowing where one was and where one was going.

When Kai led them down a side hallway, flashing the summons they'd received to the standing guards, she reached up and scratched her chin. "How do you know where the Secret Services are? Is it because you're an evanescer?"

No answer.

She huffed, but flashed a few more smiles at guards as they passed. As they made their way deeper into the palace, she started losing her bearings. Her heart pounded faster and faster, her hands growing slick with sweat. She practically bounced each step on the balls of her feet.

Succeed at this. Or lose everything.

It was so hard being still and collected when it felt like her guts were eating themselves. She'd rather burst into a run or catch hold of the solid oak beam above her and knock out a few dozen pull-ups.

Kai eyed her from the side, so subtly she almost didn't notice it. Despite the way a vein stuck out starkly in his neck, as though he were anxious about something, a tiny smile tipped the corner of his mouth.

But just when she was about to say something to make him turn fully and look at her, he straightened and swallowed, his eyes sharpening. She shut her mouth and swiveled her attention ahead.

At the far end of this hallway, a man paced outside of a closed door. Something about him made her set back her shoulders and quicken her steps; this *had* to be where they were going. Just beyond him, another man waited with his back to them, hands clasped behind his back around the pommel of a cane.

The first man spotted them and stopped pacing. He waited, hands folded into his sleeves and chin up as they approached. His garments were deep red, edged in gold embroidery—clearly a wealthy man of high rank with powerful magic.

"Sun Aranya? Shi Kai?" the man asked, his voice edged in something negative. Frustration?

They bowed. "Indeed," Aranya chirped. "We are honored—"

The second man turned around. Her heart stopped. He was of average height, with dark hair—not a streak of gray—with a blunt-nose and an unusually pink complexion.

Aranya's steps stuttered to a halt.

Lord Meng.

Of course he would be involved in the Secret Service. It fit his magic perfectly.

Lord Meng lifted his chin, regarding them beneath his prominent brow. Even Kai's footsteps stopped abruptly. "I said I would repay you, wardens. I hold to my word."

Kai tilted his head in deference and silent thanks, but Aranya just gaped. *He* got them this position. It wasn't because of Qigang's commendation. It was because Lord Meng had considered himself in debt to them and decided that this was the best way to repay them. This was why they were offered a position in the Secret Services when they were so unqualified.

But while he thought he was rendering them a service, all he'd done was raise the stakes and standards for her. If she failed here, she had nowhere else to go. She and Ye Ye would be ruined.

"Hurry, they're just about to start," said the first man.

They were ushered into a low, dark room. Candles were lit on gold-encrusted sconces along the red-paneled walls. A decorative screen blocked the only window, painted with images of magic-wielders riding qilins into battle, complete with blood and trailing fire. Her smile faltered into something more hesitant when a dozen or so faces turned toward them from the long table. She scanned the faces looking for someone friendly. Most of them regarded both her and Kai with snobbish distaste.

They were all much older.

A warm hand landed gently on her low back, urging her forward. Aranya forced herself to keep moving, to not look back and meet Kai's gaze. Instead, she found herself staring at the man in black robes at the head of the table. It was Kai's subtle guiding hand that helped her keep moving toward the two open cushions along the left side of the table. When they were seated beside each other, she chanced a glance at him, but his attention was glued to the man in black.

Everyone here was dressed so *nicely.*

Aranya wiped her clammy hands on her much simpler robes and tried to keep them from twisting themselves into the fabric. It was the effort of a hundred horses to keep her mouth firmly arranged in something close to a smile.

The last thing she needed was them seeing how out-of-place she felt here.

"Esteemed wielders of Zheninghai," the man in black began. He had to stop and clear his throat a few times.

That gave her heart enough time to skip about seven beats and fly straight into her throat.

Succeed here. Or lose everything.

And by everything . . . it was Ye Ye she would lose. He was everything.

"You are gathered for a Secret Services assignment. You have been hand-selected for this mission because you demonstrated skill, talent, and bravery in the work field."

Aranya peeked at the wielders at the table, at their uptilted chins and narrowed eyes. The air was thick with a sense of self-importance. This time, she let her smile fade into a frown. *I shouldn't be here,* she thought. If she'd been placed on this mission because of a commendation Qigang sent, she could maybe convince herself that she was even a fraction qualified to sit here. But knowing it was a favor from Lord Meng . . . She couldn't even try to pretend.

Kai's face betrayed none of the same emotions. In fact, now that she looked at him, his chin was lifted too, his eyebrows tilted to a haughty degree.

Was he trying to fit in? Or was this stroking his ego?

"This mission is top secret; leaking information is tantamount to treason and will be dealt with accordingly."

Treason? She pursed her lips, though no one else seemed to flinch. What could be *that* serious?

The man in black continued along this vein for some time, going over logistics of Secret Service assignments. A few forms were passed around and subsequently signed by all parties present. Aranya was too busy watching the people around her to notice that she'd signed her name lopsided. Had the man with the long beard across the table taught a few of her classes?

"Now, for the particulars of this mission," the man said.

She shifted forward on her mat, fighting the urge to prop her chin on her elbows. Her eyes fixed on the head of the table.

Can't. Fail.

He sniffed, adjusting his spectacles, collecting the parchments in front of him into a neat stack. With a pointed look at each wielder around the table, he waved a hand to dismiss his attendant. The door closed with a soft thud.

He began speaking. His voice pitched lower than before, quieter. It wafted over them like the steam from a teapot without its lid. It had the same slightly suffocating feeling that came when one breathed too much of such steam through their nose.

"For the past twelve years, wielders across the empire have been vanishing without a trace. Eleven high profile wielders, to date, have disappeared. With each new disappearance, new parties have been dispatched, but all have proved fruitless. This time, however," he stopped, narrowing his brows and splaying his hand wide on the stack of parchment before him, "you *must* succeed. The missing wielders, whether dead or alive, must be discovered and their mystery solved. With Fang Zedong, an Academy defector, amassing barbarian troops on the northern border, this security threat must be resolved."

Aranya barely kept herself from blurting, *"Who's Fang Zedong?"* Instead, she glanced toward Kai, trying to ask him with her eyes. He ignored her.

"Your job will be to locate each missing wielder—or proof of their deaths—and bring them back safely to Suguan. If they are deserters, traitors, then they must be tried and executed. Now, for the missing wielders."

He began listing them off. "Pen Tao, high seer, was the first to vanish twelve years ago. He resided here in Suguan. Du Liuxian, evanescer, vanished from Suguan nine years ago."

At this, Aranya shot a sharp look at Kai. Not so much as a muscle clenched in his jaw.

"The only other high seer in the empire, Cai Fu, vanished shortly thereafter, also from Suguan. Then, Xian Hanying, river-bender, from Fungxi."

A river-bender? That was an uncommon name given to those with extraordinarily potent magic pertaining to the manipulation of water. Aranya's brow wrinkled, and she tilted her head to one side as she listened.

He continued listing more off. Kang Lei, siren. Ye Min, mind-reader. There were several more, their names buzzing around her head like pesky flies on a hot summer day. She frowned deeper.

"The most recent disappearance was Lord Zuan Wan, Guardian of Ganhai, plant-wielder from Shaanet, besides possibly the most distressing loss, which happened only earlier this week—"

Her mouth opened, but she clamped it shut just in time to keep from bursting out, *"Lord Zuan Wan has disappeared?"* The sudden movement caught the man's eye, and he frowned at her. She swallowed.

A guardian had vanished? It hardly seemed possible. The guardians were the protectors of each Zheninghai territory. Their primary job was to keep the *mó guǐ* at bay and ensure magic was used only in its proper context—service to the emperor. How had one gone missing, and she had never heard of it? How had this secret been kept?

"—the only healer alive in the empire, Li Feiyan, vanished from the Academy."

At that, Aranya did actually gasp.

Feiyan had disappeared? One of her classmates? Aranya pressed a hand over her mouth, her gut sinking within her. Sure, she had never been close to the healer—no one had, for even though she was a student like the rest of them, she spent most of her days healing. But Aranya had fought her a dozen or so times over the years in arena battles. The healer was only a couple of years younger than her, with more spunk and wry humor than half the Academy students combined. Though she had no battle magic like Aranya or many other students, she'd always been a fierce opponent.

Kidnapping the healer from the Academy would have been an extraordinary feat, with so many guards and magic-wielders everywhere. Escaping by herself would have been only a fraction easier.

"What do each of these wielders have in common?" the man in black asked.

Silence.

She fidgeted with the hem of her sleeve, biting her tongue to keep from blurting what she knew was the answer.

"They all have very powerful or very unique magic," the man finally said. "This has led us to believe they are not deserting, but perhaps being abducted. It will be up to you to discover the truth as efficiently as possible. It is integral to retain the people's faith in the empire by not showing weakness now or giving them cause to doubt, especially while Butagin remains a threat. This has become increasingly difficult with these last two disappearances. Speed is imperative. You will be grouped into teams and dispatched tomorrow at first light after each missing wielder. We will expect progress reports every fortnight."

The copious amounts of instructions that followed sent Aranya's mind spinning. She tried to pay careful attention to every word spoken, but inwardly she wanted to explode with thrill, fear, and adrenaline.

Finally, the man in black began passing out assignments to groups. She waited, unable to sit still on her mat as she leaned forward and gripped her knees. Her eyes scanned the group. Who would she be paired with? Would she get a single partner, or several?

She held her breath when the man approached their side of the table.

"Lian Delan," the man in black said, peering over his spectacles at the man sitting on the other side of Kai. "You will be with Shi Kai and . . ." He squinted, looking back at the packet he held. "Sun Aranya."

He tossed the assignment down in front of Delan. "You search for Lord Zuan Wan."

"I'm with the kids?" Delan said, gesturing at Kai and Aranya. "*Both* of them?"

The man in black frowned. "They already have experience working together on kidnapping cases. You will find them capable colleagues."

Capable colleagues? Oh no. Aranya swallowed, feeling slightly nauseated. How was she supposed to not botch this when she wasn't even properly trained as a warden?

She peeked a glance at Delan. He glowered, but turned his attention from the man in black to the packet on the table, flipping it open with a puff of frustration. Kai didn't show a stitch of emotion on his face. Why was he so good at that?

Did he feel that much more confident in his ability than she did?

Once the man in black had moved on to the next group, Aranya leaned forward and forced a sunny grin at Delan. "Hello! I'm Sun Aranya. It's a pleasure to make your acquaintance."

The wielder looked up, blinked once, and then muttered, "Lian Delan." A semi-awkward silence passed, and he turned to Kai. "Well," he snapped, "who are you, stone face?"

Kai's shoulders tensed, but he said smoothly, "Shi Kai. It is an honor to work with you, Lian Delan."

Delan eyed them both warily, grunted, and returned to their file.

Aranya abandoned all semblance of propriety and deposited her elbows on the table, halfway leaning across Kai in the process to see what Delan inspected. "What does it say?" she prodded, scooting closer.

Kai shifted backward to avoid her, impatience blowing out his nostrils.

Delan didn't look up as he muttered, "Lord Zuan Wan disappeared from his home in Shaanet. Oh, there are copies for each of you." He withdrew them and slapped the stacks down on the table. Aranya leaned further across Kai to claim one. One glance at him revealed another impatient glower. She tossed him a grin and slid the pack in front of her.

Inside, she found ample details about the guardian, his family, his appointment, and history back as far as when he joined the Academy, his highly unusual magical abilities, and his disappearance.

She lost herself in reading, hardly noticing as wielders filed out of the room. She was vaguely aware of when someone handed Delan a string of coins for their journey. The man in black dismissed everyone as Kai only thumbed through the pages, quickly skimming.

Aranya intended to absorb every ounce of information in this packet.

"Well," Delan announced, climbing to his feet and wincing as he stretched. "It appears we will travel to Shaanet tomorrow. Prepare yourselves."

Her fingers turned to ice, but she braced her shoulders and nodded. She wouldn't fail. *Would not fail.*

CHAPTER 22

AFTER AN EVENING of poring over the notes she'd been given about the missing guardian and a night of mediocre sleep, Aranya was ready the next morning before dawn by the western gate of the palace. Their appointed meeting place.

Delan showed up next, and finally Kai. The latter received a pointed look from the former, which was humbly received and then promptly ignored. Kai's face shifted the moment Delan looked away, his eyebrows lowering in the vaguest expression of distaste.

His humility was never true—it was only for placation.

She turned toward her horse, tightening the saddle buckles. Kai's quietness in front of Qigang back at Zushui Wardpost hadn't been because he was particularly teachable or because he was an especially quiet person. He bided his time, carefully trying to read people so he could avoid negative notice.

But when it didn't matter . . .

An image flashed in her mind of him sprawled out on the one bed at the inn where they'd stayed. Eyes closed, arrogant grin wide. Looking at him now, all serious and stern, she never would have guessed at his true personality. What was he like around his friends? His family?

"Good morning!" she said.

"You both properly armed?" Delan asked, wrinkling his nose. "Did you bring the information packets?"

Aranya nodded to both counts, patting her robes where she'd rolled up the parchments and concealed them on her person.

"Here's the plan," Delan continued, swinging himself up onto his horse. He wasn't a tall man, but he was built for strength. His jaw was sharp, lined with a beard, and his eyes were half-hidden beneath a prominent brow. "We will ride to Shaanet—it should only take a few days—and then we will begin our investigation there. Lord Zuan Wan has only been missing for a few weeks, so our trail should still be somewhat fresh."

"Sounds like an excellent plan," said Aranya.

Delan eyed her as they rode out through the gate to begin their journey. "You're very chipper in the morning."

Kai muttered something under his breath that sounded awfully close to, *"It gets old real fast,"* but when she shot him a look, he was as impassive as always.

"And you are *not* very chipper in the morning," said Delan to Kai.

Kai merely shrugged. "One Sun Aranya is plenty for this group."

Delan raised an eyebrow and glanced between his mild expression and Aranya's darting look of irritation. He shifted in his saddle to better face them both. "I think we could all do for a good history lesson on *this.*" He gestured between the two of them. "I'm no scholar, but something tells me you two aren't exactly simpatico presently, despite whatever they said back at the palace. What turn of events landed you here?"

"We're wardens from Zushui Wardpost," Aranya said. "We solved a kidnapping case not too long ago."

"So you're here because you proved yourself brilliant beyond belief at the call of duty?" Delan asked, not bothering to hide the sarcasm in his voice.

"We're here because the government is stupid," Kai muttered sourly.

"We're here because the girl we rescued was the daughter of someone important," said Aranya.

Delan glanced at them again, tilting his head to one side and stroking his beard. "Start over. If we're to work together, I need to understand."

Aranya plunged into the tale, beginning from when she first arrived at Zushui Wardpost until now.

"Wait." Delan stopped her. "You're only a partial-shifter?"

Her ears burned, and she swallowed, even as she kept her smile from faltering too much. From betraying how her stomach dropped inside her. She nodded. "Yes, I'm a partial-shifter."

"Usually people in Secret Services have more powerful or specialized magic," he said.

It might have been an insult, or it might have been a compliment. She didn't know.

"And Stone Face here is an evanescer? What in the seven valleys were you doing as a warden? Did you flunk all your classes at the Academy?" asked Delan, aiming those last two questions directly at Kai.

Kai's jaw tensed, but he merely said, "It's nothing like that."

"But not exactly a shining pupil either, I wager." Delan smirked. "I knew you weren't the studious type the minute I saw how you read the information packet. Unlike your little companion."

Aranya raised both eyebrows, unable to help the grin that split her face as she looked back and forth between the two men.

Kai tossed a disinterested glance back her way, but his glittering eyes betrayed his scorn. "I have no need; my *little companion* is armed to the teeth with any definition or equation I might require while battling a *mó guǐ* or brigand."

Her mouth fell open. Delan laughed outright, throwing back his head.

"All right, you two, I'm skeptical of your illustrious skills, but I believe that—if nothing else—this mission will prove entertaining."

Not desiring to remain the butt of whatever jokes or insults came next, Aranya quickly asked, "What magic do you wield?"

"Feral magic; I have an augmented sense of smell and night vision."

"Sounds very useful," she replied. "Especially for searching after missing people."

"Indeed."

Silence fell, and Aranya immediately began racking her brain for questions to ask, things to start a conversation.

"Do you have a family?" she began. "Where are you from?"

"I have a wife and a handful of little rascals. I am from Heihou, toward the south."

"Long journey here?"

"It wasn't too far."

Pause. Then Aranya asked, "Is your wife a wielder, too?" It was a silly question; people with magic married other people with magic. To preserve the bloodline.

Usually.

"She does, though she works more in government than field."

"What sort of wielder is she?"

"An ice wielder."

"Oh. Nice." It was a lame response, but she couldn't come up with anything better. The silence stretching out between them, punctuated only by the clomping hooves of their horses, grated on her spine. She opened her mouth—

"One thing you'll learn about Aranya," Kai said, "is that she finds silence a very awkward thing. She considers it her duty to always fill it."

She twisted in her saddle to glare at him.

"I had already discerned," Delan replied smoothly.

Her face went hot. She opened her mouth, probably to mutter an apology, but shut it at the last minute. At her silence, Kai twisted around in his saddle and smirked at her.

"Perhaps if you offered better conversation, I wouldn't feel the need," she said.

He only grinned and faced forward again.

Delan glanced between them and muttered, "Fathers have mercy on me." Then, a second later, he sniffed, scowled, and whirled on them. "Who packed the cheese?"

"Cheese?" asked Kai.

"Yes, cheese. One of you packed it. I can smell it. Dragons, that stuff stinks! I can't think clearly near it!"

Aranya winced. "Um, I packed some."

"Get rid of it."

"Get rid of it? But it's perfectly good—"

"I don't care."

Aranya glanced back at Kai to find him looking like he'd just discovered the juiciest secret. She shot him a look that she hoped he understood to be, *"No cheese pranks, Kai."*

But he only smirked and looked away.

That night, there was no nearby town, so they were forced to camp in the middle of the wilderness. After Delan called the halt, everything was quiet as they tended their horses and set up camp.

Aranya set the rice to cooking after Kai got the fire going and passed out strips of jerky while they waited for the rice to finish. The silence made her skin itch. But she'd already asked Delan all the questions she could think of on the long road today.

"Anyone interested in some wei-chi?" asked Delan suddenly, pulling a drawstring bag out of his piled saddlebags beside him. From the bag, he pulled a board and two polished wooden containers that, when he set on the ground and opened, revealed a set of white stones, and another of black stones.

"Games! I love games!" said Aranya eagerly, scooting over toward Delan.

"Have you played before?"

"My Ye Ye taught me a little, but it's been a long time."

"You?" Delan asked Kai.

Kai, leaning back against the trunk of a tree and locking his fingers behind his head, said smugly, "I was the Academy champion of wei-chi."

"That's not a thing," said Aranya.

"Perhaps not in the circles you ran in."

She glared at him, and he only tilted his chin up.

"I'll play you, evanescer, and we'll see if you live up to your boasting," said Delan dryly.

Kai got to his feet, gestured for Aranya to scoot over, and took her spot across from Delan. She drew her knees up to her chest to watch, already rooting for Delan to win before he handed Kai the box of black stones.

"You can play black," said Delan.

Kai scowled.

"What does black mean?" asked Aranya, inspecting the crosshatched design of the board.

"It means he gets to go first."

"You don't seem happy about going first," said Aranya to Kai, swiveling her gaze up to his. "Is it disadvantageous?"

"It's advantageous. In most cases," said Delan with a spark in his eye.

Kai said nothing, only took out a stone and set it on the board. Aranya looked at that lone piece on the board and frowned. "There are so many spaces. Why did you pick that one?"

Kai spared her a brief glare, but didn't answer. Delan placed his stone. Back and forth, they took turns. Aranya watched the strange white-and-black nonsense take shape before her. Her eyes widened when Kai reached out and plucked one of Delan's stones off the board.

"Why'd you do that?" she asked.

"I thought you said you played this before," said Kai.

"It's been a long time!"

"He captured my stone," said Delan. "Because he surrounded it with his."

"Oh! I remember that now. Does that mean Kai is winning?"

Delan sighed, didn't respond. They kept putting pieces out on the board, turn for turn. Then he exclaimed, "Seven valleys, boy! You've got to get off the defensive if you're going to take any territory!"

"I know what I'm doing."

"Academy champion, my elbow," muttered Delan. Several moves later, he was pulling five of Kai's stones off the board.

Kai's jaw flexed. But he continued placing his stones.

The game progressed. Sometimes Kai and Delan placed their stones faster, other times Kai took his time studying the board.

"I'm so lost," said Aranya. "I don't remember wei-chi being so complicated."

"The rules are simple. It's the strategy that is so complex. Makes it interesting," said Delan with a grin at Kai.

Kai had a piece in his hand as he stared at the board. Then, slowly, he sighed and put it back in the box. "Pass," he said.

"Pass," said Delan with a smirk.

"Did you just lose?" Aranya asked Kai. She looked back at the board, at the seemingly random pattern of black and white stones.

"You're too reactive," said Delan to Kai. "See, look here." He took several of the stones off the board. "This was several turns ago. You could have placed your stone here, and it would have put me in a real bind. I'd have to give up these weaker stones to keep from losing these stones here, but you were too busy defending yourself after that fool move you made earlier in the game. You couldn't catch your balance after that."

"If I hadn't made that move, these stones would have been captured, and I'd have lost this territory," said Kai, pointing at the board.

"You should have moved it here," said Delan, taking one of Kai's black stones and setting it down on the board.

"That's too risky! It opens up—"

"No, look now. Let's play it out again from this point."

They went back to playing. Aranya's eyes glazed over dully. Kai's brow furrowed more and more, while Delan's expression was mild. After each play, he sat back, crossed his arms, and stared at Kai while he studied the board.

Finally, they stopped playing. Kai supported his chin on his fist, elbow on his knee, and frowned at the board.

"You see what I mean now?" said Delan.

When Kai didn't respond, Aranya scooted closer to him and bumped him with her elbow. Without moving his head, he shifted his gaze to her, saying nothing.

"My turn," she said, and flashed a grin. "Unless you want Delan to beat you again."

Kai's gaze became a glare. Then, with a huff, he gathered his long limbs and got to his feet. Aranya scooted across Delan, cracked her knuckles, and fixed her fiercest, squinty-eyed face at him.

"Don't worry, I'll go easy on you since you haven't played in a long time," said Delan. His blunt and blockish fingers sorted the colored stones back into their boxes.

"No mercy," said Aranya.

"No mercy?" repeated Delan, eyebrows raised.

"I won't show mercy to you, so you shouldn't show any to me."

"You sure have a lot of confidence for a woman who doesn't remember the rules," said Delan, eyebrows lifting even higher. "Very well, one merciless trouncing coming right up. What are you grinning about over there, evanescer?"

Aranya glanced over her shoulder toward where Kai had sat on the opposite side of the fire and was just in time to see him quickly avert his eyes from her and a slight smirk vanish from his face.

"What?" said Kai. "I wasn't grinning. I'm going to sleep, so don't be too loud."

He untied and spread out his bedroll on the ground, purposefully ignoring them. She turned her attention back to Delan and their game.

Delan leaned forward and whispered, "Is he always insufferable?"

"You haven't even seen the worst of it," Aranya whispered back. "Am I going first?"

He nodded.

"Where should I put my first stone? Does it matter?"

"You said you wanted no mercy. But now you want help?"

"Um . . ." She stopped, staring down at the board, the small black stone between her thumb and forefinger. Then she flashed a wrinkly-nosed grin up at Delan. "Maybe a *little* bit of mercy?"

Delan sighed, rolled his eyes, and pointed to a spot on the board. "This is where I'd put it."

Back and forth they went, Delan reminding her of the rules as they played. When he plucked five of her pieces off the board, her jaw dropped, and she swiveled her eyes to his. "Wait, how did you—?"

"Because you're being reckless! You're not surveying the board properly. You're not thinking through the implications of your moves. In order to succeed in this game, you have to think through what your opponent is going to do. You have to get in my brain, see the board from my perspective, and anticipate my moves. Then you can take proper, calculated risks. Less impulse, shapeshifter. Slow down."

She took a deep breath, blew out a long gust of frustration. She spent much more time on the next move, studying the board until it was a jumble of white and black rubbish. Delan continued playing quickly and decisively.

Then, quite suddenly, Delan leaned back and said, "I pass."

Aranya whipped her head up. "You pass? Does that mean I win?"

His eyelids half-dropped in a glare. "It means there are no more beneficial moves for me to make. The game is over when we both pass."

"So . . . I should keep going?"

"You should pass too."

"Why?"

"Because you lost. There are no more good moves for you to make."

"How can you be sure of that? Let me look."

Delan sighed. With a groan, he got to his feet and brushed off his robes. "Why don't you take first watch, then? You can study the board and tell me if there are any more moves. I'm going to sleep." He grabbed his bedroll and went to the opposite side of the fire to roll it out, so the three of them were arranged in a triangle around the heat.

Aranya glanced at Kai just in time to see his eyes flutter closed. She blinked. Had he been watching them this whole time? With a huff, she propped her elbow up on her knee, leaned her chin on her fist, and studied the board.

In only a few minutes, Delan snored. Kai, on the other hand, made not a single sound. Was he actually asleep, or just pretending? When she stole a glance at him, his eyes were shut, his mouth closed, and his chest rising softly.

After fifteen minutes of studying the board, she came to Delan's same conclusion. There were no moves left to make.

Aranya thought the days of traveling would be more interesting now that they had Delan with them. He was, after all, far more inclined

to answer questions and engage in conversation than Kai. But after two days of traveling, it was sinking in that she was destined to travel with boring companions. Delan would talk for a little bit, and then he would grow quiet. No matter how many questions she asked, she could scarce get a complete sentence out of him. Only mere yeses and nos.

On the third day, he finally turned to her and said with irritation, "Traveling is not a social event, Sun Aranya."

"Not with you two," she grumbled.

Kai, who was determined to say even less than Delan, quirked his lips at this, but otherwise ignored her. Ye Ye was better company than both of them combined. Even if he did get her in trouble with her landlord. Her heart squeezed. Na should be able to keep him out of trouble, right?

Their journey was far less eventful than any of them expected. Long roads during the day, long hours in the darkness, and no *mó guǐ* attacks. They relied on Delan's nose for just about everything, from locating water to picking safer spots for camping. One day they'd come in the near vicinity of a skunk, and Delan had complained of a headache for the entire rest of the day.

That was probably why, after hearing Delan complain that something had definitely died nearby, she didn't really think much of it until they stumbled upon a human corpse on the outskirts of Shaanet.

CHAPTER 23

ARANYA COMPOSED HERSELF from her sudden start, glad she had just barely withheld crying out in fright. Kai swung down from his horse, followed by Delan, who'd immediately tied one of the handkerchiefs he kept in a little container of salt and dried lavender over his nose. Together, the three of them quietly approached the body lying in the grass.

It was a horrendous sight. But Aranya was an Academy graduate, so she overcame her squeamishness and tried to ignore the signs of decay. And the bugs. She shuddered, not being able to keep herself from glancing away—just for a second.

"Looks like a warden," Delan said, reaching out and plucking the shiny pin from the corpse's belt. "Not dead very long—a few days, perhaps? It's a wonder no animals ravaged it. This stench is *quite* repugnant."

Kai pointed to the most disgusting part of the body. "Throat was slit. The body is not mauled. Probably not a *mó guǐ* attack then."

“Looks like a murdered warden to me,” said Delan.

“Why would the body still be here?” Aranya asked. “How have the other wardens not come looking? We’re not that far out of town.”

“Maybe they don’t realize the warden is missing. Say, if he was planning to be gone.” Delan leaned back on his heels, his eyes narrowing as he looked toward the direction of the village, then toward the north. He pulled off his handkerchief, winced at the stench of the body, then took a few steps up wind and sniffed the air like a hound.

Aranya shifted her stance to one leg, looking away from the body to ponder Delan’s words. “If Kai and I had been killed on the way to Suguan, no one would have known until we didn’t show up.”

“Exactly.”

“So . . . if he hasn’t been discovered yet, and we’re this close to town . . . where could he have been going? And why would someone want to kill him?”

“We’ll have to ask,” Delan said. “A murdered warden is a capital offense and merits its own investigation. The local wardens can do that.”

“Why didn’t the patrols find this?” Aranya asked.

Delan shrugged. “Too far out, lazy patrols, any number of reasons.”

Kai was still kneeling near the corpse, not even flinching as he studied it. “He wasn’t fighting when he died; he was caught by surprise. See how his weapons are all still fastened? He didn’t have time to take any out—not even a knife. But he’s wearing spurs on his boots.”

“He was riding a horse?” Aranya asked. “How was his throat slit if he was riding a horse? Especially if he had no time to pull out a knife?”

They both looked to Delan, who turned up his palms. “You think I know?” he asked. “Like I said, this is a mystery for the local wardens to solve.”

Memories of the kidnapped girl they’d rescued, spelled to leave her room without a struggle, hit Aranya’s mind.

"Maybe it was a siren," she said.

"Now that you've battled one siren, you think everything is a siren," Kai retorted.

"Enough," said Delan, flicking his hand impatiently. "Let's ride into Shaanet."

Aranya glanced at the corpse, her nose wrinkling despite herself. "Do we bring it?"

"No. The wardens need to inspect it, and they'll learn the most if it's undisturbed. Mount up." Delan gestured at their horses. "We'll leave this mystery to the local authorities and focus on our own problem."

Finding the wardpost wasn't difficult. Like the Zushui Wardpost, the Shaanet Wardpost was set in the center of the city. A young, pretty warden came to greet them as they tied up their horses outside, two long braids tossed over her shoulder and a good luck charm dangling from her throat.

"We need to speak to the supervisor," Delan said, "on several matters of importance."

"Of course!" the girl said, beckoning them to follow her.

Aranya didn't fail to notice when Kai flashed a winsome smile the girl's way. She rolled her eyes and slipped into place behind Delan.

"Was there a warden who was dispatched recently on an out-of-town mission?" Delan asked the girl.

"Yes, there was! But—oh, I don't believe I'm supposed to speak of it! The supervisor sent him off to do something. He told me he'd be back in a week or so most likely. Earlier, if things went well."

Aranya swallowed, her lips drawn in a tight firm line. She nodded, attempting a smile when the girl looked her way. Her gut churned. She hoped her face gave nothing away as the girl brought them to the supervisor's office and left.

Kai at least had the decency to look unsettled as well at the girl's oblivion. But he quickly cleared his expression and hung back a minute to speak to her, his tone low and pleasant.

Delan bowed to the supervisor as he quickly stood to greet them. Aranya followed suit as Kai caught up with them. This office—along with the entire wardpost—was significantly nicer than Zushui's, with polished wood floors and green painted walls. Bamboo accents and a red tasseled rug completed the scene. Apparently there were benefits to working in a city where a guardian lived.

"Honored Head Warden," Delan said to the slightly heavyset man. "I am Lian Delan, from Suguan Secret Services. My comrades, Sun Aranya and Shi Kai." He gestured to them. Aranya flashed a sunny grin, while Kai merely nodded. "We have a matter of great importance to address with you."

The supervisor's welcoming smile faded first into alarm, then to realization, his long, thin moustache drooping. "You are investigating the disappearance, then, are you not?" His voice lowered and his eyes darted to the door, as though to ensure no one was eavesdropping.

Aranya frowned. Did the wardens not know about the guardian's disappearance? This information was kept *very* private then. It hardly seemed possible how closely the government had protected this secret, trying to save face until Lord Zuan Wan's whereabouts were discovered.

It made her wonder how many other things she didn't know about.

"Indeed, we are. We also are the bearers of unfortunate news regarding one of your own wardens." With more tact than Aranya would have expected from Delan, he explained the discovery of the dead warden.

The supervisor listened carefully, not interrupting, but he slowly sat back down. While he maintained his composure, his skin turned pale.

"I will send a crew out there immediately," he said.

Delan nodded, expressed his satisfaction with this plan, and then informed the supervisor of his intention to investigate Lord Zuan Wan's private residence, and declined the offer for assistance.

A set of directions and a horse ride later, Aranya rode up with her companions to the gates of Lord Zuan Wan's mansion. She stared up at the towering iron-wrought gate, at the far taller mansion. It was grander than Lord Meng's residence back in Zushui. Bigger, more lush, more elegant. Its curving eaves spread far and wide, tipping upward toward the noonday sun. Cobblestone pathways snaked between crimson pillars and dark wood arches to vibrant gardens and lotus ponds.

Being one of such prominence in Zheninghai certainly had its benefits.

Her own smallness, her own *ineptness,* weighed down her shoulders as she handed her reins off to the stable hand and followed Delan and a butler inside the front doors. What was she *doing* here? On this case? In this mansion?

Mentally shaking herself, she blinked her eyes wide and let out a deep breath. She was here, and that was that. There was nothing to do except give it her best and try not to ruin everything.

"This was where he was last seen?" Delan asked when they stood outside the guardian's study.

The butler, a tall, reed-like man with a stiff topknot, pursed his lips, nodding as a muscle jerked in his jaw. "He was working late. I was about to retire for the evening, but I heard a noise from here. When I arrived, I found the room empty and the window open."

"Have you or anyone else displaced anything in this room?"

"No, sir, we have kept it exactly how it was like we were instructed."

Delan led the charge, opening the door. Aranya followed into the gloomy interior. Her lips parted as her eyes adjusted to the scene before her.

It was an absolute wreck. Tables were overturned, mats flung aside, papers fluttering in the barest draft from the open door. Worse, however, were the gouges in the wall. Like something had drilled straight through to the outside. Some of the furniture had deep scrape marks wrapping around its legs or its sides. The bright crimson curtains hung in shreds.

Kai strode to the far side of the room, kneeling to inspect one of the gouges and the floor by the window. Probably looking for dust. Delan, looking more like a dog than a human, began sniffing everything within sight.

Naturally, that left Aranya to state the obvious: "It appears there was a struggle."

Kai snorted from where he was, face inches from the floor. Delan merely paused his sniffing to mutter, "Indeed."

"I think aloud, all right?" she retorted, unintentionally wringing her hands. What was she supposed to do here? This was so beyond her experience!

"Hope you're thinking more than that," Kai said, and then winked, a tiny smirk playing along the edges of his mouth.

She was about to scowl at him when a thought suddenly hit her. A struggle meant the guardian hadn't simply decided to run off to somewhere else. This scale of destruction indicated he'd been very loath to leave.

She drew in a sharp breath through her teeth and whirled on her heel to inspect the sideways-tilted table near her. She frowned, peering closer. Carefully, she ran one finger down the scrapes. Then, catching the threads of an idea, she pushed the table into its upright position to inspect the opposite side. The same scrape marks were mirrored on the opposite side, as though whatever had caused the marks had, perhaps . . . *wrapped* around the table. And why would a kidnapper need to wrap something around a table?

She traced the marks again, cognizant of avoiding splinters, noting how the grain of the wood ran opposite the scrapes. She glanced around the ground and knelt to pluck up a few dead leaves just under the table.

"Lord Zuan Wan made the—" Aranya started to say.

"I smell blood," Delan barked suddenly, cutting her off. "Butler! I need an article of the Lord's clothing!" At her blank expression, he said, "To determine if the blood was Zuan Wan's or his assailant."

"The assailant did not cause the destruction in this room," Kai said, still crouched on the ground. "It appears that the guardian caused most of it himself."

"That's what I was going to say—" Aranya started.

"How so?" Delan asked Kai.

She huffed and folded her arms across her chest.

"Bits of plant are everywhere. Especially along these holes," Kai said, pointing. "The guardian was attacked, and he attempted to fight them off with his magic."

Aranya pointed at the table. "It looks like a huge vine grabbed this and maybe smashed it into something. Or someone."

Delan was shaking his head, but it didn't seem like it was quite directed at her. He kept sniffing the air, moving around the room, face scrunched in a wince. He shook his head again. "So many scents, but . . ."

"But what?" said Aranya.

"Three people. I smell three distinct smells. One is very . . . smoky."

Kai raised an eyebrow and shot a sideways glance at Aranya.

"One of the smells is vaguely familiar," said Delan, rubbing his finger between his knotted brows. "I caught a whiff of it a couple times just today."

"Today? Like this person is still in town?"

"Possibly . . ." Delan rocked his head from side to side, got on his hands and knees, and began smelling the air just above the floor near one of the gouges in the wall. Then he snapped upright and nearly hit the broken leg of a lattice screen. "The body. I smelled this scent on the body. It was faint, and nearly overcome by the stench of the body . . . but I smelled it all the same."

He finally stopped long enough to glance at Aranya and Kai just standing there. Did a stone just lodge in Kai's gut like one had in hers? Whoever had been here, fighting with Lord Zuan Wan, was the same person who had slit the warden's throat to stop his pursuit.

The butler came running just then with an article of clothing—a dressing robe of emerald green. Delan accepted it and held it up to his nose as he sniffed. "Not the guardian's blood I smell. Must be the assailant's."

"So the guardian was taken against his will," Aranya said, surveying the destruction. "He put up a fight but was overwhelmed."

"We can't be sure about him being abducted just yet. It seems so, but we shouldn't be hasty. *If* he was abducted . . . Subduing a mighty wielder like Lord Zuan Wan is quite a feat," Delan said somewhat absently, still holding the dressing robe up to his nose. He handed it to Aranya without glancing at her, eyebrows furrowed, then took a few more experimental sniffs in the air. His eyes cleared suddenly, and he jerked his head forward. "I've caught his scent; it's still here. Let's follow it!"

He bounded through the gaping window without glancing back to see if they followed. Kai vanished, presumably evanescing to the other side of the wall. Aranya growled under her breath as she clambered up to the opening and swung herself through.

Kai and Delan were already far ahead. She ran to catch up, cursing her partial magic once again. If she were a full shifter, she could change into a wildcat and beat them to their destination.

She ran after them through the edge of the city, out into the open fields and wilderness. Instinctively, she registered they were heading due north. She stopped up short, her eyes going wide with realization.

"This is where we found the—" she started to call.

But just then, Delan and Kai stopped too. Ahead, three unfamiliar wardens stared down at the ground. Horror was etched onto their faces. Aranya hurried to catch up, her gut twisting at the expressions on their faces. They had likely worked with this poor dead warden; they might have been good friends. She couldn't imagine the shock they beheld. She would never, ever want to see the half-decrepit remains of a friend.

Then she froze. There was no body.

Just a huge circle of black, burnt earth where the body had been only hours ago.

CHAPTER 24

ARANYA JOINED KAI, Delan, and the other wardens circling the burned spot on the ground. No singed grass remained, no shred of fabric from the clothes on the body—nothing was left except scorched earth.

Ice swept down her spine, and she turned rounded eyes up to Kai next to her. He flicked a glance her way in response, his jaw taut. Delan growled under his breath and said to the wardens, "Bring this information back to your supervisor. There is no need to remain here gawking."

The wardens shuffled off, leaving the three of them alone.

"This could only have been a fire-wielder or a *mó guǐ*," Aranya said quietly. "Nothing else could have burned so thoroughly."

"A *mó guǐ* would have eaten the body, not burned it away," Kai said with a trace of ire. "Not a *mó guǐ*."

"I don't care *what* did this; I care about *why*," Delan snapped. "Why leave the body until now, only to destroy it the moment someone happens upon it? Why not decimate it in the first place?"

"What if the first attacker didn't have the ability?" she offered. "Left it until the other could come and finish the job?"

"There's more than one way to dispose of a body, qilin-brain."

"I'm not *asking* your opinion, Shi Kai."

"Will the both of you shut up? Can't think with all of your squabbling."

Aranya glowered and crossed her arms. Kai shifted his weight to his other leg and likewise crossed his own arms.

Delan, nose in the air, sniffed ahead around the blackened spot. Just as quickly, he pulled back, his face twisting as he coughed and shook his head. "Smokey."

She chewed on the inside of her cheek, trying to decide if she should say something about that being obvious. In the end, she kept her mouth shut.

"Smokey . . . like the smell back in Lord Zuan's office?" Kai asked.

Delan's face was hard as he stared at the burned patch. "It's the same, but smokey smells aren't as distinct. Any number of fiery things could smell the same. It burns away the subtler individual smells. Did either of you find out what sort of wielder our poor victim here was?"

"He was feral," Kai said. "Similar magic to yours, but less powerful. He was sent to investigate the guardian's disappearance because the supervisor doubted the capital would send anyone within a reasonable time frame."

Aranya turned her glower on him. "And how did you find that out?"

His face split into a lopsided grin.

"That girl told you, didn't she? After you flirted with her?"

Kai merely shrugged. "Flirting can be productive in more ways than one."

"Seven valleys," she huffed, skirting away from him to Delan's side.

"If he was feral," Delan said, ignoring them, "then he would have likely caught the same scent I have. Which means . . ."

"Someone didn't want him following this trail," Aranya finished for him.

He nodded, eyes lifting the horizon. "This trail may be more dangerous than we originally expected."

Aranya followed the trajectory of his gaze, her blood simmering in her veins. Dangerous or not, she wasn't messing up this chance. She gritted her teeth and set her face north.

Mounted up, armed to the teeth, and prepared for more nights out in the wilderness, Aranya and Kai followed Delan's nose. The hours were dull beyond belief. Now that Delan was so focused, he wouldn't acknowledge a word from her. And Kai was . . . well, Kai.

Evening fell, bringing with it relief from the heat. They dismounted, hobbling their horses for the night, and set about making camp.

"These nights are getting chilly," Aranya said, drawing her cloak tighter around her shoulders. "I hardly know what to pack these days—hot in the day, cold at night. It's all so confusing."

Her companions ignored her.

"All right then," she muttered, letting her smile drift into something tighter, firmer. "I'll go fetch wood for the night."

She waited for a moment, glancing between Kai crouching on the ground, striking flint on tinder near his pile of kindling, and Delan who seemed unable to get the scent of their trail out of his nostrils. He kept pulling out one of his handkerchiefs, taking a big whiff as though to clear his scent palate, only to jerk his nose into the air a few minutes later.

She stood, patted the knife at her hip by habit, and checked her new, holstered *jiaun*. Then she strode off into the woods, refusing to glance back at the men. If they wanted to be boring, that was their problem. She wouldn't worry about it. And it wasn't like she cared what they thought of her beyond their professional esteem—which she definitely didn't have, but it *didn't matter.* All that mattered was solving this mystery and getting back safely to Ye Ye.

A few steps into the forest, and the night seemed to swallow her whole. The sounds of crooning and cricketing bugs surrounded her. Underbrush crunched beneath her feet, and she took minor pains to be quiet. After all, there *probably* wasn't anything stalking the woods this early. Most *mó guǐ* came out later in the night.

As she bent down to collect sticks, her hand unconsciously moved to touch her knife again. Just to be certain it was there. Now that she was out here, alone, in the dark, her spine tingled.

"Being Delan would sure be nice," she whispered into the darkness. "Night vision and a nose to rival wolves. Maybe I should have let him do this."

Her eyes strained. She moved quicker, collecting as much brush as she could fill her arms with. She found a fallen tree with larger branches that would be perfect for smoldering all night. A second trip might be necessary for those, however.

A light flickered in the dark. Their campfire? Had Kai gotten it going, even without her coming back with wood?

Had she come from that direction? She thought she'd come from the other direction.

Aranya paused, heart thudding too loudly in the night, and slowly turned around. Her arms braced around her pile of wood, but she flicked her right wrist and shifted her hand into talons.

The light flickered. At first, she thought it was blue, but then it softened into a welcoming orange glow. That had to be the campfire. She'd take this load back, shake off her own stupid premonition, and then return for the second.

Her feet started moving, almost of their own accord, toward the light. With each step, the light flickered, flashing blue and then back to orange. She frowned, went to open her mouth to call for Kai or Delan—

"What a pretty light," she heard herself saying.

She swallowed, clutching her wood tighter. Then, with a start, she glanced down and found her talons had vanished.

And now she couldn't make herself shift. Instead, her arms were opening. Her full collection of brush fell to the ground with a noisy clatter. Could her companions hear? Would they come find her?

Why should it matter? She was going to them—heading toward the light. Once she was there, she would simply have to tell them she'd dropped the wood.

She shook her head, gritting her teeth. What was she thinking? Her mind went muddier, and if she didn't have that light to guide her back . . .

"What a pretty light," she said. She clamped her mouth shut, glowering at no one. When she opened it again: "What a pretty light."

A wordless growl escaped her throat. Her feet kept moving. She tried to trip herself on a fallen log, but she stepped cleanly over it.

Toward the light.

Panic flared full and heady in her blood, her vision, until she nearly screamed in frustration and fear, *"WHAT A PRETTY LIGHT!!"* But she couldn't allow herself to say it again. She bit her tongue, tasting copper and sticky bile.

Think, Aranya, think!

But she couldn't. Her brain was no more her own than her stupid, dragon-eaten feet that wouldn't stop dragging her toward the qilin-scorched light.

The light was closer now. The welcoming orange leaked away entirely, leaving nothing but blue fire in its wake. Except that it wasn't fire. It was something else—something not physical at all. She drew nearer on incessant feet, her hand reaching out of its own accord, toward the dancing little blue light.

"What a pretty light," she choked, a sob clogging her throat so she could hardly breathe.

She stepped on a twig, cracking it with such resounding loudness that it seemed to split the night clean in half. Her heart sputtered within her, her arm aching as she continued holding it out toward the light.

The bugs were silent. They had been silent for some time now, but it wasn't until she stepped on the twig that she realized it. And it wasn't just that the bugs were silent—a new sound replaced them. A low humming, but not *deep*, per se. It was soft, pitched high like a mother's lullaby. Now that it caught her focus, it was almost deafening. There seemed to be words strung along those notes, buried deep beneath its melody.

She couldn't touch the flickering blue light before her. It hung suspended above the world like dancing poison, ready to strike the moment her traitorous finger came too close. She *couldn't touch it.* Somehow, she knew if she did, she would die.

She fought it, growling soundlessly as her muscles quivered under the strain of conflicting forces. Her growl turned into a cry, then a sob. Her legs were cooked strings of noodles beneath her, yet she couldn't make herself collapse onto the ground.

She tried once more to call for help. All that came out was a tremulous, "What a pretty light."

Then, out of nowhere, a face appeared before her. Cutting off the vision of the light.

It was so dark, she couldn't make it out entirely. But her hand flagged, falling to her side. Her knees buckled. Her mind cleared so suddenly it was like being dunked head-first into icy water. The relief was so profound she fell against the dark figure's chest.

Hands closed around her elbows, supporting her, and she recognized that grip. She gasped, "Kai," and could have wept with relief that her tongue was back under her ownership.

"Should have known you'd get yourself into trouble the instant you were alone," came Kai's unmistakable, irritated voice. "Get out of the lure before we both get ensnared."

"Lure?" As soon as she spoke it, realization hit. "Oh. A siren set this lure."

"And it's nearly as powerful of a lure as they come," he growled, not glancing back over his shoulder at the blue light that probably still shone. Then his voice turned wry. "You can keep clinging to me if you so please, but it's hard to walk."

She blinked. Her face was still pressed into his chest, her hands fisted in folds of his robes. "Oh!" she squeaked, pushing away from him even as he released his grip on her elbows. "I'm sorry, I didn't mean—"

"It's fine; I *did* just save your life. I can even carry you back if you'd like."

"Carr—" Aranya stopped, glancing up at the dark face before her. White teeth flashed from a devilish grin. "Seven valleys, I almost *died* and you can't be a little more . . . gentlemanly?"

"I offered to carry you."

"In your most mocking tone! For the love of the fathers, I'm not Lord Meng's sniveling daughter!"

He snorted and strode past her. "Keep up, Partial. And *you're welcome*."

She growled, hurrying after him.

"You stink at gathering brush," Kai said after a few minutes.

She probably would have retorted something, but relief still coursed heady and overwhelming through her veins. All that she managed to utter was a simple question. "How did you know to come looking for me?"

"When you took a million-and-a-half years doing a very simple task."

"I was gone that long?"

"Over half an hour."

"Fathers!" she breathed, dragging a hand down her face. "I am such an idiot."

"No one could have resisted that lure," Kai said, and she blinked at the slight softening in his tone. "We'll have to discuss it with Delan."

"A lure like that shouldn't be out here," she mumbled. When she closed her eyes, she saw that dancing flame that seemed eerily like a disembodied soul. She shuddered, opening her eyes again.

Warm, real firelight filled her vision.

"A lure like that shouldn't be set to catch any unsuspecting person," he said. "And few sirens can even set lures. Most only have simple tricks like the brigand we arrested."

He was right on both accounts.

"But even lures are set using those black stones, right?" Aranya asked. "So tomorrow, when it's light, we should hunt for the stone anchoring this lure. Don't you think it's kind of . . . suspicious?"

Her foot twisted in the uneven ground, and she yelped as she tripped. But Kai's arm darted out and caught her around the waist, keeping her upright. She shuddered out a deep breath, her legs still wobbling, as she lifted her head from where her hands had planted on his chest, to the glitter of his eyes staring down at her.

"Are you alright?" he asked, his voice painted in a shade of concern that seemed out of character for him.

"I—uh . . ." She fumbled to get her balance, ended up hanging heavier on him as she got her feet under her. Then she scrambled backward a few steps.

He let her go quickly.

"What's suspicious?" he asked, his voice slightly roughened.

She blinked. What had she been talking about? Oh, the lure. "That it's right on our trail? If we hadn't stopped for the night, we'd have walked right into it. All three of us."

Kai didn't respond, but his frown and half-glance back toward her was loud enough.

CHAPTER 25

"YOU WERE ENSNARED in a lure?" Delan burst out.

Aranya stood still, mouth drawn in a thin line. Her legs wobbled slightly, but she was steadier now than she had been before. Enough that she wasn't worried she'd collapse again into Kai's arms. He, on the other hand, seemed to be eyeing her like he was afraid she'd do just that.

"Yes, I was," she said. The next words were even more begrudging than the first: "Kai saved me."

"We'll have to investigate it," Delan muttered, tossing a log into the fire from the pile that Kai and Aranya had brought back when returning from the forest. "Very suspicious. But no use doing it in the dark. No one better fall asleep on their watch tonight; a lure like that could mean brigands in these parts."

She nodded in acknowledgement while Kai merely sat down by the fire wordlessly.

"How did you not get caught too?" Aranya asked Kai abruptly, drawing her cloak tighter around her shoulders as the air turned chillier.

"By my astute observation skills."

Delan snorted. "I'm going to sleep now. No time for wei-chi tonight. If you two are going to stay up late chattering, keep it quiet."

"We're not going to," Kai said dryly, pulling his bedroll from the pile of saddles by the fire. "Aranya will take first watch. Though I'm not sure she can be trusted to not get caught in the lure again."

Not knowing what else to do in response, she flashed him a snarl of a smile and settled herself on the ground near the fire for watch. Delan rolled over so his back was to them and promptly erupted into a chorus of snores.

Kai was about to do the same when Aranya whispered, "Really, Kai, how did you not get caught? The moment I saw the light, I couldn't escape. I didn't know how to break out of it, either, and if you hadn't—" She stopped herself. Before anything slipped between her lips that she'd regret later.

Kai, half tucked into his bedroll, glanced her way, and smirked. "Now we're expressing some measure of thanks."

"Kai."

He shrugged, laid down on the ground, and closed his eyes. "Delan asked me to go find you when you didn't come back. I wasn't about to walk straight down the path you took because if you *did* run into something, I'd run into it too. I went around and saw you following something. Your eyes were all glazed, and you looked . . ." He paused, his smile slipping into a frown.

"I looked what?" She didn't bother hiding the ire in her tone.

"Freakish. I realized it was a lure and saw that you were caught in it. That's when I appeared in front of you, to cut off your line of sight and not risk my own neck. There, that was how I did it. Are you taking notes?" The eyes-closed smirk was back.

She didn't respond. Instead, she rifled through her saddlebags and pulled out the folder with the information on Zuan Wan. In her periphery, she saw that Kai opened one eye to peer at her when she was silent. But she ignored him, thumbing through the documents.

The parchments were the worse for wear, but nothing that compromised their readability. She skimmed the first few pages, tucking stray hairs behind her ears. It was information she had largely memorized already, but something kept her flipping until the last several pages.

She had skimmed over these because they didn't have information that she believed especially pertinent, but now her brows knit as she examined them closer.

It was a record of all the missing wielders. By each name was a sketch of their face, a physical description, and the length of their disappearance.

She studied Li Feiyan's. The healer had not always been a pretty girl, but in recent years she'd blossomed into someone quite lovely. Her midnight eyes had always been her most striking feature, but the sketch didn't show that to full advantage. It did catch, however, the wry upturn of her lips. She wore that expression whenever she wasn't grinning outright—like she was silently laughing at them all.

The entire Academy had had something of a fascination for her. Being the only healer in generations, she was *special*. All the boys wanted to get her attention and marry her, which might have been the result of scheming parents trying to claim the healer's future bloodline and the prestige she bore.

But Aranya had always thought that, despite that twisting mouth and the fire in her eyes, Feiyan had seemed worn. Like the long days of healing and Academy rigor squeezed the life out of her soul.

Was the healer all right? Was she suffering under the heavy hand of her captors?

Next was the sketch of Zuan Wan. He was very serious, his bearded chin tilted up slightly. He was middle-aged, not particularly handsome, but there was a ruddy sort of power communicated through the drawing. When she skimmed the other drawings, she could not find a single one with the same determined set of jaw.

Such a powerful wielder. An image of his ransacked study flashed through her mind. The vines he spelled and manipulated had been powerful enough to tear through stone and wood. And yet they had not been enough to save him.

The fire crackled before her and, absently, Aranya added another log. Kai's much quieter snores added to Delan's.

Something just didn't sit right about this case.

Kidnapping a healer made sense—anyone would want control over the one person in the empire who could heal any physical ailment. But kidnapping one of the guardians? One of the most powerful ones, at that?

Why would anyone be so foolhardy? Perhaps even more pressing: who was powerful enough to accomplish such a feat?

Finally, Aranya's eyes drifted down to the sketch she'd set out to study.

Kang Lei. The missing siren.

She had enormous eyes, rounded and fanned with lashes. The lines of her face were soft, almost seductive. If her plump lips spread in a smile, she could waggle her finger at any man. Usually women in Zheninghai kept their hair bound up in some way, but in the sketch, her hair was free, loose, and long.

She certainly fit the stereotype of sirens; perhaps she was the reason behind the stereotype.

Aranya looked up from the sketch to the woods where she'd found the lure.

Kai had earlier said what she already knew: not many sirens could set lures, especially lures that were nearly impossible to escape. She chewed on her chapped lips.

"Could she have set it?" she whispered aloud.

She looked back down at the brief description and noted the city she had disappeared from. One far south from here, near the coast. If Kang Lei had set this lure after she'd disappeared . . .

Could she send for information from Suguan? She wanted to know exactly how many sirens in the empire could set lures and where they were all located. Additionally, she wanted to know if Kang Lei had ever been this far north.

"She should have kept a record of the lures she set to be in compliance with the government code," Aranya mumbled, glancing again toward the dark forest line. "Theoretically, I should be able to obtain a list of every snare set in the empire. But surely this one couldn't have been a legal snare. For what purpose?"

Unless, of course, the siren who'd set this was a brigand, a Hidden One like Lihua. Only far more powerful.

"A lure like that could mean brigands in these parts." That was what Delan had said.

What if . . .?

Was it possible that Kang Lei could have deserted? Become a brigand? And then used her magic to overwhelm Zuan Wan? Aided by whoever had killed the warden in Shaanet?

But *why?*

Aranya sat for hours, pondering these mysteries. She was so caught up in her thoughts that she nearly forgot to wake Kai for the second watch. Only her own aching eyelids made her remember. He groaned when she tapped on his shoulder and sat up, blinking and rubbing his eyes.

The next morning, Kai tried to block out Aranya's incessant chattering as she passed out rice cakes and jerky for breakfast. His brain was muddled from fitful sleep. The last thing he needed was all her half-brained theories about the lure she'd stumbled into last night.

She was far too eager to go investigate now that day had dawned.

Kai was only eager for one thing: more sleep.

Delan seemed to be in a similar mood, for he muttered, "I'm sure your ideas are wonderful."

Aranya's chipper tone faltered slightly, but she shrugged and settled herself on the ground. "Anyone else sore? I'm terribly sore! It's like being back at the Academy."

Kai had hardly finished swallowing his half-chewed breakfast before she was leaping up and fastening on her weapons.

"I have some ideas," she continued. "What's the nearest city? Can we stop there to send a message? I have a few pieces of information that I'd like to request. It's not about Zuan Wan directly, but I have a hunch about this lure, and I think it might be connected to him. After all, we're still on his trail. Doesn't it seem weird that it would lead right to a snare? What if this was set to ensnare anyone pursuing them? I'd like to find out how many sirens in the empire can set lures, if there are any near here, and if there's any record of Kang Lei being in these parts. Also . . . I'd like to see if there's record of this one."

Kai sat up straighter, darting a look at Delan. Kang Lei? Did she think the vanished siren set this? Delan seemed to be waiting for her to stop talking. Once she did and turned back toward her weapons, he said, "The nearest city is Zushui."

Aranya's sheathed knife slipped to the dirt. She blinked, glancing between Delan and Kai. Kai met her gaze, and something about her surprise woke him enough to give her a tiny smirk. Just enough to make her look back at Delan.

"Zushui?" she repeated, her voice suddenly breathless.

Kai watched her carefully, though trying to keep an air of disinterest about him.

"Could we . . . stop there?" Aranya asked, her voice sounding thin like she held her breath. Her eyes never strayed from Delan's. "So I can . . . send the messages?"

Delan squared his elbows on his knees. "*Just* to send messages? I smell ulterior motives on you, girl."

A flush stained her cheeks and the tips of her ears, but she simply said, "My grandfather is there, too. I would love to . . . to see how he's doing. I haven't left him alone this long . . ." She squared her shoulders and cleared her throat. "May we stop?"

Delan blinked a few times, lowering his eyes as if pondering something. Then, with a groan like he was an old man, he got to his feet and began strapping his weapons to his belt. "I can tell you right now there will be no record of this lure. Lures and snares of any type aren't meant to capture any unsuspecting wielders; they are supposed to be set for specific people or beasts. One this elaborate would have safeguards against what happened last night if it were a proper lure, made in accordance with empire guidelines. This lure was made outside of the emperor's sanction; thus, it was made by a brigand or someone like Kang Lei."

Kai stared at Delan, his mind trying to grapple with the implications of what he said. He glanced toward Aranya, who was smiling triumphantly.

"I *thought* so," she said.

He frowned, running a hand through his hair. Fathers, it could use a good wash. He didn't want to wonder how Aranya had stumbled onto that suspicion. But then his eyes landed on the folder she'd tucked back into her saddlebags. Apparently, she'd been much more productive than him during her watch. Which was fine—so long as this got done, it didn't matter who did more or less work. He only wanted to get back to his post at Zushui. Preferably with his rival having found a different position elsewhere.

An image flashed in his mind. Of her, curled up beneath a tattered blanket with a fluffy white cat in her arms, her long, dark hair falling over her head, cushion, and shoulders. Brows knit, the glimmer of tears in the shadow of her nose. And then a different image of her, eyes widened like moons in the darkness of an inn, her tears leaking between his fingers, the whimper on her lips.

Why had his mouth suddenly gone dry? Why did his chest feel tighter? He wasn't responsible for what happened to her and her grandcat when she lost her post in Zushui. Besides, if things went well on this mission, she might even find a better position.

If things went well.

Delan sighed. "Let's go investigate that lure."

"And then can we stop by Zushui?" Aranya asked, clasping her hands and grinning girlishly.

"Maybe."

CHAPTER 26

"WE'LL NEED TO determine if the lure is still active," Aranya said. "If it is, then we have to deactivate it before we investigate it."

Kai rolled his eyes, tempted to spout something snappy in retort. He held himself back, however, seeing that she only spoke to herself. As they approached, she muttered under her breath—things that sounded like an Academy checklist. One that Kai had certainly never taken the time to read, much less memorize.

"Then we find the pressure point. That's where the black stone is. If we can dislodge it, that should be enough to dismantle it," she muttered.

Delan glanced Kai's way, an amused glint in his eyes. Kai returned it.

"Alright, Miss Textbook," Delan said. "You enter the forest like you did last night. We'll see if it ensnares you again."

"But I've already been caught once. How about Kai gets caught this time?"

"His magic makes him the ideal person to ensure none of us gets too close," Delan replied coolly. "He'll watch you for signs of being ensnared and intervene before it's too late. I'll watch and determine the next step once we know whether the lure is active, and once we have an idea of where the pressure point is."

Aranya looked like she wanted to protest, but she shrugged and sighed instead. "Very well; give me some space while I go trap myself."

Kai didn't wait for the signal from Delan; he evanesced away to the clearing where he had found Aranya last night. It took him three jumps because of all the trees, but it was out of the line of sight of whatever had lured her, yet still in full view of her.

He crouched behind a tree for extra protection. Although he *didn't care*—or perhaps more aptly, didn't *want* to care—adrenaline surged in his blood. It was rather like the feeling of stepping out in the wildness of Academy hunts. It wasn't a battle, but there remained the thrill of the unknown. Like danger could leap out from the shadows at any moment.

But that was an exciting sort of danger. Not all danger was equally thrilling. He knew that fact well.

Aranya moved surprisingly swiftly into the forest, directly toward where she had encountered the lure. Had it been him, he would have skulked along the edges—trying to get close without being caught. She just plowed right in.

He wanted to call it only carelessness and stupidity. But somehow . . . That wasn't just it.

She was fearless.

The admission tasted like ashes in his mouth. She leapt into things not because she was stupid, but because she wasn't afraid. Kai had always thought his holding back was because he was merely cautious and careful.

But was that all? Or perhaps was he more fearful than he wanted to admit? He slid his fingers down the leather strap running across his chest. Just to ensure he'd remembered to strap his broadsword to his back.

Kai saw the very moment Aranya was ensnared in the lure. He straightened, every muscle tensing as he steadied his breathing into the controlled measures of a warrior. Aranya's eyes went glazed; her sure footsteps suddenly mechanical. Her lips opened, shut, opened, shut. Her brows puckered, her fisted hand upraising to touch something.

It was a strong snare. He hadn't seen many—only the ones they'd used for training back at the Academy. He could nearly smell the power pulsing in this one. Blue light flared in her drawn face.

She was resisting it. She was strong. But the lure was stronger.

"Did it catch her?" came Delan's shout.

"Yes!" Kai shouted back.

"Can we come up behind it? Or does it work every way?"

"I'll check."

Kai rose to his feet, keeping one eye on Aranya's progress as he carefully glanced around the other side of the tree. All he could see in the opposite direction were sunbeams cutting through the forest foliage. He evanesced to another tree and double checked his line of sight to ensure that when he evanesced in front of Aranya, he'd only have to do it in one jump.

"Are you finding anything?" Delan called. His voice sounded nearer, and Kai turned to see him crouching behind another tree. In case Kai got caught too.

"I don't see any effects of the lure on the opposite side, but I cannot be sure."

"No glow reflecting on the trees or anything?"

"Nothing."

"How's Aranya?"

"She's getting closer. Her footsteps are slowing, like she's fighting extra hard."

"Can you pinpoint the location of the lure?"

Kai frowned, glancing back toward Aranya's puckered face. Blue light shone brighter in her eyes. "I have a general idea. Should I intervene now?"

"Wait a bit longer. In case it's farther than we realize."

Uneasiness churned in his gut, but he remained where he was. His fingers curled into the bark on the tree he sheltered behind, digging into the dirty, sap-lined crevices. He didn't let his eyes leave his comrade. If he waited one second too late, it could spell her death. Or imprisonment in a cage nearly impossible to break.

"I think she's very close to it," Kai said, trying to keep the alarm out of his voice.

"I can see her now. She's still got a few more steps at least."

"Don't we have what we need now?"

"The more precise we have of the location, the slimmer the chances we have of getting caught in it."

Kai clenched his jaw.

Aranya's voice spilled from her lips. "What a pretty light." Her voice grew louder as she began repeating the phrase. "What a pretty light! What a *pretty light*!" Panic laced the syllables.

"Now?"

"No."

"Spitfire," Kai cursed under his breath, driving his nails into the tree bark. "Dragon-blasted *spitfire.*"

"*WHAT A PRETTY LIGHT!*" came Aranya's shriek.

"Now!" Delan shouted.

Kai evanesced in a flash, appearing directly in front of her. It was like last night, except that he could see better when her eyes cleared like clouds drifting away after a storm to reveal a blue sky. She gasped, putting up her fisted hands against his chest for support, keeping herself from stumbling into him. She was short enough that with him this close, there was no chance she'd see the siren's luring light.

"You both . . ." she gasped again, lowering her head as she braced herself.

Kai's hands hovered in midair above her back, not sure if he ought to offer stability or leave her alone. He stared down at her, waiting.

"Phoenix-spawn!" Aranya cried, her head shooting up so she could glare at him. Her fists clenched tighter around his tunic. "Both of you—phoenix-spawn! What is *wrong* with you, waiting until the last dragon-eaten second?"

"You thought I'd neglect to save a damsel in distress?" Kai smirked, ignoring his own relief. "I'm glad to see how little faith you have in me. Though if we're being technical, *I* wasn't the one who wanted to wait."

"Delan, you cracked dragon egg!" she shouted, pushing away from Kai.

"You're just fine," came the returning shout from somewhere in the trees. "Now find the pressure point of the snare!"

Aranya huffed, folding her arms across her chest, and returning her glare to Kai. Not knowing what else to do, he flashed a grin her way and said, "Would you like to do the honors?"

She stared at him, shifting her weight so she could cock one knee. Her answering smile was hardly a smile at all; it was pure challenge. "Very well, I shall."

Kai remained standing, blocking the light, as she crouched down to the ground. She kept her eyes closed as she reached a hand around him and began patting the dirt. Looking for the black stone. Hopefully, it was on the ground and not tucked into a tree knot or something else that would be much more difficult to locate blindly.

"Found it!" Aranya cried triumphantly, her grin turning genuine.

"Hand it to me and I'll take it to Delan for inspection," Kai said, holding out his palm. Some instinctive part of him made him close his eyes as her hand knocked around in the air, searching for his. Finally, there was the brush of her warm fingers contrasting with smooth cold. The stone was heavier than he expected, making his arm dip slightly.

"Now you can open your eyes," he said right before he evanesced away.

He might have said it more to himself than to her; once she had picked it up off the ground, that would be enough to dislodge the spell and make it lose its power. He forced himself to open his eyes as he reappeared in the clearing where Delan had been safely hiding, forced himself to look down at the stone he held in his palm.

It looked just like the stone the other siren had placed under the bed of Lord Meng's daughter. Except the stone itself was not merely polished black, but flecked with veiny bits of gold.

"Here's the stone." Kai held it out toward Delan.

"Perfect." Delan rolled his shoulders and stood to accept it.

The change in the older wielder was immediate and so sudden Kai almost didn't have time to evanesce backward several steps.

Delan's eyes glazed over, glowing with reflected blue light that came from nowhere. He reached out a hand, fingers stretched toward the stone in Kai's hand. His steps turned wooden.

"Seven valleys!" Kai gasped, leaping backward. He clamped his other hand over the stone, but it made no difference. He tried shoving it in his pocket. No avail.

But Delan did not move slowly like Aranya had. He pounced—a very animal movement—all while shrieking, "What a pretty light! What a pretty light!"

Kai evanesced further away, stumbling as he reappeared and falling on his backside. Aranya emerged from the trees to his right, then Delan from his left. Her face was pained, anxious, with a deeply furrowed brow over her glazed eyes. But she fought it.

Delan, however, ran on all fours toward Kai.

"Seven valleys—" Kai exclaimed again. Delan moved so fast that Kai barely rolled and evanesced away in time.

Why wasn't the spell affecting him? Was it because he bore it? Something told him that if he handed over the stone to either of them, whatever trap the spell contained would be activated. So why was he able to hold it and not be trapped by it?

Was it because he'd closed his eyes when he picked it up? Aranya had done the same.

Whatever the case, he had to get rid of it *now.* It didn't matter that they wouldn't be able to investigate it. Not if it was going to kill them.

As Delan's grappling hands came reaching for him, Kai remembered a lake they'd passed nearby. He couldn't reach it in one jump, but—

He vanished right before Delan reached the stone. And, because he hadn't angled himself properly, found himself a mere foot away on the opposite side of a tree. Growling, he evanesced again and again, cutting through the forest. Forest evanescing was just the *worst.* He finally picked up speed the thinner the trees became, until, at long last, he reappeared on the edge of the lake. His knees nearly sagged in relief. With an inarticulate cry, he raced toward the lake and hurled the black stone as far as he could into the lake.

Human eyes would never see the wretched thing again.

When he'd made it back to their camp, Aranya was saddling her mount, and Delan was furiously throwing loose items in his saddlebag, his face an utter storm cloud.

None of them said anything. Not as they disguised their campsite and mounted up for another long day ahead.

CHAPTER 27

"I SMELLED IT," growled Delan. He'd been even sourer than Kai for the last hour, refusing to talk as they mounted up and continued on their way. There had been no more investigation of the snare after Kai had gotten rid of it.

"Smelled what?" asked Aranya.

"On the lure. There was a smell that I caught a whiff of in Lord Zuan's office."

"So . . . whoever set this lure was there when Lord Zuan was abducted?"

Delan nodded grimly. "Your theory might not be far off. A siren could have aided in the guardian's abduction."

"And if Kang Lei was the one who did—"

"We don't know that," snapped Delan.

Aranya flinched unintentionally, and could almost feel Kai's eyes on her back. Judging her for being so easily ruffled. She drew in a deep breath and forced her shoulders to relax. "It seems like we should try to confirm that if we can . . .?"

"It would save us some money if we spent the night in Zushui," Kai said from the back. "Aranya and I both have tenements. You could stay with me, Delan. Then we wouldn't have to sleep outside or rent a set of rooms at an inn."

Aranya, eyes bugged, twisted in her saddle to peer back at him. One of his eyebrows raised in response. She chewed on her lip, trying to decide if she should mouth a quick, *"Thank you,"* but when he rolled his eyes, she shot him a glare instead and faced forward again in her saddle.

"We'll stop," growled Delan. "Send a message and then be on our way."

"Thank you!" she cried, a grin bursting out across her face. If they weren't mounted atop horses, she might have flung her arms around him and embraced him. But it was better this way; such a display would not be very professional.

She could hardly contain her excitement as they traveled into the afternoon. Behind the excitement, however, was a kernel of worry. What if . . .? There were too many "what-ifs" to give thought to each. She tried not to consider them, tried to focus on the relief that she could see Ye Ye again and ensure he was alright.

The result was that she grew more jittery by the hour, fiddling with her reins, adjusting her robes, inspecting her knives for nothing, and smacking her neck at the barest touch of anything that could possibly be a bug.

Finally, they crested a hill and down in the small valley lay the city of Zushui. The surface of Kankhai Lake glittered in the late afternoon sun, becoming a light source itself.

"Try not to go galloping across the plains, please," Delan said with a small smile. Apparently, the hours had taken the edge off his sour mood.

She grinned at him and tightened her grip around the leathery reins in her hands. "I'm doing my best."

A mumble from behind her made her whirl in her saddle to look back at Kai.

"What did you say?" she said, already bristling.

He fought his smile, but it was a losing battle. His face split into a full grin, his eyes dancing with amusement. "I said nothing," he replied, eyebrows arched in false innocence.

"Yes, you did! What did you say? It was mean, wasn't it?"

Delan sighed from the front and waved his hand in the air. "Enough of your bickering or you'll force me to send a message of my own to Suguan. One saying my comrades are too busy fawning over each other to do their job well."

Aranya balked. "*Fawning*? Over *him*? What is . . . How could you possibly . . . There's no way—"

Delan turned and smirked at her. He'd just goaded her! He suddenly looked more like Kai than he ever had. She shut her mouth and glared at her horse's neck. It seemed to sense the mood of its rider because its ears flattened irritably.

When they arrived in the city, and Aranya vaulted out of her saddle, Kai grabbed its lead as Delan turned his horse toward the postal station to send the message. They might have shared a brief glance when Aranya sputtered, "Does this mean . . . I can go?" She didn't know for sure, however, because she was racing away to her tenement, her satchel bouncing at her hip.

At the sight of that familiar building, her heart skipped ahead several beats until it was nearly bursting in her chest. She skittered to a stop in front of the gate, swung it open, and practically leapt across the small yard to the door.

It opened before she could turn the handle.

"Ah, Sun Aranya, it's good you're back early, because we have business to settle."

Her head jerked upward. There, in the doorway, stood the angular figure of her landlord, Xu Lim. Immediately, she bristled.

"What do you want?" she growled, forcing herself to step back and not shove past him. Forced her hands behind her back so he wouldn't see the bulge of her claws as she fought her instinct to shift.

"Six tangus. Your grandfather keeps tearing up my yard, trying to garden. It's getting out of hand, and if you don't pay the fine, I'll evict you both."

She stared at him, blinking. Injustice roiled in her blood, pounding in her ears, but she *had* to master herself. Lim noticed, and his eyes narrowed.

"Careful, *warden*, else I inform your supervisor about the fight you and your fellow warden had in my yard here."

"Six tangus?" she gasped. "But I don't . . . I don't have that. I will have it soon once I complete this . . . Once I get paid."

Lim looked taken aback, as though not expecting this submissive answer. He quickly composed himself, straightening his spine and arching his neck so he could stare down his nose at her. "You have two days."

He slammed the door in her face.

Aranya stayed there for several minutes, staring at the closed door. Then, with a groan, she covered her face with her hands. Even if she were to request advance payment for this mission, it could never arrive in two days. Especially if they were only staying one night here.

There was no time to hunt for another tenement before they left at dawn tomorrow, much less time to move her grandfather. She couldn't ask Na to move him or help with the fine, could she?

She already asked too much of Na.

But perhaps . . .

If Xu Lim really needed them to be tenants or he'd have an empty room, could she bluff him out of retracting the fine? It was risky, of course, but her options were slim.

"I'll tell him we cannot afford the fine and that we'll have to move," she whispered. "But if I'm wrong and he *does* have other people looking to rent, then I'll have to move out. *Ugh*."

She dragged her hands down her face and let them fall to her sides. She lifted her eyes to the door before her, and with a deep breath, pushed it open. Their room was shortly down the hall, and she hurried toward it.

She lifted her hand to knock, but paused. Her head drooped, anxiety and failure coiling in her gut, tight as a spring ready to explode. She couldn't let Ye Ye worry; she wouldn't let him see how anxious she was.

Tap, tap, tap.

It was strange to stand outside her own door, twiddling her fingers while waiting for admittance. But she'd given Na her key.

"It's me, Aranya," she called.

There was a rasp like a bolt sliding away, but the door didn't open. Hesitantly, Aranya turned the knob and gave a push. There, standing in his human form a few feet away, was her grandfather.

"Ye Ye!" she cried, rushing into the room and flinging her arms around him.

He chuckled, a low, grating sound. "My little sunflower is back home."

"Only for the night," she confessed, pulling back. "Has Na been taking care of you?"

"Someone's been taking mighty good care of me . . . I don't remember her name."

A whoosh of air released from Aranya's tight chest, and she wrapped her arms around her grandfather again. Hunched as he was with age, he still was taller than her and even though she took care of him, she always felt like a small girl again when they embraced.

"I wanted to make sure you were doing well," she said. "Here, why don't you sit? I've been hearing that you've been gardening recently."

"Oh yes, yes, yes." His smile was expansive, showing his few remaining teeth. "I'm glad you're home."

"Just for tonight," she reminded him.

He chuckled. "I'm glad you're home."

The corners of her mouth lifted, but she couldn't stop her brow from creasing in worry. Once she had him sitting on his mat by the fire, she stoked the flames and found that Na had restocked the woodpile. Gratitude welled in her heart.

"Have you eaten? Shall I fix you something?"

"Oh, no. I reckon I haven't." More titters.

Na hadn't fed him when she checked on him? Aranya pursed her lips but got to her feet and went to the part of their tenement that functioned as a kitchen.

"Once I'm back for good," she mumbled under her breath, "I'm unpacking this place completely. I'll make it more welcoming and comfortable."

She bustled about for a while, making soup and tidying up as best she could. When she handed a warm, filled bowl to Ye Ye, he chuckled and took it.

"I'm not hungry," he said with a grin. "But the bowl sure is warm."

"You're not hungry? Why not?"

"The other lady . . . the one who has been visiting me . . . she made me something."

"So you *did* eat?"

Ye Ye only chuckled in response.

Aranya's own soup, though little more than broth, went down heavy around the knot in her throat. Ye Ye bent happily over the steaming bowl, its contents untouched. She managed to say, "Well, enjoy the warmth, Ye Ye."

By the time she'd settled him into bed—this time in his cat form—and taken care of the dishes, she couldn't hold herself together. She picked up her cloak from the rack by the door, went to the farthest corner of the tenement, and pressed the fabric into her face.

She didn't want to wake Ye Ye with her crying.

The scratchy folds caught her tears and muffled the sounds of her sobs. Had she simply been so unaware of his decline because she saw him every day? And now that she'd been away for a few weeks, she saw the stark reality more clearly?

If she left him tomorrow . . . would he still be here when she returned?

It was Kai who knocked on her door far too early the next morning. She dragged herself away from the sleeping bundle she'd been stroking by the fire, shouldered her satchel, and drew in a deep breath through her nose.

She closed the door softly and followed behind Kai's tall form through the dark hallway of the tenement, their steps creaking on the bowed floorboards. He was like a shadow ahead of her, looming and silent.

Sometimes she forgot what they were to each other.

In the middle of battles, of saving each other's lives, of secret missions, it was easy to forget that he was the reason she had to leave her grandfather. If he hadn't shown up at Zushui Wardpost, she'd have taken her position as a warden, would have been properly trained so she wasn't making mistakes, wasn't feeling the need to prove herself. She would have studied and learned and succeeded, just like she'd done at the Academy.

But Kai, who could have had any number of appointments, being an evanescer, had wanted *this* one. Hers. A humble wardenship. And how was a partial shapeshifter supposed to compete with an evanescer? He was the reason she didn't have the appointment she earned, the reason she couldn't pay the fine.

Despite how he might act at times, Shi Kai wasn't her friend. He wasn't her comrade either. He was her rival—her enemy. And he stood in the way of everything she wanted. It was a bitter realization, but it was true.

CHAPTER 28

KAI COULDN'T HELP but notice how sullen and quiet Aranya was as they mounted up. Even Delan shot him a glance as if to ask, *"What's wrong with her?"*

At first, he thought she was just upset about her grandcat, though he wasn't sure why. Then, when she snapped at him for no reason, he wondered if he'd done something mean in her dreams last night. It wasn't until she stepped away to talk to her landlord before they left that it finally hit him what was wrong.

Right—the fine that she couldn't pay.

When she came back, her expression was bewildered and relieved. She said nothing as she swung into the saddle of her horse, and Kai tried to pretend he wasn't measuring every inch of her reaction, from her parted lips to the swollen skin beneath her lower lashes, to the slight sag of her shoulders. The way her head tilted forward.

He wasn't sure how her conversation with the landlord went, or what that fool Lim had told her, but clearly he'd kept his mouth shut about the important part.

Kai couldn't have Aranya misinterpreting his actions if she knew he'd paid the fine for her. He didn't want her trying to puzzle through his motivations, trying to figure out if there was anything between them. Because there *wasn't*. He just couldn't help his remorse that he was the cause of her difficult situation—even if *she* was the cause of *his* difficult situation.

The difference was that he could help her. She couldn't help him.

He didn't need her knowing any of that, though. So he set his face forward before she could look up and find him staring.

It was after two more days on their trail and two nights of Delan destroying both Aranya and Kai in wei-chi, that Delan shot his nose in the air, thrill suddenly ringing his pupils in white, and urged his horse faster.

Kai turned a raised eyebrow Aranya's way, but she seemed to be almost pointedly *not looking* at him as she kicked her horse after Delan's. Something had changed in Zushui, and it seemed like it was more than the fine.

"Seven valleys!" cried Aranya from ahead.

He wrinkled his forehead, then followed after them, not rushing his mount on the rocky terrain. He crested the rise, sun beating down on him, and swept his gaze over the scene below.

Delan and Aranya had both dismounted in front of a tangle of browned, twisted vines. Delan dropped to his knees, crawling around on all fours as he eagerly sniffed the area. Aranya, on the other hand, walked cautiously among them, tugging on the ones still hanging from the trees above them.

"What is this?" Kai asked, staying atop his horse.

"Zuan Wan," she said, not looking at him. "Delan said he smells him on these vines. They're magic."

"They *were* magic," said Delan, getting to his feet at the trunk of the biggest tree and pointing at its gnarled roots sticking out from the ground. "The pressure point has been destroyed. A sword or something else was thrust into the dirt here. I bet if we dug it up, we'd find the curse anchor."

"A trap," said Kai.

"And I smell three distinct scents besides the guardian's. Three I've never smelled before. They're strong on some of these vines—like they were caught."

Aranya's eyes widened, her mouth dropping open. "You know what this means, then, right?"

Delan heaved a sigh, straightening and planting one hand on his belt. "I'm afraid we don't. Care to enlighten us, shifter?" he asked dryly.

"This is *another* trap on this path north. First, the siren's lure. Now, one set by Zuan Wan himself."

"You're saying that this proves yet again that someone doesn't want us following this trail?"

"I'm *saying* that . . . it seems like, *if* Kang Lei was the one to set the siren lure, and Zuan Wan was the one to set this one, then what if we've been wrong this whole time?"

Kai crossed his arms over his chest, furrowing his brow as he tried to guess where she was going with this. His horse shifted beneath him, its head dropping to sniff between rocks for shoots of sweet grass.

"How so?" asked Delan skeptically.

Aranya drew a deep breath, eyes brighter than they'd been since they'd decided to stop at Zushui. "What if everything in Shaanet was a lie? What if the shambles of his office was staged?"

"There were other scents there besides his. Blood."

"But what if he *planted* it all? What if he wasn't taken against his will? We keep talking like Kang Lei would be the solution to overpowering him, but who overpowered *her*? Unless she was doing it of her own free will, in which case, I can't think of a single reason why she would want to kidnap Zuan Wan on her way to desert to Butagin."

Too complicated. Kai wasn't fully tracking. It reminded him of what it was like to plot how to escape Suguan after his graduation, trying to think through how his family would respond, how they would try to find him, how he could anticipate their moves and cover his trail.

It hurt his mind then, and this hurt his mind now.

"We don't have enough evidence to prove any motive at this point," said Delan. "We don't even know for certain that Kang Lei set that lure."

"But how likely is it that anyone *else* set it?"

"Unlikely."

"See?"

"Doesn't mean you can go around making assumptions! I like how you're thinking this through, but we simply don't know enough yet to draw conclusions. What we know is that Zuan Wan and Kang Lei are both missing, and a snare that was definitely set by Zuan Wan was left on the path he seems to have gone down since his disappearance. And there was another snare left, which *might* have been set by Kang Lei."

"And the dead body," added Kai helpfully.

Delan sighed. "And the dead body. Let's mount back up. There might be answers for us at the next city's postal station. When I sent that message to Suguan about our latest discoveries, I included a note saying that we would be stopping at Gebei to check for any return messages, since it was on the way."

"Gebei?" Kai blurted. His stomach dropped straight to his toes, his pulse ratcheting up a dozen notches, so fast he could hardly think.

Aranya and Delan both twisted in their saddles to look back at him. The color must have drained from his face, because she startled and her eyes widened.

"Kai?" she asked softly.

"What's the matter?" Delan said, frowning.

What was wrong? What was *wrong*? Only absolutely *everything.* His throat bobbed, and he looked off to one side, avoiding their gazes. "We cannot stop anywhere else? *Anywhere* else?"

Delan's jaw worked, staring hard at Kai. "Um . . . no. I said we would be at Gebei, so we must stop at Gebei."

Aranya watched Kai closely, the sudden twitching of his hands on his reins, his rapid blinking, the hitch in his breathing. Then her eyes lifted to his slowly. "Is your family in Gebei?"

He would have preferred if she'd taken her *jiaun* out of its holster and shot him straight through the chest than say those words aloud.

"Family?" Delan crossed his arms. "I gather you don't have the same sort of relationship with your family that our little companion does?"

Kai couldn't respond. His throat had closed, his lungs so tight he could barely breathe.

"Sorry, boy, but we've got no choice. Perhaps if you'd warned me in advance that you didn't want to stop at Gebei, I would have done another city. Alas, it cannot be helped now. Any other cities we need to avoid henceforth?" Delan asked, looking between them, eyebrow still arched.

Aranya shook her head. Kai merely glowered. No, there were no other cities he needed to avoid. Just Gebei. Just dragon-blasted, phoenix-cursed Gebei.

CHAPTER 29

ARANYA CHEWED ON her lip, the suffocating silence of their party punctuated only by the crackle of the fire. Not even she dared to say a word to lighten the mood. Kai had retreated into himself, pale as death, and hadn't spoken since earlier this afternoon. Not even when Delan spoke directly to him.

When Delan suggested a game of wei-chi, she quickly agreed. Anything to take her mind off the dark turns her imagination had taken during the uneventful afternoon, wondering why Kai would be so afraid to visit his family. Even if things were awkward, or strained, surely it wouldn't elicit such . . . *terror*.

But that was Kai. Always keeping his secrets close.

"You can play black again," said Delan.

Aranya nodded, took the little basket of black stones, and stared at the board. After a few seconds, she blinked, shook herself, and placed her first stone. Delan moved. Then it was her turn. His turn again. Back to her.

Maybe Kai had been abused as a child, and now going near his family brought back those terrible memories. Was that why he'd been running from them? Or—

"Your move," said Delan.

She blinked again. "I just moved."

He tapped his white piece on the board. "I played this. It's your turn now."

"Oh." She played her next piece. Maybe Kai's family had captured *mó guǐ* for illegal pets and Kai didn't like them. She almost snorted at that idea. Or maybe . . . hadn't he said his father had died? What if his mother had killed his father? What if Kai was afraid she'd do the same to him?

"Are you sure you want to play it there?"

She looked up. Delan's forehead creased more, and he nodded toward the stone she'd played.

"I'm being nice. Giving you a chance to rethink that move," he said.

She stared at it. "What's wrong with it?"

He sighed, placed his next stone, and plucked five of her pieces off the board. "You need to anticipate my moves. What would I do? Then you act accordingly. Catch me off guard." When she nodded and placed her next stone, Delan shook his head and sighed again, playing his piece and capturing more of hers. She went to keep playing, but his block-shaped hand landed on hers. She looked up to find him looking at her with concern. "You need sleep," he said.

He swept the pieces into their drawstring bag, folded up the board, and tucked them away, not even offering to play with the brooding Kai. "Tomorrow, we'll need to stop to bathe somewhere. You two reek so badly I can hardly breathe within a li of your presence."

She stayed up to guard the campsite, staring emptily into the dancing flames before her as the two men laid down and jerked blankets up to their chins. Delan groaned his way through his movements, like he was twenty years older than he was. Kai hardly made a single sound as he turned his back to them both. She shouldn't feel a shred of pity for her rival. Not when this was all his fault. Not when he was still her rival.

It was a miracle he could even fall asleep while Delan snored as loud as a donkey before it was fed. That was the only thing that kept Aranya awake at her post, fighting the drowsiness and trying to ignore the incessant aching of her limbs.

She should have noticed when Kai's blankets suddenly fluttered to the ground, the body beneath vanishing into nothing. But she didn't.

Not until a hand clamped over her mouth.

Aranya's every instinct flared to life, adrenaline rushing through her blood like a torrent. She flicked her hands into talons just as her wrist was grabbed, wrenched behind her.

"Don't make a sound," Kai growled under his breath. "Come with me. Sheath your claws."

She stood, whirling on him as her heart pounded so hard it pulsed against her temples. What she saw when she turned wasn't the pale, terrified façade she'd carefully peeked at all afternoon.

No, in the moonlight, Kai's face was hard as flint. Hazel eyes glittered with leaping bursts of fire, shadowed beneath his chiseled brow. He suddenly seemed taller, much taller. Was it because they stood so close? She tilted her head back, meeting the sharpness of his gaze.

"What?" she whispered.

He didn't answer, only turned and stalked toward the trees. Away from the fire. Away from Delan. In two steps, he'd been swallowed up in the night, and she could only barely make out the movement of his cloak.

Warning thrummed down her spine, prickling the back of her neck. Something knotted in her stomach—something she couldn't quite distinguish. Thrill and fear often felt alarmingly similar.

Aranya hurried after him, talons itching beneath her skin, ready for anything.

Anything . . . except Kai grabbing her by the shoulders and hissing in her ear, "*Why* did you mention my family to Delan?"

She flinched, and the burning beneath the tenors of his voice sent her claws fleeing. Shame turned her neck hot, but it didn't stop her from flinging his hands off her and stumbling backward. Into the trunk of a tree.

"You never said not to!" she hissed right back.

"Am I supposed to spell everything out for you? If I clearly don't want to talk about something, then maybe I don't want people like Delan prying into my personal business."

"Delan is our comrade! And I hardly said anything! I just asked if your family was from there. It was your face that gave the rest away!"

Not that she knew what *the rest* was.

He jerked his head to the side, a muscle feathering in his clenched jaw. And Aranya was done dancing around the truth.

"What *is* it about your family?" she demanded, refusing to let her cheeks heat any further. She hadn't done anything wrong! "Why do you refuse to talk about them? Why do you hide from them? Is it just because you don't—"

He evanesced into her face and clapped a hand over her mouth, eyes blazing. "Stop *talking* about them!"

She bit his finger. He jerked back, but only for a split second. The next second, he'd come closer, close enough that his knee bumped into hers when he snatched her jaw with his hand and forced her to tilt her head back. To look at him.

Her claws were out in a flash, one pressed threateningly against his chest, the other just beneath his ribs. Almost an embrace. Kai didn't flinch. The intensity in his eyes never faltered, not as he stared her down, lips parted enough to reveal teeth. She was so caught in that gaze, in her palm on his chest, claws slowly curling inward to pierce the fabric of his robes, that she wasn't paying attention to where his other hand went.

Not until something sharp pressed to her neck.

She sucked in a breath. Then lowered her brows into a glare, pressing her talons harder against him. Threatening him without words. Night wind caught strands of his hair, of hers, the dark tendrils dancing between them.

"Would you believe," Kai said, his voice suddenly much deeper, edged in something unfamiliar, "that I hide these things to protect you?"

She couldn't help her snort, or the wild grin she flashed up at him. "Then what's a knife doing at my throat?"

"Preventing a misunderstanding."

She chuckled—low, long, and dry.

"Lower your talons, and I'll lower my knife."

"You first, evanescer."

Behind Kai's head, the sliver of moon drifted behind a cloud, and his face grew darker. She could barely make out his nose, his mouth, the planes of his cheekbones. The only way she knew his face dipped closer to hers was the warmth blowing across her lips, and the gleam of eyes like a wild cat's drifting nearer. His hand fell from her jaw, slid behind her neck, fingers twining with her hair.

He was going to kiss her. It was a bone-shattering realization, one that dragged a gasp from deep inside her, that made her eyes fly wide and her stomach lurch.

Did she want him to kiss her?

No. Maybe?

"Promise me," he whispered, and when he spoke, his lips briefly brushed hers. "Promise me you will stop asking questions about my family."

"Why?" The word was breathless, caught up in the wind that swept the night around them.

He swallowed, the soft huffs of his breaths against her lips. Still, he did not kiss her. Did not lean forward that one fraction of an inch more and press his mouth to hers.

But he wanted to. The hand at the back of her neck, that pulled gently, tilting her face up toward his, told her he wanted to. It was the knife in his other hand, pressed to soft flesh where her pulse throbbed with a heady rhythm, that held him back.

As it should.

The clouds parted, and the dusting of moonlight that fell across the forest was enough for Aranya to see when Kai pulled away, a rueful smirk playing at the corners of his mouth. The gaze he settled on her was black with flecks of gold. His knife eased away from her throat.

"Because I think your grandfather prefers you alive."

Aranya drew her hands to her chest, talons vanishing in an instant. Strange, that her pulse still hadn't calmed even when Kai backed away another step. Stranger that she should feel any measure of loss. Of *disappointment.*

She had to clear her throat before she could manage, "And since when were you concerned about my grandfather's preferences?"

The tiny smirk on his face widened. Hardened. "You just had your hand pressed to my chest. Could you not feel my heartbeat?"

And then the shadows swallowed up her rival in one big gulp.

CHAPTER 30

IT'S JUST A quick errand," Delan told Kai as they rode into the city. "We won't be long."

Kai nodded, his face impassive. His knuckles were white, however, around the reins. "Indeed," he only said, his voice crisp.

Aranya swallowed.

Kai had put up a fight again when they reached the bounds of the city, asking if he could stay behind. Delan seemed to be still mad that Kai had withheld this information from him, because he wouldn't budge. And Kai had looked dangerously close to vanishing straight out of his saddle.

He stayed, however.

Aranya bit her lip but avoided looking at Kai. She doubted he would appreciate that. She was trying to decide if she ought to ignore him or attempt to goad him into irritation about something else—something to get his mind off his fear—when a sight on the streets of Gebei made her freeze.

It was a blind man. He was old, probably older than Ye Ye, with a white beard down to his belly. On either side of him, a man and a woman gripped his arms. Slowly, with soft coaxing, they helped him descend three steps from a house's deck to the dusty street. Bouncing around waiting for him was a little girl no more than five years old.

"Play with me, Ye Ye!" the girl cried.

"He's going to sit here and listen to you play. Oh! Be careful, dumpling! Don't knock into your grandfather!" the woman said to the girl.

The old man grinned a crinkly smile, his eyes staring off into nothing, hardly moving at all.

Aranya watched as they rode past the scene, the breath stolen from her lungs. The girl bounded around the edge of the street, practically running in circles around her parents and grandfather.

"It's time to play! Time to play!" she cried.

The scene grew blurrier by the second. Soon, it wasn't feasible to keep craning her neck to watch, and she faced forward again. That direction was blurry too.

Kai said something beside her.

"Huh?" she croaked, swallowing.

"I *said,* your hair looks horrible."

"What?" she snapped, swiping her sleeve on her nose and blinking rapidly.

"Must I repeat myself a third time?"

"No, I heard you! My hair looks *what*? Say it again!"

"Absolutely hideous."

"Seven valleys, *why* would you ever say such a thing?"

His eyes flickered, coming into clearer focus. Though tension lined his face, his mouth was turned up in a smirk. "Because it's true. I thought you should like to know."

She sniffled as she glowered at him, the hard lump in her throat easing. "It looks the same as ever."

"Not true. It's wild and matted and now that I think of it, it could use a trim. If you're not comfortable cutting it yourself . . ." He trailed off, waggling his eyebrows.

Her jaw fell open. She shoved her hand into the saddlebags, searching for anything to throw at him. Just as quickly, she stopped, realization suddenly hitting. She shoved a rebellious strand of hair behind her ear and peered at him. Then at Delan, who rolled his eyes.

She straightened in her saddle and abandoned her outrage. "I know what you're doing," she muttered.

His eyes glittered. "I'm sure I have no idea what you're speaking of."

Now it was her turn to roll her eyes. But inside, she couldn't help but be grateful. Kai said nothing more, and she could not mistake the strain he tried to hide, yet he had set that aside to make her feel better.

Regardless of his methods, she was thankful.

When they reached the postal station, Delan ordered them to stay with the horses and keep out of trouble. He gave each of them stern glances before heading inside, as if they were toddlers.

They dismounted to water their horses, and it thrilled Aranya beyond words to have a few minutes of not sitting in a saddle. When Kai's silence stretched out further, his face growing more pensive as his eyes constantly roamed the area, she exhaled through her nostrils.

She said, "Delan's beard is getting longer."

"You'll have to do better than that."

"Huh?"

"You'll not bait me on stupid conversation."

Silence.

Very well, she would try another tactic. One that would definitely work. "Why are you so nervous about running into your family? It's only the postal station. Surely they're not monitoring it."

His jaw flexed. "We're not discussing this."

"Oh?" She grinned, sidling up closer. "Come on, Shi Kai. You've created all this mystery surrounding your family. I wouldn't be half as curious if you would have simply told me a few things here and there that wasn't giving away important information. But you're determined to make sure I know that the family is off-limits for discussion. As an evanescer, one would think you'd know more about secret keeping."

His nostrils flared, and she couldn't help her triumphant grin.

"Aranya," he said, his tone humming with warning.

"What? If I'm not careful, you'll pull out a knife and—"

"Why, do my eyes deceive me?" a new voice cut into their conversation. "Could it *possibly* be that the illustrious Shi Kai has favored us with his presence?"

Kai snapped upright, his body going rigid. Aranya whirled on the newcomer, her own heart leaping.

Striding down the street toward them, in glittering robes and an ornate cloak that fluttered behind him, was a tall, thin young man. The warmth of summer had yet to wear off. Was the heavy cloak simply for show, to make his person wider and more menacing? His stride was heavy and confident, his wide smile dazzling in his handsome face. He had no litter, no horse, nothing nearby. Just him, a wealthy and beautiful man.

A man who looked eerily like the one standing next to her.

Her jaw dropped, her eyes sliding up from the approaching form to Kai's ashen face. She recognized the man from the Academy.

"Just disappear," she whispered.

"Too late," he growled back.

The man spread his arms as he came, his grin going wider and wider with each step. "Oh, my brother, how I have missed you! We've been wondering where you've been all this time! Mother has been beside herself. What a joy to see you again!"

At first, Aranya thought he must be too dimwitted to see Kai's pallor, but no, he *did* notice, and it almost seemed to make his creepy smile wider. He embraced a stiff and unmoving Kai, who didn't bother returning the affection.

"My friends told me they saw you enter the city, so I knew I had to come immediately," he said, gesturing grandly to the surrounding city. "I only wish you'd given us notice so we could properly welcome you."

Kai said nothing.

"Boring as always," the brother said, grinning. Then his attention swiveled to Aranya. "Well, who is this young lady you've brought with you?"

He didn't recognize her.

Aranya smiled hesitantly, glancing more at Kai than his brother. But Kai wasn't giving any indication of how she ought to behave, so she smiled a little brighter and bowed. "My name is Zou Ming. It's a pleasure to meet you."

Kai blinked in surprise, but she glanced his way fast enough to see him duck his head to hide a tiny smile. It emboldened her enough to flash a full grin at his brother.

"Shi Yong, at your service," he replied, fingers twinkling with jewels. "How charming you are. My, my, brother, what a pretty little thing you've brought with you."

Aranya matched his expression with just a smidge of sauciness. "You flatter, good sir."

Kai's eyes were darting between them, but he no longer looked so terrified. More . . . bewildered. He cleared his throat and said, "I trust Mother is in good health?"

Yong drew his eyes away from Aranya's face slowly, returning his attention to his brother. For a split second, his façade cracked enough for a furrow to appear between his brows. "She would be even better if you inquired of her health directly. She has missed you so."

Aranya couldn't help the shiver that raced down her spine at his tone. She maintained her smile, however, and Yong returned his attention to her. Boldly, he reached out and gently took her hand, bringing it to his lips. “You must give us the honor of your presence at our humble abode. Even if it is just for the night.”

She might have blushed, except that she was prepared for this maneuver. With a coy chuckle, she pulled her hand back and said, “To be sure, sir, but I fear we have other obligations. Otherwise, we wouldn’t hesitate to accept.”

“Other obligations?” Yong’s eyes glittered. “What, pray, could keep you from enjoying our hospitality?”

This conversation was dangerous ground. Aranya needed to watch her tongue carefully. She opened her mouth, about to respond to his question, when Delan exited the postal station, and though his face had only a second ago been hard, grim, and determined, it now flickered with confusion as he saw them.

The last thing they needed was Delan saying something before he knew what was happening. Thus, she flashed another huge grin and exclaimed, “Chang! Look who we ran into: Kai’s brother, Shi Yong! You’re just in time to meet him!”

Delan looked up, his eyes meeting hers first in confusion, then trailing up to see the tall, elegant man standing behind her. Hesitation flashed in his gaze as he glanced toward Kai. Just as quickly, however, he smiled winsomely and bowed. “Ah, Shi Yong, it’s a pleasure indeed to meet the fine brother of our comrade. He has spoken very fondly of you.”

Kai coughed.

Yong’s eyebrows shot up, but he said, “Well, I’m very happy to hear that. Please, I was just inviting you all over for tea and a meal. I can see that you are quite occupied with important things, but my mother and I would be honored if all three of you would join us.”

Kai straightened, still stiff, but seeming less tongue-tied. “I wish we could, dear brother, but—”

“Nonsense!” Yong’s smile curved upward. His attention turned to Aranya. “You must come rest after your long journey. Once you have refreshed yourself, then you can proceed on your way.”

"While your offer is generous, we could never dream of trespassing on your hospitality—" Delan started to say.

"Trespassing? Why, the notion! This is my dear brother, and if you are my brother's friends, then you are also mine."

Kai glared at the dirt.

Yong leaned toward Kai, who didn't meet his gaze. His eyes trailed up and down Kai's traveling clothes, the partially concealed weapons on his person, and he smiled devilishly. His voice was edged in threat.

"I *insist*."

Aranya glanced between the tense stares of Yong, Kai, and Delan. She had to do something so weapons didn't start flying. But what escape could be made?

"Here, my guards will personally escort you. I wish I could escort you myself, but alas I must hurry back to prepare for your reception. Mother will be so delighted!"

With a snap of his fingers, armed guards appeared seemingly from nowhere, surrounding them as Yong smiled warmly. Delan's returning smile was just as warm, and if Aranya didn't know better, she would have bought the ruse.

"We would be honored to join you for a meal," Delan said smoothly. "Then we will be on our way."

"Your generous escort is unnecessary," said Kai, sweeping past them all and striding down the street. "I haven't forgotten the way."

Aranya blinked at his turned back, barely remembering at the last second to send another smile Yong's way before grabbing the lead of her horse and Kai's and hurrying after him. She'd never been particularly adept at reading people, but staring at Kai's back, watching his firm step, she thought he looked like he walked as though facing his own death.

"Truly," Delan was saying with a laugh to Yong, "the guards aren't necessary."

"Very well. As long as no one gets lost along the way!" said Yong.

The guards withdrew as Delan and Aranya followed after Kai, and when she chanced a glance back, Yong had disappeared.

"How do we get out of this?" she said under her breath to Delan.

Though his face remained mild, there was no mistaking the clenching of his jaw. "Unfortunately, you don't just waltz away from threats like that."

"Threats?"

"He was threatening to take you and I by force if Kai didn't comply. Hence the fact that Kai is halfway down the street and not evanescing away. Stay alert, shifter. Things might get dicey. Let us hope Kai can quickly satisfy his familial obligations so that we may be on our way."

Under his breath, he cursed softly, "*Spitfire*."

Aranya tried not to look like a country bumpkin as she gaped at the mansion belonging to Kai's family. It was like a palace itself, the tallest building in the city besides the pagoda, and inlaid with nearly as much gold.

She peeked at Kai as they mounted the steps. A few strands of hair fell in his face, his eyes set before him, each movement purposeful.

Yong and Kai were night and day, two brothers from two different worlds. Though she never would have thought Kai looked poor, he seemed practically a beggar next to Yong's opulence and elegance. Now more than ever, she desperately wanted to know what had made him give up all of this. Had an overbearing brother been enough to make Kai choose to sacrifice every comfort to become a no-name warden in a random city?

Somehow, she didn't think it was as simple as that. At least now she knew that cockiness ran in the family.

"Both of you, stop staring at me," Kai muttered.

"What viper's nest have we walked into, boy?" Delan growled. "What aren't you telling us?"

"The less you know, the better."

Aranya rolled her eyes. "And I suppose the less your brother knows, the better?"

Kai's eyes were sharp when they shot to hers. "Don't tell them *anything*. And keep quiet. They've got ears everywhere in this dragon-blasted city."

She frowned, but nodded. "Very well."

"Thank you, Zou Ming," Kai said, and his half-smile was rueful. But also . . . *grateful*?

"Don't forget to thank Chang," Delan grumbled with a pointed look at her.

Aranya snickered.

Servants as graceful and elegant as peacocks ushered them inside. Suddenly, she was self-conscious of her grimy robes, her dust-encrusted skin. She reached up a hand toward her hair. Was it as bad as Kai had said it was? She tried to subtly smooth it down, to make it less *wild.*

"Your hair is fine," Kai said.

She glared at him, but when she met his eyes, she saw what lurked behind his increasing confidence. It was like he grew harder, more determined, but those things couldn't hide the fear. And if Aranya could see it after working with him for a scant month, what could his own family discern?

"You might have mentioned that you were practically the prince of Gebei," Delan said dryly.

Kai clenched his jaw. "I am no one's prince."

"Just an evanescing rogue," said Aranya.

They were led down another corridor, the afternoon light filtering through the gilded panels along the wall. The entire place was eerily quiet. The only sounds came from their own footsteps and rustling robes. It took Aranya a minute to realize that the servants escorting them were utterly silent. Their footsteps made no noise on the polished floor, their clothes made no swishing.

A chill crept up her spine, prickled the hairs on her arms.

The servants bowed and opened two grand, polished gold doors. "For your refreshment, my lady," they said.

Aranya had thought they reached the banquet hall. Instead, as she peered through the doors, she found a washroom. Her eyes widened, and she glanced back at her companions in surprise.

Kai stepped to her side and unexpectedly placed a gentle hand on her back as he leaned down toward her ear. "Don't worry, it's safe." Even lower, his voice tickling her skin, he whispered, "Keep smiling."

She blinked, staring up at him, but he nudged her forward. She squared her shoulders and refused to look back as the huge doors closed behind her.

Before her, a deep in-ground pool greeted her. Steam curled off the surface, wrapping around the petals of floating lotuses. The ceiling towered over her, painted sapphire, with glittering windows screened off with ornate patterns. The enormous room was bright, exquisite.

Aranya hadn't moved from the doors, even as Kai's and Delan's footsteps echoed into nothing behind her. She didn't have a chance to adjust to the sight of the huge room, not before silent servant girls dressed in the softest shade of blue—their robes finer than hers by far—approached from nowhere.

"We will assist you, my lady," one of the girls said.

She swallowed, forcing a smile onto her lips. "I . . . I thank you." But her feet remained rooted to the spot, refusing to budge.

The servants stared at her a long moment, as if trying to determine whether to come closer and perhaps scoot her along. Aranya drew a deep breath, and, trying not to allow her own country idiocy to influence her too much longer, stepped to the bamboo screen. When the girls followed, she flashed a wincing smile and said between tight teeth, "I'm perfectly capable of undressing myself, thank you."

They said nothing more, silently drifting away.

Heart pounding much faster than it ought, she quickly peeled away the layers of travel-grimed robes and sweat-slicked underthings.

Then, wrapping her arms around herself, she poked her head out around the screen.

Five pairs of blinking eyes met her gaze.

Aranya let out an uneasy chuckle, scooping up her clothes from the floor and wrapping them around herself. "If you don't mind, I will just slip by . . ." When they didn't move, she pursed her lips and said, "If you would be so kind as to give me some privacy?"

The girls bowed and dissipated out of the room, though Aranya knew they still hovered nearby. Probably watched.

As inviting as the bath looked, she was suddenly wondering if she ought to redress and simply explain to her host that she was afraid to keep them waiting. Would that be offensive? It seemed like it would be offensive. Possibly?

She couldn't risk offending their hosts. She didn't pretend to have a clue what was going on, and it seemed like it was better to play this carefully. Moving hesitantly, she stepped out from behind the screen, scurried to the bath, dropped the robes she used for cover, and slid into the steaming water.

It was too hot. She winced, but she couldn't wait. So she dunked her head under the surface, letting her entire body burn for a second before it adjusted.

She had to work fast. The last thing she wanted to do was linger unclothed anywhere in the house of several evanescers. She tried not to shudder at the memory of Yong's smile.

Before she realized what was happening, the servant girls had emerged and silently shuffled to her. Armed with all manner of brushes, soaps, oils, and lotions, they launched themselves at her with surprising vigor.

"Oh!" Aranya cried, trying to pull away. "I can—"

Her protests were to no avail. Even after she was scrubbed spotless, they practically dragged her out of the water to dress her.

"Wait, I can't wear that!" she cried. "It's far too fancy!"

If they were antagonists rather than servant girls, she could have landed them on their backs and dressed herself in whatever she pleased. But she couldn't use force on them, not even when they practically wrestled her onto a mat before a mirror.

But when they came at her face with paint and kohl, she staunchly refused. When they kept advancing, brushes coming dangerously close, she resorted to shifting one hand into talons and facing them.

"No paint," she said sternly, pointing a claw at each girl. "Absolutely no paint."

The last thing she needed was to be completely unrecognizable to her companions. As the servants finished their ministrations and backed away for Aranya to get a clear look at herself, a voice spoke from behind her.

"Red suits you well."

She flew to her feet, spinning to face Yong leaning against the opposite wall, ankles and arms crossed. His mouth was twisted up in a cocky smirk, and he was very nearly the thinner and taller replica of Kai. He wore rust-colored robes with sapphire and gold trim on the floor-length sleeves and sash. His long hair was partially bound up on top of his head, the rest falling down his back.

Keep smiling.

The thought barely came in time. Aranya caught herself, pressing a hand to her heart and letting out a soft gasp as she smiled. "Forgive me, but I was not expecting to see you, good sir. How long have you stood here?"

The maids were all gone. They seemed to have vanished into nothing. It was just Yong and Aranya now.

He grinned. "Not long."

Not reassuring. She hoped he would take the color of her cheeks as a maidenly blush rather than fury.

Yong evanesced to right in front of her, and if she wasn't used to it with Kai, she would have leapt back in fright. His eyes glittered with the same realization. Perhaps he was disappointed he hadn't startled her.

"The red brocade truly suits you," he said. "The gold accents bring out the fire in your eyes. Lovely. You look like a princess."

Aranya gave a laugh. "You are too kind."

He lifted one eyebrow, reaching out a hand to her face. She flinched as he caught a strand of her done-up hair between his fingers, and he grinned wickedly, clearly happy to have taken her by surprise. "I believe you are the only person to accuse me of being too kind."

A chill raced down her spine, but she chuckled anyway, determined to not let him get the upper hand. "You wish me to think ill of you?"

His eyes were darker than Kai's, and while they flashed with all the same cockiness and mischief, there was something else there as well. He ran his thumb down the lock of hair he held, as though admiring its silkiness. "Today is the first day I have seen you without pigtails."

Her breath caught between her teeth, her smile frozen. "I beg your pardon?"

He tsked. "Unfortunate that you do not remember me."

She gave an uneasy chuckle, stepping backward, so he was forced to let go of her hair. "Remember you? I daresay we only just met, good sir."

"I suppose we did. But it wasn't too long ago that I graduated from the Academy myself. You may not remember me, but I couldn't help but notice the little girl with pigtails who could shapeshift her hands into talons. It's a pleasure to officially meet you, Sun Aranya."

CHAPTER 31

SO MUCH FOR Yong not recognizing her. He grinned like a cat cornering a mouse. "Sun Aranya, yes, it is a pleasure to finally meet you. A pity the true introduction didn't come until now."

Aranya performed an exaggerated bow. At the subtle line of surprise on his brow, she said, "Ought I not bow in greeting during our *true* introduction?"

His face hardened. Her smiles unnerved him then. He must be used to being the only one playing games. He didn't know that Aranya *loved* games because a game was an opportunity to win. Despite how her blood hummed warning in her veins, she turned her back on him and started walking back toward the mirror. As though to admire herself.

In the glass, she watched his eyes narrow at her.

He appeared at her side, his long robes following his movements in a trail of silk. In one fluid motion, he extracted a fan from his voluptuous sleeves and waved it smoothly in front of him. "Please tell me: why, pray, would you introduce yourself as someone else?"

Aranya tossed a quick glance his way, before returning her attention to the mirror, running a finger down the gold embroidery on the hems of her sleeves. "What? Please don't tell me you give your real name to strangers."

"Strangers?" Yong evanesced to the opposite side of her, closer this time. "One could hardly call me a stranger; the brother of your *dear* comrade."

She lifted her chin. "Ahh, I see."

The silence was enough to indicate she'd caught him unawares again. She smiled.

"Pray tell me," she said, turning to face Yong, "when Kai flirted with all those girls at the Academy, did it cause you concern? Between training and class, were you always poking around dark corners, ensuring he only kissed girls of noble birth? Is that what this is? A worried older brother investigating the girl his wayward little brother has been spending time with?"

Yong's jaw clenched, his fanning growing faster as he smiled wider. "If only I had time to keep up with who Kai was kissing in darkened corners at the Academy."

It was a low blow, targeted to hurt. Aranya knew this, and she also knew there was no reason for it to hurt. It *did,* however, yet she laughed and returned a low blow of her own. "It's nigh an entire appointment itself to keep track of Shi Kai's doings."

He snapped the fan shut and vanished.

Aranya was prepared when he reappeared behind her, one hand darting around to grab her throat. She shifted her hands, ducked and twisted, driving her elbow into his side. He vanished. She swiped instinctively with her talons, but he was prepared and caught her wrists behind her. With a growl, she sank and yanked her hands around to her side. He was strong—stronger than she expected. Avoiding his pinning maneuver was so difficult she let out a cry as she sidestepped and landed another elbow blow to his middle.

He caught her upper arm, looped his foot around her ankle, and knocked her to the tiled ground dangerously close to the bath in a flurry of crimson brocade and gold silk. She tried to roll, tried to land a blow to his face, but he dug his knee into her back, using his other leg to stabilize him and hold her. One arm pinned both of hers, rendering her talons useless.

His other hand gripped her throat until she gasped.

"Where has my brother been all this time?" he seethed, sweat dripping off his nose. "It will go better for you if you answer. Truthfully."

Aranya glared at him. "I suppose I can't call you *kind sir* anymore now, can I?"

His fingertips dug into her jaw, the sensitive part by her ear. His smile was animal, not human.

She shouldn't goad him. Not while he had her pinned so helplessly. But adrenaline pounded in her blood, her claws twitching for fight. She grinned between choking gasps. "If you lost him so easily, perhaps you don't deserve to know."

He snarled, clenching his grip tighter. "I can kill you with my bare hands."

She rolled her bulging eyes. "I can kill you with my bare hands *and* my claws. Perhaps if you could loosen a bit, I might,"—she coughed, gasping for air—"be able to demonstrate."

He chuckled, then suddenly laxed his grip and stood up. With glittering eyes, he held out a hand to help her up. She ground her teeth into a smile that was more snarl and accepted, letting him assist her. With as much dignity as she could muster as she swallowed repeatedly and sucked in a huge lungful of air, she straightened her robes. She watched him carefully, refusing to let her guard down.

"I have many ways of getting information," Yong said easily, pulling out his fan again as if they had been chatting over tea and crumpets this entire time. "Do not be deceived, my pretty little Aranya.

I have no intention of letting any of you leave until I know where Kai has accepted his appointment. I know it's not Suguan."

She snorted with more bravado than she had, moving back toward the mirror on shaky limbs. "And what makes you think that?"

He smiled, evanesced right in front of her, and slid his hand to cup the back of her head. She tensed but kept herself from flinching. This far into this strange meeting, and she couldn't afford to show weakness now. She kept her eyes wide open as he leaned in and brushed his lips against her forehead. It took all her strength to keep her hands from shaking uncontrollably. Or from shifting into talons and relieving him of his face.

Yong pulled back with a smile.

"What's it with you two and unasked kisses?" Aranya growled.

As soon as the words left her mouth, she realized her mistake. She clamped her lips shut, desperately trying to not let her eyes close with the sudden realization. Desperately trying not to acknowledge her defeat as Yong's head tilted to one side.

"Kai kissed you?" he asked softly. Knowingly.

Phoenix-scorched tongue. "No, he hasn't," she said hastily, then shrugged in an attempt to play nonchalant and hide her flush. "He hasn't *actually* kissed me."

And those words just made everything worse. She barely withheld her wince as she forced her mouth shut, biting her tongue to force herself *not* to keep babbling. He chuckled, then leaned in again, coming so close that her stomach dropped. "Shall I show you which of us is a better kisser?"

"It doesn't matter," she retorted, twisting her head away from him, "since I'm better than both of you."

He threw back his head and laughed in surprise.

Aranya gritted her teeth and inched backward. It denied every self-preservation instinct not to turn and run.

"I think I shall call you the queen of false bravado," said Yong, still chuckling. "See you soon for our meal. I hope you're hungry."

He winked and vanished.

Aranya's shoulders sagged. She wanted to fall to the floor, quivering with fear and relief—the two far too intertwined to distinguish apart—but she dared not show weakness. Not when he could still be lurking in the shadows, watching her.

Silently, the servant girls emerged from whatever nooks and crannies they'd hid themselves during the fight and set about fixing her mussed hair.

Her nerves would never calm down until they were gone from this wretched place. What in all the seven valleys was going *on* here?

When Aranya was escorted to the meal, unsteady in this unfamiliar outfit, she wasn't expecting the dining hall to be half the size of her bathing chamber. The ceilings were low, decorative screens covering the windows on three sides of the room, with mahogany pillars rising up to meet the gilded ceiling.

It was all gold and wood. More of an intimate setting than a spectacular one.

In the center of the room was a long, low table filled to nearly overflowing with bowls of rice, dumplings, steaming vegetables, an entire roasted swan, and all sorts of other good things. Gold cushions with long glittering tassels surrounded the table.

Delan and Kai stood to one side, Delan dressed the finest she had ever seen. He wore royal blue robes, edged in silver and white embroidery. His sash was all white, a stark yet tasteful contrast to the darkness of his robes.

Kai, on the other hand, wore the same travel clothes they'd been wearing. Simple linen robes and a coarse pair of trousers, his weapons still strapped to his belt and chest.

Both of them looked up when she entered. She gave a quirky bow. "How do I look?" she asked, holding out her arms with the ridiculously long sleeves.

"Lovely, of course," Delan replied, his tone as dry as sand.

Kai said nothing, his eyes sweeping over her before looking straight ahead. At the empty side of the table. At first, she thought his scrutiny of her was disapproving—and perhaps it was—but then she saw the color rise into his cheeks. Aranya narrowed her eyes at him, gathering her skirts in her fists as she sidled up to him and whispered, "I'm going to murder you, Shi Kai."

His attention snapped down to her, his brows furrowed.

"Safe—ha! Safe, indeed," she scoffed. "Next time, I'm going to—"

His eyes flew wide, and his lips parted. "What happened?" he demanded in a low voice.

Delan stepped into the conversation, arms folded across his chest.

"Your brother assaulted me in the bathing chamber, that's all."

"He *what*?" they demanded together. At precisely the same time, they each reached for one of her elbows.

"Oh, quit with that. I'm fine," she said, shrugging off their holds. "At least he had the decency to wait until I was dressed."

Kai's nostrils flared, his jaw clenching and unclenching. He fixed a glare on the door, blowing frustration out his gritted teeth. Then he stormed past them straight toward the double doors, a murderous expression on his face.

Aranya caught his sleeve. "Kai! I said I'm fine! Don't be going off—"

"I did not think he would stoop this low," he growled, looking down at her as he shook her grip off him. But he didn't leave the room. "Fathers! I *hate* him."

Aranya and Delan both stared at Kai, startled by the vehemence in his tone.

"What's going on?" Delan said.

Kai shook his head, turning back to Aranya. "Did he hurt you?"

She barely restrained her instinct to reach up and touch her neck, the bruises hidden beneath her high collar. The last thing she needed was Kai or Delan being furious beyond containment. So, she shook her head and merely said, "He wanted to know about you."

"What did you tell him?" he asked, apprehension flashing across his face.

She glared at him. "Have a little more faith in me, idiot. I didn't tell him anything. He was asking about where you were before now."

"You didn't tell him *anything*?" Kai's eyes widened.

"Um, yes. Nothing about where you were or what we're doing."

There was a pause as he rubbed two fingers into the space between his eyes.

"You didn't tell him anything?" he repeated, as though shocked.

Aranya crossed her arms, not deigning to answer again.

Kai swallowed, eyes meeting hers with sudden earnestness. "My brother can be . . . very persuasive. How . . .?"

"Because she's not an *idiot*," Delan growled.

Aranya's heart warmed despite herself. But she pursed her lips and met Kai's gaze. "But there was one thing that I accidentally said."

Immediately, his body went rigid, eyes flaring.

She closed her eyes, taking a deep breath. "I told him you kissed me."

"You told him *what*?" Kai burst out.

"You *kissed her*?" Delan bellowed. One of his giant square hands shot out and grabbed Kai by the front of his robes, dragging him down to his eye level. "Shi Kai, what in the seven valleys is *wrong* with you? Don't you know—"

"I didn't kiss her!" Kai snapped into Delan's face, throwing his hands wide.

"You basically did! It was close enough to count!" said Aranya.

"I basically did *not*! If you thought that was a kiss, you've clearly never been kissed before. Perhaps I should remedy that, and then at least what you said would be true!"

"Excuse *me*?"

"So *did* you, or *didn't* you kiss her?" demanded Delan.

"I did not!" Kai grabbed Delan's wrist, yanked it off him, then whirled on Aranya. "For all that is good in this world, *why* would you say something like that to Yong?"

"I didn't mean to! It was just a slip of the tongue!"

Delan let out a dry snort.

"Look, I simply made an offhand comment when he kissed me—"

"HE KISSED YOU?" they both cried.

"On the forehead! Good grief—he was only trying to intimidate me! But I'm afraid, now that he thinks . . ." She trailed off, looking anywhere but Kai's face as she bit her lip.

"So . . . are we concerned he will, what? Try to break up the happy couple?" Delan asked, folding his arms and glaring at them.

Kai sighed. "If he thinks she is a weakness of mine, he could try to use her to manipulate me. At least he doesn't have her real name."

Aranya winced, making Kai groan and cover his face with his hand.

"He recognized me from the Academy," she mumbled sheepishly.

Kai scoffed, clenching his fists at his side. "Of course, he did. And if he knows your name, he can track you anywhere with his . . . *sources*. As long as he knows we're together, he can find me."

There was a long pause, and then Aranya whispered, "Why don't you want him to find you?"

The look he gave her was withering. But it was also . . . guarded, somehow. It was like he thought Yong's behavior was self-explanatory enough, even though they both knew that wasn't the main reason.

Just then, the doors opened. Aranya sprang away from Kai's side, sidling up to Delan. Kai straightened, his eyes glazing over as he stared into nothing, and his chin lifted.

The servant announced, "Master Shi Yong and Lady Shi Nuan."

CHAPTER 32

THE MOMENT THAT Lady Shi Nuan entered the room, everything stilled. It seemed the entire world waited: the servants, Aranya, Delan, Kai, even Yong. They waited for *her*.

She entered the room in a susurrus of silk—tall, reed-like, moving with the elegance of a queen, of one who knew her own power and magnitude. Her chin tipped into the air, her defined nose jutting upward. She was beautiful, more beautiful in her later years than many women half her age could ever dream. No wonder both her sons were so handsome.

Delan bowed. Aranya did the same, feeling the weight of her own insignificance pressing down on her shoulders. Suddenly, she was very glad she had opted for the finer garb provided for her rather than insisting upon staying in her filthy clothes.

Kai did not bow. Did not acknowledge his mother's entrance with even a mere blink. He was stone cold, a statue made of ice and granite. Aranya peered up at him, trying to puzzle together what was happening, why he did not address his mother, trying to figure out what he was so afraid of.

"Welcome," said Lady Shi.

Silence. Aranya did not know if she ought to say something in return, or if she should keep her mouth shut. Somehow, the presence of the elegant woman made her think that, perhaps this time, she ought to stay silent.

But Delan wasn't talking, either.

It was Yong who rescued them. "I trust you all have refreshed yourselves and are comfortable?" he asked politely, his gaze coming to rest on her.

She did not falter under that gaze. She returned it defiantly, daring him to test her, to try her, to see that she wouldn't be broken. To see that she would not betray Kai. Even if she didn't know what he hid from, what he was so afraid of, she would not betray him. And least of all to Shi Yong.

"We are much refreshed, yes," said Delan. "We are grateful for your generous hospitality."

Yong's eyes slid to Aranya's, as if looking to her for her own response. She politely ducked her head and said with probably more irony than wise, "Yes, I am much refreshed."

Lady Shi did not smile. Her mouth was drawn in a straight line across her face, her lips painted to be larger than they actually were. Kohl-lined eyes half shut, she sat as if enthroned in the heavens, looking down upon the mere mortals filling the earth.

Yong smiled however and gestured grandly to the table ladened with steaming food. "Please, sit. Let us eat and catch up on the time that we've been apart. And, of course, get to know the guests we are so delighted to host."

Aranya shot a look at Kai, who held so still he hardly seemed to breathe. Delan was the first to sit down, then Aranya followed, and finally Kai. It was Lady Shi who spoke first as they began filling their bowls from the steaming platters in the center of the table.

"My son, how I have missed you," she said with the warmth of an ice cube.

Kai said nothing in response.

When he added food to his bowl, he chose the simplest things. He did not opt for the roasted swan, or any of the other delicacies. Instead, he filled his bowl with rice and vegetables, and a scant amount of seasoned chicken. She, on the other hand, filled her bowl with whatever looked the best. After all, she didn't know when she would ever have a chance like this again to eat such fine foods. She intended to enjoy it.

"I see your manners have only improved," said Yong to Kai. "And I'm sure that that has nothing to do, of course, with the present company you keep. Ming and Chang have proven themselves to be quite delightful. I must assume, then, perhaps something else has caused this silence."

Kai exhaled, as though bored. "What should you like me to say? Shall I ask how your city is doing? After all, it *is* your city. Lest anyone be confused."

Delan glanced sideways at him.

"My dear, I'm sure I do not know what you're talking about," said Lady Shi. She dabbed her painted lips with a crimson napkin and took a dainty sip of tea.

His eyes, which had been unfocused and glazed before, now sharpened. He leaned forward on the table, fixing his full attention on his mother. "You deny that this entire city is held under your thumb? You deny that not a single person makes an independent decision without your consultation? You deny you are in complete control of everything that happens in this city?"

It took every ounce of strength for Aranya to not glance sidelong when Delan's hand froze in midair.

Lady Shi set her chopsticks down beside her bowl. Slowly, she lifted her head up to fix her beautiful, half-lidded eyes at her son. "I've missed you. Where have you been?"

It was only now Aranya realized that though Kai had heaped his bowl full of food, he hadn't taken a single bite. He hadn't even lifted his chopsticks. He was staring at his mother, fire and ice shooting out of his hazel eyes, the tips of his ears turning redder by the second. He'd never been this unnerved and uncontrolled.

She had to intervene, somehow. She had to say something, even if it was stupid.

Aranya opened her mouth. "This is a very fancy house you have here. How long did it take to build?"

Both Lady Shi and Yong swiveled their gaze from Kai to her. She pointed with her chopsticks at the door.

"That door alone must have taken months to build. I mean, look at how much gold there is! It's so intricately designed! And it's not just the door, it's this entire mansion. I've never been in a place this fine, except for the palace, but even that is not much nicer than this."

All was quiet around the table for a long moment. A moment where she felt far more triumphant and smug than she probably should. She could nearly feel Kai's gratitude emanating from him beside her as his fist slowly unclenched. For once, that cold, stone-like expression on his face softened just slightly.

Yong gave a polite nod and smiled. "Well, I can assure you that the door did not take months, but it did take quite a while. Such craftmanship—such art—is truly one of a kind. The house itself has been in our family for generations now. It is our duty to care for all the blessings that our fathers have bestowed upon us."

"Indeed," Aranya agreed. "Were your fathers evanescers too?"

Delan choked on a dumpling, but she didn't care if she was being rude or breaking customs. Yong had assaulted her in a bathing chamber, and if that wasn't cause for a little rudeness on her part, she didn't know what was. Besides, they thought she was a country bumpkin, anyway. It couldn't hurt to confirm what they already thought of her.

Lady Shi lifted her chin slightly in response to her question. Yong gave another smooth chuckle and said only, "The magic does run in our blood, yes."

He bore himself smoothly, calmly, nonchalantly. Every movement was perfectly calibrated to put them at ease. Every movement was practiced grace. But his eyes—those betrayed the intensity simmering just behind them.

Something was *wrong.* Something that had to do with Kai's comment about his mother running the city.

Delan had stopped eating. In fact, it looked like his mouth was full of food, but he couldn't find the stomach to chew and swallow. Aranya, on the other hand, continued shoveling in mouthful after mouthful.

"This is definitely the best meal I've ever had," she said.

At that, Kai's stiff neck relaxed, and his head ducked barely an inch. The movement was so slight, she almost missed it. He was trying to avoid smiling outright.

Nothing could have bolstered her courage more in that moment. Ought she to keep spewing stupid things?

"It appears most of us are not hungry," said Lady Shi, dabbing her red mouth again. "Please, do forgive the rudeness, but before you head off on your way . . ." She trailed off, looking at her son. "Kai, a word please."

He bristled, immediately going rigid.

Aranya bit her lip, glancing sidelong at him. She wanted to say, *"You don't have to go,"* but she didn't know if that was true.

Instead, she impulsively reached under the table and squeezed his hand. It surprised her when he immediately laced his fingers with hers, warm with cool, small with large. He squeezed her hand back, holding on tightly, and then his thumb swept over the skin of her hand in a brief caress.

She pulled away before his mother or brother could see, hoping her flush was not too obvious. Without a word, Kai got up off his mat and followed the two tall, elegant figures through a side door.

It shut behind them with a thud.

Immediately, Delan turned to Aranya. "What on earth was that?"

She shrugged, eyes wide, as she shoveled another bite into her mouth. "I don't know."

He growled, fisting his hand on the table. "If he had just told me to avoid Gebei, this never would have happened. That boy knows nothing about what it means to work as a team. He doesn't think through the consequences of things like this." He gave a long, snarling sort of sigh and covered his eyes with his hand.

"Maybe it's because of things like this that he avoids working in teams," said Aranya. She leaned closer, lowering her voice to a whisper. "There's something going on here, and I don't know what it is, but they want him for something. And he doesn't want whatever they want. Do you think he's going to be alright in there?"

Delan turned up his palms. "I hope so. He can always vanish if he's in immediate danger, but something about this strikes me as different."

They were silent for a while, and the food she was eating cloyed in her mouth, settling uneasily in her stomach. She set down her chopsticks.

"When you went to the postal station, was there anything for us?"

Delan exhaled, his jaw clenching. "Actually, yes, there was. And unfortunately, it's bad news."

"What?" Aranya pestered immediately, sitting up straighter. "What? What did they say?"

He sighed. Then sighed again. "Princess Meiling has been kidnapped."

CHAPTER 33

LADY SHI AND Yong never emerged from the room, not even to bid them farewell or wish them safe travels. Instead, silent and straight-backed, Kai pushed open the door and exited after a long time.

Delan and Aranya exchanged glances when he didn't look at either of them. His fists clenched tightly, and he strode past them both toward the double doors. With a mighty push, he shoved both doors open and left, leaving them swinging in his wake.

"At least he hasn't lost his flair for drama," Delan muttered as they moved to follow.

Aranya chewed on her lip as she scurried to catch up to Kai's long-legged strides. "Kai?" she called softly in the empty, opulent corridors.

"Your old clothes have been left for you both in your respective bathing chambers," he said.

"Kai?"

"Best that we change and be on our way."

"Kai!" She gripped his arm and yanked him to a stop. "Slow down!"

He stopped. He looked down at her, at her hands wrapped around his elbow, and then his eyes trailed up her arm, her shoulder, her neck, to fix directly on her lips. His earlier spoken words seemed to echo between them, silent but no less potent.

If you thought that was a kiss, you've clearly never been kissed before. Perhaps I should remedy that, and then at least what you said would be true.

She flushed, jerking away from him immediately. His rueful smirk was dark. Dark, bitter, and *so cold.* It was like looking up into the face of a stranger.

"Kai," she said firmly, refusing to touch him again. "What's going on?"

He huffed a dry, humorless chuckle and resumed his marching pace. "You remember the way to your chamber, right? It's best if we hurry."

"You have a dragon's gut full of explaining to do once we leave," Delan said. "I'm not happy about how—"

"Want to lecture me? Get in line."

Aranya growled low in her throat, quickened her pace so she could round Kai and block off his path. "Enough with *this*!" she snapped, waving her hand vaguely at him. "We're leaving, alright? And we're never coming back. *Ever*. But our first priority is our mission, and you can't forget that."

His nostrils flared, and the way his eyes flashed reminded her of when they first met in Zushui, when they were sizing up each other as rivals. She hardly reached his shoulder, but that didn't stop her from returning his gaze with all the ferocity in her soul.

"Pull yourself together, Shi Kai."

They stared at each other, a muscle in his neck ticking. It was like a string was pulled taut between them, ready to sing out if plucked. It stretched thinner, thinner. And then, suddenly, it snapped.

Kai closed his eyes. His face crumpled—just slightly; it was only visible in the shift of his eyebrows.

Aranya swallowed the abrupt lump in her throat. When she spoke, her voice was roughened. "I'm going to my chamber. But I cannot promise I will be fast, in the event of a repeat occurrence of what happened earlier."

The vulnerability on Kai's face was gone in a blink. "He won't touch you. Ever again. I've made sure of it."

She stared at him, then glanced toward Delan, who was staring at them with open concern.

"How?" she asked.

At that, *finally*—a blessed, cocky, stupid smirk.

"He doesn't like having leftovers. Especially *my* leftovers," he said.

"Leftovers?" she cried in outrage, shooting a look at Delan as if to call for backup. "*What* did you tell him about us, Shi Kai?"

His smirk widened as he shoved past her. "Nothing that wasn't true."

Delan tilted his head back to stare at the ceiling in exasperation.

It didn't take long for Aranya to make it back to the bathing chamber and change into her regular clothes. Her senses were on high alert, waiting for Yong to step out of any shadow or crevice with a too-wide grin on his face. But she dressed with no event and quickly made her way to the door.

Just as she reached out to push it open, someone appeared before her, and her hand landed on a solid chest instead of carved walnut wood. Her eyes snapped up, her hand yanking back like she'd touched fire, and found herself staring into the same smile and pair of twinkling eyes she'd been relieved to avoid only a moment ago.

"Going somewhere?" Yong asked smoothly, tilting his head to one side.

She flicked her hands into talons and smiled roguishly. "Out of my way, if you'd be so kind."

Yong merely leaned against the door, arms crossed, and let out a long-suffering sigh. "I'm afraid I cannot, my darling."

"Oh?" She took a step closer, flashing her claws in his face.

He didn't flinch. Only regarded with a mild expression that belied the intensity behind his eyes. "You're not going anywhere."

CHAPTER 34

KAI'S BRAIN SPUN wildly as he strode to the door. The hallway pressed down on his shoulders, like the air was being compressed between him and the blue-painted ceiling beams. His family's home always felt like this. Constricting, suffocating. It had never been home to him.

But he wouldn't bend. He wouldn't break.

His knee hadn't bowed when his father was alive, and it wouldn't now.

When he was within a few strides of the guarded double doors, Kai evanesced straight through them, not caring if it affected his sleep, and landed on the stairs outside beneath a pink-tinted sky. He drew in a deep breath, willing his heart to slow.

This could have gone worse. So much worse.

Since even Yong wouldn't go against orders from Suguan, he'd been allowed to leave. Not that they could keep him against his will—no one could. He was an evanescer. But he hadn't traveled alone, and as careless as he had always tried to make Yong believe he was, both of them knew he wasn't heartless.

It helped nothing that one of his companions was young and lovely.

The weight in his chest eased when Delan met him at the stables a few minutes after Kai arrived and busied himself saddling his mount and Aranya's. Of course, she would take the longest, dressed like a princess in those robes.

His ears heated, and he blinked away the image of her in that vivid red, her hair swept away from her face save for a few curling strands. She'd looked less like a snarling shapeshifter then, and more like . . . well, a beautiful young woman. One that had reached out with a warm hand to hold his before he'd even realized how tense he was. Her hand had been much smaller than he was expecting somehow. Riddled with scars like every magic-wielder's, and strong with calluses. But still tiny.

"I'm expecting an explanation," growled Delan with a very pointed look at Kai. "But I'll wait until we're out of here."

He'd be waiting a lot longer than that, but Kai said nothing.

Delan let out a deep breath as he saddled his horse, grunted in irritation when a stable boy came over to assist, and shooed him off with a flick of his hand. Kai finished Aranya's horse and led it out of the stables with his to wait in the open air. Delan was behind him a second later.

"What's taking her so long?" he asked with a wrinkled brow and a frown.

Kai went to roll his eyes and shrug, but stopped.

All the blood leeched from his face, turning to ice in his veins. He turned horrified eyes to Delan. Realization dropped like lead into his stomach, so hard, so fast his pounding heart had no room except for one word.

Aranya.

Delan was flying off his saddle even before Kai evanesced out of his. In a flash, Kai's sword was drawn, and Delan had his *jiaun* ripped from the holster and loaded with two arrows. They barely had time to glance at each other, hardly enough time for Delan to grab Kai by the collar and yank him down close to his face.

"Don't lose your head. Don't be rash," he hissed.

Then Delan was running, taking the stairs two at a time back into the mansion, and Kai vanished. He reappeared inside, and in two more leaps, he stood before the door that led to Aranya's bathing chamber. His lungs clenched so tightly he could hardly draw a full breath. Dragons blast it, dragons blast it, dragons blast it!

Don't lose your head.

Delan didn't know how timely his warning had come. Or perhaps he understood Kai better than he showed. Whatever the case, his voice forced Kai to stop before that door, to keep himself from shoving it open without a thought, sword swiping.

It gave him the heartbeat to realize what he walked into.

A trap.

Apparently, his brother had been right. He couldn't run from his family forever. Because he wouldn't leave Aranya behind to their mercy, honor and professional protocols aside. She knew where he'd been all this time, and with one slip of her tongue, all his plans would be unraveled. At least they didn't know Kai and Aranya had lived in the same city before this mission. Then they could simply track her posts and know where Kai had been.

But . . . maybe . . . maybe there were more reasons he wouldn't leave her behind.

He had the sickening realization that if his family had Aranya, they had him.

Silent as death, Kai sheathed his sword, going against every instinct raging in his blood. Then, with a deep breath, he straightened his shoulders, placed both hands flat on either door, and shoved them open.

A blade against his neck was the first thing he met.

His pulse hardly leapt in response. Because he was expecting it. He tilted his head back, baring more of his vulnerable flesh to the blades of Yong's lackeys that guarded the door, and crossed his arms over his chest.

There, by the silent and steaming water of the bath, was Aranya.

She was dressed in her normal clothes, the colorless robes of a commoner. Her wrists were bound behind her, her unshod feet tied at the ankles, and her mouth gagged. Bruises spread across her face, a cut above her eyebrow dripping blood down her temple, her hair tangled and mussed. The high-necked robes she wore had been ripped open to her collarbone, making space for a gleaming knife against the pale and vulnerable skin of her throat. One flick, and she was dead.

Dark eyes flashed beneath a swollen, furrowed brow as they met his. Her chest heaved with every gasping breath.

It was true. Every instinct inside him rebelled at this picture of her. He hated seeing her bound, hated seeing that Yong had hurt her. For this, he would make his brother pay.

He couldn't help but realize with a sinking sort of dread that he cared more about Aranya than he wanted to admit, more than he ought to.

Iron hardened his spine.

Kai lifted his eyes from the swirling vortex of fury and fear in her eyes, from the fierce edge of the blade at her neck. Up to the wretched grin of his older brother, the cunning gaze that raked over every inch of his face. Yong thought he'd won. Thought he'd played the card that would finally make his brother bend.

But Kai had spent his life matching wits with his brother. And he couldn't help but notice the blood trailing down Yong's forearm and jaw. Aranya hadn't gone down without a fight, and the fact that she'd landed blows of real pain to an evanescer gave him no lack of pride.

Kai lifted one arm and batted away the blades at his throat, then let out a sigh and rolled his eyes. "Oh *please*. It's too late in the day for this sort of nonsense."

Aranya blinked in surprise, then her eyes narrowed. Did she expect him to reveal his panic to his brother? Did she expect him to show how fast his heart raced?

"Is it?" Yong purred, his arm across Aranya's shoulders, holding her back against his chest as he tilted the knife, tickling the flesh beneath her jaw. She jerked involuntarily, but didn't whimper to her credit. "A pretty little one, this Sun Aranya. Even despite the wide shoulders."

Aranya's face colored a deep red.

Either Yong had noticed this insecurity of hers like Kai had, or he simply thought her build too strong and muscular to suit his *refined* taste. Whatever the case, the barb was clearly intended to humiliate her. To discuss her like she was a pet for purchase.

Kai let his eyes travel down to hers for a second. And then he smirked, locking his gaze on hers. "I know."

Her flush deepened, her chest rising and falling even more rapidly. Her eyes were rounded almost too wide for her sockets. *What are you doing?* she seemed to be asking. There was a tinge of something in her face that revealed a sense of betrayal.

As if Kai would ever betray her to the likes of Yong.

The door burst open behind them, and Kai didn't turn to acknowledge Delan's entrance. There was a *shing* of swords, and then the movement stopped. He could almost feel the older wielder's groan behind him.

"Anyway," Kai said flippantly, waving vaguely at Aranya and returning his attention to Yong. "You clearly want something. Otherwise, you wouldn't trouble yourself with confronting our shapeshifter. I see you discovered her claws."

Yong's blade pressed harder against Aranya's neck. She flinched when it punctured. A drop of blood beaded and then trailed down to pool in the hollow of her throat.

"It's simple, really," said Yong with a smile. "You, for her. She can go free, pretty face unmarred—"

His knife flicked toward her eye, its blade dancing against her lower lashes. She jerked away from it, but he had her pinned against his chest. There was nowhere to go. Instead, a whimper escaped her gag, and her terrified gaze shifted from the knife to Kai.

Silently pleading with him.

In all the time that he'd worked with Aranya, he'd never seen fear like this on her face. He never saw her forced to be still while death stared down its sharp-tipped blade at her.

That was when it hit him.

Sun Aranya *wasn't* fearless. Had never been fearless. It just seemed like she was because she never gave herself a chance to be afraid. She threw herself into danger so fast that she couldn't be scared. Recklessness was how she coped with fear.

Which meant this was possibly the most terrifying moment of her life.

Kai swallowed, his stomach turning over like rocks. *Don't move*, he wanted to tell her. And to himself: *don't lose your head.*

Something in his face must have given him away, because Yong's grin widened.

"See?" he purred, knife-tip dancing close to Aranya's other eye. She squeezed both of them shut. "I knew she meant something to you."

"Or perhaps I'm just not in the mood to watch someone get mutilated," Kai said dryly. "That always was, after all, more *your* style."

Yong's curling lip sent a shiver down Kai's spine. "You don't have to watch. Turn around if you have to. I can even loosen her gag, so you'll know what you're missing. Will it be your name she screams?"

Kai's control snapped.

CHAPTER 35

ARANYA TRIED TO block out the slither of Yong's words in her ears, how they trailed like a claw down her spine. She couldn't think about anything except the tip of his knife, and the memory of Ye Ye lying unconscious in their tenement in Suguan. He had no one besides her.

If she died, he died.

She'd already shifted her hands into talons, had worked one up between her bonds to slice it in half, only to discover another of Yong's tricks. The bonds didn't break—they tightened. She'd let out a surprised cry of pain.

"Spelled vines," Yong had said with a smug grin. "They come in handy for binding shifters with talons."

Then Kai had marched in, and her heart had sunk with dread while simultaneously nearly flying straight out of her throat. His face was devoid of all feeling except that wretched, wry smirk. She was glad he kept his composure. Really, she was. But also—did he truly not care if anything happened to her? Couldn't he show the slightest reflection of her panic?

Apparently not until Yong had threatened to make her scream.

Kai vanished, and Delan ducked beneath the blades at his throat, attacking the guards on either side of him. Somehow, he fired his *jiaun* with one hand, threw a knife with the other, and simultaneously landed a powerful kick to another guard. The arm around Aranya's shoulders loosened, the pressure at her back vanishing. Blades clashed behind her.

Aranya slammed her head backward, connected with the side of a jaw. There was a grunt of surprise, a yell from somewhere, and the grip on her fell away completely.

The knife was gone from her throat. She didn't have time to be relieved. Now was the time for the three of them to fight together to get out of this.

She tucked close and rolled away from Yong to her knees, then jumped and barely got her feet under herself before she fell. She jumped again, swinging her bound hands beneath her ankles so they were in front of her now. In a swift movement, she yanked the gag from her mouth and coughed.

Then she wobbled, lost her balance, and fell back to the ground. Stupid partial shapeshifting! If she'd been a full shapeshifter, she could have shifted out of these bonds. Could have turned into a wild beast and ransacked this whole chamber.

But she was nothing but a partial shapeshifter.

"Give up!" Yong shouted.

Aranya rolled, pushing up on her numb hands. A few feet away, Kai and Yong were locked in battle, swords flying as they vanished and reappeared in a deadly dance.

"Stop running! Take your place! Make our father proud!" said Yong.

"Our father is *dead*," Kai snapped and thrust his blade with fatal accuracy at his brother's heart.

Yong disappeared before the blade found its mark. "He might not be the only one dead before this is over."

And then Yong was suddenly right in front of where she was half-sprawled on the ground, his sword coming straight for her face. It happened too fast for a scream. Aranya threw herself to the side, landing on the edge of the bath. One more roll, and she'd fall in. Yong's blade came arcing for her again.

This time, she *did* scream.

A loud *chang!* resounded as she squeezed her eyes shut. They flew open, and Kai's blade hovered not even a hand's breadth above her throat, blocking the death stroke.

Then arrows were flying.

Kai and Yong both vanished. The arrows skidded across the tiles. Aranya tucked her knees to her chest and somersaulted to unsteady feet. Delan was at her side in an instant, blood spattered across his face, smearing on his beard and nose. A glance at the doors revealed he'd killed all the guards. She barely had a second to be shocked and impressed. No wonder he was in the Secret Services.

But if the pounding of footsteps outside the chamber revealed anything, it was that Yong's force wasn't limited to a handful of guards.

"We've got to get out of here," Delan said. "While Kai is keeping that wretched excuse of a human busy." He whipped out his knife, coming for her bonds.

She jerked away frantically and shook her head. "They're cursed! They can't be cut!"

His eyes widened in horror, meeting her gaze for a split second. Then her attention was snagged by a guard running toward his turned back. She used every bit of momentum she could muster, jumped, grabbed hold of Delan's arm in a way that he barely braced himself to keep from falling, and swung her bound feet toward the assailant's face. Heel connected with jaw, snapping his head backward, and Delan had enough time to whip around and send a knife flying for the death blow.

Then he was bending, wrapping one burly and bloodied arm around her knees to hoist her over his shoulder. Just as she was squeaking, the door burst open, and more guards flooded into the chamber, *jiauns* loaded and pointed at them.

"Surrender!" they barked.

Delan let go of Aranya, holding his hands up, chest heaving. She didn't move, holding onto his sleeve for balance, hating her partial magic more than ever, and glared daggers at the guards. Behind them, the constant clash and shouting of Kai and Yong.

Apparently, Kai had been justified in not wanting to pass through Gebei.

Then, suddenly, in front of them weren't the guards. Before them stood a tall woman with a gold-set ruby dangling on her forehead, robes of the deepest crimson, with long painted eyes and blood-red lips.

Shi Nuan. Kai's mother.

She lifted her chin, impassive and elegant even in the midst of battle. Those liquid-black eyes landed on Aranya for the first time today, and they skewered into her soul like blades.

"You. Come with me."

And then she merely reached out with one hand and tapped Aranya's forehead.

The world vanished around her.

CHAPTER 36

WHEN ARANYA OPENED her eyes, she was in an unfamiliar room.

It was small and dark. The only light was from round, red lanterns hanging from the ceiling, golden tassels trailing almost to the beaded edges of the cobalt-blue rug. The low table in the middle of the room gleamed gold, and fringed multicolored mats lined its perimeter. Three walls were trimmed in stained wood, shelves lined with scrolls. The fourth bore a map of Zheninghai that was so large she could have wrapped herself up in it to sleep.

In front of her—Lady Shi.

"Sit," the woman beckoned, gesturing to the mats. She glided to the opposite side of the close space and descended to sit. Aranya, on the other hand, wobbled where she stood, hands turning blue and ice-cold. She wasn't sure if she should flash her talons and leap—or hop, rather—across the room to slash into Lady Shi's face.

Don't be reckless.

She decided to sit.

It took a few unsteady hops to reach the mats. She was forced to bend down, grip the edge of the table, and lower herself into a sitting position. This was utterly ridiculous.

"Will you get these off?" Aranya asked, holding her wrists across the table.

Lady Shi's eyes flicked with boredom as she deigned to lower her gaze to Aranya's blue fingers. Just as bored, she lifted her attention away from them.

"Where has my son been hiding?" she asked.

Adrenaline hummed in Aranya's veins, but with it, a steady chill that tempered her saucy replies. Instead, she remained silent.

"Say nothing, and your feral-wielder friend will die. My guards will overwhelm him quickly; no matter his skill, he is vastly outnumbered. Then I have but to issue the command. He could lose a hand, an eye, a leg—his life."

A shudder sliced down Aranya's spine. Like mother, like son, apparently. She couldn't help the way her breath huffed through her open mouth, or the bite of pure terror at the thought of the knife that had just nearly gouged out her eye doing worse to Delan.

Then, to her surprise, Lady Shi leaned over, pressed a lily-white cloth to her mouth, and began hacking. Her whole body heaved with those coughs, and they sounded so painful Aranya couldn't help but wince.

The woman finished, delicately dabbed her lips, and set the cloth beside her, beneath the table. But not before Aranya glimpsed the blood staining the kerchief.

Kai's mother was dying.

"Where does your loyalty lie, little shifter?" Lady Shi said, lifting her chin as if nothing had happened. "Will you give a man's life to allow my treacherous son his rebellion? Do you wish for Kai to have the freedom to betray everything that matters in his life, so much that you would let an innocent's blood spill? Make a widow of his wife, take away a child's father?"

Aranya was no fool. Something very, very wrong was happening here. It wasn't as simple as Lady Shi presented it. Even so . . . whatever fate awaited Kai at the hands of his family, was it worse than what Delan would face?

"One word, little shifter. The name of the city where Kai lives, and you are free to finish your little quest with your little feral friend."

Delan would balk at being called that.

"And Kai?" Aranya asked. "Is he free to come with us, too? If I tell you?"

Lady Shi ran her tongue over her blood-red lips, tilted her head to one side, and smiled. Slowly. "Kai is always free. He is an evanescer."

Lies. From the seven layers of *diyu*.

"One word."

Zushui.

She wanted to fight, wanted to refuse. To call their bluff. But she didn't think either Yong nor Lady Shi was bluffing. Their faces flashed with the darkness of ruthless killers.

Only one word—and they would be free to go. Free to continue their quest and find out what was happening to Lord Zuan Wan and the other missing magic-wielders. Free to succeed, to provide for her grandfather. She stuffed her hands in her lap, staring down at them. They were starting to swell. A bite of panic sliced through her. How was she to ever get them off?

That was when it clicked.

Her head snapped up, met icicles beneath sweeping kohl across from her. Then she swiveled her attention to the map on the wall. At the markings trailing like black bugs up from cities like Suguan, Shaanet, and cities farther south to converge on one city, and from there, one solid line straight north to Butagin.

The city of convergence—*Gebei.*

What had Yong said about her bonds? She'd been too distressed to process his words. Now, they echoed around her mind like bats screeching in a cave.

Spelled vines.

Her breath whooshed out of her just as the eyes across from her narrowed to slits.

"You," Aranya accused and held up her wrists. "You know what happened to Zuan Wan. These are *his* vines that are binding me. Which means you have some connection to him, and your map has a trail from his hometown Shaanet straight here—"

She wasn't prepared for the blow. It landed so hard to her face she was knocked backward off the mat. She rolled, face aching and stinging, brain wobbling inside her skull, and found herself scooting backward until she hit a wall. Scrolls clattered on the shelf behind her.

She stared down the shaft of a *jiaun*, two arrows aimed right for her heart.

Everything stuttered to a halt.

She breathed hard, swallowing back a choking memory of tickling whiskers and soft white fur. Bean-padded paws and a wet, rosebud nose.

"The name of the city," said Lady Shi, face cut as though from a glacier.

Kai—or Ye Ye? Delan?

Why did she have to be a phoenix-scorched partial-shifter? Why did she always have to be a *weak failure?* Why couldn't she ever be strong enough to save the people she cared about? The people she had a duty to protect? Because while her first duty was always Ye Ye, she was honor-bound to protect Delan and Kai too, as her comrades.

One moment she was staring down those arrows, and the next, she was standing in a tenement doorway, stunned to see Ye Ye collapsed on the ground—fully believing, in that horrible second of forever, that he had died because she wasn't there. Because she hadn't been what he needed her to be.

It was the same thing now. She was just a young graduate who happened to make the right person happy at the right time and ended up on this mission that she wasn't even sort of equipped for. And now she couldn't be who Delan, Kai, Ye Ye, or Zheninghai needed her to be.

If only she and Kai hadn't both shown up to the wardpost that day.

She squeezed her eyes shut.

Zushui. Zushui. Just say the word. Just betray Kai and don't look back.

She swallowed. Opened her eyes. Opened her mouth. She was going to do it. She was going to tell Lady Shi where her son had been all this time. There was no point in sacrificing herself, Delan, and Ye Ye to save the evanescer who'd messed up her life.

And then, at the last second, realization hit her.

Lady Shi and Yong needed her. Needed this information from her. They couldn't kill her until they had the name of this city.

They could kill Delan, she thought. Sickness washed over her so strongly she nearly vomited right then and there. But then she remembered how many guards he'd taken out in the bathing chamber. How did she know they'd even managed to subdue him? Were Lady Shi's threats against him merely empty words to get her to comply? And could she trust this woman not to slaughter her, anyway? Once they had their information, she was useless.

Delan could hold his own. She needed to do the same.

Her eyes trailed up the *jiaun,* up the exquisite robes of Kai's mother, to her eyes of ice-chips.

"I won't tell you," she said.

CHAPTER 37

YONG APPEARED IN the room just as Lady Shi shifted the *jiaun* out of firing mode.

"Keep working on her," she said without preamble, turning her back to him and studying the map on the wall. Her hands clasped demurely in front of her, as if she hadn't just threatened to pluck out the eyes of an innocent man and then murder him in cold blood. She waved a hand toward Aranya, who clutched her bound hands to her chest and tried to shove away the stone that had landed in her gut. "Be swift."

But Yong didn't immediately look at Aranya. Instead, his eyes trailed from his mother to the crumpled, blood-stained napkin on the table. He swallowed visibly. "Mother, are you—"

"The shapeshifter, boy."

Was that a sigh that just escaped Yong? Did his shoulders drop the barest smidge? She wasn't sure, because when he turned his attention to her, his face was like flint. Her heart seized within her.

Where was Kai?

Yong grabbed her by the forearm and tugged her to her feet, despite her yanking against him.

"Take these off now," she growled, thrusting her wrists in his face. "You can't keep delaying us as wielders of the empire!"

He merely raised an eyebrow, bent, and heaved her over his shoulder. She grunted and kicked until something sharp pressed against the back of her leg.

"Keep wiggling," said Yong, "and I'll slice through the tendons in your knee, and you'll never walk again."

Aranya stilled.

"Very good." He chuckled. Then they were out of the room. Heading somewhere that she didn't know, and with each step she became more worried about what *"keep working on her"* meant.

"What do you know about Lord Zuan Wan?" she asked, pressing her bound hands against his back so she could lift her head. "He was here, wasn't he?"

"Your curiosity will get you in trouble, Sun Aranya," said Yong. He didn't even try to soften his steps when he went down a flight of stairs, and each movement sent his shoulder stabbing into her hipbone.

If Kang Lei had been trying to desert Zheninghai, if Zuan Wan had been too, and they'd stopped here . . . Did that mean Yong and Lady Shi were planning a revolt? Had they allied themselves with the barbarians in the north? Were they trying to make Kai join them?

That had to be it. And Kai wouldn't betray his empire, so he ran from his family.

Footsteps sounded ahead of them. Aranya craned to look, but something sharp tapped her knee again. With a surge of fury, she stiffened and stilled.

"Clear out," said Yong in a sharp, authoritative voice. Not to her.

"It's *night*," replied an irritated, raspy, smoke-filled voice.

A fire-wielder. Aranya would bet her life on it.

"Yes, well you stayed too long in Shaanet, now didn't you? Out. Now. I don't like royalty in my dungeon for long. Besides, Fang will be anxious for her."

Royalty?

The princess was kidnapped.

And also—Shaanet. A fire-wielder. Was this the fire-wielder that had destroyed the body of the warden they'd found? Aranya's mind spun. It felt like she had the pieces of the puzzle. But how did they fit together?

When Yong turned a corner, and several figures passed him, she used her core to lift herself just enough to catch a glimpse of them. Three people, wearing heavy, obscuring cloaks, yet somehow they were familiar.

Then one of them glanced back at her, and Aranya's eyes widened to behold a face she knew. It was a man's face, handsome with a sad sort of hopelessness shining in his eyes. They hardened when they met hers, and in a flurry of cloak he'd turned his back on her.

He was the illusionist she and Kai had battled in the rain outside the inn on their way to Suguan.

Just when Yong started down a flight of stairs, Aranya caught sight of a fourth cloaked and hooded figure. She wore no royal garments, only a simple set of travel-soiled robes. But there was no mistaking the grace with which she moved, the subtle elegance. Aranya was not a girl of refined taste by any means, but even she could tell the difference.

The girl's hands were bound, and she was yanked after what Aranya guessed was the fire-wielder. She stumbled, fell to her knees, unable to brace her fall. But she didn't make a sound. Not even when she was roughly yanked to her feet after her captors.

The cursed princess. The one born without magic.

Then Aranya's view was cut off, swallowed up in dimness as Yong descended further down the stairs. Her breathing came faster with each step, but her mind was spinning too fast for her to have time to panic. What could Yong and Lady Shi want with a cursed princess? Or was it someone else—this *Fang* that Yong had mentioned?

Suddenly, a memory clicked into place. What had she heard in that Secret Services meeting back at the capital? That they needed to find out what was happening to these wielders because of the barbarian unrest in the north, because of someone named Fang Zedong amassing troops.

The name meant nothing to her, but it still tasted wrong on her tongue. Another flash of that map in that room with the red hanging lanterns. Of a path going north. Straight to Butagin. Converging here, in Gebei.

Here, at the Shi mansion.

Keys jangled, then echoed. A dank coolness washed over her, sending her spine tingling and her chest tightening. Then, abruptly, something hit her.

"Where's Kai?" she asked, unable to hide the thread of panic in her voice.

No answer.

He'd been fighting Yong last she'd seen him. But that fight was clearly over. Did that mean Kai had lost? He wasn't dead, right? Yong was trying to get him to comply, not to kill him.

Right?

Her gut sank as her brain scrambled for possible explanations. Had he . . . left? Left them? Had he made his escape without them? No. He wouldn't. Kai wouldn't abandon them. Wouldn't abandon her. After all, he'd come back for her earlier, in the bathing chamber.

"Where's Delan?" she asked.

Yong snorted and readjusted his grip on her. "He's being dismembered because you wouldn't talk. Would you like to go watch?"

The seed of panic blossomed into a frantic surge that swept through her body. She bucked, slamming her knees into his ribs as hard as she could. But she was off balance, rendering the blow impotent. Yong only grunted and tightened his hold. She shifted her hands back into talons and tried to stab them straight into his back as she squirmed.

But she couldn't hurt him, because just then he flung her to the ground. She landed painfully on her tailbone and only managed to roll slightly to the side to keep from injuring herself.

Yong stood before her, his form almost entirely in the shadows cast by a lone lantern. It hung on the wall of what appeared to be a dark, dank cell. Aranya scooted into a better sitting position, scowling up at him.

"You're bluffing," said Aranya. "You're bluffing to get me to talk."

"You're gambling a lot on this being a bluff."

"Delan is too skilled for you."

"Unfortunately skill doesn't matter when you're outnumbered twenty to one."

The blood drained from her face, dread dousing the fight that had previously flooded every inch of muscle and bone in her body. Yong crouched before her, studying her face. He reached out with one hand as though to take her chin, but she knocked his hand away and snarled.

"All I need from you, Sun Aranya," he said, unfazed, "is the name of the city where Kai accepted his appointment. If you tell me now, I'll say the word and my guards will stop the feral-wielder's torture."

Aranya squeezed her eyes shut and drew a deep breath between clenched teeth. "I told you. I'm not talking."

"So you and Kai are that involved, then? Hmm? That you would give the life of your comrade for Kai to shirk his responsibilities?"

"Why do you want to know the city so much?" she snapped, refusing to answer his stupid question. "Why do you want Kai? He's just fulfilling his duty to the empire!"

"Does duty to empire outweigh duty to family?" Yong spat. "You have family, don't you, Aranya? Would you abandon them?"

Would you abandon them?

Aranya jerked back involuntarily, hitting her head on the cold stone wall. "Wh-what?"

Yong's eyes glittered. "You do, don't you? Have family that you're responsible for. Don't you want to go back to them? Take care of them? You saw how our mother is suffering. She just wants Kai to visit her in her final days. You, of all people, should understand!"

He was manipulating her. Yet knowing it couldn't quell the rising burst of fury, frustration, and utter helplessness in her chest. She turned her face away from him, fixing unfocused eyes on the shadows playing across crevices of the wall and the dark grout between each stone.

"I'm not a fool," she said, her voice low. "I know this isn't just about visiting during the festivals. There's more at play here, and it has to do with Fang Zedong, doesn't it?"

One minute she was speaking. The next, pain exploded across her face. Her neck snapped backward from the shock of it. For a split second, she was too stunned to realize he'd just backhanded her.

Then he was dragging her close, his nails digging into her upper arm. "What is it you want? Do you realize the power that I have? The things I could grant you? Money, appointments, status, opportunity, connections—I can give you so much. Things Kai can't dream of giving you while he runs from the Shi name. You have family. Do you want them cared for? Medical bills paid, comfortable housing? Do you want servants to take care of them while you are running around on your little missions? All you have to do, Aranya, is say the word. The name of the city, and then say what you want. I'll give it to you, whatever you ask."

He was shockingly earnest. To her utter horror, Aranya believed every word that he said. Not just that he *could* give her those things, but that he *would,* if she betrayed Kai. No matter how her eyes searched his for the slightest glint of malice or trickery, she found none.

But she did glimpse that veiled desperation she'd seen when he'd noticed his mother's bloody handkerchief.

He could give her the money, the help, the security, the *everything* she needed to take care of Ye Ye. All this desperate flailing she had been doing for the last seven years to take care of Ye Ye—could it be over in a second? With one word, could she have everything she'd been trying to gain?

"Anything you want, Aranya," he whispered. He must have read her hesitance in her face. "Just say the word."

Aranya met his gaze. Lantern light flickered across his dark, dilated irises, and in their reflection, she saw herself. Someone who felt too small for the weight she bore. She and Yong understood each other in a way that she and Kai would never understand each other. And he could give her what Kai could never give her.

Tears welled up in her eyes. She hated them—hated herself for them. Slowly, she drew a deep, shuddering breath. And then she opened her mouth.

"No."

Yong blinked once, twice. Then again. His brow twisted, his lips parting in shock. He'd thought she was going to give in. He'd apparently been sure of it.

Aranya lunged forward and, with a snarl, grabbed his collar with her bound hands. "There are many things that I want, evanescer, but I'll get them myself. The right way. I won't sell my loyalty."

The easy thing to do—and possibly the wise thing—would have been to give him what he wanted and take what she could. To do *whatever* it took to take care of her grandfather. But Ye Ye would have wanted her to stand her ground, and she never wanted to be too ashamed to look him in the eye.

But more practical than that, she was only valuable to the Shi family so long as she held this information. If she gave it up now, there was the chance they'd have her killed and be done. She couldn't risk it yet, no matter how much she was inclined to believe Yong's promises.

She wasn't fully sure if she'd just doomed herself and her comrades—and possibly even Ye Ye himself—and she didn't know how she would pay for this decision, but she couldn't deny the thrill of taking a stand. Of refusing to bend or back down.

The thrill was short-lived. Yong had her by the arms again, dragging her up so he could seethe in her face, "Fine. Your loyalty stands up against gifts. We'll see how it stands against pain."

With that, he flung her against the stone wall and strode out of the cell. He snapped his fingers as Aranya caught her balance, panting. She dug her talons into stone, gritting her teeth against her spinning head.

A cloaked figure filled the doorway.

Yong slammed the door shut with a clang that rung in her ears like the drawing of a blade in the stillness of an empty cave.

Aranya's gut plunged all the way to her toes. Nevertheless, she dragged herself to her feet, her heart pounding faster and faster. Was she going to be tortured? Oh fathers, she couldn't last against torture.

For a brief moment, she closed her eyes and reconsidered. Maybe she *should* just give the name of that city up. Just betray everything and be done.

You're only valuable to them with this information.

She sighed, and a dry sob worked its way through her chest. There was no other option. No option but to endure if there was to be any hope of escape. She steeled her shoulders and faced the figure slowly approaching her.

Her eyes flicked beyond him to Yong, standing outside her cell with an expression of iron. Utterly gone was that slip of vulnerability she'd seen in him.

She glanced back just in time to watch the figure throw back his hood. Apparently she was expecting a face of scars or something else fierce and unyielding. Instead, it was the unremarkable, bearded face of a man.

If her feet weren't bound, she would have taken an uneasy step backward. As it was, she could only stand, bracing herself against the wall.

Then, the worst thing happened.

He didn't pull out some torture device meant to wrench screams from her until her throat was raw, her vocal chords shredded. Instead, the man's face shifted. His whole body shifted as he bent forward. His arms became front legs, his nose lengthening into a long, gray snout. The cloak melted away into silver fur that caught the erratic dancing light of the lantern. Teeth lengthened, lips pulled back into a feral snarl.

Worst of all: his dark eyes shifted until they were nothing but black marbles, void of all human reason and compassion.

A wild, bloodthirsty wolf stood before her. Growling as he prowled closer, teeth flashing like daggers of fire.

"Dragons *blast* it," Aranya moaned.

Yong had set a full shapeshifter on her. One that would shred her to pieces until she talked.

CHAPTER 38

KAI'S LUNGS HEAVED alongside Delan's as they tore through the gates of the mansion on horseback. Arrows whizzed toward them as guards chased after them. He pulled Aranya's horse behind him, forcing it into a gallop.

"Ride in front of me!" Kai yelled to Delan. "They won't shoot me! And here, catch this!"

Kai threw the lead to Delan, who snatched it out of the air as he tossed Kai an incredulous look before urging his horse faster, taking the lead through the streets of Gebei. People scattered, screamed, loose chickens squawked and shot into the air in a flurry of feathers.

"Left!" shouted Kai. If Delan hadn't heard him, they were heading straight for the central market and it would be impossible to not hurt anyone.

Delan veered to the left down an alley, Aranya's horse nickering and flattening its ears as it slowed to follow.

As they fled through the city and out into the wilderness, Kai's mind tripped over itself. He was so distracted he almost forgot to give Delan directions. Aranya was back there, and even if he had a plan to rescue her, and even if he *knew* his family wouldn't kill her if they thought she would be a tool to manipulate Kai, he couldn't help his frantic pulse.

What if they *did* hurt her? Or what if things had changed, and they simply killed her outright? What if getting Delan out would cost Aranya everything? What if Aranya talked? What if she told them he'd accepted an appointment in Zushui? That's what they would want to know, after all, so that they could find his specific appointment and maneuver a way to get him dismissed so he had nowhere to go.

"You should come home," his mother and brother would say. *"Where you belong."*

And why shouldn't Aranya reveal that information? If it meant keeping her eyes? What loyalty did she have toward him? He'd messed up her appointment. Fathers, he'd held her at knife-point last night!

They were well out of the city by now, entering the familiar forest wilderness. Delan drew up short.

"I am going to murder you, boy!" he said, whirling in his saddle while their mounts foamed at the mouth and heaved for air. "Aranya—"

Kai was already swinging down from his saddle. "I can save her. There are these secret passageways. Built by my father. I'll find her, get her out through one of those tunnels, and meet you back here."

"If there are tunnels out of there, then you can be sure they've blocked them so you can't escape that way," snapped Delan.

Kai shook his head vigorously, still panting. It was taking everything not to evanesce away. Every moment he delayed was another chance for something to go wrong. For Aranya to get hurt. "No, my mother and brother don't know about those tunnels. Just me."

"You expect me to believe that? How could you be the only one who knows?"

"Because my father only trusted me." It was the most honest answer he could give without delving into too much detail. *My father had plans for me.*

"You can't operate on the assumption that you're the only one who knows about the tunnels or you could walk right into an ambush and it's Aranya who will be the one to suffer. You can only use them if you *first* verify that they're empty. Move fast."

Kai nodded, relief that Delan wasn't challenging him any more running like water through his limbs. Quickly, they coordinated a meeting spot, and Delan said he'd get the horses there and stay there for only ten minutes.

"If you're not back, I'm leaving the horses to come help you. And if anything happens to her, I will have your head. Understand?"

Kai would cut off his own head if his family did anything to her. His gaze met the older wielder's, and though only a moment before, they were experienced wielder berating new graduate, for the span of their locked gazes, they were comrades. Of the same mind and same goal—*get Aranya out of there.*

Then Kai turned and vanished into the air.

The wolf pounced.

Aranya threw herself to the left, toward the bars of the cell. The wolf snapped its jaws, pouncing again. She rolled, gasped, grabbed hold of the bars. Frantically, she pulled herself upright and flung her talons in front of her, barely in time to slash away the wolf's maw as it came for her face.

There was no time for screaming, for hardly any sound, barely a scrap of any emotion save utter panic and desperate instinct.

The wolf snarled, jumped—and landed with sharp-tipped paws on her shoulders, knocking her straight to the ground. Aranya gasped as her back hit the floor of the cell hard. She rolled so its teeth barely missed her shoulders, then immediately flung herself into a roll in the opposite direction.

Full shapeshifters always win, she thought, frantic tears pricking at her eyes. *Stupid, stupid partial magic.*

Never in her life had she hated her magic as much as she did now. If she was a full shapeshifter, she could get out of these wretched bonds. If she was a full shapeshifter, she wouldn't be so disadvantaged. She could tear claw and fang into her opponent, letting wild animal instinct take over her body and mind. She was only delaying the inevitable, only putting off her fate until she was too exhausted to keep fighting.

The wolf caught her between its paws. She looked up into those black, soulless eyes, the snarling mouth and incisors gleaming in the lantern light just inches from her face.

Using her bound wrists, she stabbed upward with her talons, aiming for its neck. She only succeeded in knocking aside its bite. It snapped again at her neck, and she let out a cry as she barely knocked it aside again.

"Say the name of the city and I'll call him off," came Yong's voice from somewhere.

She needed to get out from beneath it. If she was to have any hope, she'd need to go on the offense. With a vicious swipe, she clawed with her talons at the wolf's face, while bringing up her knees sharply to land a kick to the wolf's lower abdomen.

It snarled in her face.

Another cry—this one of fear—sliced through her body and ripped free of her gritted teeth.

Those powerful jaws came snapping for her again, utterly relentless and impossible to fend off for long. It was so fast she barely had time to react, barely had time to get her talons up to spare her face.

The wolf's teeth clamped down on her bound wrists.

Teeth punctured her skin. Blood flowed down her arms. The magical bonds wrenched tighter. Aranya screamed.

Have to get out. Have to get out.

Using all of her strength, as the wolf bit harder, she flung her arms to one side and kicked her knees at the same time, barely rolling the wolf off her. It let go of her wrists, immediately coming for her face again. Aranya scooted so her back was to the bars and kicked her legs out hard, knocking away the wolf for a split second.

How could she beat it? That was the only way she wasn't going to be mauled to shreds here. She had to overcome it. In order to do that, she had to get ahead of it.

How could she get ahead of something that was so much stronger, fiercer, and wilder than her? Its bloodthirsty instincts were uncontrollable, its desire for her blood insatiable. How could she overcome it if she knew how strong those instincts were and had a hard enough time controlling them just as a partial shapeshifter?

How could she ever—

Wait.

Its instincts.

How many times had Qigang and Kai told her to put her claws away because they were messing with her ability to think straight?

What if she used the wolf's instinct against it? Even though wielding her talons brought out the animalistic instinct inside her, she was still mostly human. Could she use her partial magic to outsmart it?

As the wolf came charging for her again, she reached up, grabbed the throat of the wolf with her bound hands, and brought up her knees again to drive it forward and slammed its head into the cell bars above her. Blunt tipped nails dug into her shoulder, making her cry out.

She rolled to the right, getting out from underneath it. Frantically, as it leapt for her again, she caught hold of the bars and dragged herself to her feet. Gripping the iron in both hands, her wrists aching and bleeding, she jumped and swung her feet to connect straight with the wolf's jaw.

It was the heartbeat she needed to hobble and swing herself into the corner, standing with her back pressed into the cold bars and stone wall. She held her bound hands out in front of her defensively, slightly crouching. She panted, meeting the black-eyed glare of the wild animal cornering her and snarling. Foam dripped from its jaws onto the floor. It approached slowly, torchlight gleaming on its silver hide and casting a long, terrifying shadow against the opposite wall of the cell.

She saw the look in its eyes. It wanted to kill her, despite the orders she was nearly certain it had been given, which was to keep her alive. She would use that desire against it. She cowered in that corner, letting it savor its victory over her as it prowled closer.

Oh please let this work. Please let this work.

She was quickly draining her strength, gasping and barely staying upright even now. If this didn't work, there would be no hope left for her. Her muscles quivered, her eyes too wide and her lungs expanding and shrinking like kitchen billows.

The wolf pounced.

Aranya dropped to her knees, nearly losing her balance on her bound ankles, and shoved her talons straight upward. They sliced through flesh. Blood rushed down her hands, her arms. A startled yelp sounded from the wolf as its body stiffened.

She shoved it off her, leapt to her feet, and grabbed the lantern from the wall. With a sudden burst of adrenaline and terror, she smashed it over the wolf. Glass broke. Metal bent.

Fur caught fire.

But the wolf was already dead.

In the light of the licking fire, Aranya lifted her eyes to see Yong standing outside her cell. Tall and stiff like a statue.

She hobbled as far away from the wolf's body as she could, caught hold of the bars with her shaking, bleeding hands, and sunk to her knees. Yet she met that stony evanescer gaze with her own between strands of hair fallen out of her braid.

"Apparently being only a partial shapeshifter isn't that bad," she said.

She wasn't surprised when Yong evanesced through the bars, landing in a crouch before her gasping self, a knife in his hand catching the light of the dying tongues of fire on the wolf's body.

"If I could crawl into your mind and take whatever information I wanted, I would. But if you kill my men, then I will simply resort to old-fashioned torture. You've heard of slow-slicing, haven't you?"

The blood drained from her face. Even her fast inhales slowed, almost completely stopped.

Yong's eyes glittered as the tip of his knife danced along the skin of her arm. "Death by a thousand cuts. Made one by one. Slowly. With plenty of time to reconsider your decision to protect Kai. My earlier offer stands, to give you whatever you want in exchange for the name of the city."

She was weak, exhausted, and *frustrated.* That frustration burned hot, overcoming all else. "You think I'm trying to protect Kai?" she snapped. "If this was just about Kai, I'd have told you long ago."

Yong paused, his knife stilled against her elbow. "What?"

"You're asking me to betray my empire. My people. My family. Myself."

"No—no!" he said quickly. "You're confused. How would this betray Zheninghai?"

"Because you're allied with the man rumored to be raising troops against the empire. You're *helping* him, which means that helping you is betraying everything I love. I don't know what kind of man you are, Shi Yong, that you would think I'd do that." Her gaze darted to his knife. "Under any circumstance."

Yong blinked, lips parting—clearly taken aback. With a growl, he put away his knife and stood. "No wonder my brother has feelings for you. You're just like him. All *noble.*"

"Kai doesn't have feelings for me," Aranya blurted with a frown.

His eyes met hers for one long, hard moment. "If you think that, then you're even more of a fool than I thought." In a flash, he evanesced beyond her cell. "Better get comfortable. It looks like you'll be here for a while. And don't expect Kai to save you, since there is only one key to this cell—I have it—and Kai can't evanesce you out of there. *If* he even comes back for you."

The question was on the tip of her tongue, begging to be asked, wound up in anxiety. *Is Delan alright?* But to ask would be to betray herself. She kept her mouth shut as Yong strode out of the dungeon, his fancy boots clinking on stone as he left her alone with the stench of burned flesh.

Kai appeared in his mother's study, just *knowing* she was going to be here, with all her scrolls and her giant map of the empire on one wall, cooking up a wicked scheme to use Aranya against him in a way that would guarantee his permanent cooperation with her.

She was there, just like he'd known she would be. Sitting on her colored mat, her chin lifted haughtily, her crimson lips set in an elegant pout. But though she'd taken her from the bathing chamber, Aranya was nowhere to be seen.

His chest heaved, his hands balling into fists at his side. "Where is she?"

"So Yong was right," said his mother airily, glancing idly at her floating lantern lights. "You do care about the shapeshifter. In a way, you never cared for those Academy girls. It seems that you have a heart after all. A pity. There was a reason I raised you to be heartless. Caring makes you vulnerable, son. If you care about her, she's all we need to bring you home."

Fire burned in Kai's lungs. Of all the things his mother had done to him—and all the things she hadn't been for him—he thought he might hate her the most for this.

"No matter what threat you make," said Kai, grinding out the words through his clenched jaw, "I won't be your heir. I don't care about Father's will. Make Yong the heir. He's your favorite, anyway."

And he always had been.

"You know we cannot do that," said Lady Shi.

"Find a loophole," snapped Kai. "That's what you're good at."

"Your father made sure of it. He knew I'd try. Not even your death will transfer the inheritance to Yong. We need you, son. And we will have you."

She'd actually looked into the possibility of killing him. Her own son. He met her gaze—how had he ever called her mother? Then he evanesced out of the room.

She wasn't helping, she didn't have Aranya, and he needed to find her before they hurt her. Now that he'd shown himself, everyone would be warned to expect him, to watch for him.

Kai ducked into the shadows behind a stairwell, catching his breath and clutching his head, as though that would make everything better. Where would she be? Would they have put her in the dungeon already? Or was Yong working on her somewhere else? His mind spun through all the things that could have happened to her while he was gone. His blood pounded frantically. Where, where, where?

This panic was nearly paralyzing.

He'd start with the dungeons. Then he'd go from there.

It took several leaps, and a unit of guards spotted him on his second one. Cursing, he kept going, hating all these barriers between him and Aranya. Then he landed in darkness. A horrid stench filled his nostrils. One of burned flesh. There—ahead, was the light of a fire. His heart stopped.

Then he'd evanesced straight to the cell with the fire and landed hard on his feet, nearly stumbling into a burning corpse. *Oh fathers, a corpse—*

It was a wolf.

This only fractionally relieved his panic. He spun around.

And there she was.

She crouched in the corner, her bound hands gripping the iron bars, blood streaking down her bruised and dirty face, down her hands and dripping off her elbow. Her dark eyes were too wide in their sockets as she stared up at him, her mouth falling open.

Kai nearly choked on his relief. Fathers, she was the most beautiful thing he'd ever seen.

Aranya first thought the tall shadow that appeared in her cell was Yong and braced herself for another fight. She'd been given just enough time for her adrenaline to die down, for all her injuries to start aching and stinging, enough time to remember how much her feet and hands hurt despite being numb.

Just enough time to wonder if she was trapped here forever.

But someone evanesced into her cell, and every exhausted muscle in her body tensed, ready for fight, ready to—

Then he'd turned around. Even with the dying fire behind him, even though only his silhouette was visible, she recognized him.

Kai.

Her heart skipped a beat while her lungs dropped all the way to her stomach in relief. Her mouth fell open, and it was his name on the tip of her tongue, and she just wanted to say it over and over again. And maybe cry too.

She sucked in a sharp breath, only to blink and find that dark looming form just in front of her, crouched in the shadows, and two warm fingers pressed against her lips. Silently bidding her quiet. A tear pricked the corner of her eye.

Kai glanced away from her, back toward the rest of the dungeon, as though watching for guards or evanescing family members. Then he turned back to her, grabbed her shoulders. "Are you alright?" Panic edged his hushed voice. His hand slipped up to cup her face, making her draw in a sharp breath. "They *did* hurt you. You're bleeding. Aranya—"

Kai doesn't have feelings for me.

You're a fool if you believe that.

Aranya blinked, startled. Kai was withdrawing a knife. He took her forearm, bringing up his knife. She jerked back and shook her head. His grip tightened as he tilted his head to one side. She grabbed him by the collar, dragging his face to hers, so she could whisper in his ear, "They're spelled. Can't be cut."

He twisted his face to look at her, very close. The whites of his eyes, ringing black pupils, were barely visible in the darkness. He sheathed his knife and, with another glance over his shoulder, gripped her upper arms and pulled her to her feet. She clung to the front of his tunic with both hands, trying to keep her balance. His grip was tight on her, almost painful with intensity. But it was a pain she didn't mind.

She lifted her eyes, met his. "You can't get me out of here. Yong said there's only one key, and he has it. Can you sneak it off him? If he knows you're back, he'll come to here to make sure—"

"I don't need a key to get you out of here."

"But you can't take other people when you evanesce. We'd be caught if we tried to cut the bars."

"Hush," he whispered, reaching out and pressing his finger again to her lips.

She frowned at him, biting her tongue. Carefully, he let go of her, leaving her holding onto the bars for support. Then he vanished, and her heart seized up at his sudden absence.

She was alone again with the wolf carcass.

Until—scratching.

It was so soft at first she almost didn't notice it. The sound blended in with the silence, growing only fractionally louder with each hollow thud of her heart. A soft but high-pitched whine struck her next. Made her feet tingle, her breathing grow stronger. She tightened her grip on the bars she held and turned to look over her shoulder at the back of the cell.

She was just in time to watch the stone wall shift. And then there was Kai, a dark silhouette again, standing in the doorway of a . . . secret passageway? Her heart lifted.

Dare she hope? Dare she—

A door farther down the dungeon banged open. "He's here! He'll come straight for her—"

Suddenly, Kai was right in front of her just as torchlight came around the corner. His eyes were wide, bits of hair falling in his face as shadows cut his profile in sharp relief. Swiftly, he bent, gripped the back of her knees, and hoisted her up over his shoulder with a grunt. The world spun. She let out a small gasp, grabbed fistfuls of his cloak for support, and then they were moving fast, ducking through the opening.

"Hey—hey!" came shouts behind them. She looked up to see Yong's face, stark with horror, staring at them as though in shock.

"He saw us!" Aranya said.

Kai half-glanced over his shoulder, then broke into a run, kicking the tunnel door shut behind him. It bounced partially open again, but only a sliver of light was visible through it.

It didn't matter; doors couldn't keep evanescers out.

Cool air swept down her spine, drier than the dungeon. Deeper darkness permeated the air, but Kai didn't slow one bit.

"Don't make a sound," said Kai, and ducked sharply to the left.

She might as well have her eyes closed with how dark it was.

Behind her ran clattering footsteps, alarmingly close. They abruptly stopped. Yong's voice—again, unnervingly nearby—rang out back toward the door. "Get a light in here!"

Kai ran faster, utterly silent, taking turns so sharply she dared not lift her head for fear of it getting slammed into the wall.

"Split up—find them!" called Yong to his guards. "Turn this place upside-down!"

Kai was breathing hard, but his grip on her never faltered. It almost seemed like the squeeze on her knee was his silent reassurance that he would get her out of this. It was the worst feeling; being unable to do anything except try not to move or make a sound. She gripped his cloak in both hands and hung on as tightly as she could.

The further Kai ran, the thicker the darkness. Yong's pursuit grew quieter, and for the first time, she started to truly hope. Hope that they could get out of here, that they could escape, that she could be free—

Then, Yong's voice cut through the caverns, far away but carried through the tunnels so it rung in their ears.

"Don't think this is over, Kai! We will track you down! I swear it on our father's grave!"

Kai gave a soft huff in response, and then he slowed to a stop. He kept one hand tight around her knees, while the other moved something that made a sharp whine in response. She cringed.

And then—

Light.

"Thank the fathers, I was just about to come after you," came Delan's rough voice.

Aranya shoved herself up, head twisting so she could find Delan—who was whole and hale with all appendages intact. "You're alright!" she gasped.

"Of course I'm alright."

She sagged, still on Kai's shoulder, and her breath shuddered out of her.

"They followed us," blurted Kai, each breath a gasping pant. "We only have a few minutes before they find this exit."

Delan growled something inarticulate, and then Aranya found herself wrestled atop Kai's horse. Just as soon as she was sitting sideways, wrists and ankles still bound, Kai mounted up behind her, slipped an arm around her waist, and drew her back against his chest.

She only had a fraction of a second to be stiff and embarrassed before they were galloping off at breakneck speed. And then they were moving so fast none of it mattered. So she turned her face into the crook of his shoulder and neck and tried to breathe, to calm her racing heart. She felt when he tilted his head down to look at her and then lifted it to keep focused on their flight.

CHAPTER 39

NO ONE SPOKE a word. Not until they were a safe distance from Gebei. The sun rose, turning the forest from green to golden, spilling across Aranya's exhausted eyes. She leaned heavily against Kai's chest, listening to the raging rhythm of his heart. It never slowed, even when they were hours from the city.

It was the only distraction from staring down at her wretched bonds.

Suddenly, Delan pulled a halt. Kai's heart leapt in response against her cheek, and she peered at the older wielder. Delan's face was so red, his jaw so tight, his fists so clenched, she thought he might explode.

He did.

"What in the seven layers of *diyu* was *that,* boy?" Delan demanded. "You don't tell us to avoid Gebei, then you choose not to tell us why, let us walk into a dragon-blasted trap—"

"I told you not to go to Gebei!" snapped Kai in return. "I *said* to go anywhere else—"

"After I'd already committed to! Even then, we could have stopped, but you didn't give any real reason to not go, now did you?"

"I *couldn't* give you a reason!"

"My elbow you couldn't! How about, *'If you step foot in Gebei, you'll end up fighting for your life'*? That might have been nice to know!"

"And what would you have done if I'd said that?" Kai demanded, his grip tightening on Aranya's shoulder. "You would have—"

"—asked to know what was going on? Yes, we would have! Just like I'm asking now. So tell me once and for all, Shi Kai, *why* was Princess Meiling bound and locked up in your family's dungeon? Hm? Is that what you can't tell us? That you are all traitors to the crown?"

Delan had seen that? She'd lost track of him when she'd been taken by Lady Shi, but apparently he'd also seen the princess being dragged away.

Kai stiffened so sharply that she glanced up at his face. She expected to see the same look of rage that was written across Delan's face on Kai's, but instead he'd gone pale. Deathly pale, his lips suddenly bloodless in the dawn.

"*Who* was in the dungeon?" he asked, voice wavering. His grip on her slackened.

"Princess Meiling," said Aranya. "I heard your brother say they were taking her to Fang."

Kai swayed on his saddle. His hand trembled on the reins, enough to make Aranya's brow furrow.

"I didn't . . . I didn't know anything about this," he said.

She wanted to believe him.

Delan, however, looked much more skeptical. "Give me one reason why I shouldn't contact Secret Services and turn over your whole family."

"There's no proof," said Kai.

"She's proof," spat Delan, gesturing at Aranya. "She heard what they said."

"Don't," said Kai immediately, almost breathlessly. His chest heaved against her. "*Please* don't mention anything that Aranya heard."

"Why not?"

His deep breath shuddered out of him. "Because then she will be killed."

Aranya stiffened. Delan growled, "By whom?"

"By Yong."

"But then that would only prove—"

"Yes, and Aranya would be *dead*."

"They don't have her. *We* have her."

"That won't stop him. There's no catching my family in their crimes. They're evanescers. You can't catch them. Can't bind them. I don't understand how they're connected with Fang—truly, I don't. And while I haven't gone about this in the best way, I hope you both can see how hard I've tried to avoid them. I took my appointment in Zushui as a warden for the one and only purpose of staying below their radar. If that doesn't show where my loyalties lie, then I don't know what will."

Even Delan was quiet at that. But Aranya's pulse had kicked up several notches, dread coiling heavily in her stomach.

"Kai?" she said softly.

"Yes?"

"They wanted me to tell them where you'd gone."

Kai's head snapped down to hers, his hands suddenly on her shoulders, twisting her so he could look at her. "Did you tell them?" His voice was a mix of desperate hope and terror.

She lifted her eyes to meet his rounded ones. "No, I didn't."

The tension in him was gone in a split second, leaving him almost sagging against her. His sigh of relief could have blown a ship ashore. Then he muttered something under his breath that sounded an awful lot like, *"I could kiss you."*

"What?"

His eyes snapped up to meet hers, and then he was shaking his head. "You didn't tell them anything? Is that why they did this to you?" He reached up, carefully touched her forehead near her temple.

Dried blood cracked as she winced away from his touch. His gaze hardened, his mouth thinning as his jaw flexed. His grip on her shoulder dropped, and his arm looped back around her waist, holding her against him.

Did she imagine he held her closer than before?

She blinked against the rising swell of uncertainty and tried to block out the warmth of his arms around her as they rode. It was better to focus on the sun rising higher and higher into the sky, marking the start of a new day. Exhausted as she was, it was time to set their sights forward to the rest of the mission ahead of them.

"I saw a map of Lady Shi's," said Aranya. "It had a path marked from cities all over the empire, converging at Gebei. Then heading north, to a city or something marked Khaiduk."

Delan cast her a sideways glance. "Khaiduk is the name of the enemy fortress on the border of Butagin and Zheninghai."

"I guess we're heading north, then?" said Aranya.

"But first," said Delan, "we need to free you from those phoenix-scorched bonds."

CHAPTER 40

IT WAS DUSK before they reached their destination, a city called Haihai that Delan knew had a curse breaker.

They rode into the city, found a patrolling warden, received directions to the curse breaker's office, and proceeded thus. When they dismounted, it was another community effort of wrestling and awkwardness to get Aranya to the ground in front of the wooden deck outside the curse breaker's hut. It looked like the other huts on the street—bare and dusty with a thatch roof.

Delan held her steady on her feet, his grip driving into her biceps whenever she wobbled. By this time, blood from chafing stained her sleeves, and she was torn between desperation and apathy. She'd been like this all day; might as well wait a few more minutes. At the same time, she was nearly gasping with anticipation of relief.

Kai strode up to the door and knocked. No answer. He knocked again, much louder.

Still no answer.

He fisted his hand and pounded into the wood.

"Go away! We's closed for the day!" came the shriek from inside.

"Open up! We need your help!" called Kai.

"I's *says* we's *closed* for the day!"

Delan ground his teeth, dragged Aranya to the deck so she could catch hold of a splintering pillar. Then he marched up the steps, banged on the door, and shouted wrathfully, "Open this *door,* witch! We've got a girl here in a nasty predicament with spelled bonds we can't cut. O—" *Pound.* "—pen—" *Slam.* "—up!"

Aranya bit her lip, fighting the sudden despair coating her throat. Kai glanced back from the door to her. Briefly, they held each other's gaze. He looked back toward the door where the curse breaker inside berated them.

"The sign says CLOSED!" she shrieked. "Comes back tomorrows!"

"She's in pain!"

"I don'ts serves peoples who calls me witch!"

Delan looked skyward, his jaw working. "I'm sorry I called you a witch. Will you just look at her?"

"I's making no promises! We's closed!"

But the door clicked—a bolt being drawn back. Then another, and another. Seven bolts in all. After the last bolt, silence.

The door flung wide open.

Delan barely leaped back to avoid getting his face smashed by the door as a hook-nosed crone peered out from the building, eyes narrow and sagging skin pinched and leathery. She peered from around the door, clutching it with knobby fingers.

"Hows this?" she growled. "You broughts me what?"

Aranya pushed herself upright and, balancing carefully, held up her hands. "We cannot cut them."

The crone's eyes narrowed, and the door creaked as she pushed it open further. She scuttled out a few steps, her knot-like elbows on display around the edges of her patchwork cloak. "What's *this*?" she croaked.

Aranya licked her lips and held the bonds out to her, trying not to let her face brighten too much with hope that might only be dashed a second later. "If we try to cut it, it tightens."

The woman gripped Aranya's thumb and raised it up, turning her hands this way and that to view the bonds. "Hmmm." A few seconds later, after a painful poke at her wrists, too near where she'd been bitten by the wolf, that made her hiss, the woman said again, "Hmmm."

"You can break this spell?" Delan prodded. "We can pay, of course—"

The crone scoffed, dropping Aranya's hands. "I don'ts work for free, *boy*."

Delan glared at her.

She scooted up the steps, making odd smacking sounds with her mouth. "But no, I cants help her. This isn't a true curse—I don't works in those kinds of spells. You'll need to find the spellcaster and get him to undos it."

"Wait, but—" Delan started, leaping toward the door.

The crone was shockingly fast. Too quick for Delan, she slammed the door behind her and, in quick succession, threw each bolt back in place with punctuated emphasis. All three of them stared at the locked door before them. Then Kai and Delan both turned to Aranya. She stared back at them, trying not to sag hopelessly beneath their gazes.

"Stay with her," Delan growled, turning on Kai. "There's got to be another way. I'll be back soon."

With that, he mounted his horse and rode away into the sunset falling over the city.

Kai shifted his gaze to her, all mirth mercifully gone from his face. Except that what replaced it only made her bristle more—*pity*. She swallowed and shrugged. "I'm sure Delan will find something."

He heaved a sigh that was the opposite of agreement. He descended the stairs, not looking at her, and muttered, "Want to wait here or somewhere else?"

She forced a smile and said, "Here's fine."

"Would you like to sit?"

"I've been sitting all day."

"Very well. Hungry?"

She nodded. He started for their horses. But the moment the twist returned to his lips—before he could say anything—she snapped, "If you say anything about me being heavy or eating too much beef jerky after you had to carry me so much last night, I'm going—"

He turned, holding up his hands innocently as he continued walking backward toward the horse. He couldn't suppress his grin, and the sight of it eased something tight inside her chest. "I wasn't going to say anything."

She huffed but had to turn away to keep from revealing her own smile. Perhaps a little fun was what they needed now, when everything was looking so dire for her and their mission. They could pretend none of the problems with the Shi family had ever happened and just return to being antagonistic comrades.

She armed herself with a sly grin when he returned with a rice cake. It quickly faltered when she saw the meager offering.

"What? This is it?"

He opened his mouth to respond, his eyes glittering wickedly, when they suddenly darted over her shoulder down the street. All amusement fled his face. He slipped the rice cake into his pocket. She tried to follow his line of sight, but she startled when he grabbed her shoulders, bringing his face suddenly close to hers. She was about to snap something about personal space, but his jaw clenched so tightly she could hear his teeth grinding.

"What's wrong?" she asked in a strained whisper. "*Please* don't tell me your brother is behind me."

His gaze flicked from beyond her down to her face. "Oh, no, definitely not." But he didn't relax. She twisted to look behind her, but he tightened his grip on her shoulders, keeping her fixed in place. His words came tumbling out: "Remember that fine your grandfather accrued that you couldn't pay in Zushui?"

"Yes . . .? Wait, how do you know about that? I didn't tell—"

"I paid it. Now—"

"You *what*?"

"—I'm calling in my debt."

"You're—"

"Just forgive me in advance, alright?"

"Kai, what in the seven—"

Her question was cut off. The hands gripping her shoulders tightened and drew her close—far too close. It all happened so fast she couldn't even squeak as her eyes flew wide . . . and Kai kissed her.

It was lightning to her gut.

Her bound fists flew up to grip the front of his shirt and shove him away. But his hands moved to cup her face in a strangely tender gesture, and then he *really* kissed her. It swept through her like fire, then water that made her limbs go liquid. She stumbled, losing her balance on her bound feet. One of his arms wrapped around her, catching her against him. She forgot her painful bonds, her swollen and bruised face.

She had never been kissed like this.

Was that why her heart suddenly ached so sharply in her chest? Why tears sprang behind her shut eyelids and a painful lump formed in her throat?

He pulled back, and belatedly her eyelashes fluttered open to find him searching her face. Could he read the sudden and unexpected burst of emotion inside her? There was something flashing in that hazel gaze—something vulnerable, something almost pained.

His brows came together in a pinch, and then he leaned in again. His nose brushed hers softly. Almost a nuzzle, definitely a question. She couldn't help herself; she closed her eyes and tilted her chin up with a tiny whimper on her lips—her answer. Her hands were still fisted in his tunic, but she couldn't push him away. Not in this reckless, bewildering moment.

Not in this moment when it was like being simultaneously torn to pieces and knit back together as a tear slipped free and his lips found hers again.

His second kiss was not at all what she expected. It was the sort of soft, lingering kiss a couple would share after being married for twenty or thirty years. The kind that spoke of promises, of endless days ahead, and half-finished stories behind. It was a kiss that called to the deep craving of her soul—to hold and be held without the fear of imminent loss. It held a magic that could make her lose her head, turn her into a lovesick fool with no will or mind of her own.

How many girls had he kissed to be this good?

Her senses came roaring back. She found the strength in her arms to push him back, to break the kiss, even as he tightened his arm around her to keep her from falling.

"What was *that*?" she sputtered, dashing angrily at her wet cheek with her bound hands.

His answering grin was triumph itself. Except—it wasn't at all. That grin wasn't the least bit true. It was like the cool expression he'd worn in the bathing chamber when Yong had his knife to her throat. Distant, detached, like he didn't care at all. After the tenderness of his kiss, she could tell the difference. Could read his twitching eyebrow, the way his eyes seemed to darken as he withdrew from the vulnerability of affection.

What was she supposed to think or feel now? Should she be angry because he'd kissed her without her permission? Should she be embarrassed because she'd enjoyed it, and had asked for the second? It was too much. She felt it all. Rage at herself for her own vulnerability in front of her rival. Confusion about why she had the sudden and overwhelming urge to crawl into a ball with her fluffy white cat back in Zushui and cry—over how long it had been since she'd been with her grandfather, over what she'd faced in Gebei, over knowing it was only a matter of time before she had no one else in this world.

She hated herself for the inexplicable longing for Kai to be something . . . *more*. It was ridiculous, really. This just went to show how much unexpected kisses could ruin everything and why he should *not* have kissed her in the first place. She squared her shoulders, scowling, ready to spout off a rebuking tirade.

Her bonds fell off.

Aranya startled, her chafed and bleeding wrists suddenly free. The vines trussing her ankles broke away too, leaving her jaw gaping like a codfish. She pried her hands free of Kai's shirt and held them up before her. They looked horrible and felt even worse, but she couldn't feel pain in the flood of relief.

"The kiss broke the spell on the vines," she breathed, trying to rub the feeling back into her hands. "The Yanzhao Technique . . ." It was something they'd been taught at the Academy, but it hadn't even occurred to her that something like the Yanzhao Technique, a kiss to break the spell, would work in a situation like this.

"Fathers," Kai gasped, clearly as shocked as she was.

Her head shot up, and she snapped, "*Why* did you kiss me, Shi Kai? What is wrong with you? I'm not one of your dalliances! Seven valleys, I'm your *colleague*!"

But his attention flitted back over her head. Now, limbs finally unhindered, she turned to see what he looked at.

Oh.

A young woman—clearly a warden on patrol—stared from the opposite side of the street, her mouth open and eyes ringed in hurt. Her gaze darted between Kai and Aranya.

"Come on," he said, a bit gruffly, and took her arm to steer her away. His face was determined as he snatched the leads of their horses.

"Who was that? Do you know her?" Aranya said, stumbling after him on numb feet. "Why was she—why did you—"

"She and I . . ." He let out a frustrated exhale. "We were involved. Back at the Academy. I didn't . . . She thought . . . I guess she thought it was serious—"

"Wait, you *courted* at the Academy?"

"I didn't court! At least, *I* didn't think it was—"

"And you just used me to get back at her?" Aranya's cry was near outrage. "You used us both—"

"She's been insistent. Years later! I've told her *no* a thousand times and she won't listen, and she knows my family and—look, you saw my family—" He broke off, cursing under his breath. "I'm sorry, Aranya. I shouldn't . . . It was all I could think of. She's gone behind my back more than once to tell my mother—" He stopped, didn't start again. He scratched the back of his neck, watching her.

Aranya stared at him, not knowing what she should be thinking or feeling.

He turned wincing eyes to hers. "At least . . . you're free now."

At least? She ground her teeth, working her jaw, eyes fixed unseeing down the street—away from Kai. Anywhere but Kai. Her chest heaved with each breath, frustration mounting on every inhale.

Then her gaze snapped to his. He stood still, long legs planted widely in the dirt. He'd folded his arms across his chest, losing the vulnerable posture and instead meeting the force of her gaze with his. As if to dare her to hate him for freeing her from those impossibly wretched bonds.

There it was again. That closed-off expression. It was like they were back at the Zushui wardpost only moments after they'd been told they would be competing for the wardenship. Sizing each other up and refusing to back down.

She tilted her chin up. "This isn't over, evanescer."

He gave her a dark smirk. "Who said it was?"

They'll save their empire . . . or be each other's downfall. The adventure and romance continues in Warrior of Blade and Dusk.

BONUS READING

Want to read Kai's POV of Aranya's nightmare? Download it for free when you sign up for Anastasis Blythe's newsletter at:

AnastasisBlythe.com/Kai

MORE FROM ANASTASIS BLYTHE

THE ZHENINGHAI CHRONICLES

Maiden of Candlelight and Lotuses

Warrior of Blade and Dusk

Princess of Shadows and Starlight

Captive of Twilight and Treachery

ABOUT THE AUTHOR

Anastasis Blythe makes her home in central Texas with her husband and their two adorable but rather whiny cats. When she's not writing, she is reading an unhealthy amount of fantasy novels, daydreaming about future books, and trying to keep up with the laundry.

If you would like free novels, regular behind-the-scenes updates on her writing, and an early peek at new book covers, join her community at Patreon.com/AnastasisBlythe.

CONNECT WITH ANASTASIS ONLINE AT:

Website - AnastasisBlythe.com

Instagram - @AnastasisBlythe

Facebook - Anastasis Blythe

Goodreads - Anastasis Blythe